By Jo Walton from Tom Doherty Associates

The King's Name
The King's Peace
The Prize in the Game

THE
KING'S
NAME

JO WALTON

A TOM DOHERTY ASSOCIATES BOOK
NEW YORK

This is a work of fiction. All the characters and events portrayed in this book are either products of the author's imagination or are used fictitiously.

THE KING'S NAME

Copyright © 2001 by Jo Walton

Edited by Patrick Nielsen Hayden

A Tor Book
Published by Tom Doherty Associates, LLC
175 Fifth Avenue
New York, NY 10010

www.tor.com

Tor® is a registered trademark of Tom Doherty Associates, LLC.

ISBN: 0-765-34340-1

First edition: December 2001
First mass market edition: November 2002

Printed in the United States of America

0 9 8 7 6 5 4 3 2 1

Here's the rest of it, Gangrader. I hope it's what you wanted.

This volume is especially for the participants of the newsgroup rec.arts.sf.composition, both for specific help and for just being there, a community where it's normal to want to talk about writing.

Thanks once again to Graydon and Emmet and Hrolfr for reading chapters as they were written, Julie Pascal for suggesting the title of this volume, Michael Grant for all the semicolons, Mary Lace for having such appropriate reactions, David Goldfarb, Mary Kuhner and Janet Kegg for helpful readings, Sketty Library for getting me books, and Patrick Nielsen Hayden for doing all the difficult stuff.

Introduction

I greet the appearance of this second volume of the translation of the Sulien Texts with the same pleasure with
which I greeted the publication of the first. (*The King's
Peace*, Tor Books, New Caravroc, 2753.) It was past time for
a translation of the work into modern Yalnic, more than a
hundred years after the discovery of the text and the publication of the first Vincan edition. This is not an unapproach-
able work; indeed it is an exciting and readable one. The
delay in translation is for reasons of political controversy
which we would all do well to put behind us in these more
liberal times.

This, like the first volume, consists of merely the text, with
no scholarly annotations. Serious students seeking such will
be able to read the Vincan and would be better to purchase
my *The Complete Sulien Text* (2733, rev. 2748, Thurriman
University Press, New Caryavroc). I am honored, however, to
say a few words about the work, for those unscholarly read-
ers who read this vernacular edition for pleasure but for
whom the bare text is not enough.

The book, whoever wrote it and for whatever purpose, is
set against the troubled and all-but-undocumented history of
the thirteenth century. It deals with a period that we know
better from myth and legend than from sober historical accounts. The Vincan legions had departed the island of Tir
Tanagiri forty years before the opening events of the book.
The time between had been one of chaos, invasion, and civil

war, as the island became once more a collection of petty kingdoms and as the barbarous Jarns crossed the sea to raid, invade, and settle. King Urdo, as every Tanagan schoolchild knows, united the island and brought peace.

In the first volume published in this edition were the first two "books" of a document which claims to be the memoirs of Sulien ap Gwien, one of the legendary armigers of King Urdo. This second volume contains the third, longest, and last "book." The first "book," *The King's Peace*, begins with the assertion that the writer is Sulien ap Gwien, Lord of Derwen, writing at ninety-three years of age for the purpose of setting records straight.

At the time of writing, she says, the Jarnish invaders from overseas were at peace with the Tanagan and Vincan inhabitants of Tir Tanagiri, and she wishes to give an account of how they came to be one people. The book documents Sulien's career, beginning with her brother's murder and her rape by the young Jarnish raider Ulf Gunnarsson, the nephew of Sweyn, king of Jarnholme. She was then dedicated against her will to the Jarnish god Gangrader, and left to die of exposure, which she escaped by her own efforts. Unknowingly pregnant by Ulf, she entered into the service of the High King Urdo ap Avren. The baby was born and named, shockingly, Darien Suliensson in Jarnish fashion. Many people believed this child to be the son of Urdo, because of a night Sulien and Urdo spent in the same room in Caer Gloran. He was fostered in the monastery of Thansethan, whereupon Sulien returned to one of Urdo's cavalry regiments, or "alae," and became leader of a pennon of twenty-four riders. After an invasion of the island by Sweyn and a disastrous battle at Caer Lind, in Tevin, she became praefecto, or general in command, of the ala. Meanwhile she earned the enmity of and later killed Morwen, witch, queen of Demedia, and sister of Urdo. There followed six years of war, culminating in a great victory for the High King's forces at Foreth Hill. At this victory Urdo did not accept a truce from the defeated Jarnish kings, but forced them into making an alliance and recognizing him as High King, with all the island henceforward to live under law.

The second "book" contained in the first volume, *The King's Law*, covers the first seven years of Urdo's Peace. On the first afternoon of the Peace, Ulf Gunnarsson received a trial for rape, before Urdo and Ohtar, a Jarnish king. He admitted his fault and offered to make reparation, then refused to defend himself in a judicial combat. Sulien decided to let him live, and he entered her ala.

The victory at Foreth was shortly followed by an invasion of three large groups of Isarnagans, the barbarous people who lived in the western island of Tir Isarnagiri. Sulien successfully persuaded one contingent of Isarnagans, led by Lew ap Ross and his wife, Emer ap Allel, the sister of Urdo's queen, to become vassals and settle in an empty part of her brother Morien's realm of Derwen. During the negotiations Sulien discovered that Emer was secretly involved in an adulterous relationship with Conal ap Amagien, all the more shocking because Conal had killed Emer's mother. The other two contingents of Isarnagan invaders were eventually defeated militarily. One, led by Black Darag and Atha ap Gren, retreated back to Tir Isarnagiri. The other was treacherously slaughtered by Urdo's Malmish praefecto, Marchel ap Thurrig, after they had surrendered. Marchel was exiled to her father's homeland of Narlahena for her crime: but for Thurrig's long and faithful service she would have been executed for it.

Meanwhile a Feast of Peace was held in Caer Tanaga for all the kings of the lands that made up Tir Tanagiri, Jarnish and Tanagan alike. Not all the kings were happy about this, but an uneasy peace held. A few years later there was an attempt by one of these petty kings, Cinon of Nene, on the life of Sulien's son Darien, still fostered at Thansethan. The attempt was foiled by the intervention of the great boar, Turth, one of the powers of the land. Sulien believed this attempt to have been instigated by Morthu, the son of Morwen, who hated her for killing his mother. Urdo refused to act against Morthu without proof. Two years later, Urdo's queen, Elenn, miscarried of a son. She suspected this of being Morthu's doing, but he passed the examination of the priest Teilo, who should have been able to detect a lie. Urdo and Elenn and all their court then made pilgrimage to Thansethan to pray for a son. This visit, and this volume, concluded with two terrible duels—the first between Sulien, as the queen's champion, and Conal ap Amagien for the honor of Elenn, whom Conal had jokingly insulted. The second was between Ulf Gunnarsson and Sulien's brother Morien, after Morthu revealed to Morien that Ulf was the killer of their brother. Ulf won his duel, and the news was brought to Sulien as she preserved the queen's honor without killing Conal, that her brother was dead and she must leave the ala and return home to become Lord of Derwen.

The present volume takes up the story five years later.

I have here recounted the events of the first volume as if they were indeed the words of Sulien herself, and of definite historicity. Unfortunately, we can by no means be sure that this is the case.

The manuscript we have fills the last seven volumes of the compilation known as *The White Book of Scatha*. The history of the White Book would itself fill volumes, but suffice to say that the White Book as we have it came to the island of Scatha sometime in the twenty-first century, and has certainly not been tampered with since that time. It languished, neglected until the first three volumes, consisting of Tanagan prose and poetry, were published with an acclaimed translation by Lady Gladis Hanver in 2564. There was then pressure to publish the rest of the book, and though additional volumes appeared, the "Sulien Text" remained invisible. The middle volumes of the White Book consist largely of uninteresting Vincan poetry of the fourteenth and fifteenth centuries, and it was generally believed that there was no more of interest in the work. The publication of Professor Malaki Kahn's Vincan edition of *The King's Peace: An Extract From the White Book* in 2658 came as a complete surprise to everyone.

What was not surprising was that Kahn chose to publish his edition in Vincan. The text, which contradicts almost all known facts about King Urdo and many about the Early Insular Church, could not at that time have been published in Yalnic. Even in Vincan it was immediately denounced by many as a forgery. Professor Kahn's application to excavate at Derwen was greeted with derision, and it is true that it would require the destruction of large parts of what is now an attractive twenty-first-century port to discover the thirteenth-century home (and possibly the original manuscript) the author of the "Sulien Text" describes.

From stylistic and scribal evidence in the White Book itself it appears that the "Sulien Text" was copied in the mid-twentieth century, probably either at Thansethan or at Thanmarchel, and at the request of the Haver family of Scatha, who commissioned the White Book. The scribal note states that it is a copy of an earlier copy which was certainly made at Thansethan, very probably for the Great King Alward. This would be the sixteenth-century Alward of Munew who reunited the whole of Tanager under his leadership while holding off the Norlander invasion. He was a great scholar and may well have been interested in the life of Urdo. There is no intrinsic reason to disbelieve that the White Book scribe told the truth as he knew it. (See Jeyver, *The Scribes of the White Book,* 2723.)

It is to Alward's sixteenth-century scribe that we owe the chapter division of the work as we have it, the commonly used title ("I found in the library of Thansethan a work on the King's Peace" the scribal note begins) and also the quotations which are used to head each chapter. Some of these quotations have been described as "of more value than the text itself." (Prof. bint Kerigan, "The Poetic Fragments of Anirin ap Erbin From the So-called Sulien Text.") These fragments have been attested by many scholars as undoubtedly genuine. Some of them are very well known while others are not found elsewhere. They, at least, unmistakably date from the age of Urdo, or not long after.

Those who claim that the text is a modern forgery, especially those who attacked Prof. Kahn's religious or other motives, are no less than delusional. The manuscript exists and has been extensively studied in modern conditions. While there would have been many reasons one could imagine for someone to forge an account of Urdo's life—especially one as different from the accepted version and as pro-pagan as Sulien's account—there would have been little purpose in doing it without circulating it and stirring up difficulty. "If someone went to the trouble of forging this book, why did they then not go to the further trouble of disseminating it?" asked Dr. Enid Godwinsson. (In "The Sulien Text: Whose Agenda?" in *Journal of Vincan Studies*, Spring 2749.)

This is not to say that the text is indeed the work of the shadowy Sulien ap Gwien. Very little is known about her except for what appears in this book, and that little is often directly contradictory to her own text. Without wishing to enter into religious controversies, it should be noted (see Camling, "Irony in 'The Glory of Morthu,' " *Urdossian Quarterly*, Autumn 2685) that the Vincan word "pius" which is almost universally applied to Sulien in the later chronicles and poetry dealing with Urdo, meant at that date "faithful," and not, as it means now and is generally translated, "pious."

In the five hundred years between Sulien's time and Alward's the work may have been written by anyone. Yet, who would have chosen to do it? Indeed, who would have had the skill or the time to do so? Without need of Godwinsson's whimsical conclusion that the forger died on or before completion of the manuscript, it is worth considering her point about the sheer time such a forgery must have taken: we are not talking a few pages but a weighty work that covers two volumes of modern print. It must have taken years. The text is written in an almost classical Vincan, the sure sign of someone very well educated. Few outside the monasteries in those centuries would have had that skill. Few inside the monasteries would have had the desire.

One of the most controversial points in the text is, of course, the treatment of religion. The monks of the Insular Church were remarkable in their kind treatment of manuscripts from other traditions, but they did not go out of their way to forge works that would bring discredit on themselves. Sulien's general view of the Church as being suited to idiots, her portraits of St. Gerthmol as a fool, St. Dewin as a manipulator and, worst of all, St. Marchel as a short-tempered bigot, indicate an agenda of someone who disliked the Church. Only in her treatment of St. Arvlid and St. Teilo do we see anything approaching the hagiographic work typical of the period, and even there they are engagingly human saints, as Brother Ivor of Thanmarchel points out about Arvlid (*Sulien and the Early Insular Church*, 2722), "This picture of the blessed martyr helping out in childbirth and making honey is not the one the church gives us, but it is one the church should be very slow to reject." Indeed the Church has been quick to claim the picture of life at Thansethan as "Sulien" shows it, while rejecting other parts of this "eyewitness" account out of hand.

There are many parts of the text which show an intimate familiarity with the thirteenth century in which it is purported to be set. Sulien always calls the islands Tir Tanagiri and Tir Isarnagiri, though these "Tir" prefixes had ceased to be in use by the time of Gwyn Dariensson's *Code of Laws*, and the island was already the familiar Tanager by the time of Alward. Yet she calls the islanders "Tanagans" and "Isarnagans" and not "Tirtanagans" as we find in the Vincan period, for example in Decius Manicius. This is precisely as we would expect for the transition period. In many other ways—for example the description of the training of the alae and the growth of villages—she has been vindicated by archaeology. Martinsson's (*Proof of Forgery of the Sulien Text*, 2731) denunciation of the name of the otherwise unknown "Masarn" because the word "masarn," "a maple tree," was not in use until the discovery of maples in the Trans-Iarla lands in the twenty-second century, must be dismissed. The book cannot have been tampered with since it came to Scatha and the possession of the Hanver family a hundred years before the discovery of the New World. The name Masarn must have some other origin. Hartley's ("A Possible Southern Connection" in *Journal of Vincan Studies*, Summer 2745) fanciful coupling with the common Sifacian name "Massinissa" must regrettably be dismissed, as, unless he had come, like Elhanen the Great, on an elephant across all the Vincan lands, how could a Sifacian have been in Tanager at that time?

Yet to place against these historical accuracies we have typical miracle tales of the period. What are we to make of a work which, on the one hand contains a detailed description of a stable block that has been excavated precisely as described, and on the other repeats miracle stories like the three days' night and the magical water on Foreth? Brother Ivor's comment that "She cannot even decide consistently which set of Heathen Gods she worships" (Ivor, op. cit.) is unfair, but certainly the personal appearance of gods in the text takes it out of the realm of history into that of fable.

We must regretfully dismiss the idea that this may be the famous "boke" on which Galfrid of Thanmarchel claimed to have based his famous "The King and the Kingdom." For one thing, Galfrid states clearly that his "boke" was written "in the ancient Tanagan language," whereas the Sulien text is in Vincan and certainly has not been re-translated back into Vincan. There is also Kunnarsson's (*The Sulien Text: A Reconsideration*, University of Stellanova Press, 2751) very well-considered point, "If the author of the Sulien text was attempting to give us the history behind the myth, they made a mistake and gave us the wrong half, explaining the things that nobody believed anyway and leaving out the plausible parts of the story most beloved by the poets." I believe, with Prof. Kunnarsson, that these omissions are evidence for the genuine, or at least very early, nature of the text.

The burden of proof that the work was not written by Sulien ap Gwien under the circumstances she states in the text, lies with those who would suggest otherwise. Until we have permission to fulfill the late Prof. Kahn's dream and excavate at Derwen, unless and until we discover the lead casket she says she wished to place in the walls (and which her great-nephew says he had done to her desire), then we will have no proof either way.

   —Prof. Estin Jonson,
    Dept. of Sub-Vincan History, University of Dunidin,
    2754 AUC.

Up to now they used to shiver every time they heard mention of the Romans' skill in warfare, but now they are victorious, and we die, nobly, as befits brave men, but perishing all the same.

—Libanius, 378

Let the dead be carried gently;
let them wonder, who are living,
what choice shall be tomorrow.

—Graydon Saunders, "The Pebble," 1998

— I —

The swallows fly low tonight,
swooping and soaring,
soon the rain will come.

I trudge uphill to the dun,
children run past me.
My breath comes slowly.

They all held me mighty, then,
blood on the spearblade,
death in bright sunlight.

Better the spear had caught me,
in my youth, my pride.
Before my defeat.

It brings me grief, not comfort,
he died long ago
upright, like a man.

Very few care for me now.
Rain makes my bones ache.
My deeds forgotten.

The swallows recall to mind
time gone, chances missed,
and my only son.

> — "The Lament of Atha ap Gren"

The first I knew about the civil war was when my sister Aurien poisoned me.

I was in her hall in Magor. I spent most of my time at Derwen, but half the ala were stationed a day's ride away at Magor and I rode down to see them and exchange troops quite regularly. I enjoyed going, it made a break in my routine. I had nothing to do there but the work of a praefecto. Aurien needed no help running Magor. She was always cool and polite toward me but never more. Her boys, however, were always pleased to see me. She did have the decency to wait until they had gone to bed before poisoning me, which probably saved my life. It meant she had to put it into the cider, not the food, where anyone would have just thought she had been heavy-handed with the spices. It was the very end of spring, never a good time for meat, and she had four extra mouths to feed.

I had brought Conal Fishface and Emlin with me and Emer was there, too, on her way back from a visit to Caer Tanaga. As soon as I saw her there I thought that Conal had known she would be and felt angry with him for using me like that. He did not eat with us, of course, but he joined us in the eating alcove afterward. I was saying good night to the boys. Galbian, the fifteen-year-old Duke of Magor, bowed like the adult he almost was. Thirteen-year-old Gwien, the heir to Derwen, was still young enough to go off reluctantly, begging for rides and stories tomorrow. Aurien over-protected them. If I said anything to her about it she would reply by saying she would bear in mind all my experience of child-rearing. But the consequence of her fussing was that they ran off to the barracks when they could and didn't tell her their adventures. I was glad Galbian would be in the ala next year; both the discipline and the training would do him good. Aurien set her lips and said nothing when they talked about winning glory at war.

Conal sat down beside me, and Aurien poured out the cider. She had brought out a board set with beakers and a heavy stone jug. She poured for Emer first, then for me, then Emlin, Conal, and for herself last. None of her people were sitting with us that night, not even Father Cinwil who was usually her constant companion. She raised her beaker to me, and drank. I drank in return. I noticed the bitterness almost at once, but I had still in politeness drained almost half the cup before I set it down. I could feel my tongue thickening in my mouth.

"What news from Caer Tanaga?" Aurien asked Emer.

"Very little," Emer said. "Some of the allied kings are late sending their taxes this year, it seems."

"And how are Urdo and your sister?" Aurien asked.

I leaned forward to pick up my beaker to drink some more and see if it would clear the strangeness in my mouth and throat. As I did so I realized that my body wasn't responding the way it should. "I don't feel well—" I began, but the words came out slurred.

"I think the cider has been too much for Sulien," Aurien said, and laughed. "She went off drinking with the armigers before dinner, and that cup has set her over the edge."

I tried to protest that I had taken no strong drink since the night before, but instead I slid down toward the table. My eyes were half open. I could see, but I had lost control of my body. Conal leaned toward me and deftly sniffed at my cup while his body shielded him from Aurien. He lifted me so I was sitting up again. "It wasn't with the armigers she was drinking but with me," he said. "We were having a contest and it seems I have won." Again I tried to protest that there wasn't a word of truth in it, but my mouth wouldn't obey me. My mind was working slowly, because it was only now I knew I'd been poisoned. Being poisoned at meat at my own sister's table was something that I had never feared.

"These soldiers, I don't know how they put up with each other," Aurien said to Emer. Emer laughed politely. I couldn't see her. She must have known Conal was lying. "I'll call for some water," Aurien went on.

"I think, as it is my fault she's in this condition, I'd better take the praefecto to bed," Conal said, heaving me to my feet.

"She can walk, the legs are always the last to go. Perhaps you'll give me a hand, ap Trivan?"

"Just put her straight to bed, she'll be all right," Aurien said. "She often does this, and it always passes off by morning."

I couldn't speak to deny this. I felt Emlin heave up my other shoulder, but I couldn't feel my legs at all. "My apologies, Lady," he said to Aurien.

"Really, it isn't you who needs to apologize," she said. "No doubt I'll hear enough excuses from my sister in the morning. I'll send some water to her room, but I don't expect she'll recover consciousness tonight now; she never does."

"It must be very hard on her to drink so much," Emer was saying as Conal and Emlin half carried and half dragged me out of the hall. As soon as we were outside I felt as if I was being pulled in half.

"It's this way," Emlin said.

"The midden first," Conal said. "She has to be sick."

"If she's had that much to drink—" Emlin began, when Conal interrupted him in a savage whisper.

"She hasn't had anything beyond that half cup. I was lying to give myself a reason to take charge of her in time. She's been poisoned and we need to get it out of her."

"Poisoned?" Emlin echoed. "Poisoned? Why?" They started to drag me again, this time out toward the midden. It was twilight outside. A chill wind was blowing. I tried to breathe deeply but couldn't even manage that. I wasn't sure if I was breathing at all, I couldn't feel it.

"Why, I can't think; it's ridiculous to poison someone at your own table but I know who, and what. It was henbane. I could smell it. From the look of her it was a strong dose—it doesn't usually act quite that fast. Water given after that would finish her off; it would take it right through her system, and she was twice offered it." My head lolled back against my shoulder. I wondered how Conal had come to know so much about poison.

"But why would Galba's lady poison her own sister?" Emlin asked.

"Because she wants her dead for some good reason," Conal suggested.

"Why should I trust you?" Emlin asked.

"What is the worst that can happen if you do?" Conal asked. He sounded furious. "Your praefecto, with a sore head, will be angry you did too much. Have you ever seen her in this condition, by the way? I thought not. If you don't, well, she'll be dead. She'll also be disgraced. Dead of drinking is no fit end for a hero's story." We had reached the midden. I could barely smell it. "Now, stick your finger down her throat."

"Why me?" Emlin asked, but he took hold of my jaw and did as Conal told him. As his finger went down I retched and the cider came back out, and my dinner with it, splashing Emlin's boots.

"That's why," Conal said, holding me as far forward as he could. As I retched I began to feel a little better.

"Do it again," I said, but it came out as a gargle.

"What's that?" Emlin asked eagerly. I tried again, but nothing happened.

"See if there's any more that can come out," Conal suggested. Emlin did, and I managed to empty myself. Then Conal wiped my face with his sleeve and pinched my cheek, frowning. I could see his hand but I could barely feel the touch. "We'd better get her out of here," he said.

"Why?" Emlin asked. "How would that help?"

"Partly because the lady of Magor may well try again," Conal said. "And partly because Sulien may yet die of this if it spreads so she stops breathing. Worse, she could live but like this, paralyzed or part paralyzed." I jerked and twitched in his hands, trying desperately to move. He was right, I had rather be dead. "We need to get her home to Derwen. The land will help her there."

"How can we do that?" Emlin asked. "She's in no state to ride."

"Tie her on the horse like a sack of meal," Conal suggested. "I know. I'll take her to her room, in case anyone comes checking. You saddle up horses for you and for her, and bring them around under the window. I'll lower her down to you when I hear you coming, then you can ride for Derwen."

"I—" Emlin hesitated. He looked at me. "Praefecto?"

I tried to speak, to tell him to do what Conal said, but I couldn't say anything but inarticulate grunts. With all the strength I had I concentrated on my right hand, and managed to make the ala hand signal to tell Emlin he should take Conal's orders. It was the best I could do.

"Understood," he said. He looked worried. As he went out of sight he was chewing on his beard.

Conal lifted me over his shoulder and went back through the house toward my room. We passed some servants who looked baffled but said nothing. When we got inside Conal propped me against the wall in a slumped position. "Breathe as deep as you can," he said. "Water wouldn't be a good idea yet." I sat and breathed. He took my armor off the armor stand by the bed. "I'm going to see if I can get this on you," he said. "It's more sensible for riding, and safer in case of arrows. I wish I knew what was happening; she can't have hoped to get away with that. There must be something going on."

I grunted agreement. Conal hauled me up and unwound my drape, dropping it on the floor. He put one of my arms into the armor and stared confused at the breast strapping. I would have liked to laugh; but I would have liked to be able to move my arms even more. Just then there came a tap at the door. In one swift movement Conal picked me up, dropped me on the bed, and dropped my cloak on top of me. I couldn't turn my head, so I could see nothing but my armor stand and beyond it the arched Vincan window and, outside, the darkening sky and one branch of a sycamore, the trefoil leaves very dark against the twilight blue.

"Yes?" Conal said, somewhere I couldn't see him. "My lady?" I wished I felt more confident in his ability to stop Aurien from politely poisoning me again. I couldn't think what I had done to her recently to make her hate me so much. It was twelve years since I had brought Galba home after Foreth.

"It's me," Emer's voice said. I heard the door open and someone come in. "What game are you two playing?" she asked, and then, "Conal!"

Conal laughed, and shut the door, still laughing. "Do you doubt me so much?" he gasped, between gales of merriment. "No, I am not sneaking off to betray you with Sulien ap Gwien, dreadful as it seems to see me alone here in her room and her drape thrown on the floor."

"What then?" Emer sounded impatient. "Sulien?"

"She can't talk," Conal said. I flopped my head a little and made a noise that was supposed to be agreement. I was drooling; it disgusted me to feel it. "She's been poisoned. Ap Trivan and I are going to get her out of here. You can help me get her into her armor. You probably have a better idea of how the confounded fastenings work."

At that Emer gurgled with laughter, and came around into my field of vision. She was carrying a jug of water. She set it down on the floor and pulled down the cloak, and she and Conal began to dress me. I felt terrible, and worse, I felt sleepy. I knew if I slept, the drug would take me. "Where are you going to take her?" Emer asked.

"Ap Trivan's going to take her home to Derwen," Conal said.

"Ah, yes. The land will help," Emer said, fastening the straps. I felt like a large, ungainly baby as she forced my legs in.

"You don't seem surprised that the lady of Magor would do such a thing," Conal said.

Emer glanced at me, sighed, then looked up at him. "I have quarreled with my sister. She knows about you, and she has cast me off. A red-cloak came to Aurien this morning with letters."

Conal drew in his breath sharply. "That's nonsense," he said, very gently. He took one of Emer's hands and held it for a moment. "Elenn may well wish you dead, and certainly me, but why Sulien? She was her champion. She is Urdo's friend, and his praefecto and the mother of his son. Death in disgrace would not serve the High King."

"Elenn is not Urdo," Emer said, still looking up at him. "Elenn is an Isarnagan and a woman. Poison is a woman's weapon."

"Aurien is a woman," Conal said. "If Elenn wanted anyone dead it would include me, and probably you as well if she knows. It would be too good a chance for her to miss when we were all together, but none of the other cups were touched. In any case Aurien is no particular friend to Elenn that I have ever heard. Who are her friends?"

"Thansethan," Emer said, unhesitatingly. "That could mean Elenn. Kerys ap Uthbad and her brother Cinvar, the lord of Tathal. Veniva and the people of Derwen, but why would any of them want Sulien dead? Beyond that I do not know."

"Thansethan could mean more than Elenn," Conal said. I was dressed; he walked over to the window and looked out. "But it is not a thing the Pale often do, poisoning their families. I know the White God gives a shield against a great many dangers, but surely not against kin-murder?"

Emer turned to look at him. A strand of her hair was straggling loose down her back. "I think it gives a shield against any perils encountered in their cause," she said. "And they have never been friends to Sulien."

I tried to speak, but it was pointless. I found it hard to imagine Father Gerthmol poisoning me. It would be an act of war against Derwen, and that would break Urdo's Peace. Whoever killed me he would avenge me, and so would Darien. Darien was a signifer now. I was more inclined to believe that Aurien had done it to stop Gwien coming to Derwen to spend the summer with me. It was disproportionate, but it was a comprehensible reason.

They both turned to me. "What is it?" Emer asked. She looked at Conal. He raised his eyebrows.

"Do you know why Aurien did it? Do you think Thansethan would poison you?" he asked. I rolled my eyes; it was about all I could manage. Conal snorted. "I don't think so either."

"What are we going to do in the morning when she's gone?" Emer asked, practically.

"Assume she's eloped with ap Trivan and sympathize with Aurien for the scandal of having a sister who drinks so much and shares blankets with her subordinates," Conal said. I rolled my eyes again.

"Should we leave tonight as well?" Emer asked. "Are we in danger here? If she wanted to poison us she's missed her best chance."

"Not if she wanted to get away with it. That story about drinking too much could easily have worked if she'd died in the night. An ignominious end for Urdo's praefecto, but not incredible. Less convincing if it was all three of us, don't you think?"

"It wouldn't have worked on Veniva," Emer said. "Veniva knows how much Sulien drinks, who better? It wouldn't have worked on Urdo either, though Aurien might have thought it would. I suppose if she suspected me she wouldn't have let me bring the water up."

"She can't have been expecting us either," Conal said. "Maybe she only had one dose prepared? I only decided to come on the flick of a wing. I came to Dun Morr with messages to Lew, and as I was bored waiting for you I rode to Derwen, and when I heard Sulien was coming here I came with her. And she must have known you'd be coming through, but not when. You know how surprised I was to see you, my heart." He smiled very deliberately.

"She is awake and listening," Emer said, glancing at me, embarrassed. "I think it would be safer if we all leave tonight."

"I shall have to send ap Trivan for more horses," Conal said. He leaned out of the window. "This is a very convenient tree. Ah, here he comes."

I forced my hand to move, to give the hand signal that meant the whole ala. Emer saw, but of course she didn't understand. I couldn't leave them here in danger. Then there were the boys—but I knew Aurien would never hurt her boys, even if she had gone quite mad.

Conal came around behind me and heaved me to my feet. My balance was terrible. I couldn't have stood without being held but my legs seemed to move of themselves. He walked me to the window. I looked down and saw two armed and mounted men, and Beauty. I was glad it wasn't Glimmer. He hadn't been happy with anything that wasn't routine since the time we met Turth. One of the riders was Emlin, the other was Garian. I wished I had been practicing belly flopping onto horses from a height, though it would have done me little good if I had. Conal lowered me down, and Emlin caught hold of me and steadied me into the saddle. I fell forward over Beauty's neck at once. Garian tied my legs to the saddle so I couldn't fall off completely. I caught Emlin's eye, and made the hand signal again. "The ala," I signaled. "To Derwen. At dawn." Moving them now would probably be more dangerous than staying the night; a dawn move wouldn't seem so suspicious that anyone would go and wake Aurien. Or so I hoped. Emlin looked puzzled.

"But how can I move the ala at dawn if I go with you now?" he asked.

He couldn't, of course. "You stay and move the ala," Conal said. "We'll go with her. Could you get another horse for me? The queen of Dun Morr can ride yours."

I had told him to obey Conal. Conal, for all his faults, was quick-witted and good in an emergency. Emlin dismounted hesitantly, looking at me and up at Conal. Conal lowered Emer out of the window into the saddle of Emlin's horse. Garian steadied her. She muttered something under her breath that included the word "greathorses," then straightened in the saddle. Emlin went back toward the stables. He came back much more quickly than he had the first time, when he must have had to wake Garian. It still seemed like a long time, slumped and still on Beauty's broad back. The night air seemed to be doing me good. I was breathing more easily. I struggled to straighten myself but I still couldn't manage it. Beauty stood without complaint. He was too good-mannered to object if I'd decided to sit on his back like an awkward parcel.

As Conal jumped down into the saddle, people carrying torches came running around the corner of the house. "Stop thief!" they called. I could see the light shining on weapons.

"Come on, ride for your lives!" Conal shouted. I could only see behind, not in front. I caught sight of Emlin running back toward the stables. They had no chance of catching us. We were mounted and they were on foot. He was a different matter. I hoped the darkness would cover him. I managed to nudge Beauty with my knees and we went off after the others as fast as a lightning bolt.

— 2 —

When putting a traitor to the question, banish all emotions and
pay close attention.

—Caius Dalitus, *The Relations of Rulers*

I knew we could make it home to Derwen in a night without
killing the horses. I had done it before. I sat in the saddle
and let Beauty carry me after the others through the night. We
rode as fast as we dared, and for the most part in silence. Garian didn't ask a single question. I think he was born without
any curiosity. After we had left the pursuit far behind, Emer
and Conal sang together quietly for a while. They sang old
Isarnagan songs about feuds and battles and impossible
quests. Their voices blended well together. Then they trailed
off and we rode on in silence again.

I could have slept if I had let myself. I did not seem to be
getting any worse, but nor could I detect any improvement. I
hated being carried along like a sack of turnips. From time to
time I tried to sit up and failed. Occasionally I coughed. I
could twitch my knees and move one hand, the whole arm if
I tried really hard. It was horrible to be so weak. The worst of
it was not being able to talk at all. I had always been well until then, and had suffered no more hurt than battle-cuts and
bruises, which soon healed. I had thought aging meant being
slower at thirty-eight than I had been at eighteen, which
could be made up by having better technique. That poisoning
was my first taste of real infirmity. I hated it. I tried not to
think what I would do if the land could not help me and if I
must live in this state forever. The Vincan answer would have
been to kill myself. I could not take that way out. I had responsibilities; I had made promises to Derwen, to my people,
and to Urdo. There was nobody else ready to care for the
land. It would be five years before Gwien was old enough.

Five years of only being able to twitch my fingers, grunt, and drool seemed a daunting prospect.

We were near the borders of Derwen but not yet over them when we heard the pursuit. They were mounted and noisy. I could see nothing but dark branches, but they sounded to me like half an untrained pennon crashing along, ten or fifteen people. Without discussion we all put on a spurt. They continued on after us. After a while I heard a voice calling out: "Who rides in Magor?"

That was not an ala challenge. "I think the truth will serve best," Conal said. "That way it will be more difficult for them to say they took us for brigands or raiders in the dark. In any case, it may be Emlin and his people."

"We are not at war with them, and you are a herald from Atha," Emer agreed. I tried to shout a warning and managed a few strangled syllables, but it was too late.

"Ap Gaius, armiger of the ala of Magor, Emer ap Allel, the queen of Dun Morr, Sulien ap Gwien, praefecto of the High King and Lord of Derwen, and I am Conal ap Amagien, herald of Oriel, called Conal the Victor."

I could hardly believe that he had forgotten the prohibition Emer had placed on him, that to give any part of his name when he was with her would mean death. I tried to spur Beauty on, and he found some more speed from within him somewhere as a shower of arrows fell around us. One of them skittered off one of the shoulder plates on my armor.

"Annoying," Conal said.

"I do wish there had been time to go for my sword," Emer said.

"Take Sulien's, she can't use it at the moment," Conal said. Then Emer was beside me, drawing out my sword. I grunted permission, but when it was gone I felt naked and disarmed. My shield was on the side of the saddle, but she didn't take it. I hoped she had Emlin's.

Then the first of them were among us. That is the only battle of my life in which I did nothing. I gave no orders, killed nobody, and suffered no wounds, I simply rode straight on as

fast as I could. I caught glimpses of Emer and Garian and
Conal fighting. Conal leapt from the saddle straight at one of
them, knocking him back onto the ground. That trick would
never have worked on an armiger who was used to his horse,
and only a madman would have tried it. Conal laughed and
brandished a sword he had acquired in the encounter. He
must have been practicing riding since that duel at
Thansethan. I saw him take down another man with the
sword. He had no shield, and of course he was still wearing
the tunic and breeches he had worn for dinner in the hall.

None of the pursuers seemed confident on their horses.
Some of them had bows, and most of them had swords, but
none of them seemed to have spears. They were not armed
like armigers. They did not give the battle cry of our ala,
"Galba!" but rather called "Magor!" to let each other know
where they were. I worked out after a while they must be Aurien's household guards got up on greathorses. Garian seemed
to be doing particularly well against them. He was the only
hale and trained armiger there. I saw him take down two of
them, and then Beauty jumped a stream and we were in Derwen.

It was like falling into dark water. The land came over me
like a wave. It was not just the sense of being home, known
and knowing. There is a sea tide and a land tide, and it was
the land tide that drew me down to where the trees and I are
brothers and the slow shifting of the rock on the world's skin
makes a song I can hear. I did not ask for strength or reach for
strength. What charms could there be against poison? But the
land knew me and recognized me. There was a moment of
deep belonging there, and for the instant between the drifting
of a dandelion seed and the growth of an oak tree I sat
straight on Apple's back in deep forest in the first glimmer of
spring dawn and knew the land as the land knew me. There
was a great disturbance along the borders of Magor, and distant rumblings of disturbance mixed with a new song from
the waterwheels grinding at Nant Gefalion. Still, all grew as
it should and the land was well. As for me, something was
choking me. I hawked and spat, and all the poison that had

been running through my veins fell from my mouth in one sour, twisted lump. A tingling pain ran through my body, followed by agonizing cramps as I sat up. Poor Beauty stopped as I did so. He was sweating and trembling and his ears were flat against his head. I felt more thirsty than I have ever been in my life. My strength was back, and I thanked the land spirits of Derwen with all the words I knew.

The sounds of pursuit had fallen behind. I spoke to Beauty reassuringly and reached down for my waterskin. I drained it in one draft. The sky was graying in the east but it was still very dark under the trees. I untied my legs from the saddle. Then I turned Beauty's head and let him walk back slowly to where we had last seen the others. I did not know what good we could do. He was almost at the end of his strength and I had no sword.

I found Conal first. He was lying at the brook, filling a helmet with water. His eyes widened when he saw me sitting up in the saddle. "You made it into Derwen, I see," he said. "Then this expedition was not entirely futile."

"You saved my life," I said directly. Beauty forded the little stream and halted beside him. "Thank you."

"It was only polite," he said, and smiled. "I should have done it rather better had I known what I was getting into. Whatever have you done to anger your sister so much that she is poisoning you and sending armed men after you?"

"I don't know," I said. "I don't understand this at all."

"What a shame," Conal said. "It would have been nice to know what was going on. I'm very sorry to tell you that ap Gaius is dead. He and I were fighting the last of them."

"Turth's tusks!" I swore. Garian had been a good armiger. "You've killed them all?"

"None of them will be going back to tell tales," Conal said. "Do you think you could take this water to Emer? She's a little way down the track back there." He gestured a little with the helmet, spilling some of the water.

"Of course," I said, dismounting. My legs felt very wobbly. I wanted to drink more water myself. Beauty put his head down to drink as soon as I was down. "But why don't you take it yourself?" Then I saw that his other arm, the one not holding the helmet, was barely attached to his shoulder. "Oh, Fishface, you idiot!" I said. "You've got yourself killed! Where's the weapon that did it?"

Conal snorted. "I am dying with a woman who despises me," he said. "That is about what my father and my uncle always thought I would deserve. The weapon is back there near Emer. I already sang all the charms I know, which is what has kept me alive this far. Beyond that the gods are laughing at me. I broke the curse, and I will die for it. I should have told them my name was Fishface."

"I'll carry you back there and try my charms," I said. It must have been a heavy blow from on top after he was already unhorsed. It could have been a sword or an ax, there was no way to tell. Armor might have helped, but probably not very much. "And anyway, I don't despise you. You infuriate me a lot of the time but I've never despised you."

"That's good to know," he said, and smiled, gathering together all his charm. "I'd really much prefer it if you took the water to Emer. She may be destined to die as well, but her foot appears to be reattached so there is likely hope for her. Do tell her—well, tell her I love her more than breath, if you would. She will know that I am dead, if she is alive to know it. I grant you it would make a better song if we both die, but I'd really rather she didn't. I suppose as far as songs go it should have been the three of us. Strange that you should be here, after all these stories of terrible debauchery you and I are supposed to have committed. But you prefer leprous female dead cod, I recall." He smiled at me again.

"You're babbling," I said, gruffly, to hide the lump that had come into my throat. "Hold onto that helmet, I can carry you and it."

"If you like," he said indifferently. The dawn birds were starting to sing loudly all around us. I took Beauty's head to stop him drinking too much too soon. "When I told my father Black Darag was dead he asked me why, in that case, I was still alive," Conal said meditatively as I bent down toward him. I hoped it wasn't far to where Emer was. I wondered if I could put him up on Beauty.

"You told me that at Thansethan," I said, getting my arms underneath him.

"Well, if you get the chance, let him know that I managed to die in a not unworthy cause, nor entirely without dignity."

"If I have to," I said, and lifted. Conal laughed and drew breath to say something. Then his bad arm flopped away from his body and a tremendous amount of blood ran out of it, all down my armor and into the stream. Beauty made a little whuffle of disgust. I set him down again, gently, though there was no need. He was unquestionably dead.

I took the helmet and set it carefully on a stone. Then I wiped my armor as clean as I could with the flowing water. Then I filled up my waterskin. There would have been enough water in that for Emer, but somehow taking the wretched helmet had become an obligation I owed to Conal. I led Beauty back down the track. That left both my hands full so I had to let my tears run unchecked. It was strange that I wept for Conal; I had not even known I had liked him.

Emer was sitting propped against a bank. She appeared to be alive but very weak. I gave her the helmet of water.

Garian's horse was cropping the grass nearby. Garian himself lay on his back. His eyes were wide open, staring at the sky. He had been stabbed through the thigh and his life had run out of him. There were six other bodies in sight, and four dead horses. I looked at the bodies one by one. I recognized all of them as Aurien's people. The last of them was Cado, whose father Berth was my trumpeter and whose daughter Flerian was one of my scouts. It seemed terribly wrong that he should have been trying to kill me. I stared at him for a moment and then looked back at Emer. She lowered the helmet.

"Conal?" she asked, as if she already knew the answer.

"Dead," I confirmed. She closed her eyes for a moment, then took a deep breath. "It was as good a death as any warrior could wish," I said. "He told me to tell you he loved you

more than breath. He said it in that way of his but I know he
meant it."

"Much good it does me," she said bleakly. Then, while she
wept, I caught Garian's mare. There didn't seem any point in
the two of us making a pyre now. If we rode on a few hours to
Derwen we could come back with plenty of people. Besides,
if anyone else was going to approach from Magor I wanted
the troops behind me.

I helped Emer onto Garian's mare and got back up on
Beauty. We went on together in silence. When we came to the
stream Emer drew in her breath but did not dismount. We
went on, into Derwen. The trees and the track were no different, yet everything was different, because I knew it and it
knew me.

After a while Emer wiped her eyes. "I killed him as sure as
if I'd held the sword," she said. "Don't ever curse anyone unless you know what you're doing."

"I don't know any curses," I said.

"They're not like charms you have to learn," she replied.
"There are so many things you don't seem to know in Tir
Tanagiri. I suppose it comes of having no oracle-priests."

"Tell me how to curse, then," I asked, less because I
wanted to know than to distract her from her grief.

"You can only give a prohibition to someone who is close
to you; a lover or a relative, or a personal enemy. They have
to be there in front of you; it is better if you are touching
them. Then you reach out to the gods and set a prohibition on
them that if they break it they will die. If the gods will have
it then you can feel it become part of the way the world is. It
binds you to them, and you will know when it finds them. It
is warding as well as curse, because they will not die of other
things that might have found them. Some people set prohibi-
tions on their children to protect them. There is a story of a
mother who set a warding curse on her son that he could not
be killed indoors or out of doors, by weapons or of any sickness. He died when the house collapsed as he was in the
doorway. The whole family was crushed."

"You just reach out?" I asked.

"Perhaps it is better that people don't do it so much here," she said. "Conal—" Her voice broke.

"Or I might have killed him that morning before the walls of Derwen," I said harshly.

"I should have trusted you," she said.

"You had little reason to," I said.

I was worried about Emlin and the rest of the ala in Magor. As soon as I got home I would have to send word to Urdo, making sure the messenger went through Nant Gefalion and Caer Gloran, not the faster way through Magor.

I had filled and emptied my waterskin four times before we came to the town walls, and still my thirst seemed never ending. I was also exhausted and had no expectation of sleep. I told the gate guards to close the gates and send the decurios to me. Then Emer and I rode up and dismounted at the stables by the house. I wanted to talk to Veniva before doing anything.

Daldaf ap Wyn, my mother's steward, came forward to greet me. "Welcome home, Lord; you have come earlier than we looked for you?"

I didn't want to tell him anything at the moment, so I just said, "Yes." He handed me and Emer steaming beakers of hot apple juice. This was faster than he normally managed a hot drink, even on a cold day. I thought that he must have started heating them when he heard we were at the gates.

"Peace in this hall," he said to Emer. I raised my beaker to my lips, then, despite my thirst, waited as she murmured the response, to drink with her. Then I caught the smell and dashed it down, knocking Emer's from her hand. My cup was copper, it dented and rolled, making a ringing sound. Emer's was my mother's precious red Vincan cup, and it broke into many pieces. I grabbed Daldaf by the upper arms and lifted him off the ground.

"Nobody plays that trick twice!" I said. His look of terror was enough to convict him in my eyes. "Who told you to poison me and why are you doing it?"

Just then Veniva swept into the hall. She smelled of rosemary, and had green stains on her apron; she must have been making up a salve. She took in the scene in a moment and raised her eyebrows. "Whatever are you doing to Dal?" she asked.

"Stopping him from poisoning me and my guest," I said. It was only then that it struck me that if Emer's drink had also been poisoned then he had actually poisoned the guest cup. It was an enormity that made Aurien's attempted kin-murder at her own table look almost acceptable.

Veniva came forward quickly. Daldaf was struggling in my grip. I had thought I was weak and tired, but I had no trouble keeping him pinned. "Did you do that?" she asked. He said nothing. I shook him, and he still said nothing. Veniva stooped to the broken pieces of her precious red cup and sniffed at one. "Henbane?" she said, in a horrified voice. "Daldaf? Why?"

"I'll never speak," he said. "The White God will protect me!" He tried to spit at me, and missed.

"It's even worse than that," I said, holding him at arm's length. "Aurien tried to poison me yesterday. Then she sent troops after us when we were on our way here, and killed Garian and Conal the Victor." I think it was the first time I'd ever referred to him as anything but Fishface, and it was then I really believed he was dead and I'd never hear his outrageous statements again.

"Aurien did?" Veniva said. "And Daldaf is invoking the White God?"

"I'll make him talk," I said.

"He is my steward, Sulien," my mother said. "I think I know my duty. *I* will make him talk."

"I'm entitled to a fair trial," Daldaf said, looking frightened, as well he might.

"So you are," Veniva said. She clapped her hands, and the hall was suddenly full of servants and people of the house. I expect they had been listening around the corners. My three decurios were shuffling their feet on the porch; she called them in as well. I gave Daldaf to ap Madog, who took a firm grip on him and pinned both his hands behind his back.

"Before all the gods who care to listen!" I said, in my loud lord's voice. "Daldaf ap Wyn, you stand accused of attempted murder of your lord and of a guest of the house by poisoning the welcome cup." This was the most impromptu justice I had ever given, but it was all quite legal. "Have you anything to say?"

"I won't speak," he said.

"The pieces of the cup are here and the smell of henbane is still on them," I said. "I am witness to this act, and so is your other attempted victim, Emer ap Allel, queen of Dun Morr. If any would smell the cup, come and do it. That the poison is in it is not in dispute. If you did not set it there, tell me who did."

Daldaf just shook his head and said nothing.

"I ask you again if you will name the others who conspired with you in this act, or if you have anything to say that can mitigate your offense?"

"I won't speak, you can't make me!" he said again. Veniva took the curved gold comb out of her hair and twisted the loops up without it. She ran her fingers over the sharp points and smiled.

"The punishment for attempted murder is death, and the punishment for treachery is death, and the punishment for the impiety of poisoning the guest-cup you will find after death."

"The White God will protect me!" Daldaf said. There was a murmur among the onlookers, many of whom had taken the pebble.

"You are no martyr, Daldaf, only a murderer," I said. I picked up the copper cup he had given me and set it upright so anyone who wanted to could come and smell it. "I sentence you to death. As the conspiracy you are concerned with touches on matters of deep importance, and since you will not speak, you will be put to the question before you are executed. Ap Madog, take him—" We had never had to torture anyone before that I could remember. I couldn't think where would be a good place to do it. "Take him where my lady mother tells you." Ap Madog dragged him off, struggling. I gestured to two of the other armigers to go with him in case he needed help. They made their way toward Veniva. She stood and watched him for a moment, her hand on the teeth of her comb.

"You have brought disgrace on my hall," she said to Daldaf, loudly, so that everyone could hear. Then she went off toward the store rooms, the others following.

I found another cup and welcomed Emer properly to Derwen. Then I sent out Hiveth and her whole pennon to bring back the bodies and to look out for Emlin and the pennons from Magor. I sent a messenger to Dun Morr to inform Lew of Conal's death and Emer's safety. I gave him another message for Govien ap Caw, who was in charge of the pennons stationed there, to tell him to bring them to me as quickly as he could. Then I sent everyone back to work, making sure the guards were alert and that there would be sentries out.

Then, although I was very tired and it would have been better to wait until after Daldaf had spoken, I began to compose a message to Urdo.

Stir to life, my exiled heart,
far down the mountain I see the horse
of a messenger bringing letters.

News is coming to stir my blood,
news from ever-bustling Vinca,
politics, literature, scandal, and love.

No longer is everything I care for out of reach.
The messenger is drawing ever nearer.
Outside my window the snow is melting.
　　　　—Naso, "The Banks of the Vonar, Number 61"

I went into the little accounts room, sat at the table by the
east window, and took up pen and parchment. I had spent
many days in that room in the last five years, working on accounts, writing to Urdo, and watching the square of sunlight
creep across the stone flags. Everything in my life was complicated, and only writing to Urdo was simple. He had long
wrestled with the problems of kingship and knew ways of
dealing with questions that had only begun to perplex me.
Therefore I wrote to him not just with news but with all the
questions that came to me. Angas had told me years before
that it was lonely to be a king, and now I felt it for myself.
Had it not been for Urdo's letters I do not know how I could
have borne it. I went to Caer Tanaga for half a month or so
every year, usually at midsummer. The rest of the time duty
kept me at Derwen. I had Veniva for company, I had Emlin
and the ala, but it was hard and lonely. I was doing work that
did not suit me and for which I had never been trained.

After Morien's death I had suddenly found myself responsible for the whole land of Derwen, for everyone and everything on it. I do not think I was a bad lord, even then, but

there was so much I did not know. I learned a new respect for my father and Duke Galba. I learned administration and justice. I tried hard to be fair and to learn how to be a lord. I read Urdo's laws and now I began to understand them. Sometimes things Urdo had said about them years before when he was first thinking about them came back to me. Often our letters were about law and justice; the red-cloaks would carry discussion of some point in Dalitus back and forth for a month. Other times I would simply pour out everything that was troubling me in one long letter. Often enough, just writing it would ease my heart, and his reply would set me quite straight again. He always replied, often within a day or two of when my message reached him. Once, when it was a problem with Cinvar ap Uthbad of Tathal about the border above Nant Gefalion, he came himself, unannounced.

Now I sat chewing the end of my pen and slowly stripping off the feathering. I had written the salutation so many times that I didn't have to think: "From Sulien the daughter of Gwien, Lord of Derwen, at Derwen, to the High King Urdo, War-leader of the Tanagans, at Caer Tanaga or where he may be, Greetings!" I dipped the pen again and left enough space so that when the sheet was folded and sealed the salutation would be all that was visible. "My sister Aurien," I wrote, and stopped and stared at those three words, alone with space all around them. How many times in the last five years, I wondered, had I written them thus to Urdo? How many different sentences had they begun? "My sister Aurien doesn't want her boys trained with weapons—" As if there was any choice for a nobly born child, or would she have us all defended against the raiders by monks of the White God? "My sister Aurien objects to my naming little Gwien heir to Derwen—" Although what else could I have done? Darien was promised to Urdo, who still had no other heir. Veniva kept on sighing for more grandchildren, saying that she had not expected this when she had borne four children. In the end I had outright told her I would never marry. Gwien was as good an heir as any child of mine and the land accepted him. Anyone would have thought Aurien would be pleased to see her two sons both become kings, but since Galba died nothing pleased her.

I ran my hands through my hair and looked at the words again. "My sister Aurien." Oh, I had known for years that Aurien hated me, and had known it in part my fault. Still, why did she think she could get away with poisoning me now? The story about drink would never have worked on those who knew me best, on Veniva or on Urdo. She was no fool. There must be something I was missing, something happening I didn't know about. She had not acted like someone mad or possessed by evil spirits, and Daldaf had been in league with her. I kept staring at those three words, as if expecting them to develop answers instead of more questions. I stood up and paced. The little accounts room was cluttered with chests of accounts and receipts, and there was only enough clear space for three strides. One of the chests was marked in fresh, clear letters, "taxes." The summer before we had passed twenty years since we had given our hoarded gold to Urdo, and now Derwen paid tax like all the kingdoms. My mother groaned and complained and said she would have argued the gold was worth more if she had ever imagined any of us would be alive to see the day.

I looked out of the window. I could just see the gates, shut and guarded. There was no sign of the pennon coming back with Conal and Garian's bodies. The sky was full of threatening low clouds but there was no rain yet. I looked at the couch and longed to fling myself down and sleep. Things might be clearer when I woke up. I went back to the table and sat down; those three words were waiting to ambush me again. "My sister Aurien." I shook my head at them. I could feel my eyes closing and I let them. When I woke up Veniva would come and explain why Aurien hated me and what I had done wrong.

I knew I was dreaming, and yet it seemed as if it was no dream but just what I had been expecting to happen. Veniva was in the room, dressed in a drape, white with a dark blue border. It was folded perfectly and pinned with Aurien's pearl brooch from the hoard. I noted idly that her carefully pinned hair had returned to the black it had been when I was a child. She looked entirely calm. She was holding a big leather pouch like the ones the red-cloaks carried. "Sulien, I have come to ask your permission to send these to Aurien." She drew out of the pouch a coil of rope and a dagger. I drew in my breath. I had read in Cornelien about this ancient custom of sending the implements of suicide as a mercy to the nobly born. It had been a custom, never a law, even in Vinca long ago. I could not remember a time it had been done in living memory. "She is the mother of my grandsons," Veniva said. "Let me send these as my personal gift. Treachery needs repayment. I have raised a fine set of fools and traitors. At least let hers be a Vincan death." Then she reached into the pouch again and drew out Daldaf's head, dripping blood from the neck. He appeared to be quite alive; he looked up at me and said, "And the life of the world to come."

I woke with a start, to find not Veniva but one of the house servants bending over me. I rubbed my eyes. I felt slow and sick and stupid.

"They've brought the bodies and they wanted to know what to do with them," she stammered.

"Has my mother—is my mother there yet?" I asked, stretching and yawning.

"The wife of Gwien is still—" She hesitated. "Still in the old dairy with Daldaf."

There was a horrible taste in the back of my mouth. I did not want to watch Daldaf being tortured. "Bring me hot mint water to the hall," I said, and she scurried off toward the kitchens.

I went out into the hall, where suddenly I was being asked a hundred questions by everyone. Most of them had to do with the daily routine of the house, which had been so terribly disrupted. I could see that we were going to need a new steward immediately. I had never quite thought how much Daldaf did.

The question of what to do with the bodies was not a simple one either.

Garian was a follower of the White God, and he had a mother, a wife, and two children at Magor. Conal, of course, was Isarnagan. His nearest relative was Lew, at Dun Morr, but his father was still alive in Oriel and might want his body sent home. He was one of Oriel's Royal Kin. I thought of asking Emer what she would want done, and then realized how inappropriate that would be. Yet I knew nothing about his personal relationship with the gods. I gave orders for both bodies to be laid out honorably for the time being. I sat down on the windowseat to sip my mint water and think. People kept coming up to me with questions, which I answered as best I could. In between interruptions I dozed and fretted. Despite the irritation of the interruptions I didn't want to go to bed or to try to get on with my letter. I wanted to sit in the sunshine and watch my people as I had done so many times in the last years. Through the window I could see Second Pennon drilling, and a ship unlading at the wharf. In the hall people kept coming and going.

Well into the afternoon, Veniva came back. She was still wearing the russet overdress she had worn that morning. It was flecked with blood where her apron had not covered it. She looked distressed.

"What news?" I asked.

"We must speak privately," she said, glancing around the hall. I followed her back into the little accounts room, where the three words of my letter were waiting ominously.

"What did he say?" I asked as she closed the door.

"Civil war," Veniva said tersely, and her lips closed on that single Vincan word as if she would say no more. Then, as I gaped at her, she drew breath and spoke again. "You must write to all the kings and tell them it is not true and keep them from rising."

"What isn't true?" I asked.

Veniva looked drawn and hollow-eyed. "It is just like that time when Flavien wrote to all of us that Urdo was become a tyrant and meant to depose him," she said. "That time your father and Duke Galba and old Uthbad wrote letters to all the kings and they were reassured. It may work again, if we are quick."

"But what are they saying, and why has nobody said it to us?" I asked, feeling as if I was riding full tilt through a forest in a mist.

"It is this Breghedan affair. But that is just the spark. Some of the kings are restless with Urdo, and say he is a pagan and a tyrant and he prefers the Jarns to his own people. Daldaf told me there is a conspiracy between Cinvar ap Uthbad, Cinon ap Cinon, and Flavien ap Borthas, with Ayl and Angas and Custennin wavering about joining in. Aurien, of course, the fool, is deeply implicated."

"We're in a terrible position here," I said, reaching for a map. It was one of the new sharp ones Raul's people had drawn up. "I don't believe it about Ayl and Angas, but Custennin might be idiotic enough. What's happening in Wenlad?"

"He didn't mention it," Veniva said. "But wait. Marchel ap Thurrig is due to land in Magor with two alae of Narlahenan horse. Apparently they hoped that, if you were ignominiously dead and Aurien urged it, our ala would join them. Then they could take the whole center of the land and the others would join them."

"Emlin has more loyalty than that," I said automatically. But Emlin had served under Marchel once. I didn't think he would have done that, but it wasn't impossible.

"That part of the plan failed. Daldaf was horrified to see you coming back and decided to poison you."

"He would have done better to stab me, if he wanted to get away with it. I wasn't expecting anything and it would have been less impious." I felt detached from the whole thing.

"He was never noted for strategic thinking, though he was a very good steward and I will miss that." Veniva smiled grimly. "He admits he has been intercepting your letters."

"My letters?" I echoed inanely. My letters to Urdo? But I had been getting answers, Daldaf certainly wasn't capable of forging them. The thought that he might have been reading them was dreadful enough. I wondered who else might have written to me and what they might have said. I hadn't heard from ap Erbin for some time.

"We trust the red-cloaks so much," Veniva said. "We think what we have written will be delivered. It seems many things have been going astray. We will have to check his room. He said he had destroyed most of them but there were some he was saving to send to Demedia."

"To Morthu?" I asked, though I knew it was true. Our eyes met, and she raised her chin in affirmation. Veniva had hated Morthu as much as I had since the day of Morien's death. I felt ill at the thought of Morthu reading Urdo's letters and knowing so much of what he thought and dreamed. I took a slow breath and tried to clear my head. "The most urgent thing is Marchel," I said, putting my hand on the map again. "Did he say exactly where she would land?"

"He didn't know," Veniva said. "But you're wrong. The most urgent thing is writing to the kings. If Marchel lands that is an invasion; that doesn't break the Peace. If the kings rise—it will be the way it was after Avren's death. I have lived through that once, and we so barely saved anything of civilization that time. If it happens again that will be the end, I think, the end of everything that was good about Vincan ways of life, the end of Peace, and the world will go down in darkness and petty squabbling forever." She leaned forward and gripped my arm with surprising strength. "Even if Urdo wins he will not be able to hold the country without the trust of the kings. If there is constant war, the next time somebody manages to stop it there will be nobody left who knows how to make pipes for hot water or who can remember how to make laws people will keep. We must hold onto this fragment of Peace whatever happens or there will be nobody left to understand what Peace *is*."

I had never realized how much it meant to her. "I will write to them," I said. "But I am only one person, and I am not sure how much they trust me. I don't know if they think of me as a king like them or if they think I am the High King's Prae-

fecto first and Lord of Derwen afterward." I knew that some
of them at least thought that. Custennin had never made any
secret of it.

"And are you?" Veniva asked, never taking her eyes off
mine for an instant.

I hesitated. "I never wanted to be Lord of Derwen, but I
have always done my best for land and people, as my father
did. I *am* Lord of Derwen; I stand between land and people,
before the gods. They are my responsibility, and I accept that
as I have accepted it since we came home after Morien died.
But I still serve Urdo the High King, and always will."

"That would go very badly with Flavien," Veniva said, re-
leasing my arm. She stood up. "Still, you must write to them
for whatever little good it may do to hold the Peace. Tell
them you support Urdo and he is no tyrant, whatever he is
doing in Bregheda."

"What choice does he have in Bregheda?" I asked. "Glyn
is—"

"If the kings won't accept it, and it seems they won't, then
Urdo is being stupid," Veniva said firmly.

"There is nobody alive who is the child or the grandchild
of a king of Bregheda," I said. "Cyndylan's horse tripped and
he broke his neck, then old Penda died of grief for the last of
his sons. Urdo had to make a decision."

"Make a decision, yes. He didn't have to make one that
would antagonize half the kings. Glyn is the great-grandson
of Minmanton of Bregheda, yes, but he is also Urdo's own
man, and everyone knows it. It looks as if he is trying to control the kingdom."

"Why ever would he need to bother to?" I threw up my
hands. "When I heard, I thought it was another burden he was
putting onto Glyn and Garah, and I wondered that he was
prepared to manage without them at Caer Tanaga."

Veniva gave a brief choked laugh, and turned to look out of
the window. "You may be sure this is not what Cinvar of
Tathal or Cinon of Nene thought when the news reached
them. They know their fathers and grandfathers back to the
days when they married the trees. Glyn is being raised to be

their equal, and he is Urdo's own man and his wife was a groom and the daughter of a farmer. I knew the kings would hate it. But whatever Urdo is doing, there is no choice but to support him."

"Is it better to argue it in the letters to Cinvar and Cinon or not?" I asked.

"There is no use writing to Cinvar at all," she said, turning to look at me. "If Uthbad One-Hand were still alive he might pay attention to you, but Cinvar will not. We have killed Daldaf ap Wyn, who he considers a kinsman. He and Marchel will never forgive us for that. But if it is only Tathal and Magor that is not so bad. Magor will be safe in any case; Aurien will have been careful to make sure the boys know nothing."

"Good," I said, and meant it. I took up my pen and a fresh parchment, fit for writing to kings. "So should I mention Bregheda, and my friendship with Glyn?" I hesitated, looking up at her. "Oh Mother, will you write as well?"

She blinked at me, surprised. "What good would that do? I am not a king. I am not your father."

I smiled. "No, but there is power in your name. There are those among the kings who may pay more attention to you than to me. You know what arguments will move them. You are respected, and you are one of them."

"One of them?" She stared at me across the little room as if I had gone mad. "I have never been one of them. I was born in Rutipia, in Bricinia that is now Cennet, in the year the last Vincan legions left Tir Tanagiri. When I was twelve years old Avren banished us from our land and our towns and gave all of Cennet to his new Jarnish father-in-law, Hengist. He made an alliance with the very Jarns we had been fighting outside our walls all my life. The Tanagan lords fought Avren and each other but cared nothing for us, no more than Avren did. They gave us no help at all. My father was the magistrate of Rutipia; he was killed when we opened the gates to leave. The people scattered like chaff. There were no towns left. Towns need so many different kinds of people, and they were all scattered and helpless. Gwien . . . your father—" She hes-

itated, and clearly thought better of what she was going to
say. "They call me the last of the Vincans. There are none of
my people left now. There are monasteries instead of schools,
clusters of farmers' houses around lords' houses instead of
towns. My own child thinks it is splendid that there is acknowledged law and very few people actually die fighting
before they are grown up, at least most years. And what is
worst, you are right!"

I didn't know what to say. "You never told me any of that,"
I said, at last.

She laughed. "What good would it do you to know? I
brought you up safely and properly and taught you as well as
I could. And I never think of any of that, never think about
the time before I came here. For years I believed the Vincans
would come back one day, but now I know they will not.
Only the raiders come from over the sea. Narlahena is fallen
and Lossia is overrun and Vinca itself is fallen to the barbarians, and there are only Caer Custenn and us with a sea of
them between us, squabbling and killing the people who
know and care what civilization is."

I had never really thought about where Veniva had come
from. She was my mother. She was a Vincan, yes, I knew
that, but I had not thought she meant it so literally. All my life
she had always been at Derwen. "You could still write to the
kings," I said, hesitantly. "They think of you as one of them."

"Not those of them who remember where I come from,
which will be few enough by now," she said. "Very well, I
will do it, if you think it will be any help at all. I would do
anything that can sway the straw in the wind to help this
Peace hold."

So we sat there the rest of the afternoon writing letters to
all the kings. I wrote first to Cinon and Flavien and Custennin, difficult letters all, trying to stop them rising treacherously while avoiding accusing them of intending to. Then I
wrote to all the other kings. To my surprise the easiest letters
were those to Alfwin and Ohtar, who I had no reason at all to
distrust. It was very strange that distant Jarnish kings were

easier to understand than my kin close at hand, but that was the way of it. I knew what to say to reassure them.

I was in the middle of writing to Ayl, and yawning over my work, when a servant came in to tell me that Emlin was here, with the half ala from Magor. I was glad to take a break, although I left Veniva still writing. I have rarely done anything so difficult or so completely useless as writing those letters to the kings.

— 4 —

My running child, from your first step you passed me,
stretched out your arms and charged across the field.
What could I do? You would not heed my warning,
the more I called, the more you would not yield.

How fast you ran! How much you wanted glory!
How brave you were, the world stretched out before.
A name you won, my child, all know your story,
No deed of mine could make you safe once more.

How far you ran, my laughing child, beyond me.
How great you grew, my child I could not save.
How bright you burned, how little you have left me;
nothing but ashes cold within the grave.
— Isarnagan Lament

Emlin was sitting on the window ledge, looked tired but
unhurt. He stood as I came up. When I saw him I felt as
if a weight had been lifted from me. If Aurien was prepared
to murder me then she might have been prepared to bar doors
and burn barracks. The safety of my armigers and my horses
had been on my mind all day, though I'd pushed the thought
away every time it surfaced.

"Sulien! You're better!" he greeted me.

I waved him back to the seat and sat down beside him. So
much had happened that the poisoning and paralysis seemed
long ago by now. "The land healed me. But Garian and Conal
the Victor are dead, killed by some of Aurien's household.
How about you and the ala?"

"They're all here safe," he said. "I spent the night in the
stables and left at dawn as you said."

"Any trouble?" I asked.

"No. Well, Galba's lady asked us to stay. She said those who had more loyalty to Galba and the White God than to you and Urdo should stay. When she saw we weren't going to she seemed glad to let us go, almost hurried us out."

"Did any of them want to stay?" I remembered how they had all cut their hair for Galba. Even the recruits who had come into the ala after his death knew all the stories about him, and one of the stories was his great love for Aurien. I had never tried to discourage this love of Galba. He had been my friend, too; he had formed this ala and given it much of its spirit. I tried to command them well, I had expanded them from six pennons to nine, but they were Galba's ala still and fought with the Rod of Magor on their ala banner. As for the White God, many of the armigers had taken the pebble. It was interesting that Aurien was making that claim. I wondered where Thansethan stood.

Emlin looked awkward. "One or two looked to see what their friends were doing, but nobody moved."

"I'm not asking for names," I said, as gently as I could. Emlin himself had been Galba's tribuno before he was mine. Aurien might well have got some of them if I *had* been dead of drink. "That's all right. So, you left without being attacked?"

"Who could attack us?" Emlin looked puzzled. "I can see that Aurien could send her guards to fight four people in the forest, but I had three pennons with me, half an ala!"

"Did you see anything of Marchel?" I asked.

"Marchel?" His eyebrows rose in astonishment. "No. Isn't she in Narlahena?"

As I was explaining the new situation to him as best I could, a servant came up and announced that the dinner I had ordered was ready. I remembered the cook asking me about it that afternoon and agreeing to all his suggestions.

Veniva came out of the accounts room, announcing that she would need to find a new steward. Emlin and I followed her to the eating alcove, where Duncan and Emer soon joined us. Emer looked terrible, her eyes red-rimmed from weeping and with shadows under them so dark they were almost blue. The old scar on her cheek showed angrily red as if she had been scrubbing her face hard. Duncan was looking tired, and I suddenly wondered how old he was. He still went out to the practice yard regularly, though he had not been war-leader since my father died.

We talked about the troubles as we ate. Emer ate nothing but bread, sometimes dipping it in her broth for politeness. I was hungry, but with so many questions I talked more than I ate. When I mentioned Marchel's supposed invasion, Duncan clicked his tongue.

"Where are her children?" he asked. "Are they at Nant Gefalion with ap Wyn the Smith? We should send swift riders up there to seize them as hostages for her good conduct, and ap Wyn as well."

"What good conduct?" I asked, swallowing. "She is exiled on pain of death, she can't be here in honor."

"No," Emer agreed, "but Duncan is right. Having hostages might well prevent her moving against us directly."

"If she doesn't move against us, she will still move against Urdo, which is as bad; nothing will work but defeating her. She needs to be killed. Her alae could leave, but how could we persuade her to pretend she'd never been here and just take her alae right away back to Narlahena or off to Caer Custenn or—or Rigatona!" I said.

Veniva raised her chin. "Well. But a threat to her children might be enough to do that. Without her what could the levies of Magor and Tathal do against the alae?"

"I don't like it," I said. "Either the boys are our enemies, in which case they won't be at Nant Gefalion but away at Talgarth or Caer Gloran preparing to fight us, or, if they are there, then they are innocent or very stupid."

"We needn't harm them," Veniva said. "Only tell Marchel that we have them in our keeping."

"And Urdo has taken hostages into the ala many times without harming them," Emlin said.

"People usually have a choice whether or not to give

hostages," I protested. "They are given as a pledge of faith, not kidnaped."

"These days, perhaps," Duncan said, looking sternly at his plate.

"She is an exile, and has no faith." Veniva shrugged. "And we're not talking about little children; the boys are grown men now. They are our enemies by their connections, and we should take them if we can. We have killed Daldaf; all his kin will be against us."

"If they mean us harm they won't be waiting there tamely to be taken," I said. "No. That is wrong and I won't have anything to do with it."

"Maybe we could invite them," Veniva said. "It would be safer for them here than up in the hills, if there is trouble. They would not be hostages, but honored guests. And if there is any restraining Marchel then it serves the same purpose."

I chewed and swallowed the last of my preserved apples, thinking about this. When I looked up all their eyes were on me. "I will send a pennon up to see if they are there, and to warn Nant Gefalion of the danger coming. If Cinvar invades from Caer Gloran they will come that way. I will have them offer ap Wyn and his sons our hospitality, but there will be no coercion in it."

Duncan sighed, but none of them argued with me.

When we finished eating I went out to the center of the hall and looked at my household, gathered in the alcoves. Being Lord of Derwen and obliged to do it often hadn't made me any better at making speeches. "You will have heard the news whispered," I said. "Better to hear it said plainly and by me. There have been attacks, and there may be invasions and up-risings." I didn't want to use the word war, though it burned on my tongue. "My sister Aurien ap Gwien is no longer our friend. Do not trust any messages coming from Magor. I will be riding to Magor in arms soon, but I will be calling the levies and enough force will be left here to protect you. I know you are all loyal, and I know you will do what you can. I will speak to the ala in the morning when the rest of the pennons come here from Dun Morr. A hard time may be coming, but we will uphold the King's Peace and win through."

I went back to Veniva and the others among a rising buzz of speculation. I would have gone straight off to read the letters in Daldaf's chest, but Emer put her hand on my arm. "I will sing, if I have your permission," she said.

"Of course," I said automatically, my thoughts catching up with my tongue too late. Sing? Now? It was true that we had just eaten, but it didn't seem the right time for singing. It was already too late to call her back. I sank back on the cushion next to my mother.

Emer went out into the center of the hall and sat on the stool by the great harp, which had been sitting there covered since Morien had died, except for occasional visits by musicians. She took up the little lap harp that sat beside it, removed the leather cover, and tuned it. The conversation rose for a moment when she went out. The people knew her, of course. The queen of Dun Morr was often here, but she was not one of us. Then it slowed and ceased as she tuned the strings, and the hall was silent when she spoke, though she did not raise her eyes from the harp.

"I was thinking," she said, quietly, "of the first time I ate in this hall, new come to Derwen, twelve years ago now. That was a night we had not dreamed, after the day that had been, when my people were come in arms, a night of friendship made and war averted. So many of those friends are dead now, or scattered. Morien ap Gwien lies under the earth and Conal the Victor lies unburned tonight." She plucked a string and let the echoes die away before she went on, perhaps to hide the tremor in her voice. "Garian ap Gaius is dead beside him, fallen together in one defense, though on that day they faced each other as enemies. So strangely time and alliances move, and here I sit in this hall tonight to hear that war is coming again."

Then she plucked at the harpstrings and played the tune of an old Isarnagan lament, a parent singing of a child who is dead. We all knew the song, had heard it many times. When she had played it through she played it again and sang the words, and when she had sung it she played it over again in silence. For the first time I knew in my heart that I had a son who could die in war—Darien was a signifier, he would be first in any charge Urdo's ala made. Then, immediately, I knew that it made no difference. Every armiger was someone's child, and my responsibility, and in this war with raised levies from Derwen every one of my people who fought and fell was like a child to me. I could not hold them back and keep them safe because someone's heart breaks when everyone dies, no more than a child can be kept from running free. There are wars that have to be fought whatever the cost, however much the true cost should be remembered. Every battle since Caer Lind I had written letters to the survivors of my fallen. While that task never grew easier, those who chose to fight were not children; they were grown warriors who had chosen to hazard themselves to protect those safe at home. More people would have died had I left those battles unfought, and many of them would have been children and unarmed farmers. Their deaths were heartbreak, yes, but they were a price they had paid willingly for the Peace. Emer had a right to mourn, but I suddenly felt angry with her for diminishing Conal's death like this. He had died laughing and, as he had said himself, in no unworthy cause.

Veniva leaned over. She had a tear on her cheek, I don't think there was a dry eye in the room by then. Emer was still playing the tune on the harp, and weeping. I thought Veniva was going to say something about Morien, or even Darien, but what she whispered was, "Who does Emer ap Allel have to mourn like that? Her daughter is eleven years old and safe in Dun Morr with Lew."

I was jerked out of my mood by the question. "Her mother, Maga—" I began feebly.

"That is *not* a song you sing for your mother dead more than ten years ago," Veniva hissed in my ear. "That is a song you sing for a child or a lover lost—" She paused. "Surely not Conal? He killed her mother!"

I moved a little away and looked straight at her. "It would be a great impiety," I said, gravely and very low.

"It would indeed." Veniva's look spoke volumes. "Well, if anyone remarks on it to me I shall tell them about the war the poor woman lived through in Connat before she was sixteen years old, and how personally she takes these things."

When Emer came back we congratulated her on her singing, and then I took a good lamp and went off to search Daldaf's possessions.

I had never had cause to go into his room before and I looked around curiously. It was just off the hall, as any steward's room would be. The walls were limewashed white, like everywhere else. There was one small window with tendrils of ivy poking in, a bed, and a chest at the foot, much like my room or anyone's room. I found it hard to picture him plotting treachery in this pleasant place. I set the lamp on the windowsill to add to the late light coming through. There was a soot mark there to show that it was where Daldaf usually put a lamp or a candle. I sat down on the bed and opened the chest.

The packet of letters was right at the bottom, under his clothes and jewelry. It was a thick pouch and I drew it out reluctantly. There were copies of my last three letters to Urdo and his to me on the top. This made me immediately furious. If Daldaf had been in front of me at that moment I would have been hard put to it not to run him through. How dared he read my private letters! I put them aside. The next letter was addressed to me but I had never seen it.

"From Ayl the son of Trumwin, king of Aylsfa, at Fenshal, by the hand of his clerk, Arcan of Thansethan, to Sulien the daughter of Gwien, Lord of Derwen, at Derwen, Blessings!"

So Ayl had a Jarnish clerk at last, though a monk. He had never been able to learn his letters, from starting too late and not applying himself enough. The few letters I had had from him before had been written by Penarwen. I opened the letter and read it through. Then I read it again, puzzled. I could not see why Daldaf had kept this from me. It was rambling and full of pieties I could not believe Ayl had uttered, but there was nothing in it but vague expressions of friendship and loyalty. On the second read I caught the tone, and put it down, shocked. This letter was like the ones I had spent the afternoon writing, but further clouded by Ayl's need to use a clerk he did not entirely trust. He was trying to feel me out about rebellion without openly saying anything of the kind. I was shocked. I had not thought Ayl could be drawn into this quarrel. I could not see what would make him line up beside Flavien and Cinvar. He seemed to want me to reassure him about something. Whatever it was, I had not; the letter had sat for half a month unanswered.

I took up the next letter and blinked at the salutation.

"*From Rigga of Rigatona at Caer Custenn to her cousin Sulien ap Gwien at Derwen, upon the island of Tir Tanagiri, Greetings!*" I had not heard from Rigg since she had left with ap Theophilus for Caer Custenn four years before. She was not the sort of person to write letters, even had sending letters across that vast distance not been difficult almost to impossibility.

> "*Sulien my cousin, I write to you rather than to Urdo because I was an idiot and allowed Lukas to forbid me to write to Urdo. As it is a thing without honor and against the borders of hospitality I should have written to Urdo in any case except that the stratagem of writing to you occurred to me, that I need not break the promise my husband extorted by force nor yet the sacred bonds of kinship and hospitality I share with you and with Urdo alike. It did not occur to him to forbid me to write to you.*"

I almost laughed at the words and the thought of ap Theophilus imposing anything on Rigg by force. She overtopped him by a foot and could have broken him in half with one hand.

> "*The Jarnsmen of Jarnholme and their king Arling Gunnarsson have sent to Caer Custenn for help against*

*the high kingdom of Tir Tanagiri. The Emperor Sabbat-
ian, badly advised by my husband Lukas ap
Theophilus, has made alliance with them, and has sent
them some devices of war."*

Her Vincan had improved markedly, I noticed, but whatever the devices were she either didn't know the word for
them or wasn't telling me.

*"This is his business and none of mine, even should
Arling attack you. You are strong in arms, besides having horses which he does not. But I learned privily what
it was that the Vincan Empire gained in exchange and
this is a concern. It seems that Urdo's nephew Morthu
ap Talorgen is allied with this Arling and he is sending
Sabbatian plans and models of many things used in
your country such as waterwheels and flails for thresh-
ing wheat. Lukas says it is known that Urdo would keep
all such knowledge for himself and refuse to share it.
Further he says that we give arts of war and gain arts
of peace, which is a loss on our side. Truly men can be
fools sometimes. However all this may be, this Morthu
is a traitor and you and Urdo should withdraw all trust
in him. He is the man the queen believed had harmed
her; it seems she had good reason to hate him."*

I stared at this dumbfounded for a moment. This was
something I had wanted for years, proof of Morthu's treachery which Urdo must believe. Yet it said nothing of the alliance I knew of, with Marchel, and everything about a
different alliance nobody knew about, with Arling.

*"With this I send my respects to you and to your fam-
ily, and to Urdo and his queen, wishing her safe in-
crease. I should say that Lukas and the girls join me in
these good wishes, and I am sure they would if they only
knew I was writing. The girls are too young yet to understand secrets. The younger I have called Laris after*

*my aunt who was your grandmother, so you see family
is not forgotten even so far away! The elder is called
Helena after Lukas's mother. Oh, but we had a fight
about that and I let Lukas win that time. They are riding
already. The new baby will be born soon, and I am
weary with waiting. I am warleader of Sabbatian's cavalry, what time I am not too great with child to ride. My
horses are well and also foaling. I will send this letter
with a friend of mine who will be going to Jarnholme
with the devices, and he will contrive to send it across
the narrow seas on a Narlahenan ship. So you will have
this news not long after they have their machines."*

I would have to send this news to Urdo at once. An alliance
with our open enemies would condemn Morthu even in the
eyes of his supporters. Flavien and Cinon might hate Urdo,
but surely they must hate Arling more? I blessed Rigg in my
heart and was glad she was happy and thriving in distant Caer
Custenn.

There was only one letter left and it was a great, thick one.
My heart sank to see it. I had to turn it to the light to read the
salutation.

*"From Gwyn ap Talorgen, Lord of Angas, King of
Demedia, at Dun Idyn, to Sulien ap Gwien, Lord and
King of Derwen, at Derwen, or to her hand wherever
she may be."*

Angas. I knew there must be something terribly wrong for
him to write to me at this length. I opened it reluctantly.

*"Sulien, this is the hardest letter I've ever had to
write, and it doesn't seem right I have to write it twice.
It was bad enough the first time. It seems impossible
not to trust you, but then it would have seemed impossible not to trust Urdo, or other people I trusted and had
proof, real proof, before my eyes, that they were deceiv-
ing me and in league against me.*

"*But Sulien, old comrade, even if I don't trust myself or my own judgment, I still trust you. I remember when I first met you, you were gangly and overgrown and your hair was all spiky and you came out of nowhere with your sword in your hand ready to fight anyone as long as you got to fight. Everything seemed so simple then. I was young and there wasn't any question who the enemy was. In those days I thought Urdo was true and just and honorable—I can't believe he wasn't, however much he may have changed since. We were all so young, you and me and Osvran, dear Osvran, and Eirann, so beautiful.*

"*Forgive me rambling, Sulien, but you probably have the other letter that says it all clearly. The mead helped me write that one, but I'm not sure it's helping me now, because I'm wishing I was that young decurio prince with nothing to worry about but keeping my lance pointed in the right direction. Yet they call me "the Lucky" because of Quintien. Nobody is lucky who has to live in a house with Morthu and hear his poison in my ears all day long. And once you give in to him, even a little way, then you give in more and more until he has fingers everywhere, he will not be content with enough. I don't know whom to trust!*"

I could feel his pain coming through the words. But what could Morthu have done to turn him against Urdo? I skimmed down the page; more pain, examples of friends who had betrayed him, warnings against trusting the mails because Urdo was interfering with them. Urdo? How could he believe that? He said Urdo had come to want power and control. I just shook my head reading it. Then I came to a piece about Bregheda and read more slowly.

"*This latest insult is meant to take me straight in the teeth. I have written and written to him about it and he either ignores my letters entirely or writes to me slightingly ignoring my concerns and saying he is sure I will understand. Penda of Bregheda died, as you will have heard. His son and heir Cyndylan died before him, having no children. Cyndylan died in Dun Idyn in fact, he had come here with his wife to make a pilgrimage to Thandeilo in the hope she might conceive. So there is nobody living with an undisputed claim to be king of Bregheda. Naturally Urdo must choose, and of those possible he chooses a commoner, and not just a commoner but his own man, a nobody he has raised to be great, whose wife was a groom and who will be loyal to Urdo only and not to the land. This Glyn has an older brother who is lord of Clidar, a part of Bregheda. He could not rule the whole land, but he had children who would be suitable, with the lord of Clidar as regent. Or if this did not suit Urdo, my own grandmother, though not his, Avren's first wife Branwen, was Minmanton's daughter, and so all my kin have a claim on Bregheda. Any of my children save my heir would be ideal, or any of Penarwen's save the eldest, or, as my first thought was, it would be something for Morthu to do which would give him responsibility suited to his station and get him out of my house! He could even marry one of Clidar's girls, when they're old enough. But no. I wrote to Urdo suggesting this, and I know Morthu has written. He has not even refused it, he has ignored me and appointed a man of low breeding without consultation, either with me or with the land. You know how important it is that the land consents, and Urdo must know, yet he appoints some quartermaster who has not lived there since he was fifteen years old."*

He went on in this vein for some time. Angas was clearly wounded deeply. It was all nonsense. He did not know Glyn as I did; if he had he would have put aside all this talk of low breeding. I remembered him throwing an acorn cake out of the window and bellowing on the night before his wedding. I remembered him laughing with Osvran in camp. How had that joy gone to this bitterness? He was right that the land of

Bregheda would have to consent to any king, but the land was more likely to want a grown man with children of his own than a half-grown boy. And how could he know? Nobody could speak for the land without being the king already, except Urdo, who was high king of the whole island. As for Morthu, I couldn't see why Angas didn't realize what a terrible idea it would be to give him power. I would have to reply to this straight away. Angas was confused and unhappy, he could be set straight—if only I could get through to him. I realized that any letter I sent would not reach him, as this had not reached me. Morthu was like an impenetrable barrier between us. I would have to send someone I trusted, and someone Angas trusted too, all the way to Demedia, before any message could get through.

I shook my head. The feeble "proof" of Urdo's "tyranny" was all invented by Morthu, cleverly playing on Angas's weaknesses; his pride, the intolerance of the low born he had inherited from his parents, his loneliness.

"There is nobody I can turn to," I read. "Osvran and Eirann are dead, Marchel is exiled, and you and Penarwen are far away. My decurios are not my equals. My children are too young to understand my mind. Hivlian is gone to Thandeilo to be a monk. I would not let her go, but when Eirann's fourth birth was twins she said that Quintien was a replacement for her in the family and a miracle. I could not keep her back then. She would not stay even when Eirann weakened and died. She has powers, like my mother, and she said she would be safest inside a monastery. I do not know if she feared madness like my mother. Sometimes I fear that even though I have no such powers. I have thought to taking the pebble myself, in memory of Eirann and as a shield against the night."

Poor Angas. What he needed was a strong friend nearby to talk sense into him. Morthu was enough to drive anyone mad. Urdo should have thought of that before sending him to Demedia. I wished I had killed him when I first saw him. Angas couldn't do it himself, of course. If only Osvran had lived and been there to do it for him.

"Maybe Morthu is mad; I have often thought so. He tells me he knows through his powers that Urdo means to diminish all the kings, and there is other evidence as I have said. But he has grown a hatred against you that is beyond all rationality. He says, forgive me Sulien, that your son Darien is not Urdo's son but was conceived incestuously with your brother Darien. No matter how many times I tell him that we all know you spent the night with Urdo at Caer Gloran, and no matter how often I remark on the resemblance between Urdo and Darien, whose skin is half as pale as a Jarn, like his father, Morthu will not listen. I fear that people who do not know you and do not know Darien may believe him. But I know this is a lie, and it makes me distrust other things that my brother tells me.

"This is why I am sending two copies of this impossible letter. (I will never call you tactless again after the things I have written here!) The first copy I will send by the red-cloaks. If it does not reach you and this does, then you will know that Morthu is speaking the truth when he says that Urdo is reading everything they carry and that is why some letters I send to the kings go ever unanswered. This one I shall entrust to my servant, Vigen the Dumb. You, with your famous memory, may remember Vigen from when we were stationed at Caer Gloran—I had found him work in the bathhouse there. He lost a leg long ago fighting the Isarnagans, and then my father cut out his tongue because he would not speak against me and Osvran when we were boys. I have looked after him ever since, and I know he would not betray me. He is not much of a counselor, as he can neither speak nor write, but he can hear and he is loyal without doubt. Give him your answer and let him bring it to me."

I dropped the letter and cried out. Vigen was dead. Daldaf had accused him of attacking him to rob him late at night in the town on a day after a market, almost a month before. I had indeed recognized him from long before at Caer Gloran, but a tongueless stranger can ill defend himself in court against a respected local liar. He had grunted fiercely and made threatening gestures toward Daldaf and imploring ones to me. Nobody had spoken for him and one of the merchants from a ship said he had caught him thieving in the market and sent him off with a beating. I had not thought long before I condemned him; I thought him a landless outlaw of the type I least wanted in Derwen. Angas had sent me the last person he could trust, and I had killed him in form of law. I could not even think what he must think of me now, what he must believe. If only I could go to Demedia myself, or Urdo could, I knew Angas would believe us. I wondered what Morthu would do if we did. But we could not, we were needed at home. Marchel was about to invade, and possibly Arling as well.

I finished the letter, read it through again, then took my lamp into the accounts room. The hall was dark; everyone was in bed. I had to write to Urdo. Yet was there any point? Would a letter get through? How much correspondence was being stopped, and where? I realized I was baring my teeth and hissing. None of those letters I had spent the afternoon on could be sent, or if they were then there was a strong chance it would be only Morthu who would read them. I sat down and wrote to Urdo—a brief account of what had happened, and enclosing the letters I had found. I sealed it, then I went out to the barracks. There was a chill in the night air, even though it was summer. The sky was dark except in the west, where it was deep blue and the evening star burned as bright as a beacon.

The guard greeted me with surprise. I wished I could take a horse and ride straight out the six days to Caer Tanaga. Brighteyes was rested, and so was Evenstar. Yet I could not; my duty to my land and people prevented it. I went into the barracks and looked at the sleeping armigers. Who among them could I trust utterly with this message of life and death? I had meant to wake Flerian ap Cado, my best scout, but seeing her asleep I remembered seeing her father dead only that morning, fighting for Aurien against me. The man in the bed next to her had a pebble of the White God gently rising up and down with his breathing. Who among these my people might have ties and allegiances elsewhere that meant they might betray me? After only one day I already hated civil war, hated it with all my heart.

I prayed to the Lord Messenger to guide my choice, to get my message through. Then I knew I could trust them all, or none of them; those were my choices. I could be like poor Angas and retreat into trusting nobody, in which case Morthu would have won already. Or I could trust my people, my oath-sworn armigers, who had sworn to have no enemies save as they were Urdo's enemies and to harm none of his friends, to strike and go and do as he should command. I should not be foolish with traitors, but unless I knew them for such I should trust them. If I trusted them not to betray me then that trust would bind us all, bind the kingdom together. Rigg and Ayl and Angas had all written because they trusted me. I would be as worthy of that as I could. I bent and shook Flerian's shoulder gently.

"Wake up," I said quietly. "I want you to take an urgent message to Urdo at Caer Tanaga, to go at once and as fast as you can, and to give it only to him, do you understand?"

She struggled into wakefulness and sat up carefully. "Yes, sir," she said, pushing back her hair sleepily. "I will go at once."

— 5 —

What did you think the sun meant
poking up so cheekily
not decently veiled,
dappling her trail of flaming glory
far out across the sky?

Only you could be surprised
at rain before nightfall.
> —Heed, attr. Alswith Flamehair

I spent the morning talking to the ala and raising the militia. The levy of Derwen had been almost nothing in my father's day. Even now it would not compare to the militias of Tinala, Bregheda, or any of the Jarnish kingdoms. Infantry and cavalry do not mix well together; to put it at its simplest, people on foot cannot keep up with horses. Whenever I had to fight with infantry it always seemed that we were sacrificing all our mobility for a very small gain. Nevertheless I had instituted a proper militia from among the strong young farmers of my kingdom. They came and trained in the seasons when there was little to be done on the farms, and I counted it as good as a tenth of their tax paid, or a fifth if I kept them away from home for very long. Most of those who were fit for the work thought it a good bargain. Duncan usually took care of the specifics of the training. They all knew which end of a spear was which and had spent at least a little time drilling with the ala. This meant they were not afraid of horses and they knew our signals and commands. They knew each other and understood who could give them orders. They would not run away on a battlefield, at least not straight away, and that was as much as I had asked of them. That was more than I had ever thought they would need to do. Infantry are for holding land cavalry has taken, and I had need of only enough of them to serve as guards around the town. If we were attacked, well, I had the ala.

My main use of the militia was as a source of recruits. Every season a few of them would come to me shyly and ask if I needed armigers. If they had strong shoulders and could ride I would make sure they could be spared from their homes. Then I would usually start them as grooms or scouts and begin their training. After a year or so if I felt they had earned a horse and weapons I would take their oath. In this way over five years I had raised three more pennons. The whole ala had three halves—one usually at Magor, one usually at Derwen, and one usually at Dun Morr.

The land could support them. Derwen was thriving. The harvests were good and there were plenty of foals. Trade had increased as well; we could sell as much linen and linen-paper as we could make, and we made more every year. We were making enough iron and smithgoods at Nant Gefalion to sell those too. In return we got tin and lead and silver from Munew, books and grain from Segantia, Jarnish beer from Cennet, dyes and mordants from Aylsfa, leather goods from Tevin, apples and cider from Tathal, gold and roofing slate from Wenlad. We even had traders coming with salt from Nene, honey and blown glass from Tinala, fleeces from Bregheda and Demedia, and worked wooden goods from Bereich. We had ships come often from Tir Isarnagiri and from Narlahena, and even sometimes from Varnia, though most of our Varnian goods came to us through Munew and Segantia. These days what my mother called Imperial goods were mostly books, wine, spices, and preserved fruits. We bought little oil now, as we had linen-seed oil in sufficient quantity for our own use.

People who had been driven out of the eastern lands by the Jarns had come to us and settled, bringing their skills and increasing everyone's comfort. We did not need to bring in pottery and iron as we had before, we had our own. The single potter my mother had enticed to the town fifteen years before was now one among a whole street of potters. One of them made nothing but tiles for roofs and floors, and insisted on being called a tiler, not a potter. If a farmer broke the one pottery cup they kept for blessings it was a shame but not a disaster for them, it could be mended or replaced. There were shops in town all the time, workshops which sold their goods; a candlemaker and a tinsmith and a cobbler. We held a market four times a year, not all that much smaller than the ones at Caer Tanaga.

All these enterprises throve within the town itself, which consequently grew all the time and was beginning to press on the walls my father had so wisely built wider than they were needed. This last year I had moved the press for crushing the oil from the linen seeds a little way upriver from the town, with a waterwheel of its own. This kept the waterwheel above the docks free for grinding corn and sawing wood. All the retting of the flax was done upstream as well, beyond the walls. This dirtied the river of course. I had been considering a plan Glividen had suggested of building an aqueduct to bring clean water into the town from the stream in the woods. It would make it much easier to water the horses than using wells and troughs. But until now this had seemed the worst of having that work out there. I had not thought about needing to defend it. This was Urdo's Peace; no raider would land near a town so well defended. Now I fretted about it. My father had meant the walls to hold all the local farmers if necessary, as they had when the Isarnagans attacked. Now, if we had to take in the people, there would be no room for them inside unless we crowded them into our hall, and maybe not then.

Everywhere I went, people wanted to ask questions. Mostly I could not answer them. First thing that morning I had sent Hiveth's pennon to Nant Gefalion, and to warn the people of the countryside on the way. My plan was to gather the militia and wait for the rest of the ala to come up from Dun Morr. Then I would leave the militia with one pennon under Duncan's command to defend the town if necessary, and take the rest, amounting to seven pennons, to Magor to try to prevent Marchel from landing. I had sent scouts out down the coast at first light.

All the way along the coast between Derwen and Magor there are shingle and sand bays where a ship can be half-beached safely enough to disembark people through the surf. But Marchel was bringing horses, which can scramble ashore well enough but cannot climb cliffs. I could only think of half a dozen places she could unload them. Magor was not near enough to the water to have docks inside the walls the way we did at Derwen. She could unload them at Aberhavren and bring them down the high road, but I thought she would be more likely to bring them to shore somewhere quieter, and plan a day or so for the horses to recover before they would be seen. They were bound to be half sick and weary from the journey. It was eight hundred miles straight across the open sea from Narlahena, or so the Malmish merchants delighted in telling me whenever I tried to haggle with them. It wasn't like taking animals across a river or even the fifty miles from Tapit Point to Tir Isarnagiri. I hoped to prevent her from having that time, to catch her as soon as she landed and make her fight before she was ready.

Govien and his three pennons arrived in the late afternoon, when I was out in the yard talking to Nodol Boar-beard about supplies. To my surprise, Lew arrived with them. My first thought was that he had come to escort Emer home, and to claim Conal's body. I went up to greet him and helped him dismount.

"Greetings, and welcome to Derwen, Lew ap Ross," I said when he was down, bowing. He bowed back, looking as plump and self-important as ever. He still had the ridiculous long mustache. I wished he hadn't come to waste my time. I was already looking around for Veniva to take him off my hands and take him into the hall for the welcome cup so I could talk to Govien.

"Lord Sulien," he said as he straightened. "I came as soon as I had the news. I have left ap Ranien to gather my forces. They will leave tomorrow and come as fast as warriors may come on their own feet. I thought I would take advantage of the horses and come more swiftly to let you know what strength you can expect. Ap Ranien will bring four thousand fighters, armed with spears and shields, and fifty of my household warriors, armed with swords as well."

I gaped at him. It had never occurred to me to ask Lew to call up his people, nor that if I had he might have obeyed. He was sworn to me and to Urdo, and he did have that fighting strength, but he was a king and an ally. Before I had ever met him, Emer had told me Lew was an old fool and strongly implied that he was a coward. I had never seen anything of him to contradict this impression, until now. He was fat and he fussed, and he consulted his advisors frequently and at length. But he was neither fool nor coward, and when he had to act he did. He could have stayed quite safely in Dun Morr and let the half ala come to me. Indeed, he need not have stirred out of his fortress at any time. The rebels would most likely have left him alone. Instead he had stripped his own land of troops to come to my aid, and I had not even asked him to. "I am overwhelmed," I said. "I don't know what to say. I had not expected such great help." I wondered if he even knew who we would be fighting. I wondered how I was going to feed four thousand extra infantry. "This is an act of honor which will be remembered with your name forever."

Lew bowed again at that, looking terribly pleased. "It is no more than I have sworn to do," he said.

"I hope you have left enough defenders for your own home," I said, as the thought struck me.

"There are enough people there to man the walls. My daughter and heir is in charge, with three of my most experienced counselors to help her. I will defend Derwen or go where you want me."

I suddenly remembered Demedia, invaded from Oriel as Angas was busily invading Bereich. If Lew were left in charge he could take Derwen while I was away. Trusting good faith could be taken too far. I wished I really knew why Lew had stripped his country of troops. "We should make sure to leave enough people to defend our homes," I said. His daughter and heir was only eleven years old. "Come with me." I gestured to Nodol to accompany us. "I will call your wife and my decurios and we will have a council of war."

In the end I waited another day to see ap Ranien's army arrive, and yet another to see them safely leave again in the direction of Magor. My militia were raised and ready by then. I sent some of them west to Dun Morr and left most of them to defend Derwen. I left Lew in charge of them, Veniva in charge of the town, and Emlin in charge of the pennon I left there and general defense. I had Emer make it clear to Lew that he would take general military orders from Emlin while I was away. She could put it diplomatically, as I could not. Emlin was capable of conducting the defense and of dealing tactfully with Lew; none of my other decurios were. I wished I had two of him. I tried to squelch that thought before I caught myself wishing for all my friends, living and dead. Among that list, even though I knew perfectly well that if he had been there I'd have been cursing him for making my life difficult, I wished Conal was there to offer suggestions. I also wished most strongly and just as vainly that Emer and Duncan would be content to stay behind.

Emer insisted that she wanted to fight and that her place was at the front. I don't know what arguments she used on Lew; the ones she gave me were senseless and plainly amounted to the fact that she wanted to be doing something because Conal was dead. I had some sympathy for not wanting to sit and wait, but I couldn't see what getting herself killed would help. I could and did prevent her from riding with the ala—she was not trained and would be a liability. As Lew gave her permission, I could not stop her riding with ap Ranien's army, which had a few mounted scouts.

Duncan was even more of a problem. I had meant to leave the militia in his hands and take Lew to Magor where I could keep an eye on him. But at the war council, after Lew had revealed that he had heard disquieting hints of the rebellion already and I had made my dispositions, Duncan begged leave to ride to Magor. He sat stiffly, rubbing his thumbs together and avoiding my mother's eyes.

"But your duty is here," I said impatiently.

He stood up, bowed, and stared straight over my seated head. "If I have ever done anything to deserve the gratitude of the Lords of Derwen, then let me ride with you," he said. I could not refuse a request phrased like that. But it left a gap in my arrangements. Riding to battle, Duncan was just another armiger; with infantry he was a reliable commander. I bit my lip and left Lew in charge of my people, where he could do little harm even if he intended any. His own people, under ap Ranien, were following me east. But I rode off heavy-hearted. I had wasted two days, I was going with uncertain allies against friends turned enemies, and I wondered how many others were riding with me seeking death.

I was still in a bad mood when we stopped for our noon rest and food. Ap Madog came and sat by me as I was eating some good cheese Garah's mother had made. "I was thinking," he began.

I bit my tongue and managed not to commend him for the strenuous mental activity. "Yes?" I asked, as encouragingly as I could. It can't have been very encouragingly, he gave me a nervous glance.

"About supply," he said. "I know Nodol's performed miracles getting us ready to go out so soon, and I know where the caches are and what I was thinking is that they're the same caches we've been using all this time."

"Yes?" I said again, not following him. A pigeon whirred out of the trees and I stared at it blankly as it disappeared back into them. Then suddenly I saw what he meant. "Yes," I said, in an entirely different tone. "And Marchel commanded the ala here before Galba, didn't she, so she will know them too."

Ap Madog jerked up his chin in doleful agreement. "I was hoping you'd thought of something," he said.

"It was very good thinking on your part," I said. "I'll write to Nodol and tell him, and tell Lew to set some of our militia to guard them."

"Why can't he use them to move them?" ap Madog asked. "Guarding on foot against mounted enemies is really tough."

"I know, but if he moves them we won't know where they are either. Think why we make the caches, think how easily we can find them? What's the first assignment a new armiger gets, eh? Nodol could move them and he could send me a map of where they are, but could everyone who might need them find them from that? Supplies you can't find might as well be on the moon."

"Right." Ap Madog looked downcast. "The other thing I was thinking—are we planning to attack Magor itself? Because my wife's parents are there and—"

"We will do what is necessary, but I'm very much aware that many of the ala have family in Magor," I said. "They're unlikely to walk onto a battlefield by mistake though. Don't worry."

Just then I saw a scout hurrying toward me. I stood up so he could see me better. "They've landed," he blurted. "We found signs. They've headed inland for Magor."

"How many?" I asked.

The scout frowned. "It's hard to tell. A lot. I'd say a whole ala at least, maybe more. A lot of horses, four or five hundred, but they were being led, not ridden, so I can't guess how many are spares. There were a lot of people as well."

"Most importantly, when?" I asked urgently.

"This morning very early, when the tide was high."

"Then we might still catch them and cut them off before they reach Magor," I said. I gave orders to remount and we set off at once.

We pushed on as rapidly as we dared and came to Magor in the late afternoon. I was riding toward the rear of the column as we came out of the woods. The track is quite wide there, with ditches separating it from the fields on either side. In that season they held standing barley, nearly ripe. There was a shout from the first rank as they came out of the trees and caught sight of Magor. Marchel had reached it before us; there was a column of horse going in through the main gates in the wall Duke Galba had built. We were in column and the first pennon took off at a canter down the track toward them. I signaled to Berth to sound the attack, though it was almost unnecessary. Everyone knew what to do. Only the first pennon could engage now, the rest of us rode behind in support. It was all we could do without trampling the barley and risking our horses' necks on the unseen and uneven ground.

The main body of them kept on filing inside Magor as we approached. Our front ranks had their lances lowered. I signaled to the decurios to spread out by pennons and attack on their own initiative. Berth relayed the orders. Everyone behind readied their weapons and prepared to spread out when there was an opportunity. We thundered nearer. Evenstar put back her head and neighed as she scented them.

They were mounting and forming up with admirable speed. Two pennons came toward us rapidly. As they came nearer I could see that they were all Malms, pale-skinned, long-nosed, and dark-eyed. They could all have been Thurrig's children. They were armed much as we were but wore lighter armor. They had charge and rally banners like ours and they were clearly organized the same way we were. Their horses were much smaller than ours, but real horses, not ponies like the ones Sweyn's horsemen had used. They seemed all gray or dappled or black, with not a brown hair among them. They were tall, but not as tall as greathorses. The tallest were perhaps a hand's width shorter, and most were two or three hands smaller. They were much more delicately built, nothing like as broad or strong. They were fast enough, as we saw when they charged toward us. The Malms were shouting and howling as they came. It took me a moment to realize that it was not "Glory and Death!" they were shouting but "The Glory of God!" I could feel Evenstar speed up of her own accord, although we were nowhere near them. I saw the impact when the two lines met.

They could not stand before us. They must have known that when they came out. There were two pennons of them against a whole ala, even though we could not spread out, and their additional speed could not make up for our strength. They fought like fiends, aiming for our horses. If they had been slower, or if we had not been confined to the narrow track, we would have killed them all almost at once.

As it was, they were fighting to buy time to get their friends to safety, and they did that, at the cost of their own lives. They probably did better against us than they should have. They had been practicing, and fighting against people on horseback was still strange to us. I wanted to come up to them and fight. There was just no room. It was one of the most frustrating skirmishes of my life.

Eventually they broke and we surrounded them. I signaled to Cadarn to wait in case they broke for the walls, and went closer myself. They were still fighting, though they could not maneuver. Then the last of their friends passed inside and the gates of Magor closed firmly behind them. A trumpet blast came from the walls, and the Malms who were still outside cheered to hear it and fought harder, if anything. Not one of them surrendered; we had to kill them all.

I stared at Magor, firmly in the hands of the enemy. The stables and the barracks, clearly visible as their walls formed part of the outer wall, had been ours only two days ago. I knew it all so well. It felt wrong for it to be against us. Duke Galba would have cried to see his hard work in building the walls abused like that. There was nothing for it but a siege, and I knew how well supplied they were. I had made sure of the supplies myself. I realized I was grinding my teeth loudly, and stopped.

I set Cadarn and ap Madog's pennons, who had been in the rear, to watch the town, and the rest of us retreated to the edge of the woods, patched up our wounded as best we could, and gathered up our dead. There were plenty of wounded; I saw that everything was in hand, and checked to see if anyone needed my help singing charms. One or two of them did, so I saw to that. Then I turned to Govien for the death tally. There had been time.

"Ten horses, another ten too badly wounded to survive, though the grooms are trying with the weapons." It is always more difficult with horses, who cannot say which weapon hurt them. "Only three armigers," he added, uncertainly. He wasn't used to being tribuno and we were both used to Emlin doing this.

"Good work," I said.

Then I went to look at the dead as I always did. Govien had pulled them out of the battlefield and had them brought to the edge of the woods. Elidah was a girl who had been one of my first volunteers when I instituted the militia. I remembered visiting her parents on their farm near Derwen, and their pride at the thought of their daughter being an armiger. I had been meaning to promote her to sequifer soon. Mabon was a man who had served for many years under Galba. He had fought at Caer Avroc and at Foreth, only to die within sight of the place he had been born. The third corpse was Duncan.

He had been killed cleanly by a spear thrust through the neck. He looked old and confused, as if the world had confounded his expectations again. I remembered him long ago teaching me to fight. He had come here to die and he had what he wanted. I brushed away tears that helped nothing. If only Marchel had lined up her alae at that moment, I would have been ready to mount up and charge straight at them.

"Where are we going to camp?" Govien asked, coming up behind me. It was just starting to get dark and the rain was beginning. I knew as well as he did how vulnerable we were dismounted, and how any ditch we could build to keep them out would also keep us in. I frowned.

"We've got to keep them in there. Tomorrow ap Ranien and the Isarnagan army will be here and we can besiege them properly. For tonight, I think we rest here until it gets properly dark and they can't see us leave, and then press onto Aberhavren, which has shelter and walls and supplies. We need to secure it in any case, and tomorrow we need to block Marchel's route to Caer Gloran."

Govien sighed. He was from Magor originally; he had been promoted to decurio by Galba. He was a broad, squat man, one of the shortest of the armigers but very strong. He was looking tired to death. Mabon had been a friend of his. "This is awful," he said, looking not at the bodies but at the walls and the gate.

"You cannot," I said through gritted teeth, "hate it worse than I do. But we'll stop them. We can do it. Don't worry."

I was almost surprised to see him comforted by this, and sound confident and heartened as he rode off to relay my orders.

— 6 —

This is a time of war, we must stand firm
against the fearsome foe, not waste our lives
for empty dreams of glory or of skill.
All lives have worth, including this of mine
I lightly held so long, and those who die
are spent to save the fire in the corn,
the hungry winter, homes and farms destroyed,
more deaths than these we count, the land aflame
and all the Peace we built so long, forgot.
　　　　—From "Thirty Sword"

I t took ten days to lure her out.

I held a council of war at Aberhavren at dawn the day after we arrived there. The place was not a town, just a little settlement that had sprung up around the spot where the ferry crosses the Havren. It had no walls, only a wooden stockade. Galba had widened this to make room for the ala when he had first been based down here. We also kept a supply dump here. I had been afraid to find that Marchel had taken it or that Aurien had given orders to the locals to forbid me entry. The whole spirit of civil war is caught in that fear, riding up to a strong place you know well and not knowing if the inhabitants are for you or against you. Fortunately the inhabitants of Aberhavren were indifferent. The man on the gate had inquired why we were riding so late, but made no move to stop us entering when I gave my name. He would probably not have tried to stop Marchel either. I did not know if the local people even knew about the civil war.

I gathered my decurios together in the shack where I'd been sleeping and they crowded around, leaning against the walls. As the day brightened I could see that in some places the plaster was wearing off and the willow wattles showed through. I had Talog bring breakfast, and we all ate porridge while they offered me their views and suggestions.

"The problem is that we want to get her out but not to let her escape," I said.

"We can starve her out," objected Govien, gesturing with his bowl.

"There are almost two months' supplies for an ala inside Magor," Bradwen said gloomily, putting hers down. "I put them there myself." She had been the sequifer of Garian's pennon before I promoted her after Garian's death. It had been her job to deal with Nodol Boar-beard about supplies for Magor.

"That's not counting anything Aurien might have been stockpiling," I added. "Did any of you who were stationed at Magor see any signs she was doing that?"

Bradwen and Golidan shook their heads. I wished I'd thought to ask Emlin before leaving him at Derwen. "It's a bad time of year for it," Golidan said.

"We always keep supplies for the horses in case we have to move in a hurry," Bradwen said. "But the cabbages and the turnips will be ready in ten days or so—if she'd done this after harvest she'd have had a whole winter's supplies."

"Summer is a better time to fight," I said. "But if she has two alae in there with a month's supplies, then starving her out is a possibility. That might take too long if there is trouble elsewhere."

"Is there any news?" ap Madog asked. He scraped around his empty bowl for the last morsels, then set it down.

I shook my head, swallowing the last of my own breakfast. "None. But Cinvar could come south at any time. More Malms could land. We have no idea what Flavien or the other kings are doing. There is the possibility of a Jarnish invasion, which could come anywhere."

Cynrig Fairbeard stirred uneasily, then realized we were all looking at him. He was a Jarnsman of course, one of Sweyn's more distant kin, who had been taken into the alae after Foreth. Like Ulf he had learned fast and become a reliable armiger. I had made him a decurio when I formed the ninth pennon. I had thought long and hard about doing it, but I had never had any reason to doubt his loyalty and he was the best of the possibilities. It would have been unfair to pass over him because of the color of his skin or because he had fought against us twelve years ago. "I haven't heard anything," he said. "Arling hates me even more than he hates all of you; he calls those of us who ride with you traitors. But I can tell you this; he won't land just anywhere, he will land where he thinks the land will be with him, and that is Tevin. Sweyn made the sacrifice there and Arling will think that the gods will listen to him because of that. Also, Sweyn's son and daughter by Gerda Hakonsdottar are in Caer Linder with their mother, and Arling will want to secure them."

"I'm surprised he won't want to kill them as rivals," ap Madog said. "The daughter must be what, eighteen or so by now? And the son was born the year before Foreth, so he'll be twelve or thirteen? That's old enough to be worrying, considering both of them have been brought up by Alfwin and in our Peace."

Cynrig looked shocked. "No Jarnish king would ever kill his nephews. Even apart from the impiety, which Mother Frith would punish, who of his huscarls would risk his honor to stand beside a man who would do such a thing?"

"Sweyn killed his own daughter!" Govien objected. "You just said so and we all know it. He slaughtered her like a deer as a sacrifice."

"That was his daughter, not his nephew," Cynrig explained, then, seeing our faces, he laughed. "It does make a difference! But it's hard to explain. And that was a sacrifice, which is a different thing. In any case many of us thought Sweyn was wrong to do that, and we were right, as events proved. Sweyn's old wife, Hulda, never forgave him for killing the girl or for marrying Gerda."

Govien opened his mouth, but I beat him to it. "If Arling is likely to land in Tevin then it makes it less likely we are going to get reinforcements here," I said, dragging them back to the point before they went off on a long digression about Jarnish customs. "How are we going to get Marchel out?"

"What would get us out if we were in there and being besieged?" Bradwen asked.

"Good question," I said. I thought about it. Cynrig grinned at Bradwen and she preened. I ignored them and considered what would get me out. Nothing would unless the walls were likely to fall, except lack of supplies. "Nothing. I'd wait until they'd gone away."

"We could send the Isarnagans up against the town," Golidan said. "I remember when they came against Derwen. We thought the sheer weight of them would have the gates down, and there was nothing we could do but sortie out now and then and throw things from the walls."

"They'll be there tonight," I said. "We can try that. But if we could get the walls down and the Isarnagans into the town there would be no restraining them. None of us have forgotten we have friends inside as well as enemies."

"What if we did go away?" ap Madog asked. "What would she do?"

"Probably go up the highroad to Caer Gloran to join up with Cinvar," I said. "The last thing we want is two hostile alae on the loose and out of reach. They're not strong enough to stand against us, but against infantry the light horses may not make much difference."

"What happens if they come out and try to run past us?" ap Madog asked. "They're very fast. They might try to form up and make a run for it."

"Good point," I said, leaning forward intently. "We need to keep her engaged and stop her escaping. We've got to stop her from forming up and getting away."

"We could keep trying to flank them," Govien said. "By pennons. Whenever any group of them tries to form up. That would work."

"It might," I said slowly, thinking about it.

"I think it would," ap Madog said, moving his cup toward

his bowl consideringly. "If we can keep between them and the road, and make sure we don't charge through them."

"I don't know," Golidan said. "That ought to work. But how about if we ambushed her? If we let her come out and make toward Caer Gloran, north up the highroad, and then caught her on the way? There'd be no problem with forming up, we could take her from both sides if we found a good spot, which we could scout out well in advance."

"Tempting, but too risky," I said after a moment. "If she went to Derwen or across the river here, instead, we'd be sitting there like a saddle on a cow while she started ravaging the country. We don't know for sure that's what she'll do."

"Ambush is a good idea though," Cynrig said, stroking his beard. "If we pretended to leave and didn't." Bradwen smiled at him admiringly. Those two had shared blankets on and off for a while, before he had been promoted off to Dun Morr. I resisted the urge to pour cold water on them.

"We could destroy the crops in the fields," Govien said. "That might get her out, and we could be ready."

"We need to be closer," I said.

"If we built a stockade on the hill with the cache just to the north of Magor," Bradwen said, "the one with the good spring. Then we'd be close enough but not too close. And we could have the Isarnagans build it and guard it when they come up. Then, rather than burning crops we could start to gather them in the fields, even if they're not quite ready. We could use the cabbage and turnips for the horses, even small. If she saw that it might make her sortie out, especially if she only saw the Isarnagans."

"We have to think like a fox," I said. "What would we do if we thought the besiegers had gone away?"

"Send out scouts," everyone chorused, then we all laughed.

"So that won't work," I said, leaning back on the rickety wall. "Because scouts would find out the real situation. But what if we tried to make her think that we had gone and were pretending we hadn't?"

"She'd still send scouts," ap Madog said.

I thought about what could get me out of there. "If we acted as if we'd left half an ala that was pretending to be a whole ala, with the Isarnagans, she'd think she could take them. She wouldn't want to send out scouts then, because half an ala would be enough to get scouts, and scouts might scare them into the stockade to stop them bluffing."

"We could have someone else in your praefecto's cloak so she thinks you've gone and have left someone pretending to be you. Someone not as tall," quiet Cadarn said. It was the first thing he'd said all day. "I'll do it if you like."

"I will," Bradwen said. "It'll look more likely on a woman, but I'll go close enough that someone will recognize me, or at least see that I'm not Sulien."

"Why would you go, though?" Ap Madog protested. "I mean, she'd guess it's a trick. You've no reason to go off anywhere."

I thought for a moment. There wasn't much that would get me away from Magor at the moment. "If Derwen was attacked, or if Urdo called me away," I said.

"So we need a messenger!" Govien said, excited. "A messenger arriving very obviously from Aberhavren, a red-cloak riding up exhausted and rushing up to the camp, and then that night you sneak away. She'd believe that I think."

Between us we worked out all the details of the subterfuge. Then we rode back to Magor and secured the hill and the roads. I left half a pennon at Aberhavren under ap Madog with strict orders to send for me if there was any trouble or any troops sighted from any direction. We brought up the supplies from two of the nearby caches and added them to the cache on the hill. We spent most of the day demonstrating as showily as we could what a whole ala looks like and pretending to threaten the walls. They threw spears but were otherwise helpless. I gave orders that no local farmers were to be hurt and that as much as possible we should try to avoid damaging crops and property. We would need to cut trees and gather some crops later but I explained we would compensate the farmers for them. This had been close to our standard way of operating in the war, so the ala took this calmly.

I had no herald so I sent my trumpeter, Berth, under herald's branches to try and negotiate. Aurien, or Marchel, sent Father Cinwil out to ask us to go away and stop invading Magor. The negotiation was as pointless as I had known it would be; it just wasted an hour of the morning.

When the Isarnagans came up that evening we set them to building the stockade around the hill. Ap Ranien and Emer came up to me in the long dusk. I was standing by the newly driven posts of the stockade, gazing down the valley at Magor and the distant line of the sea.

"There's just no possibility of holding them, sir," ap Ranien said, as soon as I greeted him. "It was hard enough on Derwen land, but here? How can you expect it? They're out in arms, they're bound to loot."

It took me a moment to realize they were talking about the rule on looting. "But this isn't an invasion, it's a civil war," I said, as calmly as I could.

"We know all about civil wars," Emer said. "More than you do, I think. The people have come to fight, and they won't understand what you mean by restraint. I've told them they mustn't kill the farmers of Magor, that it would be dishonorable, and I think they heard that. But as far as property goes—if we try to say that they should harm nothing they'll just go home, probably looting all the way back to Dun Morr."

"It's barbaric!" I exclaimed. They said nothing. I looked from one to the other of them. Ap Ranien was standing as stiff and bristling as a pine tree. He looked desperately unhappy.

Emer wasn't looking at me at all. "It's our custom," she said. "We will need to be in the land longer than this to change it."

So the next morning I went around the local farms warning them about the war, explaining that nobody could restrain the Isarnagans, and offering the farmers the protection of Derwen if they cared to go there. More of them headed west than I expected. I did not think they would be so afraid. It was going to be very crowded at home. I hoped Veniva could cope.

I set scouts to watching the two gates of Magor in case Marchel or anyone ventured out. Then I set the other half of ap Madog's pennon, with all the scouts, to scouting the whole area to give warning of any approaching troops from anywhere. They would be based at Aberhavren under ap Madog's command and use the supplies and the stables there. This left me with six pennons and an Isarnagan army. I tried to keep the army inside the stockade as much as I could to minimize looting problems. I ordered some of them to gather the ripest cabbages nearest to Magor. They could have done with another ten days or half a month in the ground, but the horses were happy at the addition to their diet. I hoped to make Marchel think we would gather all the crops as they ripened, leaving her nothing.

All that day I kept half the ala rested and ready to mount if she came out. At noon, the fake red-cloak arrived with what looked like an urgent message. Then, on toward twilight but when there was still light to be seen, I led three pennons quietly away north up the highroad as if we were sneaking off toward Caer Gloran. When it was completely dark I led them even more quietly back around to the hill with the stockade and inside.

For the next seven days we tried hard to make six pennons look like three trying to look like six. Bradwen wore my gold-leaf praefecto's cloak and rode about as if she were trying to keep out of direct sight of Magor, but actually hoping to be recognized. I stayed in the stockade. The deception made my head hurt, especially as time went on and there was no indication that Marchel was fooled at all.

On the tenth day she came out, as the Isarnagans started to gather the turnips. What she could see was half the ala waiting unmounted but ready under the trees, and the disorganized Isarnagans. The rest of us were in the stockade, and likewise ready. I felt we had been ready so long that the sortie would never happen and we would remain there until the Malms started to get hungry.

The hardest part was letting her get them all out before we attacked. We had arranged the palisade so that we could

move out a section and ride downhill. I knew that if she noticed us before she had her pennons committed she would
pull back behind the walls. Waiting just the right amount of
time was agonizing. Evenstar was restless under me and I
tried to speak soothingly to her. Marchel's armigers advanced through the gates, and I waited and watched. The half
ala under Govien mounted up. Bradwen discarded my spare
cloak to avoid confusion. More of Marchel's forces came
out. Then, as soon as they were all there, I gave the orders.
The Isarnagans swung out the wall section, and we charged
downhill, spear points lowered, ready to take them in the
flank.

It was a glorious moment pounding down toward them. It
seemed as if it was going to be like the charges we made in
the war, until we were nearly there. Then it was clear that
they were mounted and mobile, and they could also wheel
about and charge. They were faster than I had thought, even
after seeing them fight before. And then we were among
them and there was no time for thought, only for attack and
evasion and blood and death. Evenstar shouldered the lighter
horses hard, though they tried to duck and dodge away. That
left me dealing with the riders. We were not used to fighting
mounted opponents, and they were not used to fighting
against people riding horses larger and stronger than theirs. I
tried to take as much advantage of that as I could.

I fought with the spear until it was dragged from my hands
by a falling armiger. Then I drew my sword, the sword I had
owned so long it felt almost like an extension of my arm, except that I never forgot it had belonged to my brother Darien.
It was the sword that had killed Morwen and many another
enemy. I took an instant to brandish the sword toward the
light of the setting sun and dedicate the slain to the Lord of
Light. Then Evenstar reared and kicked out at one of the
Malmish horses and I was back in the endless moment of battle, and there was nothing but the press and my companions
and the enemy.

I did not direct that battle well. I did not know how to direct a battle against cavalry. I had plans, and I gave orders,

but once we were engaged we fought by pennons, rushing in if they seemed to be forming up. The Isarnagans kept her away from the walls of Magor and the ala stayed between her and the highroad. As soon as she was committed I signaled for all the Isarnagans, those who had been picking turnips and all the ones from the camp. They poured around the walls and blocked her from retreat. They kept their spears up and used their slingstones to devastating effect. This forced her away from the walls and out onto the uneven ground. I glanced around now and then to make sure they were staying where they should be, and they were, their raven banners catching the breeze. People on the walls were throwing things down onto the nearest and some of them had their shields up. I had a glimpse of Aurien once, standing on the wall by the gate above them, bareheaded. I looked away quickly. I did not want to see her. The Malms who were trying to kill me were strangers.

It was a long, hard fight. We kept on fighting, rallying, holding, and drawing back until we were all exhausted and our horses were foaming at the mouth. Even I could hardly spare a thought to the wider strategy. We were starting to get the upper hand, and with the Isarnagans between Marchel and the walls, in theory we could change horses and they could not. But the Malms kept pressing on, preventing us from disengaging. At last I saw Marchel across the battlefield. She looked angry and was fighting furiously, engaged with Cynrig. As I watched she got in a cut on his arm and then a rush by his pennon forced them apart. I rallied my pennon and tried to find a way toward her across the field. We were facing due east by this time; the whole battle had twisted around. I was about to sound the advance when I saw sunlight flashing on something up the road toward Aberhavren. I held the advance for a moment, thinking it might be a messenger from ap Madog.

Then I saw them thundering toward me, and tears came into my eyes. It was my ala, Urdo's Own Ala, coming in perfect order and as fresh-looking as if they had just left their barracks in Caer Tanaga. They were in a spearhead forma-

tion, aiming to split the Malms. They were flying all their
banners, and in the center were the great purple banner I had
carried at Foreth and Urdo's gold running horse on white and
green. Then they were closer, wheeling to their own signals,
one half ready to take Marchel from each side. She must have
known they were there, for there were trumpet calls, but she
just kept on giving her own signals and rallying her pennons
to her. I brought my pennon into another advance then, thinking she was coming toward me.

As we went forward I saw the first pennon of Urdo's Own
Ala charging to the fray. Close to the front of the charge, with
the gold signifer's banner set in his saddle-cup, was my son
Darien, riding a golden summerhorse. He was full-grown
now, twenty years old, in the prime of his youth. He had his
sword in his hand. He was smiling, and he reminded me of a
monk so far gone in worship he was barely aware of the
world around him. There was a strange light in his sea gray
eyes. Then he hit and he began fighting calmly with an assur-
ance I had never seen in him. He made it seem like a holy
thing. I did not know if what I felt was pride or envy. He
looked like a joyful young god in the morning of the world. I
had to look away from him then to block a blow coming from
my left which jarred my arm hard so that I almost dropped
my shield. I was fighting for my life for a moment then. It is
very bad to become distracted in battle.

I knew we had them. It became a slaughter. I caught sight
of Ulf quite near me. He was using his ax, paying no attention to the Malms' light armor and going straight through it
wherever he hit. I was annoyed to see how effective it was; ax
heads sink deeper than swords, and never once did Ulf seem
in danger of having his caught in a falling body.

About half of the Malms were caught between my six tired
pennons and the fresh troops. They fought bravely, and few
of them surrendered even when we called upon them to do
so. The other half of them were between Urdo's Own Ala and
the river. That was where Marchel was, and at the moment of
the first attack she rallied her pennons and made a dash north
for the highroad. We had forgotten she might want to break

for the north. She was pursued, of course, and many of her followers were brought down. She had about two pennons with her by the time she got away, no more than fifty mounted armigers, and no remounts. They left with a burst of their surprising speed, though the horses must have been tired almost to death. Urdo could not have guessed how fast they were, not having seen them before. Against any of our slower alae his strategy would have worked perfectly and let us roll up both halves of them.

After Marchel left, the Malms around me started to surrender.

I would have changed horses and gone after Marchel, but I heard Grugin blowing the rally call for all armigers, and turned Evenstar's tired head away from the trees and back toward Magor. We walked across the bloody trampled field, occasionally going around a fallen body, horse or rider or sometimes both together. So it was that I came up to Urdo on the middle of a won field, as I had met him the first time so long before. He was riding Thunder and he looked like himself, as he always did.

"My lord," I said, as the alae formed up around us. I could see Darien, wiping his face. Near him was Masarn's familiar broad grin. I was amazed. I couldn't think what he was doing here; he said he had given up fighting. I looked back at Urdo, not knowing what to say. "You came."

"I have come," he said, and smiled.

7

Then Tovran raged at his daughter and swore that she would marry Drusan, whether she would or no. He did not wish to be thought a barbarian by his Lossian and Tirtanagan subjects so he did not kill Naso as he had threatened but gave him work that kept him far away from Vinca on the north-east border of the Empire.

But Helen still said, "What though my lover be only a poet, he is true to me and I love him. That is worth more than Empire to me."

Drusan said he would not have the maiden if she be unwilling, but Tovran would not see his plans for dynasty fall away. After two years in which Helen did not change her mind, he set a date for the wedding. On the morning on which she was to be married her father went to her rooms and found the poor girl dead in her bath, her wrists cut and all her blood drained away.

Then Dalitus said to Drusan, "Helen has done only what our noble ancestors thought it good to do when faced with an intolerable situation. You and I should consider our principles when faced with an Emperor who demands such sacrifice. Is it wise that we give it to him, or should we consider some other course?" Drusan refused to pay attention then, but afterward when Dalitus would say such things he began to listen.

—From Cornelien, *The Annals of Imperial Vinca*

We should go after her," I said, gesturing uphill toward where Marchel and the majority of her surviving armigers had disappeared into the trees.

"Some of us. On fresh horses," Urdo said, signaling to Grugin. The call went out for those who could to change horses. "Will four pennons be enough, do you think?"

"If they can catch her," I said wearily. I pulled my helmet off and rubbed my head where it had started to hurt. There was a new dent in the helmet.

"Her horses may be fast, but they must be nearly foundered,"

Urdo said. He beckoned to Masarn. "Take four pennons of unwounded armigers on fresh horses and pursue."

"How far?" he asked, looking warily northward toward the hills. "Are there tracks?"

"Not that way," I said. "The highroad goes north; she'll have to stay on it. You couldn't get horses through the high hills, and she has no supplies; she'll have to make for a base." I turned to Urdo. "I'm sorry. I thought we could lure her out to fight without her getting loose."

"She's loose with two pennons and no supplies, rather than two alae and well equipped," he said. "I call that well enough. Masarn, follow her as best you can, keep near to the highroad. I will send scouts along there. You keep sending messages. Come back on the road when it gets dark, that will be an hour or two yet. But don't stay out all night; camped by the road you would be very vulnerable."

I glanced around for my decurios. "Take Bradwen's pennon," I said. "She knows the land around here well. And—" I noticed something. "Did ap Madog's pennon come up with you?"

"From Aberhavren, yes," Urdo said.

"Then take some of them as well; they have been scouting but not long in the battle."

Masarn raised his chin. "I'll do what I can," he said.

"But what are you doing here anyway?" I asked.

"No time," he said, and grinned. "Like a lot of our people, I've come back to the banner for the *emergency*."

I smiled as he went off. His words brought back the war so clearly, and all the good times then.

"We have to get inside," Urdo said, bringing my mind back to the moment. "Come on."

I settled my helmet back on my head and took up my shield again. It was beaten and battered so that the painted figure of a demon was almost unrecognizable. Even the iron rim was dented where I had brought it down hard on a gauntleted wrist. "What terms do we offer?" I asked.

"Aurien must stand trial. The rest of them were obeying her orders and can be forgiven if they ask pardon now and

swear not to oppose us any longer," Urdo said. He signaled to
Grugin and to Raul, who came up from where he had been
waiting with the baggage train. He had herald's branches
with him. My pennon came and formed up behind me. I
looked them over briefly. We were seven down. I hoped they
were mostly wounded, not dead. I would have to find out
later. I'd never lost so many at one fight. We just weren't used
to fighting other cavalry.

We raised our banners and rode toward the gates of
Magor, still resolutely shut against us. As we went, Grugin
blew the command to the rest of the armigers to stand
down. Govien started to sort out the wounded and the dead.
The few Malmish prisoners were being roped together. I
had no idea what we were going to do with them. It didn't
seem likely that we would get a good ransom from their
families in Narlahena. Golidan had set half his pennon to
catching the loose Malmish horses, who were beginning to
gather unhappily into groups as horses will who have lost
their riders.

The Isarnagans were shouting and banging their shields
with their spears. They quietened as we drew near, impressed
by the banners and Urdo's bearing. They moved out of the
way to make a path for us. I saw Emer among them, alive and
unwounded.

I recognized the people on the wall by the gates. Two of
them were Aurien's regular hall guards. The third was Father
Cinwil. The fourth was my nephew Galbian. How could Aurien be such a fool as to have the boy there? My stomach
clenched as I looked up at him. If he offered defiance then his
life was forfeit. The law said fifteen was old enough to know
what he was doing personally, though not old enough to be
expected to try to control his mother. Aurien knew that; she
had to.

"The invaders from across the sea, whom Aurien ap Gwien
chose to harbor, are dead, fled, or defeated," Raul said loudly.
"Aurien ap Gwien, who has poisoned her sister and conspired
with the High King's enemies against the Peace and the Law,
must stand trial for her crimes."

I glanced at Urdo, who was looking up at Galbian. I was so glad he was here to conduct the trial and relieve me of that burden.

"You people of Magor who will swear to uphold the King's Peace and the Law from this day forward, may have mercy, and return to King's Peace by so swearing, though you should dread to swear falsely in the name of the White God ever merciful, or in the name of any god of the land."

Raul paused, and took several breaths. What he said next was not so loud, but it carried. "Open the gates, in the name of Urdo ap Avren, High King of Tir Tanagiri!"

"We will open the gates," Father Cinwil said. I breathed a sigh of relief. "But the heathens must not enter."

"The folk of Dun Morr will remain outside, but you must send out food and drink to them," Raul countered quickly.

"We do not have enough to send," Father Cinwil said. "Come in and we will show you."

I frowned. There should have been plenty. Raul glanced at Urdo, raising his eyebrows. Urdo must have signaled something I did not see, for Raul went on smoothly. "Very well, if you do not have enough you cannot. But open the gates and accept our pardon, or suffer the consequences."

"We will accept your offer of clemency," Galbian said, his voice sounding strained and high as he forced it to carry. I wondered if Aurien had sent him up there so she could avoid saying that. Then the gates were opened from inside and we rode in.

Galbian came down at once and knelt to Urdo. I did not hear what they said to each other, but Urdo raised him and embraced him without hesitation. Then young Gwien came and knelt, and again Urdo forgave him easily. Gwien came up to me afterward, as the people of Magor came up one by one. "Will I still be going to Derwen for the summer?" he asked, with a child's self-centered view of the world.

"You'll probably be coming to live at Derwen to learn how to be my heir," I said.

"Oh good," he said, and started to pet Evenstar. After a moment, awkwardly and without looking up, he said, "I'm ever so glad Mother didn't manage to poison you, Aunt Sulien."

"Where is your mother?" I asked. She wasn't anywhere in sight.

"She said when you were ready she'd be in Grandfather's room, but you should go there and not us. She made us promise."

I knew then, and my dream came back to me in a flash; Veniva holding out a coil of rope and a dagger. Suicide, the Vincan way out. All she would be avoiding was a trial and an execution. In many ways it would be better. Still, I had to try to stop her. She might have information we needed about our enemies' plans. Urdo was still accepting pardons. I could not distract him. I signaled to Raul, who walked his horse over to me.

"I need to go into the hall to find Aurien," I said. "Gwien, tell Raul what she told you."

Gwien repeated it. Raul's hand went to his pebble, but his eyes met mine. "I will come with you," he said.

"Look after Evenstar, Gwien," I said. I dismounted, feeling my legs wobble as I took my own weight. I had not realized how tired I was. Evenstar suffered the boy to take hold of her harness self-importantly. Galbian stood under the portico outside the hall and looked at me with shadowed eyes as Raul and I passed. Unlike his brother, he knew.

The hall seemed empty; all its people were outside. I pushed open doors, and walked through the dining hall with the Vincan couches. I longed to lie down on one and sleep; the exhaustion of the days of waiting and of the battle was hitting me hard. I pressed on, leading Raul to the great stairway leading upstairs. I knew the way. Duke Galba's room was the great upper chamber, hung with tapestries showing the lives and noble deaths of the Dukes of Magor. The newest and brightest showed Galba killing Sweyn at Foreth. Aurien had made it herself; it had taken her two years. The spears and swords were made of real silver-gilt thread that came all the way from Caer Custenn.

She was sitting before it in one of the red padded chairs. For a moment I thought we had been in time. Her eyes were open and she seemed to see us. She was wearing a red linen overdress fastened at the neck with her gold-and-pearl brooch. She had let her white hair down to straggle loose about her face. I could not remember the last time I had seen her with her hair disarranged. She had shorn it for Galba, not let it straggle. Seeing it like that set off deep feelings of uneasiness; it was almost frightening. I took a breath and walked into the room toward her.

"Aurien?" I said. She had her pebble around her neck on a cord, as usual. There was a beaker in her hand. She neither moved nor spoke. I froze, halfway across the room. Raul came past me and went up to her. He put his hand to her neck to check if her blood was still moving. As he did so her hand opened and the beaker fell to the floor and split in two. A few drops spilled out onto the woven carpet. Raul began murmuring prayers over her. I picked up the bits of the beaker and sniffed at them. Henbane.

Raul came to a break in his prayers. "Too late," I said in a hushed voice.

"Oh no," he said, turning to me. "She is poisoned, paralyzed by the poison, but alive."

I looked at her in horror, remembering how I had felt when the poison had hold of me, how I had been able to see and hear but not respond. She could live for years unable to move. Conal had said so and he knew about poison. She could not stand trial like this. I thought about the boys. I glanced at Raul. I knew followers of the White God thought suicide a terrible sin, denying all chance of the world they believed was to come. I almost wondered that she had been so Vincan in the end. I felt sure Raul would not let me put a cushion on her face to end it for her kindly. I wondered how much he knew about poisons. He wouldn't have had much chance to learn at Thansethan.

"We must give her water," I said, surprised to hear my voice come out evenly. "We may be able to wash it out of her system." Raul looked at me quickly, then agreed quietly. As I left the room he was praying over her.

I ran downstairs, snatched up a beaker, and ran out of the back of the hall to fetch water from the well. I wound the handle as fast as I could, slopping it everywhere. I poured it from the bucket to the beaker, not worrying how much I spilled. I had taken two steps across the yard back toward the hall when I smelled the henbane in it. I stopped dead. She had poisoned the well. Or, to be fair to her, someone had. I could not believe Aurien would have done it without telling the boys to be careful, and they would have told Urdo. I wondered briefly where henbane came from and how expensive it was. I didn't know if it would take a lot or only a little to poison a whole well. Conal would have known. Maybe I could ask Emer.

I turned back to the well and started to laugh. I had come to get water to poison my sister, and found poison in the well. Yet I could not take her a cup of poison, whatever my intentions and however much she had done the same for me. I emptied all the water I had drawn back into the well and set the beaker down on the rim. Then I calmed myself and sang Garah's charm for water, naming the Mother as Coventina; as I had done in Caer Lind when the wells were poisoned, as I had done on the top of Foreth Hill. There came a gurgle from the depths of the well. I could feel the charm working on the world, driving out the poison and setting the rising water as it should be. There would be a charm that drives poison out of people that way, if any god loved people as the Mother of Many Waters loves water. Then I drew up the bucket again, slowly this time, aware of the holiness of water and of all things. I filled the beaker carefully. I sniffed at it. It was good, clear water. I poured a little from it, carefully, then drank it, praising the Mother. I poured it full again, and turned toward the hall.

Again I stopped. How could I use this water, sacred as all water is sacred, to kill my sister? Yet killing her now was a kindness to everyone. I took another step toward the door. I raised the beaker toward the sky. I would take it in. It would be the gods' choice what came of it. Death can also be a holy thing.

I hurried up through the hall and back to the tapestry-hung room. Raul broke off his prayer and turned as I came in. "I think—" he began. Then Aurien choked a little and he turned back to her. It seemed to me that she was looking at me, and the expression in her eyes was hatred.

"I'm sorry I was so long, but the well was poisoned," I said.

I kept my eyes on Aurien's face, but detected no changes. I could not tell if she had known it or not. "Where did you get the water, then?" Raul asked.

"I cleansed the well," I said. "I have used the charm before. This is pure water. I drank some myself before I brought it up. There might have been clean water in a jug but I couldn't leave it like that; anyone might have come along and drawn water."

He looked at me, surprised, then shook his head a little and put out his hand for the beaker. I gave it to him and he set the beaker to Aurien's lips. She opened them a little. She was staring at me and I could still not make out the expression on her mouth. Raul stroked her throat and she swallowed. She kept on swallowing. "Marchel must have poisoned the well," Raul said. "Aurien must have taken some of the water and drunk it without noticing." In that case, why had we hurried in here, I wondered. Also, the liquid in the broken beaker had been wine and not water. But Raul went on, "I am glad. If it was suicide she could never find her way to God. This way she has her chance of forgiveness." He made the sign of the White God and touched his pebble to her forehead and lips.

I didn't say anything. The beaker was empty. Raul put it down. Aurien looked at me an instant in what appeared to be deep concern, and then she just stopped being there. Her head lolled back on her neck, her heart stopped pumping, and her breath stopped. I killed a dozen people on the field of battle that day, or more. In a way I killed all of them, by giving the orders I did, and most of them deserved it far less than Aurien. I have never felt any guilt for helping her find the death she wanted.

"Ah," Raul said. "I wondered if that would happen. It sometimes does, with henbane." We looked at each other for a moment. Then Raul began the prayers for the dead.

8

O Lord, give of thy Ever-Living Spirit to these people, that being now born again and made heirs of everlasting salvation through God Made Man they may continue to be thy servants and attain thy promises and dwell with thee in eternal glory, ever more praising thy glorious Name.

—From the Baptism of the White God, early translation as used at Thansethan

When we came out, the courtyard was full of armigers and grooms watering their horses and walking them. It was only the two pennons we had come in with; the others had gone down to the river. All the same the courtyard seemed like Caer Tanaga at a fair. Gwien had given Evenstar half a bucket and was walking her. I was relieved to see he had been able to stop her. Too much cold water can kill a hot horse. She was a very well-mannered mare but he was only thirteen.

I let Raul explain to Urdo his theory about the well poisoning. When he heard his mother was dead, little Gwien flung himself weeping against Evenstar's leg. She gave one startled huff and swung her head around to nose at him, then stood patiently. Galbian just kept very still. He was young to have the whole weight of Magor fall onto his shoulders. Urdo took the boys off into the hall. I looked enquiringly to see if he needed me, but he shook his head.

Once the horses were cool and watered I brought both alae inside the walls. I warned Dalmer that the other wells might also be poisoned and he went off to check the supply situation. I checked on the wounded and the dead. When I came back inside, I started settling disputes about how to assign billets. There was barely room for all of us inside the walls and definitely not going to be enough room for all the horses in the stables.

I spent a few minutes with Darien in the stables where he was settling his summerhorse, whose name, appropriately enough, was Barley. I left him and came out to a dispute between Golidan and Rigol about who had first claim on the barracks. Golidan was stalking off to set up tents and I was drawing breath when Dalmer came up to me, looking furious.

"Where's Urdo?" he asked without preliminary as soon as the decurios had gone off. "The food has all been deliberately destroyed. Trampled by horses, thrown in the midden, or generally fouled. Some of the roots may be salvageable for the horses; it's hard to hurt a turnip, but that will take time. And if there's anything that will ever be fit for people to eat, that we didn't bring in ourselves, then it's well hidden."

"But they could have won!" I said, trying to take it in. "I'd assumed that someone poisoned the well at the last moment, but that must have taken time. What did they think they were doing?"

"I've no idea. I don't know if thinking came into it. But the waste of it! I could cry to see it. If I ever get my hands on Marchel, killing will be too good for her. Murdering prisoners and invading the country and destroying good food!"

"That's why they said they didn't have enough for the Isarnagans," I said, my mind catching up slowly.

"And we shall have to send something out to them as well," Dalmer said. "Celemon? Hey, Celemon!" Celemon ap Caius, who had been ap Erbin's quartermaster the last time I had seen her, had been unpacking supplies from packhorses. She set down a heavy pack and came over to us. "What have we brought we can feed four thousand Isarnagans who are likely to destroy the countryside if we don't feed them?"

Celemon shrugged. "Porridge?" Dalmer swatted at her with the wax tablet he was carrying. She dodged and pretended to cower, though she could have picked Dalmer up in one hand if she'd wanted to.

"There are some cows on a farm a mile or so south of here," I said. "If you give them half a dozen cows they'll be so delighted they won't mind if they take half the night to cook and they'll get less food out of it than if they had porridge."

"I can see you have experience of Isarnagans," Celemon said to me. "I'm only used to feeding armigers and horses. I'm doing Glyn's job since he got to be king of Bregheda."

"I expect ap Erbin misses you," I said. "A good quartermaster is hard to find."

Celemon shrugged again. "We've been training people as well as we can. I am hoping to get back down to Caer Segant eventually; my husband likes it there. But for now, will you give me a scout so I can find this farm and deal with the Isarnagans?"

I signaled to the nearest of my armigers to find me one of our scouts. "Shall you bring some cows back for us as well?" I asked.

"How many cows do they have?" Dalmer asked.

I shrugged. "I didn't count, I was too busy getting the troops away. More than a dozen. Fine, big beasts."

"That must be some farmer's whole livelihood," Dalmer said. "They might sell one or two for silver, but never the whole herd. It's terrible that we need to do this."

"Why do we?" Celemon asked. "We have what supplies we brought. I know harvest is due, but shouldn't there be enough?"

"Marchel destroyed it," Dalmer said, anger in every line of his body. "We'll have to feed the local people as well, most likely."

I looked away as he began to detail the destruction and saw Emer and ap Ranien standing just by the gate. Emer looked as if she had every right to be there, but ap Ranien looked uneasy. As he caught my eye he said something to Emer.

"There are the Isarnagan leaders now," I said, interrupting Dalmer. "By the terms by which the gates were opened they should not come inside. Will you come and greet them with me?"

"I should speak to Urdo if I can," Dalmer said. "But you go, Celemon, you might be able to get an accurate count of their numbers from them."

I led Celemon over to the gate, where I made the introductions and everyone bowed low and very politely.

"We were just arranging to have some cows brought in for your victory feast," Celemon said.

Emer and ap Ranien exchanged glances. "There may be no need," ap Ranien said.

"We understand your people will want to celebrate—" I said. But I had misunderstood.

"Are we to stay in the stockade again tonight?" Emer asked.

"Yes," I said. "The people of the town are afraid of your troops."

"In that case we can easily set up roasting pits," Emer continued. "We have been clearing the field, and there are a great number of dead horses. Unless you have any need of them, they will suffice to feed our people."

My stomach heaved, and I bit my tongue to stop myself saying something offensive and undiplomatic. I needn't have bothered.

"That's the next thing to cannibalism!" Celemon blurted. "Our greathorses are our battle-companions! They are honored dead and their bodies are treated with honor."

A memory came to me of Glyn's sober face over a well I had purified, long ago. "Come, Celemon," I said. "Remember Caer Lind? We would have eaten our own horses there rather than starve, and they were still alive." I was as horrified as she was, but I had spent time with the Isarnagans and their barbarism could not horrify me as it would have once. I had even had to judge one case of horse-stealing where the motive had clearly been much the same as the thief would have had for stealing a cow.

"Besides, we weren't suggesting we eat your dead companions, just the horses of the enemy," ap Ranien put in quickly.

I opened my mouth, while trying to find a polite way to suggest that eating the fallen enemy was only marginally better. Celemon was looking quite green and leaning against the wall. While I was looking for words I heard Urdo's voice from behind me. "You and your people may feast on the Malmish horses, though you should know that it will cause many in the alae to have the same reaction as ap Caius here."

I spun round. I had no idea how long he had been there. He came forward and took up a place beside me. He was looking and sounding very weary. Celemon cleared her throat uneasily.

Emer smiled. "We are accustomed to being considered barbarians," she said.

"I would have that change," Urdo said. "You are all my people now. This is a good time to make the change. Tonight, feast as is your custom. Make sure it is only the Malmish horses you eat. Then, tomorrow, I will gift you and your people with some of the Malmish horses that are left alive. There should be two horses for each of your household warriors. This victory feast will mark the change from your people seeing horses as cattle to seeing them as companions."

Emer frowned and drew breath, but did not speak. "What about the spoils of the field?" ap Ranien asked.

"Your people may have what they have found on the bodies of our enemies," Urdo said. "We know the difference between an army that fights even partly for plunder, and one that fights for the Peace and the glory of their names." He paused, and looked from Emer to ap Ranien. "The cabbages and roots will be ripening in Dun Morr as they are here. Your troops will need to be home to gather them. How many can you spare me for a longer campaign?"

"I can lead five hundred who would rather fight than farm," Emer said, without even glancing at ap Ranien. "You are right that many of them will soon be needed at home."

I looked at poor ap Ranien, who was biting his lip. He shrugged a little when he caught my eye. I guessed he would not be glad to be away from Emer. He was a steady man for an Isarnagan, but I would not have liked to ride in his saddle. Lew listened too hard to advice, and Emer did not listen hard enough.

"Very good," Urdo said. "Set up camp in the stockade for tonight, and arrange who will be going home. Tomorrow five hundred of your troops will begin marching up the highroad toward Caer Gloran."

While they were smiling and bowing and exchanging politenesses, Urdo added, almost as an afterthought, "Send some of your horse-collecting parties down here—we have some more dead horses in the stables and you may as well take them, too." They took this without a murmur, but I turned to Urdo, startled. He ignored me and kept smiling evenly at Emer.

After the Isarnagans left us, Urdo sent Celemon off to get on with her work. "Oh well," she said, wanly, as she left. "Think of the food we'll save. Not only the supplies we don't need to feed the Isarnagans, but the porridge we'll save on the armigers. Nobody will be able to eat a bite when they know."

"Better not to spread the news too widely," Urdo warned. Celemon rolled her eyes and made the hand signal that meant that she would follow orders.

"*What* dead horses in the stables?" I asked, quietly, as soon as we were alone.

Urdo ran his hands through his hair. "Marchel's armigers have all gone, sure enough. Her grooms were left in here and decided to cause what havoc they could. They poisoned the wells, spoiled the food, and went to the new stables over beyond the hall and started to kill the spare horses."

"How many?" I asked queasily. I had to know, whether I wanted to or not.

"About fifty dead. Two stables' full. Ap Selevan caught them as they were going into the third stable. They are presently barricaded inside there, demanding their lives in return for not slaughtering any more horses."

I gasped as this hit me like successive blows to the stomach. "Their own horses?" I said.

"Indeed," Urdo said between his teeth. "Ap Selevan sent a message to me. They are refusing to surrender unless you and I are both there."

"They could have surrendered at any time," I said. "Are

they mad to do that, killing horses and destroying supplies to put themselves outside the law?"

"A horse is a weapon, and a horse in our hand is a weapon against them," Urdo said. "But I wonder what these Malms know of surrender. They may be zealots, fanatics, the worst kind of enemy."

"Very few of them surrendered in the fighting," I said. "And Marchel was exiled for slaughtering those Isarnagans at Varae—" I hesitated, and Urdo raised his chin grimly. "But I do not think it is a custom of their people."

"Thurrig has honor," Urdo said.

"And Larig did. But what I was thinking was Marcia Antonilla writing about them two hundred years ago when they first attempted to cross the River Vonar. They had honor then, as a people."

"That's good to know," Urdo said soberly. "Now, they are waiting for us to get there, so we will go. Have you a fresh horse?"

I looked around as if expecting a fresh horse to be standing at my side and saw Urdo's groom, ap Caw, with Thunder and one of the summerhorses, both saddled and ready. "Not nearer than the stockade," I said.

"Then take Thunder," Urdo said. "He will remember you."

"Why do they need me there?" I asked, belatedly realizing that this was strange. "You, yes, but why me?"

"There could be all sorts of reasons. In the worst case they want to kill us both in a charge. But we will have two pennons there, so they cannot do it." He signaled to ap Caw, who brought the horses up.

I was tired already. All my bones ached. I wished I could summon up a fresh body as easily as a fresh horse. I swung up onto Thunder's back, talking to him reassuringly, all sorts of nonsense if I should write it down afterward, just making noises to let him know that he knew me and while I wasn't Urdo I was still someone he should take notice of.

Urdo smiled to hear this stream of nonsense as he mounted the summerhorse. "This is Harvest," he said, patting her face.

"Did Dalmer find you?" I asked, the name reminding me uneasily of the destruction of the supplies.

"Yes, he did," Urdo said, looking grim as we started to move off. "There is no stored food here at all. I think Marchel meant Magor to be a problem for us. I have no intention of getting caught up down here longer than I have to. But we can't leave it empty to be reoccupied either. I had wondered about leaving the Isarnagans as guards, but I suspect they'd terrorize the countryside. We'll have to leave a pennon at least, preferably one of those which is usually here. If Masarn does not catch up with Marchel we should leave two. What did you do with the farmers?"

I rode close beside him so we could talk without being much overheard. "Sent them off to Derwen, out of the way. I can send them back again."

"We're going to have to go to Derwen anyway," Urdo said. "Since there's no way from here over the mountains to Nant Gefalion we have to go up the track from Derwen. We also need to get hold of supplies. The problem with moving alae around like pieces on a fidchel board is feeding them on the squares they get to. I will set Dalmer and Celemon working on the problem, but it is a problem."

"There are some supplies at Derwen, but you will have to speak to Nodol about them," I said. "Why do we have to go to Nant Gefalion? Is Cinvar coming down that way? I sent Hiveth's pennon up to block it. The last news I have there was no trouble there. Oh, and he had invited Marchel's sons to join us, and sent them to Derwen where they are safe with my mother."

"Invited?" Urdo frowned. "You haven't been taking hostages?"

"No. Duncan and my mother wanted to, but I insisted it would be an invitation."

"Good." Urdo sighed. "I'll have a word with them when we get to Derwen and see if they'd like to join the ala. I would have done it years ago, except they never let me know they were back here, so I felt they might not want my attention." We threaded our way past the house, along to where the new stable blocks were. "Marchel isn't the real problem though. Nor is Arling, even armed with mysterious machines from Caer Custenn. In some ways he's a blessing because he's an obvious foreign invasion."

"Morthu," I said.

"Morthu could be brought to trial for treason with the evidence of Rigg's letter," Urdo said. "The real problem is the kings, and you know it. We have to put this revolt down as quickly as we can and let them know that having civil wars just isn't an acceptable way to settle differences anymore. By the latest news I have none of them have done anything beyond raising their levies, which is no crime. None of them, that is, except Cinvar, who has killed two men of Cadraith's who happened to be visiting him and declared that he will have none of my rule. I have sent Luth and ap Erbin up into Tevin to help Alfwin against Arling when he lands. I have written to Cadraith and ap Meneth to come to Tathal to join us there. If we crush Cinvar quickly then maybe Flavien and Cinon will see the folly of their plans."

"What about Ayl?" I asked.

"Ayl can learn from example," Urdo said grimly.

"You don't think he might join Arling?"

"It's not impossible. But there was no news of Arling landing when I left Caer Tanaga, and Marchel and Cinvar were already a problem. I think this is the right order to tackle them in. I've written to Ayl, for whatever good that will do. I've left half an ala in Caer Tanaga for all that I have a whole ala here—I recalled all the veterans who live nearby." He grinned. "Like Masarn. They all came. I'm proud of them. Most of them are here, and I left three pennons under Gormant who are used to fighting together."

"And what about Angas?" I almost didn't want to ask.

Urdo sighed again. There was a guard on the door of the first stable block; we returned his signal that all was well as we rode past him. "Angas is another sort of problem. I need to talk to Angas. As you said in your letter, Angas needs someone to sort things out for him. We need to bring Morthu to justice and then Angas's problems will go away, I think. In any case, Angas is right up in Demedia; it will take him half a month or more to get anywhere he can be a problem. Invading Bregheda, well, it's possible, but he knows the terrain well enough to know how foolish it would be. The land is packed thick with mountains. Everyone knows that in all Penda's wars with Borthas, Mardol was the only winner, nibbling away at the south instead of going head-on at the hills. Invading Bregheda from the north would be even more foolish."

"I wish there was some way of knowing what's going on far away," I said. "I'm worrying about Angas and Arling, and we just can't know, it's too far. And if Morthu has infiltrated the red-cloaks then we don't know what news to trust."

"Elenn is looking after the messages for the time being," Urdo said. "And I have sent to Garah to ask her to come back to Caer Tanaga and do her old job for the emergency. Nothing is likely to get lost or copied at Caer Tanaga with them there. It does no good to worry about it anyway."

"You still haven't said why Nant Gefalion rather than up the highroad to Caer Gloran," I reminded him as we exchanged signals with the guard on the second door.

"I'm going to send the Isarnagans up the highroad. They can hold it; they can prevent people coming back down it at speed. But we ought to go through Nant Gefalion to get the supplies from Derwen, send the farmers back here. And also, if Cinvar isn't invading south, that way we'll be more likely to surprise him coming up there."

"If we head off for Derwen in the morning, and spend tomorrow night there, we won't be pushing the horses too hard. Then Nant Gefalion is a day from there, and we can be at Caer Gloran the afternoon of the next day," I said.

Urdo raised his chin. "I also want to take your nephews to your mother. Galbian is too young to rule here without help, and he's been spoiled, you're right. He needs a few years in the ala to sort him out. I thought when all this is over we might leave your man Duncan as steward of Derwen and I might take Galbian to Caer Tanaga for training. What do you think?"

"Duncan's dead," I said. "Ten days ago, in the fighting. But there must be somebody who can do it."

"I'll think about it," Urdo said. Then he drew Harvest gently to a halt, for we were almost around the second stable and could already see a press of armigers outside the third. I halted beside him. "Will you stay down here or come up to Tathal with me?"

"I will certainly come," I said, without hesitation. "Veniva can look after the day-to-day affairs of Derwen. And the ala is ready, of course. I have also raised the militia, and though some will be needed for the harvest we could take the rest. They know our signals and they may be a help against Cinvar."

"Are you sure Derwen can risk them?" Urdo asked.

I thought of the militia for a moment, all those young and eager farmers who came to fight at my word. They were my people, my responsibility, even as my armigers were, even as the land was. They trusted me to make choices for them that might kill them, that would kill some of them, inevitably. "Yes," I said, after a moment. "If we lose, then there is no holding Derwen alone, no matter how many troops are there. I would not risk my people for glory, nor myself neither, not now I have a duty to the land." I looked over at him, sitting still and patient on the summerhorse, listening to me. Then I bit my lip and looked away, seeing and not seeing the two pennons clustered outside the stable. "I joined the ala because I wanted to fight, and for a long time that's all it was for me; the glory, the skills, the comradeship. Most of the war I was fighting for the Peace because you said it was a good thing and I was prepared to leave the thinking to you. But eventually I did realize what it was we were fighting for, what the Peace is, what the Law is; it is more than any single person, and better for everyone. You said after Foreth that our honor lay in how well the Peace was kept, breath by breath, all our days. If I were to throw away my peoples' lives that would be a terrible thing. But if I were to be too careful of them and risk the Peace, that would be even worse. Having come so far I will not throw away the honor of Foreth now, and everyone's future choices."

I looked back at Urdo, and saw to my amazement that there were tears on his face. He smiled at me. "Then we will take your militia with us," he said. "Now, let us deal with these Malms."

We rode on. The stable doors were closed, but not barred on the outside. Ap Selevan reported to Urdo that nothing had happened while they were waiting. I greeted old friends in ap Selevan's pennon, and in Elwith's. I was exchanging a few words with ap Padarn when there came a movement from within the stable.

Everyone turned and lowered their spears toward the doors as they swung open. I was expecting a suicidal rush forward and moved Thunder ahead, between Urdo and the doors.

Instead a single tiny woman walked out, her bare head held high. Her hair was completely gray now but I would have known her anywhere. Many of the armigers recognized her, and even those that did not fell back a little before her. She ignored them as if they did not exist. I had known that Amala had gone to Narlahena with Marchel, but had never thought she might have come back with her. She walked in silence across the muddy stable yard toward us and stopped in front of Urdo. She was wearing a white drape embroidered in blue and gold, and she did not look in the least as if she had been killing horses in it. She seemed as fresh as if she had just come from the bathhouse.

She stood there in silence for a moment, looking at us. Always before Amala had made me feel ungainly and barbaric. Now, even though I was wearing battle-stained armor, I was only aware how very frail she was. She must have been almost seventy years old.

"Why are you here, wife of Thurrig?" Urdo asked, with no warmth in his voice.

"I was not exiled from Tir Tanagiri," Amala said, biting off the words in her familiar way.

"True," Urdo said. "You left of your own choice, and were free to return in peace at any time and rejoin the rest of your family. But your daughter was not so free, and nor were you free to return and take up arms against me."

"Take up arms?" Amala said, raising her bare arms almost as if she were about to take an oath, and making it abundantly clear that she was weaponless.

"Enough of this," Urdo said, frowning. "Marchel has invaded us and you came here with her. You, and those with you, stand accused of well-poisoning, horse-murder, and destruction of supplies. By the law you have earned death, and I have force enough here to take you all. What is to prevent me?"

"Will you speak with me in private?" Amala asked, looking around at the waiting pennons.

"Are you here as a herald?" Urdo asked.

"I have no branches, but we shall say I am if it pleases you," she replied. The question now was where we should go. These stables were right across Magor from the hall, which was the only place we could really offer any hospitality. It was even further to the stockade. Urdo solved this by dismounting, giving Harvest's reins to Ulf, who was the nearest, and leading Amala off toward the place where the memorials for the dead dukes of Magor lay. I gave ap Padarn Thunder's reins. I told ap Selevan to keep the rest ready at the stable doors and to kill the Malms if they made any attempt to break out. Then I hurried off after them.

We sat down on the carved rock that recorded the dates of Duke Galba's life, and of his wife's. Young Galba's stone was nearby, and I realized that soon we would be burning Aurien, and cutting her name into it beside his.

"So," Urdo said when we were settled. "Tell me why I should not just set fire to that stable block and solve my whole problem?"

"Even if you cared nothing that Thurrig would avenge me," she said, crisply, "would you have war with Narlahena?"

Urdo made a sound that was cousin to a laugh. "It would seem that I have it whether I would or not. Two alae landed is a little much for a fishing trip gone astray."

"Then you have thought about the fleet it took to bring them here?" Amala said. I frowned. I had not. "King Gomoarion is supporting Marchel's venture, yes, in hope of easy gain, plunder, and a victory for the White God. Also, it is the payment he has made her for acting all these years as his cavalry commander. But he has many more alae, and a strong fleet. All who came here are volunteers, and he has declared no war on you."

"A nice distinction," Urdo said. "So why does that change if I treat you and your people as you deserve?"

"His son is among the rabble of grooms and cooks taking refuge in that stable. Gomoarion did not know he was here, and nor did Marchel. He stowed away on board, he was so full of zeal to see the victory of the White God in another land." Amala touched a hand to her hair, looking suddenly weary. "All of this well-poisoning and slaughter of horses was at Gomoarionsson's instigation. His father will pay you a fine ransom for his safe return to Narlahena, but he would lay the land waste if harm came to him."

"He could try," Urdo said. Laying the land waste, even with alae and a fleet, was far from easy. It would be difficult for him to do even what we had done in Oriel in the way of destruction, as he had no nearby base. But even if he only stopped the Narlahenan merchant ships from crossing to trade with us, that would be very bad. An outright invasion, with such a long supply line, would be costly for us, even if he could only win if he had allies here. Though that idea did not seem as comforting as it might. "So what do you suggest, wife of Thurrig?" Urdo continued.

Amala smiled wryly. "I have been suggesting that we entrust ourselves to your honor since before the gates were opened. Some among us have been longing to spend their lives winning the praise of the White God for killing pagans. Is Raul here, Urdo? It might do them good to talk to him. But I would beg of you to give us a ship that we might return to Narlahena in peace."

Urdo frowned. "Impossible," he said. "But if you will all

surrender fully I will spare your lives, counting these crimes but excess of zeal."

Amala pursed her lips, and I guessed that she had never really thought she would get a ship. "And if I were to accept that, and if we were to swear not to make war upon you, would you send us all to Thansethan?"

Urdo hesitated. It was too far, across too dubious ground, and Thansethan's loyalty was not certain. Yet what else could he do with them, to keep them secure? I could not offer to keep them here or at Derwen; the ala would not harbor horse-killers and here there might still be people who sympathized with them. The association of ideas gave me the answer. "We could send them to Dun Morr," I said, turning to Urdo. "There are enough Isarnagans there who could do with help on the farms and could keep an eye on them. They won't mistreat them and Lew would be delighted to have the duty. Also, there isn't anywhere to land on that coast until you get all the way to Tapit Point, so it's unlikely the Narlahenans could mount a rescue."

"Good," Urdo said. "That will do for the mass of them, if they will only be induced to surrender. That would also be a good thing for those who surrendered in the field." He turned to Amala. "Would you accept that?"

"For those who surrendered in the field and for the rabble in the stables, yes." She hesitated a moment. "Some of them are young and foolish and wish for a martyr's crown. You should ask them to give up their arms and swear by the Holy Father that they will not fight. Make sure priests are there, Raul and Father Cinwil. They are very young, and they may not see life as preferable." She hesitated again, looking down at the gravemarker she was sitting on and then up at Urdo. She looked old and frail and tentative. "I know you would not wish to kill them after showing such leniency. But for myself, and for Gomoarionsson?"

"I would send you to Thurrig," Urdo said, "but the times are very uncertain. I will send to tell him you are safe, and that your grandsons are safe at Derwen. You may wait there with them if you choose, or you may go to Caer Tanaga until I can deliver you to your husband. As for Gomoarionsson, I suppose it would be an insult to expect him to labor for Lew, though if he is as you have represented him it would do him good. I shall write to his father and say that we announce royal visits differently in Tir Tanagiri, but for all that, his son is safely arrived in my keeping. Gomoarionsson himself I shall send to Caer Tanaga, where Elenn and Gormant can entertain him until we hear his father's wishes. If his father wants him back after he has been such a fool."

"Will we give the Isarnagans the ransom when it comes?" I asked.

"Half of it," Urdo said. "And we will set it high."

"Where is Thurrig?" Amala asked.

Urdo laughed. "In Caer Thanbard, or sailing against the pirates, where would he be? Have you heard different?"

Amala smiled, thin-lipped. "I will accept your conditions," she said. "But you must let me go back into that terrible stable and make Gomoarionsson see this as a way forward."

— 9 —

Here long ago
light was born
as every morning
light is born
thy gift,
ever renewed
as each day brings
a new dawn.

This is the world's
axle-point
as is each step
on the turning world.

Standing here still
as the world turns
toward red dawn
I know
light is how I see
light is what I see
I know myself
seeing the light.

Thanks from my heart
Albian, Radiant Sun,
thy gift
to see myself
in thy light.
   —Hymn to Dawn

Amala went back into the stable and eventually came out
with a sullen-looking bunch of Malms. They all looked
very young. I heard afterward she had needed to get two of

the others to sit on Gomoarionsson before he would agree to surrender on Urdo's very generous terms. We sent most of them out under escort to the Isarnagans in the stockade, but Celemon managed to fit Amala and Gomoarionsson into the hall.

Masarn arrived back late in the evening. Marchel appeared to have vanished. The only sign he had seen of her was a handful of foundered horses.

She must have known of a track we didn't know, or of somewhere nearby to hide out of sight. She had spent two years as praefecto down in Magor, and longer in Caer Gloran; she had had time to get to know the land well. I had to send Masarn and his people out to the stockade for the night. There really wasn't enough room for another four pennons inside the walls of Magor—it would have been a squeeze to make room for another four armigers at that point. Marchel's two alae must have been very cramped. I didn't want either people or horses to spend the night outside with Marchel loose. I couldn't find the optimism Masarn had to hope the land had eaten them. Masarn was quite prepared to take the risk of being outside; he was far more horrified at the thought of sleeping near the horse-eaters. Word had spread, and he had heard the rumor as soon as he was in the gates. I mollified him with the promise that if he caught the Isarnagans so much as cutting a hair from a greathorse, living or dead, he had permission to kill them on the spot.

I slept in my tent and woke late. I hadn't missed anything but breakfast. Urdo was still settling the affairs of Magor and wasn't anything like ready to leave. I hadn't even really missed breakfast; Talog had saved me some cold porridge. I went to the stables to see to my horses, and found Darien and ap Caw there.

Ap Caw was leaning on the wall next to Barley's stall, chewing on a piece of straw. Darien was fussing over a long-maned Narlahenan horse. They both looked up as I came in. "Look at my new riding horse," Darien said. I came up and gave it a closer look. It was a gray gelding, probably nine or ten years old by the teeth.

"I thought Urdo was giving them to the Isarnagans?" I said, making friends with him. He was a very good-tempered horse, quite happy to become acquainted.

"Lots of them," ap Caw said, spitting out the straw. "Waste of good horses if they eat them, but no arguing with Urdo when he's using that voice. He swears their eating days are over after last night, but I'll wait and see what they do. I was up before dawn sorting the horses for him, choosing the youngest and making sure they all had sound wind, not that the Isarnagans will be able to tell more than that they have a leg at each corner. Two each for all the household warriors, four for their captain, six for the queen, and a dozen to go back to the king. Every one of them in breeding condition, mostly mares but a fair sprinkling of stallions, too. Urdo says he wants to set them up a herd at Dun Morr."

"I'm sure he's right that they won't eat horses anymore," Darien said. "I hope so anyway. They're not greathorses, but they're very fast and they fought very well, I thought." I looked over at him, and realized that he had grown again and I had to look up to talk to him. At his full height he over-topped me by three or four fingers. He was taller than my brother Darien had ever been. He was older than my brother Darien had ever been, too. I was only just taking in that he was an armiger and not a child, old enough to fight in the first rank and give other people orders, and now I had to cope with the fact that he was taller than I was. We smiled at each other, a little uncertainly.

"They fought very well indeed," I said, looking back to the gray horse. "And the rest are being shared out in the ala?"

"In both alae," ap Caw said. "Yours as well. Every armiger should have two good riding horses now, and not have to ride their greathorse unless we're expecting battle unexpectedly, if you catch my meaning."

Darien and I both laughed. "I catch it precisely," I said, "I have fought a number of such unexpected battles."

"I've seen you fight," ap Caw said, shaking his head. "Both of you, come to that, exactly the same look on your faces, fighting as if you were off in a lovely dream and all the broken heads and smashed bones only happen to someone else. I've looked after too many hurt horses to believe that sort of thing myself."

"I've looked after hurt horses, too," said Darien, and there was pain in his voice. "You remember how awful it was when Pole Star broke his leg, and that wasn't even in battle. He is well now," he assured me hastily. "This was two years ago. He stepped wrong and fell in training; it was my fault, not his at all, I was confusing him. We splinted it and ap Caw and I sat beside him singing hymns, but it was ap Gavan who saved him—she knew a charm to St. Riganna, Holy Mother of Horses, which could keep him still long enough for it to heal."

I was just taking a drink from my water bottle as he said this, and I choked. They were both looking at me with concern when I had my breath back. St. Riganna indeed. I didn't say anything. If I hadn't wanted Darien brought up to believe in the White God I shouldn't have left him at Thansethan, and better that he should learn Garah's Horsemother charms than not. "I am glad he is better," I said. "Many horses with broken legs can never heal at all. And ap Caw, you will not find that anyone is less careful with their horse than with their own body in battle."

"That's as may be," ap Caw said dubiously. "Well, these Narlahenans are a blessing for us all. There were a fair few packhorses into the bargain. Now that's what I call useful, and I told Celemon so. She just shrugged and said they would be tomorrow when there was something to pack onto them."

Darien turned to me. "When are we leaving for Derwen?"

"When Urdo is ready," I said. "Later this morning I think, then we should be there before it is quite dark. I have sent messages already so they will be expecting us."

Both groups of Isarnagans set off before we did. Emer went first, leading her five hundred north up the high road. It seemed to include most of the people who had been given horses. Ap Ranien's group made a start on their way back to Derwen and then Dun Morr.

We left two pennons to hold Magor and Aberhavren. Urdo

did not name a regent for the land; there was nobody of sufficient standing and sufficient trustworthiness. Whoever he had named the kings who hated us could have used to claim he was taking the land to himself. So he named none. Instead he made Bradwen, decurio of the Second Pennon of Galba's Ala, key-keeper of the fort of Magor—although in truth Magor and Derwen were never forts or Vincan cities, only the homes of lords and their people with new walls built around them. Then he named Golidan war-leader of Magor. They would report to Urdo only, until Galbian grew old enough to rule for himself.

Bradwen came up to take oath first. She knelt to Galbian and swore to be key-keeper in his name. She had a scrape on one cheek from the battle the day before and, combined with her frown, it made her look like a ferocious warrior rather than a steward. She had complained to me that she did not want to be left behind to count turnips, even though she had been trained in quartermaster work by Nodol. She wanted to come with the ala and lead her pennon to battle. Golidan assured her that he would let her take turns leading patrols, and I assured her it was her duty. I was not close by at the oath taking—many of the people of Magor and those of the local farmers who had not fled had come in to see it. I could still see her face clearly. Golidan took oath afterward, looking very solemn. I was sorry to leave them behind; they were both reliable decurios whose initiative I could trust. I wished I could have left Cynrig Fairbeard in place of Golidan. It would have made Bradwen happier to have someone there she wanted to share blankets with and he would have done just as well. But it would not have gone well with the local people to have a Jarn as war-leader, and it would have made Cinon faint if he had heard of it.

They stood outside the gates with their two pennons drawn up in full parade order until we were out of sight.

It was a weary ride back. I felt as if I had been riding to and fro over this ground too many times recently. We left Magor in the late morning and came to Derwen late in the long summer dusk.

The messengers had served their purpose, and the scouts had let them know exactly when we would be arriving. The first person I saw as we came through the gates was Emlin, a wax tablet and stylus poking out of the top of his tunic. Nodol Boar-beard was beside him, holding a lantern.

"You two look cheerful and organized!" I called down to them. Emlin grinned. I could see the lines in his face even through the grin.

"Most of the horses will have to go outside," Nodol said. "But there should be room and food inside for all the people who have come from Magor."

"The horses ought to be safe," Emlin added. "We have my whole pennon on sentry-ring, and half the militia camping out as distance defense. I suppose you saw some of them, coming in?"

"I did indeed, and Lew out there with them," I said. We had stopped to greet him, and Urdo had presented him with his twelve dapple-gray horses, which had pleased him greatly. "Well done. Do you know what you're doing with the two alae then?"

"We know where to put them for tonight, anyway," Nodol said.

"And are you ready for tomorrow?" I asked.

"As ready as anyone could be," Nodol said, shaking his head. "Let's leave tomorrow until tomorrow, and get on with the quartering."

"Yes, you can leave that to us," Emlin said. "Welcome home, Sulien."

There was a noisy moment then as the alae split into pennons, each going where Emlin told them. Their decurios went with them.

I left them to it and dismounted to go to the hall. I waited a moment for Urdo and Raul. Raul had Father Cinwil with him. Urdo signaled to Darien. Darien brought up Aurien's boys, and with them Amala and a sullen young Malm who I guessed immediately must be Gomoarionsson.

Veniva was waiting for us outside, alone by the top of the steps. Some of the people of the house were standing watching from just inside. The yard was full of armigers clattering about.

I went forward first and she embraced me. "Welcome home, Lord," she said. Suddenly I remembered the first time she had said those words to me, when we had come back from Thansethan with Morien's body. Urdo had been here then, too; and now, as then, I could feel his eyes on me, giving me the strength to accept my responsibilities.

Veniva moved onto embrace and welcome Galbian and Gwien. Then, without hesitation, she embraced Darien and greeted him as kin. She had done it each time he visited, but I saw his face light up when she did it now. Even now, he was not used to feeling he belonged.

I expected her to call one of the waiting servants for a cup to welcome Urdo and the others. I felt a pang of guilt for breaking her special Vincan cup, even though I had had no choice about it. But instead she moved forward to where Urdo stood and embraced him, as she had done with the rest of us.

If it had been true that he were Darien's acknowledged father, she would have been perfectly entitled to do so. As it was I wished the ground would open and swallow me. I felt the hot blood burning in my cheeks. Urdo started for an instant, then hugged her back. Such an embrace at departure would have been nothing unusual among friends, but as a welcome it went clean against custom. I wondered whether I should say anything, do anything. Then my eyes met Darien's over their heads. He still looked pleased, and I realized that anything I said would threaten that. I smiled back at him and did nothing. Urdo was kin by any measure but that of blood.

Then Veniva signaled and a servant limped out with a cup. It was Seriol ap Owain, whose left foot had been crushed between two horses at Foreth. I had found him a place serving my mother after he was no longer fit to ride as an armiger. I had never seen the cup he carried before. It was silver and double-handled, like Elenn's welcome cup at Caer Tanaga. There was gold inlaid on it, forming letters, but I was not

near enough to read them. I could not think where she had
got the gold. I looked at Veniva and raised my eyebrows. She
smiled, and I guessed from the smile that all the jewelers in
Derwen had been working day and night to have the cup
ready for my return. Veniva took the cup from Seriol and offered the welcome of the house to Amala and Gomoarionsson, and then to Raul and last to Father Cinwil. They all
accepted the peace of the hall. As Seriol led the way inside I
took the cup from Veniva and looked at it. It read "Maneo,"
and on the other side, in Tanagan, "I shall remain." I stopped
dead and looked at my mother. She was wearing her best embroidered overdress, but the golden comb was not in her hair.

"Nobody insults the welcome of my house," Veniva said
quietly.

"Of course not," I said, turning the cup in my hands, and
touching the letters. It was beautifully made. "But in Tanagan? From you?"

She smiled again. "That is exactly what Glividen said
when I asked him to put that."

I blinked. She had made Urdo's architect design her a cup?
He hadn't even been here when I left. "And what did you say
to Glividen?"

"I said, if I am the last of the Vincans then my welcome
cup would have the gold Gwien's ancestors buried, and our
strong words would be set in Tanagan *too*." She smiled, and
took back the cup from my unresisting hand. "Now let us go
and attend to our guests."

I followed her inside in silence.

The lamps were all lit. The hall was swept so clean there
was scarcely a cobweb to be seen, even up in the high corners. A servant was taking around Narlahenan wine on a tray.
Veniva was clearly making an effort to impress Urdo and
Amala.

Glividen was sitting in the hall and came up to greet us. He
had come by ship from Caer Thanbard. It would have been
foolish to ask him for messages in front of Amala and Gomoarionsson, however much they were being treated as honored guests. Amala asked him if he had seen Thurrig and he

bowed and informed her courteously that Thurrig was in Caer Thanbard and very well, indeed prodigiously well for a man his age, still fit enough to command the fleet or even fight in the line of battle if required. I had never really thought about how old Thurrig was. He had always been there, always older and wiser but always a strong fighter. He, too, must be almost seventy; he had been an admiral for more than forty years.

As I was thinking this his grandsons came out. Amala embraced them, then led them up to be introduced to me. I wished she had used names rather than just calling them her grandsons. It made it awkward to know how to address them. I didn't know their father's name. If I had ever been told ap Wyn the Smith's own name I had forgotten it. They had been small boys when I had seen them in Caer Gloran, now they were young men, older than Darien. They both had the same broad shoulders and blacksmith's build as their father, who was there behind them, bowing to me. The older one's face was like Thurrig or Larig, and the younger like Marchel and Amala. The older one had a wife with him. She was delicately pretty and seemed very shy; she did not want to let go of the support of her husband's arm. She was six or seven months pregnant. She seemed very cautious of Amala. They all four kept repeating how much they appreciated my hospitality and how good I was being to them. I did not like to think that I had even considered for a moment that I was taking them hostage.

Just then the music began. I was hungry and would rather have eaten directly. I danced with Urdo, and for a moment almost forgot I was tired. In the lamplight it felt almost like old times in the ala at Caer Tanaga, when we would dance on a winter evening. Then I danced a very fast dance with Darien, at the end of which I was a little out of breath. After that Glividen came up to me. He led me a little nearer the musicians to make sure the music covered the sound of him speaking quietly. He didn't make any attempt to dance. He looked at me to be sure he had my attention and spoke quietly. "Why did you send for me?"

I blinked at him, surprised. "I didn't send for you," I said. "I was going to ask you what had brought you here unexpectedly."

He hesitated and stroked his beard, clearly perplexed. "I thought at first it was some urgent need for the aqueduct. Then, when your mother told me about the invasion and that she had no idea what you were planning, I thought I had best wait in case you needed some military engineering done. I waited here because if you had wanted me at Magor you would have said Magor, I thought."

"I didn't say anything," I said. Behind his shoulder Marchel's older son was swinging his wife carefully. "Who told you I wanted you? Thurrig? Custennin?"

"No." He frowned. "I was doing some work for Thurrig, designing a new dock. Urdo knows all about it. But it wasn't Custennin but his sister ap Cledwin, Bishop Dewin's lady, who sent for me and told me you needed me urgently."

"Linwen of Munew? Why in the world?" I said. If it had been Dewin it would have clearly been the Church's plot. But Linwen could mean either that or Custennin and Munew.

"There was a ship just arrived that was coming here," Glividen said, shaking his head. "It seemed very plausible that you needed me. I can't think why she would say that if you didn't."

"Maybe she just wanted you out of Caer Thanbard," I said. This seemed the most likely explanation. Glividen, what time he paid attention to what was going on and wasn't swept away in his ideas about making something, was known to be loyal to Urdo. "Whose side is she on? Had you seen her recently? Or Custennin? Could they have been planning an uprising?"

He frowned again, looking very unhappy. "I never thought of any such thing. I don't know. It isn't impossible. I had feasted with them when I first came there, naturally. But I was staying with Thurrig; I didn't see them often."

"And how did Thurrig seem?"

"As he always is, less full of life than when he was younger, but full of concerns for my new dock and for an idea he had for changing the curve of the bows of a ship. It wouldn't work, unfortunately, the thing would swamp. We built a model." He stared past me at the musicians, not seeing the harp and the drum but some boat in his mind. "I have been thinking about it since though, on the boat here. There might be a way of doing it if the keel were deeper." He gestured proportions with his hands.

"It would sink," I said doubtfully, distracted by his enthusiasm despite myself.

"No, no," he said. "At least, I think not. There is a mention in Quintilian of a Tigrian boat with a deep keel. The bows would come up like this—"

"I need to speak to Urdo about Munew," I interrupted.

"Ask him what he wants me to do," Glividen said. "He knows I will go anywhere he can best use my talents."

Urdo was sitting in the windowseat talking to Veniva and Amala when I came up.

"Ah, Sulien my dear," Amala said, smiling at me. "Looking so military as always. I remember the first time I met you I had to teach you how to wear a drape."

Veniva smiled a thin-lipped smile. "That illuminates a little matter for me about how Sulien wears her drape," she said. Her Vincan was always perfect but just now, in comparison with Amala's clipped accent, it sounded especially mellifluous. Or maybe she was doing it on purpose. "And yes, military is the right word; my daughter is known for being one of the three greatest battlehorsemen of the island of Tir Tanagiri. But I have heard it said of your daughter that she was born in the saddle."

I winced, but the two old women kept on smiling at each other as if they felt nothing but the greatest amity for each other. Urdo was staring straight forward with absolutely no expression on his face. I ran through the possible ways of getting him alone without them noticing and gave up immediately. "Shall we dance?" I asked.

Urdo raised his eyebrows, Veniva smiled, and Amala pursed her lips. I could feel myself blushing, but Urdo took my hand equably and we went out onto the floor. As we danced I told him what Glividen had told me. Urdo did not seem surprised.

"It doesn't necessarily mean Custennin's about to revolt," he said. "I don't think it changes anything much. We knew Custennin was uncertain—that's the one thing that's always sure about him. I don't think he will commit himself to anything unless it's quite clear who has the advantage. The same goes for Dewin and the large parts of the Church. If we win they will always have been on our side, and if we were to lose, well, they will always have been on the other side. As for Thurrig, who knows. He has always been loyal to his word until now."

"I like Thurrig," I said. "He has been a good friend to me."

"But Marchel is his daughter," he said, taking my hands. "I think I should write to Thurrig if I had a reliable messenger. And I had better send Amala to Caer Tanaga tomorrow. She and your mother will tear each other to shreds if I leave her here."

I winced again, letting go of his hands and dancing away. "I was hoping it wasn't all as bad as it sounded."

"You missed a wonderful discussion of what marvelous grandsons they each have," Urdo said, leaning toward me. He smiled. "I like both of them. And you needn't be embarrassed. My mother would be doing just the same if she were there."

It was only too easy to picture Rowanna with them. I shuddered. "Give me a Jarnish shield wall bristling with weapons rather than that sort of barbed conversation."

"You're not still afraid of your mother, are you?" he asked.

I thought about it for a moment. "Afraid isn't the word. But I know I can't manage talking like that without slashing right through all the layers and saying exactly what everyone's trying to avoid. It's all right in the alae, and really my mother is used to me, but when it comes to diplomacy I'm still a disaster."

"Not a disaster," Urdo said. "You've done very well as Lord of Derwen these last five years. And you've done magnificently with Lew ap Ross, better than I would have guessed. He is an Isarnagan king and he is proud to look to you as his lord." Urdo swung me and I suddenly remembered dancing with poor Conal here in the hall, and how he had been such a terrible dancer. Then I remembered that I had never got around to telling Urdo about him and Emer, though she had said Elenn knew.

"You know about Emer and Conal?" I asked quietly.

Urdo looked sad. "Elenn told me. She was very angry at the insult to her mother. But now Conal is dead that should be an end to it."

"You didn't say anything to Emer?"

"She is leading an allied army north for me. If her husband chooses to send his kinsman to her bed and she agrees, then it is none of my affair that there is a bloodfeud between her and that kinsman unless she complains about it, whatever my wife might say."

"Who told you Lew knew?"

The expression on Urdo's face would have made me laugh if it had been possible to laugh at something like that. He said nothing for a moment. I heard Glividen's voice from behind me, raised over the music, "No. I went to Thansethan specially to read it, but I have been all over the heating ducts underneath Caer Tanaga and if you ask me he doesn't understand the principles . . ." and then Amala's reply, "You should write a book yourself."

At last Urdo said, quietly and flatly, "Lew doesn't know? Then I should have spoken to her. Still, unless her husband complains, why should I reproach her about her private life that is conducted in private and causes no scandal? It is over. He is dead."

"Lew has sent his body back to Atha and his father so that his ashes can lie in his own country. He saved my life again and again when Aurien poisoned me."

"Elenn hated him because he killed her mother," Urdo said, absently swinging me again as the dance came to an end. "I liked what I saw of him and I am glad he found a good death. He certainly fought well and bravely that time at Thansethan."

"It is over now in any case," I said as we bowed to each other.

"I had better keep Emer away from Caer Tanaga for the time being," he said, straightening up.

"Pieces on a fidchel board are a lot easier," I said. "They never quarrel with the other pieces of the same color."

Urdo laughed.

Just then Seriol came out of the kitchen to say dinner was ready. The smell that came out with him made my knees weak. Poor Seriol looked hot and flustered, but I thought he would make a good steward when he had settled down to it. I looked around for Darien, for him to take my arm and walk into the dining hall with me as he usually did when he visited. To my surprise Veniva was already holding his arm. She gestured to me, incomprehensibly. Then Urdo moved nearer to me and I leaned down a little, thinking he wanted to say something in private. But he just smiled and took my arm. I suppose I should have been expecting it after that greeting. Clearly my mother wanted to make a point before the guests. This strange status she was wishing on me was something I had agreed to in theory years before, letting people believe Darien was Urdo's son. It had never really been anything I had needed to take notice of before. I became aware of Amala's gaze and straightened my back. I could just picture Elenn being furious when she heard. I wished I had had a moment to change out of my riding leathers. Most of all I wished Veniva hadn't decided to do this.

Seriol arranged everyone in the alcoves with a minimum of fuss. Somehow we ended up with Glividen, Gomoarions-son, and the younger of Marchel's sons, as well as family in our alcove. I saw Raul settling himself between Amala and Father Cinwil. Then a servant brought the food and I stopped paying attention to anything else. We were each given a whole roast duck stuffed with onions and roots and plums and oats. It was the most I could do to eat politely and keep my knife hand clean. It tasted as good as the smell, which is saying a great deal.

We didn't talk much at first. Marchel's son and Glividen

told us how they had been up river with the militia, snaring the ducks we were eating. From the way he said this I gathered that Glividen had been here several days already. I admired their skill with the nets and we talked a little about good places for fowling. None of them had been to Tevin. I wondered if Arling had landed there and how Alfwin was doing if he had.

Then Urdo complimented Veniva on the stuffing and she talked for a long time about the importance of sunlight and sloping ground for plum trees. Little Gwien made some remarks about the orchards at Magor. Galbian glowered at him. He was hardly eating anything.

Gwien, who had eaten most of his duck, looked back at his brother miserably. He looked around, clearly trying to think of something to say. Unfortunately he noticed Gomoarionsson, who had been silent until now. He had eaten the breast meat of his duck and a little of the stuffing. "Do you have plums in Narlahena?" Gwien asked politely.

The Malmish prince frowned. "Of course we do!" he said, in bitten-off Vincan. "Gold plums and blue plums and green plums and apricots and damsons, and also grapes, oranges, lemons, and olives, and other delicious fruit that are quite unknown here where you must eat disgusting tubers." He poked at his stuffing disdainfully. "The trees are heavy with fruit and the land is rich with golden corn. These are the sort of blessings the White God brings to a land. You would see sunshine, the clouds of shame would roll back, and this wet and benighted place would overflow with vines and olives if you were to accept him into your hearts and your lives."

I would have laughed, but for his obvious sincerity. He was very young, only a year or two older than Galbian. The thought of any god using their power to cause a climate to change so much, and the devastation such a change would occasion, was almost too much for my composure. The gods keep the balance of the world, and however little time I had for the White God and however crazy some of his worshipers were I had never heard that he was completely insane. I filled my mouth quickly and avoided meeting anyone's eyes.

"How have the harvests been in Tir Isarnagiri these last ten years?" Veniva asked, as if she were showing a polite interest in some slight matter.

She was looking at Urdo, but Glividen answered. "Good, lady, but I can report no wonders of fruit like what grows around the Middle Sea."

He shook his head at Gomoarionsson, who tossed his own head in response. "Come to Narlahena and see how a kingdom can flourish in the light of the Lord. We tried here and though you won with the aid of demons, we have God on our side and cannot be wholly defeated. We will try again and bring this land into light and honor yet."

When he mentioned demons his eyes flicked to me, and then away again. I sighed.

"You are stepping on the borders of courtesy," Urdo said warningly. "I am treating you as a guest rather than a prisoner for your father's sake and because Amala asked it, but if your actions warrant it I shall not hesitate to take a captive's oath from you and keep you imprisoned."

Gomoarionsson lowered his eyes and looked away.

Then Marchel's son spoke up, surprising everyone. We all turned to him, but he was looking at Gomoarionsson. "I have been to Narlahena, as you know well enough. It is true that there are grapes, but in all other ways it is a terrible place. It is too hot, and the Malms there are mostly fiery of temper and care little about making things and much about destroying them. Smiths have no honor there, nor does anyone but priests and warriors. They say everyone has their place under the White God, yes, but they would fix them into that place as stones are fixed into a tower where they have no choice but to stay. There is slavery there still, and farmers go in fear of their lords. I have seen that sunlight, and I think rather that God's light is the soft light that shines through the clouds of Tir Tanagiri, or the light at my father's forge, the red forgefire He gives me as a tool I use to make the best iron tools I can. For that work I have respect here and a good place. And when trouble came, though my uncle was a traitor and my own mother came across the sea in arms, Lord Sulien invited us here to be safe. Would that happen in Narlahena? Or would I have been used as a pawn in civil war or executed for what my family have done without my knowledge? I have seen things like that happen there."

He stared at Gomoarionsson until the prince looked down. "You may have seen my father wipe out traitors to the White God, yes, perhaps," he said.

Marchel's son shook his head. He looked so much like his mother that I could hardly believe he was talking so sensibly. "I have been brought up to worship the White God Ever Merciful all my life, and the hymns of smithcraft I sing name him, although my grandfather Wyn used to call on Govannon. I would like everyone to come to know the White God, come to praise him, to understand his mercy and through his sacrifice come to eternal life praising him. But I think bringing that mercy with a sword, as if to force something that should be a good choice on everyone is—" He hesitated, looking around and seeing us all looking at him. He swallowed, then continued much more quietly: "Very wrong."

"That is well said," Urdo said. "I have always said I would have people worship as they would."

"And for people to choose how they shall live, and not be blamed for the faults of others or trapped by their birth," Darien said, looking at Urdo and smiling.

Urdo smiled back. He turned to Gomoarionsson. "Here we have law and justice, and many people in Tir Tanagiri have taken the pebble, as you can see."

Marchel's son, Darien, Galbian, little Gwien, and Glividen touched their hands quickly to where their own pebbles hung. Gomoarionsson's eyes followed their gestures. He frowned, and for the first time he looked a little uncertain. "I thought you had all rejected his mercy," he said.

"Did my mother say that?" Marchel's son asked.

Gomoarionsson jerked his head downward, a curious gesture. "Yes," he said. "She told us she was exiled for speaking his word."

"She was exiled for killing people after they surrendered," I said quickly.

"I had also heard that story," Gomoarionsson said, looking at me and then down at his feet. "But there are always stories about people who are exiled. She told us there would be no mercy at all for anyone who was captured, that we would be sacrificed to demons. Now I see this was mistaken."

"This was an outright lie!" I said angrily. "Nobody but Marchel has ever done anything like that."

"I wanted so much to bring the light of the White God, the way St. Diego brought it to Narlahena or Chanerig Thurrigsson to Tir Isarnagiri," Gomoarionsson said. "My father doesn't know I am here."

"Marchel would have forced that light on people unwilling," her son said, leaning forward. "And that is wrong, even if it covered the land in soft fruit knee-deep so that we needed shovels to harvest it."

We laughed; even Gomoarionsson smiled a little.

"My mother would have as well," Galbian suddenly said, unexpectedly.

"I don't know why Aurien wanted to do that," Veniva said. "She is dead and cannot answer. But will you follow her?"

"No," Galbian said. "I am no traitor to the High King, and he knows it." He looked at Urdo, then back at Veniva. "I have taken the pebble. But that is for myself. I will not force anyone to do that when I am Duke, though if I can bring Magor to God I will." He looked at Urdo again, a little defiantly.

"As Custennin did in Munew," Urdo said. "As Guthrum and Ninian have done in Cennet, and as Cinvar has done in Tathal. I have not objected. It is between you and the land and the people. When this war is over you should have two years in the ala, at Caer Tanaga. Then you will be old enough and experienced enough to be Duke of Magor in your own name, though still very young for it. If you speak to the land at that time and the land is willing then I have no objection to you bringing Magor to the White God."

"Father Cinwil says it is willing," Galbian said.

"It is for *you* to say, and no priest nor anyone else," Urdo said, very sternly. "That is part of what it means to be a lord. Your grandfather knew that. Magor has been waiting patiently the seven years since he died for you to be old enough to speak for it. It is a great responsibility, that has come to you early."

Galbian drew a breath, let it out again, straightened his back, and looked at Urdo. "I will let you know if the land is willing," he said. Veniva smiled.

"The land and the people will come to the Lord when the time is right," Darien said with great confidence. Gomoarionsson looked at him curiously. Marchel's son, Galbian, and Gwien were raising their chins in assent.

I looked at Veniva, and suddenly I realized how she felt when she called herself the last of the Vincans. I had heard Urdo say to Raul that this would happen and I hadn't believed it, but here were all the young people, my son and my nephews, and all of them had turned away from the old gods. But what could I do? I couldn't take up a sword in the gods' defense; that would be as wrong as what Marchel had done. Nobody was going around saying how wonderful they were and how they could save your soul, they were just there, part of the way the world was, and maybe that wasn't enough for people. I think I must have made some noise, because Urdo and everyone was looking at me. I was halfway to my feet. I sank back again, shaking my head.

"Maybe the light of the White God will indeed come to shine here," Gomoarionsson said. "Perhaps Marchel was too hasty."

"I am delighted you realize it," Urdo said, sounding entirely sincere.

"But will you not take the pebble?" Gomoarionsson asked. He looked at me and at Veniva. "Will you not understand that the White God was born into the world to live and die with us, and through his sacrifice we can all live eternally praising him? Will you not come into the light?"

"I don't think that's any way to live, eternally or otherwise," I said. This clearly put me back into the category of demon for Gomoarionsson. He touched his pebble contemptuously.

Urdo just sighed. Veniva stood up, as straight as a sword

blade for all that she was old and thin. She raised her arms and sang, quite loudly. People in the other alcoves stopped talking and turned to look. She sang a hymn I had heard hundreds of times, that I had sung myself many times, the hymn to dawn, thanking the Radiant Sun for the light and the knowledge a new day can bring. It was a strange thing to hear at night, indoors. Veniva's voice had never been strong, and now it was old, but still there was power in it. I found myself standing again, beside her, and Urdo beside me, and Darien on her other side. Then I saw Govien standing on the far side of the room, and other people, until when she had finished perhaps a third of us were on our feet. She bowed to Gomoarionsson then, and sat down, and said, "There is more than one light."

Gomoarionsson just sat there with his mouth slightly open, looking ridiculous. When I think of all the trouble we went to with him it makes me want to weep. He never amounted to anything after all, and was killed at a banquet twenty years later by his sister's husband, who is king in Narlahena still.

"It can all be part of the White God, too. It can," Darien said, sitting down again. But Veniva shook her head, and I didn't understand what he meant then.

— 10 —

"Before setting out on a journey, pack supplies, check the map, and make sure you know why you're going."
—Tanagan proverb

Not even oracles know what's going on somewhere else, only what happened to people in other worlds. I asked ap Fial about this, afterward, when "if" was drilling into my head over and over like a demented woodpecker on an iron bar. He told me that nobody could change the past, and the only way to change the future was by changing the present, one day at a time. After that he relented a little, drank some blackberry wine with me, and became slightly more human. He told me that he had been taught to be wary of thinking he knew the future because the many futures oracle-priests can see are other worlds, more or less like our own, and bound to our own by the great events, but not by the lesser events, nor even by the significance of those great events. He said it's hard to tell which are the great events.

When he was quite drunk he told me that some oracle-priests are surprised when things come out differently from the way they expected, and others are surprised if they come out the same. I suppose the Vincans were right to ban them. I don't know how they can bear it, even after training for twenty years. He told me then what Morwen had told me long before, that I was not in any of those futures, those other worlds he could see; there is only one of me. I find that comforting sometimes. It would be too painful to think that there are worlds somewhere where I got everything right.

We left the next morning and rode uneventfully through the hills all day. It was not all uphill, no matter what Masarn said, but each ridge was higher than the last, and as the day went on we saw more trees and fewer farms. For all that, there was more cleared land than there had been when I was first Lord of Derwen. Some fields were planted with crops, but as we got higher more of them were dotted with sheep. Some of the farmers waved, and their children came running to watch us go by. Some of them cheered and called my name. I always waved back. When we had passed one group of children, watching the sheep far out of sight of any farmhouse, Urdo smiled suddenly.

"I wonder what they will say when they get home," he said. "Do you think they will say to their parents that they saw two alae of armigers with bright banners go riding up the track this morning?"

"And if they do will their mother scold them for making up stories?" I said.

"Or will they tell stories when they are old and bent, and say that they remember when they were children and they saw the High King Urdo go up the hill with the Praefecto Sulien at his side, and the sun shining out of a cloudless sky? Then their grandchildren will laugh at them," Masarn said. The sun was indeed shining for once, though there were a few clouds around the western horizon.

"Their grandchildren will not laugh," Darien said. He was absolutely in earnest; nobody can be so serious who is not also young. The rest of us just smiled, and rode on.

We were not riding fast, to spare the horses. We came at last to Nant Gefalion in the long twilight. We had long since lost the sun behind the hills we had been climbing all day, but back at Derwen he would still be slipping into the sea. High summer had crept up on me; it was only two days before midsummer day.

Nant Gefalion was quiet. Hiveth had the place well in hand. Nobody at all had come down the track from Caer Gloran, and nobody had come up the track from Derwen except my own scouts and messengers. The forges were quieter than normal, but the smiths I spoke to were not disturbed. They were glad to have a pennon to protect them in case of trouble. "Thank you for taking thought of us," one old fellow said, speaking for them all and bowing in Jarnish fashion. He was the carpenter who had moved here from Caer Segant, I remembered. They wanted me to leave Hiveth with them. It was hard to explain that they would be better defended if my ala was whole even if it was elsewhere. Everyone can understand a pennon in front of their eyes.

The next morning we set off north and east again toward Caer Gloran. We crossed into Tathal almost at once. The border was clear to me though there was nothing here to mark it. Urdo set an easy pace again, although now we were over the watershed and headed downhill. We reached the highroad in the afternoon. Every time I came over the little rise there I remembered the first time I had ridden this way and the skirmish I had interrupted between Marchel and the Jarnish raiders. This time, despite all reports, I half expected to see Cinvar's militia drawn up to meet us, but I was disappointed. The highroad was empty in both directions, and there was no army between us and the river.

Urdo and I conferred for a little while, while the alae had a short break; watering the horses, stretching, and working out the stiffness riding all day will cause in even the fittest. "We could camp here tonight and send out more scouts in both directions," I said. "There is some hope Emer might reach us late tonight, if they have made good time up the highroad. They had fewer miles to cover than we did."

"I don't think they are nearby," Urdo said, frowning. "I want to know what Cinvar is doing."

"Is there any chance he might be sitting at home waiting until we do something that looks aggressive?" I asked.

"I think the time for scoring that sort of point is over," Urdo said. "In any case, he killed those two men of Cadraith's household. We are entitled to come and inquire into his conduct."

"What are we going to do with him?" I asked. The pennon cooks were handing out cold bannocks they'd cooked before we set off in the morning. Talog brought us one each, and I bit into mine hungrily.

Urdo sighed, turning his in his hand. "Raul and I have been

talking about this endlessly. There's no denying Cinvar is in open rebellion, if he is. Whatever I do, it's very difficult for me not to look as if I am acting tyrannically, exactly as my enemies say I am doing. I will do as I did at Magor, if I can. Assuming he takes arms against us, Cinvar has to be executed, but his son Pedrog, who is blameless and away in ap Erbin's ala, can inherit."

"So what he does now makes no difference?" I said, with my mouth full.

"If he comes and asks pardon without fighting at all, that would make all the difference, but I somehow doubt he will. We are going to have to go to him." Urdo took a bite of his bannock at last, and chewed thoughtfully.

"There is a problem with riding up to the walls of Caer Gloran and demanding entry," I said, pulling out the map. "We have nowhere to retreat to if they close the gates, and then they could come out at night and attack us when we are dismounted."

"We have two alae, and the ironwork for some war machines that could be assembled if needed. We can make a proper camp and sleep by numbers. In any case, he may be in Talgarth."

"Have you been up there?" I asked.

Urdo shook his head. "Uthbad always came to Caer Gloran to see me, if I was anywhere in Tathal, and so does Cinvar. Caer Gloran is properly one of my fortresses, not one of the king of Tathal's. Though, since the Peace, since I disbanded Marchel's ala, I have kept no forces there."

"I have only been to Talgarth once myself," I said, remembering the winter journey from Caer Avroc with Galba and two pennons. I pointed it out on the map, northwest of Caer Gloran. "It's not a proper fort, for all that they call it the Fort of Tathal in poetry. It's an old earthwork fortification on top of a hill. Old Uthbad's father retreated up there when the legions left, according to my mother. It's completely untakeable, I should think, but it would be very easy to ignore anyone up there. If he's there we can safely leave the Isarnagans to besiege him and eat the countryside clean, while we go off to deal with whatever's happening in Tevin."

Urdo glanced east as if he could see all the way to distant Tevin, and sighed. Then he saw something close at hand. "There's a scout coming back," he said.

It was Flerian who came up to us, looking pleased with herself. "Nothing moving, southeast down the highroad three miles," she said. Her horse looked exhausted; she must have come back very fast. "But I found a farmer who would talk to me. She said that Cinvar had gone away down the highroad yesterday morning, very early, taking her son with him." She paused and took a deep breath. "That is, he took his whole army and all his militia, which included the farmer's son. She said her son said they were going to Caer Tanaga. She said her son hadn't been expecting to go so soon; a message came the night before telling him to be ready to leave at dawn."

"Any chance it was a trap, the farmer lying?" Urdo asked.

"I don't think so," Flerian said. She took a drink from her water bottle, then retied the top carefully. "She was worried about her son going off with only one shirt, she was worried the wars had come again, but she wasn't afraid of me especially, and when I said I'd come from the High King she praised the White God and said that you'd bring peace again. She didn't seem clever enough to be lying that well."

"Good work," I said. "Now get a bannock, change horses and rub that poor tired creature down, and make sure he doesn't drink too much too fast." She went off to follow orders, smiling. "Who would he leave in Caer Gloran if he has gone off?" I asked.

"I don't know," Urdo said. "But why would he go? Caer Tanaga? And the night before last—that's the day we fought Marchel, no, the day after? Too soon for him to have had any news of it, because she didn't have any rested messengers to send."

"She didn't," I agreed. "There's only half an ala at Caer Tanaga, you said?"

"Gormant should be able to hold the place against whatever infantry Cinvar can field, and in any case, if he left yesterday morning on foot we can overtake him long before he reaches the city."

"What if Flavien and the others are going down there to join him?" I asked.

"Much more difficult, but still possible," Urdo said.

"So what now?" I asked, looking at the alae, who had mostly finished watering their horses. "Camp or go?"

"Caer Gloran," Urdo said decisively. "I need to know what's happening in Tathal. We couldn't catch Cinvar tonight in any case. It's four days' ride from here to Caer Tanaga, without killing the horses, call it seven days' march for him. Caer Gloran and news tonight, then tomorrow we follow Cinvar."

Before we reached Caer Gloran our scouts reported meeting scouts from Cadraith ap Mardol's ala, coming down the highroad from the north. We met up with Cadraith just outside the town as the sun was setting behind us in a blaze of red and gold. The great dark walls loomed up ahead, and we followed the road around toward the gates. Cadraith had no news we had not sent him. He had seen nothing of ap Meneth and had suffered no problems except the two men Cinvar had killed. It was good to see him again after so long.

The lookouts on the walls saw us approaching and blew signals. We drew to a halt out of range, unless they had large engines on the walls above, and sent forward the advance party, under herald's branches; Raul with half a pennon as escort. They rode toward the great closed gates confidently. They were well armored, but no missiles fell on them. As they drew nearer, the gates swung open.

Raul was out in front, ready to do his herald's duty. He turned to Urdo for instructions. As he hesitated an old woman stepped into the middle of the open gateway, full in the light of a pair of torches set inside the gates on either side. Even at that distance I recognized her. She was Idrien ap Galba, old Uthbad's wife, Cinvar's mother. I had not seen her since Morien's funeral. She looked shrunken and tired. She was leaning on a cane. She bore no other visible weapons, but she was not holding a cup of welcome either. She just stood in the doorway, waiting.

Urdo signaled to Raul to go on. Raul went forward, branch in hand. Idrien said something to him, quietly, and his shoulders stiffened. Then she said something again; maybe he had asked her to repeat it. He said something else and she shrugged her shoulders, wearily, and spoke again. Then Raul rode back toward us. When he came close I could see that he was frowning.

"Idrien ap Galba, Dowager Queen of Tathal, informs us that Caer Gloran is an open city and that we may rest here but may not use it for military purposes."

"What!" Urdo said. I had never seen him so astonished. I could feel my own eyebrows rising and Cadraith's were up to his helmet already.

"She reminds us that Elhanen the Great respected the neutrality of open cities," Raul said, absolutely calmly.

"That being the latest precedent she can remember?" I asked, and laughed. "I don't think there has ever been an open city in Tir Tanagiri, and it was a very old custom when Elhanen respected it in Narlahena seven hundred years ago."

"I don't believe it is even practiced in Lossia these days," Urdo said. "But we are not living in the pages of Fedra. I can't imagine what Idrien's thinking. I will speak to her myself."

"I said that these were not Fedra's times, nor Elhanen's, when a city could declare itself no part of a war," Raul said. "Idrien replied that whatever times they were, declaring Caer Gloran an open city was the only course she could think of which would not dishonor any of her vows, for her son made her promise not to surrender Caer Gloran as a base, but she has neither troops nor desire to defend it against us."

I looked at Urdo, who for once was completely at a loss for words. If Idrien's intention had been to throw us entirely into confusion she could not have done better.

"We could do it, but it would be a very strange precedent," Cadraith said.

"In either direction," Raul agreed, and his voice sounded

strange in my ears, recalling battles of a war that was won and lost a thousand years ago. "When Petra rose up after declaring itself open, everyone within the walls was killed or sold into slavery, but when the Sateans violated the neutrality of an open city the priests called on the gods to blast them, and they had no victories after. Fedra called Larissa a whore among cities for declaring itself open to each side in turn as the war passed over it."

This, or something, stirred Urdo into one of his immediate decisions. "Go back to her, Raul, and tell her that open cities are no part of the law of Tir Tanagiri and never have been. Ask her if her son is in rebellion against us. If he is, ask her if she supports him and if the city does. If she does not, and the city does not, then say we will come in for tonight and leave in the morning, taking supplies but neither garrisoning my city nor doing any harm."

"What's the difference between that and what she's asking for?" I asked.

Raul and Urdo both looked at me with identical expressions of exasperation. "We have not accepted the precedent," Urdo explained.

"And if she should say they are in rebellion," Raul added, "then we are not obliged to treat them as neutrals. We will have a statement of loyalty from her, if she is not, though she will not have broken her word to her son."

"I see," I said, as meekly as I could. Urdo laughed. "Unless it is a trap," I added. "They might mean to lure us in and kill us. We don't know for sure that Cinvar isn't there. There seem to be plenty of people on the walls. Inside the town an ala can't maneuver easily. I remember that nightmare fighting inside Caer Lind."

"There haven't been many farmers around in the fields," Cadraith said, "They could all be inside, waiting to ambush us."

"Three pennons first to check everything, then," Urdo said. "Elwith's and one of each of yours."

"Cynrig's," I agreed, and Cadraith named and signaled to

one of his. I gave the orders for the three pennons to be ready as Raul rode back to the gate and spoke to Idrien again.

"She wouldn't have got far trying to declare an open city to a Jarnish king," Urdo said as we watched them talking in the torchlight. It was quite dark now.

"She'd have got her head cut off," Cadraith said. "I'm not sure she wouldn't have with some of our praefectos. She was risking it anyway."

"That's part of why I'm agreeing, as far as I am agreeing," Urdo said, watching Raul and Idrien intently. "Though I should think if she knew I was here she'd know I wouldn't be likely to harm her personally. She was one of my father's warriors, after all."

"Nobody tells me anything," I said. "I wouldn't be inclined to hurt her either; she's always been friendly to me and she's a sort of relative, and in any case her daughter, Enid, was my friend."

"Enid was a very brave armiger, and as loyal as the day," Urdo said. "She saved my life once. If she hadn't died at Caer Lind a lot of things would be different. She might have been able to make her brother see sense."

"Bran ap Penda too," I said. "He'd have made a good king, when he'd grown up, if he'd needed to."

"Ah?" Urdo sounded interested. "I never really knew him well, but he was in your pennon, wasn't he?"

"Yes. He was one of the first people to fall at Caer Lind, in the ambush."

"If he'd lived there would have been no pretext for saying you were interfering in Bregheda," Cadraith said regretfully.

Raul was leaning toward Idrien, and now they were embracing.

"Ah, good, warm baths and hot food tonight," Masarn said cheerfully, from behind us. We all turned to look at him. "Reporting the three pennons ready when needed," he said. "And delighted to see that we're going to be going inside."

We waited in the cooling evening while the pennons checked that the town was safe.

"Safe, and practically deserted," Cynrig reported. "It seems like there's almost nobody there."

"It's creepy," Elwith said. "I've been at Caer Gloran before, and it's always been quite a busy place, but not now. It's like a town when people leave because there's a fever."

We went in and settled ourselves and our horses in the dusty stables and barracks that had only been used by redcloaks since Marchel's ala were disbanded. Cinvar must have kept whatever horses he used himself in stables somewhere else. There was almost room, even with three alae. The cooks started making supper for the armigers, but before I could join my pennon a messenger came from Idrien inviting Urdo, Cadraith, Raul, and myself to eat with her. The messenger, who was a child of six or seven, waited for a reply.

"There's no way to refuse such an invitation," Raul said.

The meal was one of the most uncomfortable of my life. The food was barely adequate, undercooked roast lamb with herbs and hot bread. The service was appalling and the conversation terribly strained. I would far rather have eaten with the ala, and I was sure Urdo would have. We sat on benches by a table, as the ala often did, but in all other ways it was a very formal meal. Idrien had a priest with her whose name I didn't catch, and there were no other guests.

"I was hoping to have the pleasure of seeing your daughter, Kerys," I said, as soon as the first painful formalities were over and we had started eating. This was the most neutral thing I could think of to say. I could quite reasonably have called Kerys my sister; she had been married to Morien long enough, but I did not want to appear to be pushing a relationship Idrien might no longer wish to acknowledge.

"She is in Talgarth," Idrien said. "Along with the greater part of the people of Caer Gloran, whose absence you may have noticed. Cinvar has made her key-keeper of that fortress and she believes it may be defended if you attempt to reduce it." Much suddenly became clear. I winced. Had he sent his mother here with no troops to defend the indefensible while leaving his sister in the strong place?

"And Cinvar?" Urdo asked.

Idrien looked at him sharply. "Cinvar?"

Urdo spread his hands. "Your son is in rebellion, you are loyal; it is a difficult situation for us all. But I need to know what the rebels are doing so they can be stopped."

Idrien's lips thinned. "This is why I sought neutrality," she said, looking at her priest, who raised his chin sympathetically but said nothing. "Are you really asking me to betray my son?"

"I am asking you to save your daughter and your grandchildren," Urdo said emphatically, leaning forward. "You are old enough to remember the civil wars. I know you will have counseled Cinvar against rebellion, and he has not listened. If there is to be any peace it will not be through victory for your son. In such a victory everyone loses."

There was a long, heavy silence. I drew breath to speak once, though I was not sure what to say, but Urdo, not even taking his eyes away from Idrien, put his hand on mine to silence me and I let the breath go again. After a long time, Idrien spoke again. "I suppose whatever happens it makes no difference what I tell you. Cinvar, yes, acting consistently against my advice, has taken all the militia he can raise and gone to Caer Tanaga."

We knew this already, of course, but it was good confirmation. "And who are his allies?" Urdo asked.

"Cinon of Nene, Flavien of Tinala, Gwyn of Angas, and Arling Gunnarson of Jarnholme, for sure," she said, quite calmly. "Some of the other kings were wavering about joining them. Cinvar went off to Caer Tanaga because he heard that Arling had landed and they were all to make an attack on the city."

"Landed where?" I blurted. Idrien looked at me as if she had forgotten there was anyone in the room but Urdo. He could have that effect on people.

"Where?" she murmured, as if this was an unimportant detail. "Oh, down in the south, I forget where exactly. Othona, would it be?"

Othona, on the coast of Aylsfa. From there it was hardly half a day's sail up the Tamer to Caer Tanaga if the wind was right. I could remember Ayl telling me so. We had all been so sure Arling would attack Tevin first.

"I will send messengers tonight, and we will leave at dawn," Urdo said, bowing to Idrien.

"I don't have many supplies to give you, I told your clerk," she said, gesturing to Raul.

"We will not wait for supplies," Urdo said. He turned and looked at me, and at the same time made the hand signal that meant I should take care of things. Of course, he could not leave the table without giving Idrien insult, but I could.

I rose and bowed to Idrien. "If you will excuse me?" I said, putting my hand to my stomach as if I were unwell. She bowed to me, and smiled. She knew perfectly well what I was doing, leaving the table when my food was not half finished.

"How many troops did Cinvar take?" Urdo was asking as I left the room.

As soon as I was outside I ran, as if I could make up for lost minutes. Masarn saw me and followed. He assembled the messengers, not red-cloaks but reliable scouts from our alae. I wrote the messages, to ap Erbin, to Luth, to Alfwin in Tevin, and to ap Meneth, who I guessed must be somewhere between Caer Rangor and here, urging them all to come with all speed to Caer Tanaga. Then, when they had set off, I gave orders that everyone was to be ready to start at dawn.

By the time I was done I thought Urdo would probably have finished eating, so I went to his room. He was there, with Raul and Cadraith. I explained what I had done, and Raul went off to send more messages to Thansethan, and to Custennin and Rowanna. Cadraith went with him; he wanted to make sure his ala understood the orders, and would be packed and ready to leave. Urdo and I sat for a while, looking at the map. Maps and papers were already spilling out of the box he used for them when traveling.

"She cannot possibly hold off Arling and all those infantry," Urdo said. Gormant was in charge in Caer Tanaga. I knew Urdo meant Elenn.

"They can hold the citadel for as long as they have supplies, unless there is treachery inside," I said, as confidently as I could.

"They are very few to do it against a really determined assault," Urdo said. "Cinvar could not take them, but Arling has war machines."

Just as we were starting to discuss how we would take Caer Tanaga if we were Arling, with or without machines, there was a slight scratch at the door and a young girl slipped in. She was perhaps sixteen or seventeen, and she was wearing only a thin linen shift. "Excuse me, Lord, my lady sent to ask—" she began, then caught sight of me and stopped.

"Yes, what?" Urdo asked gently. But she tossed her head and ran out of the room.

"Idrien sent her to ask what?" I said, walking to the door and watching her run down the corridor. "What could she want?"

"To know if I am cold in bed, no doubt," Urdo said, laughing. "Well, whatever shreds of reputation your mother has left us, that will be the end of them. Elenn is going to kill me." Then he stopped laughing and, looking at the map again, he spoke quietly. "If she is safe, I will be happy to take whatever insults and hard names it pleases her to throw at my head."

I did not linger long after that, but found my own bed and slept until it was time to be on our way again.

— II —

My skill in arms grows great,
I make war on whole hosts,
fine armies cower away.
I crush the heroes one by one
until I weary of fighting.

One stick can't make a fire
let me have a battle-companion
a shield-strong warrior,
a friend to watch my back,
a wife to bear me sons.
   —"Black Darag's Lament"

We rode down to Caer Tanaga as fast as the horses would take us. In some cases we went faster. Darien's new Narlahenan horse foundered and I left one exhausted riding mare at a farm. She survived, by Horsemother's blessing, to bear foals for the farmers' children who nursed her back to health. She would never have had the wind to carry my weight again, even if I had had the heart to take her away from them. I hate to think how many horses our three alae left behind us, dead or half dead in a trail down the highroad from Caer Gloran. Nobody rode their greathorses; they came along as lightly burdened as possible. They needed to be fresh to fight, so we were careful with them. Often, as we rode down the highroad, one of the stallions would put his head back and issue a great challenging huff. We were going to war, and we were going as fast as anyone could.

We passed Emer and her troops on the first day. We had sent messages to her so she knew what was going on, and had changed the direction of the Isarnagan march so that they, too, were heading for Caer Tanaga. They drew back from the road and cheered as we passed through them. It put heart into us to see them, after the cold welcome at Caer Gloran. "I liked your barbarians," Cadraith said to me when we stopped at noon to rest the horses and to eat. "I would never have guessed that their leader was the queen's sister. She looked so grim and scarred, like a real veteran."

"She's had the scar since I've known her," I replied. "I think she got it in the war between Oriel and Connat."

"All the stories about that war are about Atha and Black Darag, but I suppose some other people must have fought," Cadraith said, indistinctly, around the piece of cheese he was chewing. "They looked ready for a fight anyway, enthusiastic. That's what I like to see in allies."

"Oh, Isarnagans are always ready to fight," I agreed.

Then the signal came to remount, and we rode on again. The highroad unwound before us like a skein of yarn. It is not possible to ride hour after hour and day after day at white heat. All the same, so far as we could we did. Caer Tanaga meant something to all of us. Not even Masarn joked the way he usually did. He was one of the many of us who had families there.

The second day we found the body of a red-cloak, hung in a tree at the side of the road. We were out of Tathal, in the eastern part of Magor, almost in Segantia.

"Someone in Caer Tanaga wanted to give us news Cinvar didn't want us to have," Urdo said grimly, looking at the dangling body as I came up.

When they cut him down I saw that it was Senach Red-Eye, who had fought in my pennon long ago. He was iron-haired and iron-bearded now, and all his face was purple and engorged, not just his wounded eye. He was carrying no messages now; whatever he had been bringing us had been taken from him.

"It is Senach," I said. "I remember him interrupting Galba's funeral to bring me word that the Isarnagans had invaded."

"He brought me the news that Elenn's mother had died,"

Urdo recalled. "He served well, as an armiger and as a red-cloak. We cannot wait until sunset to send him back, and he would not have wanted it. Red-cloaks know the meaning of urgency, none better."

"He worshiped the White God," I said. "He will not mind if he does not lie where he fell. Isn't there a shrine along this highroad somewhere where he could be buried tonight?"

So we took up his body on a packhorse, and left it a few miles on at a little place at the roadside where there was a little square church of the White God, a priest's house, and a cluster of farmhouses. Raul spoke to the priest, who promised to do what was needful for Senach. He took his name and some clippings of hair from those of us who had been his friends. That was where I left my poor, exhausted mare. The last time I had news from there, they were calling Senach a saint. No doubt he would have been surprised to hear it. We didn't guess that then, we just rode on, swearing to revenge Senach on Cinvar when we caught him.

On the morning of the third day, we gave the horses oats and dried fruit that Celemon had brought us from a supply cache near where we had camped. "I'm worried that we have heard nothing from ap Meneth," Urdo said, when we had heard the scouts' reports. "Nobody we have sent looking for him has come back. I know Morthu has been subverting my messengers. I wonder how long Cinvar has been hanging them?"

"And who else he might have hanged?" Cadraith muttered into his beard, only just loud enough for us to hear.

"Ap Meneth has an ala," I protested. "Senach was one man on horseback. If there had been a battle we would have seen signs."

"If it had been here," Cadraith countered. "Ap Meneth was off in Caer Rangor."

I suddenly remembered my fears for Emlin and the ala in Magor, the terrible thought that Aurien might set fire to the stables. An ala is a very good weapon in the field, but dismounted and unwarned ap Meneth was as vulnerable as anyone else. Some of this dismay must have showed on my face, for Urdo patted my shoulder. "Nothing we can do about it for now," he said.

We caught up with Cinvar late on that third day, well into Segantia. We were past the turning on the highroad that leads southwest to Caer Thanbard, in a region of gently rolling and well-grazed downland. We were perhaps three or four hours easy ride from Caer Tanaga, and it was early afternoon. Our scouts warned us in plenty of time, so we were not at all surprised. He had five thousand troops under arms, or so Idrien had told Urdo. But most of those were farmers who fought in his militia, not real warriors. We had three alae.

He knew we were there. The scouts said he had his forces drawn up on a rise at the side of the road, threatening the road and threatening us. I talked to my groom about the horses. Brighteyes seemed the most eager to fight, so I decided I would ride him and keep Evenstar armored and ready in reserve in case of a second charge. I tightened my wrist straps and went to get my orders from Urdo.

The alae were drawn up already; they had eaten in position and by numbers. Urdo was dismounted and standing next to Thunder, with the standards set up around him. He smiled at me as I slid down beside him. Darien was there, with his summerhorse, frowning at a blemish on his sword. Cadraith and Masarn came up almost as soon as I had dismounted.

"So, have you sent Raul out?" Masarn asked, looking around for him.

"There's very little point," Urdo said. "It's well past noon already. Cinvar's got his militia drawn up on the top of a rise just ahead. He's sitting there threatening the road. He's in open rebellion. There's nothing to talk to him about. We want to kill him and get to Caer Tanaga today."

"We don't just want to hammer into his people," I said. "He's got what has to be pretty much all the able-bodied people in Tathal with him. They're farmers, not warriors. If they're dead, nobody will be getting the harvest in."

"I know," Urdo said. "They also have what high ground there is, and we don't know for sure how many of them there are. The land tells me there is a great weight of strangers, but cannot count numbers. We don't know where Cinon and Flavien are; it's possible they may have come this far this quickly if they wanted to join up with Cinvar."

"Surely if they have any sense they'd go straight down the highroad that runs pretty much straight from Caer Avroc to Caer Tanaga?" Cadraith said.

"If they had any sense they'd have stayed at home," Masarn said, rolling his eyes. "If you could count on people acting as if they have sense the world would be much easier to understand."

Urdo laughed. "Indeed. I think all we can say is that we don't know where anyone is beyond the three alae in our sight. We could wait and send out more scouts, but there isn't much cover for them to get around behind Cinvar. The lie of the land isn't conducive to seeing clearly—all these rolling downs. We could easily waste hours, and this is not a comfortable place to delay."

"Our three alae are ready now," Masarn said.

"So how shall we attack? Straight up the hill will kill a lot of Cinvar's troops but risks getting bogged down among them," I said.

Urdo smiled. "Cinvar does not respect our honor either. My ala will go past him on the road."

Masarn frowned. "Farmers or not, there are a lot of them."

"There are," Urdo said, still smiling. "Which is why we will run away, half a mile or so, until we are well clear and the ala can wheel out of column into line."

"To face a great confused mass of farmers out of their lines and off their hill." I did not say this loudly; I was thinking that perhaps even Cinvar was not so much a fool as that.

Urdo shrugged. "Or we will be behind them, and Cinvar will be trying to decide what to do with foes on two sides. If that happens, we will all ride north, and turn up onto the down well north of Cinvar, then charge south. My ala will curve north, whether or not we are running away, once we are past Cinvar; Cadraith's ala will start north as we start down the road. With any luck, Cinvar will be so certain I am a coward and trying to escape him that he will not think about what to do for long enough."

"So we go off the road, and far enough that we have the slope with us rather than against us?" Cadraith asked.

"Yes," Urdo agreed. "If the militia chase us, Galba's Ala charges down the road into their flank and rear; if they don't break, pull back. Don't risk getting stuck in among them, Sulien. Cadraith, if they charge off the hill, don't wait for us; sweep up onto the down-top, then charge Cinvar from behind. Tell your people to kill him if they can, anyone who has not broken bread with him and can do so in honor. As for his people, all of you tell your armigers that any of the militia who throw down their weapons and run, let them run. Anyone in arms, kill."

We all raised our chins in agreement. Urdo turned to Darien. "You will take the great banner," he said. "We want speed at first, and then once we get through, what happens depends very much on whether Cinvar is fool enough to chase us."

Darien drew out the great purple banner. "I carried that at Foreth," I said, looking at it. It seemed very long ago and in another world, and at the same time as if it had been mere hours ago.

"I know," Darien said, and laughed a little. "Everyone knows that! I wish I could have been there." Cadraith looked from Darien to Urdo, and then to me, and smiled. I laughed with Darien, and embraced him, and then Urdo, and went back to my own ala, passing on Urdo's orders to my decurios.

We walked the horses up to the crest of the nearest down, ready to take our places. We could see Cinvar's troops drawn up on the hill. All the slopes were gentle and covered in short grass, except where the highroad cut through them in stone. The further slope was steeper, but it did not seem very steep; certainly it was nothing compared to the hills of Derwen or of Bregheda. The militia of Tathal waved their weapons and shouted at us. They made a hedge of weapons against the sky.

I could see swords and spears and axes, and also scythes and clubs. Cinvar was in the center with his household warriors around him; he had a single great banner with the Brown Dog of Tathal on a yellow background.

In a flurry of trumpet calls and hand signals Urdo's ala went down the road, going quite fast. Cinvar's troops really did fall for it and came rushing down the slope. Cadraith's ala was already moving north. I signaled for Galba's ala to follow me and charged down the road to take Cinvar's troops in the rear.

It all went splendidly until I realized it wasn't only Cinvar. We were quite a way down the road when I saw Flavien's banner up ahead, and Cinon's. They were drawn up behind the hill, where they had been out of our sight. They stood firm, blocking the road ahead of Urdo's ala, who were caught between them and the mass of Cinvar's troops, the ones we had hoped would break and scatter at my charge. I signaled to Cadraith straight away, in case he had not seen, then I pulled Galba's ala close around me and we charged up the shoulder of the hill, straight through the remaining bulk of Cinvar's troops.

There is no time in battle to wonder whether the young man impaled on your spear is the farmer's son who went off to war with only one shirt. There is no time to count your enemies when they are still coming at you. There were a lot of them, and they stood better than I would have thought. We had to hack our way through them to get to Urdo, there was no other choice. It was possible that they could swamp his ala through sheer force of numbers. I saw ap Selevan pulled down by three Tathalians. I kept moving, signaling to my pennon to stay close to me, and to the ala to keep formation. We had discipline and kept together; our opponents had no such habits. We kept moving, never quite bogging down, until we got through them.

They kept trying to harass us, but as soon as we had joined up with Urdo's ala and made some space to maneuver we ran north to join Cadraith. Dalmer and Celemon brought up the supplies and the spare horses to join us straightaway. We re-formed quickly, the three alae together again, with the supply train in the middle. We changed horses; then, safely on Evenstar's broad back, I drew breath and looked around to consider the position.

As usual, the battle had taken more time than I had noticed. The sun was drawing down the sky in the west behind us. We were well north of the road. East, a little way down the road, Cinon and Flavien were still drawn up, blocking us entirely from going east toward Caer Tanaga. Behind us Cinvar and his troops were attempting to form up and close us in. We had outrun them, but that had bought us only a little time. Cinvar kept trying to call them back to re-form. If Cinvar had a proper system of signals like ours he might have been on us already.

One of the quartermasters delivered the fresh spears to the ala. I heard the steady clicking behind me as the bundle was passed from armiger to armiger along the lines.

Urdo signaled and the three alae formed up individually, ready to ride as soon as we had orders. I rode over to Urdo to find out what the orders were, and saw Cadraith doing the same. Poor Cadraith had been wounded in the leg and looked pale. He kept looking southeast. I turned my head to see what was attracting his attention, and closed my eyes for an instant, as if that could help.

On the top of the southern down, clear against the sky, fresh and drawn up in battle order, stood Angas's ala. He couldn't get to us unless Cinon and Flavien made a lane for him, but he was there. The Thorn of Demedia showed clearly on his banners even at that distance.

"Angas," he said, gesturing as we came up together.

There was nothing I could say to that, except yes, so I ignored it.

"We could charge back at Cinvar's troops?" I suggested. "They're shaken already; another charge might scatter them."

"But where are we heading?" Masarn asked.

I realized then that we were trying to think of a way out of a trap, and we had no strong place close to retreat to. Between the three kings there were as many foot soldiers as at

Foreth, maybe more, and now there was Angas's ala. We could all die, I thought, and the Peace with us. I had always known that I could die in battle. I had seen friends fall and had enough close escapes to know myself mortal. But it had always seemed that, although I could die, it would be in victory, to help build the Peace, the way Urdo had spoken about the fallen of Foreth.

Urdo was about to speak when there came a great cacophonous roar from ahead. It was so loud and discordant it spooked the horses, but we all turned to face it. I saw a woman advancing up the little stream that ran in the valley bottom below us, an army behind her. She had a spear in each hand, and her hair was spiked with lime so that it stood out almost an arm's length from her head in all directions. She was quite naked, and painted blue all over, with spiraling designs drawn in black and white on top. Her stomach had a red mouth drawn on it and her breasts were painted so that her nipples looked like eyes, outlined in white and black. She was howling like the ghosts of a thousand neglected ancestors come for vengeance. Her people, who seemed numerous and well armed, followed behind, blowing war trumpets that made a disconsolate bellow rather than playing discernable notes. Many of them were also naked and painted, others wore sensible armor. All of them were carrying stabbing swords, spears, and round shields, which they beat on as they approached.

"Back to your alae, and charge Cinvar now," Urdo said urgently. I went back at top speed, and gave the signals. There was a moment's hesitation, then we saw that Darien was leading Urdo's Own Ala down on the Tathalians, and we came down after them to drive the hammer blow home. I don't know if I even killed anyone in that charge, it seemed as if they broke instantly. They were only half-trained farmers after all. We hit them, and the army of blue-painted howling Isarnagans hit them just afterward, and they scattered, fleeing south or east toward their friends. Even Cinvar ran, and the men of his household, whatever they said afterward.

They scattered eastward toward their waiting friends, who had still not moved.

We obeyed orders and let them run once they had dropped their weapons. The foot soldiers pursued until called back by a loud, discordant blast on their war-trumpets. Then they came back and started looting among the fallen.

We rallied and re-formed again. Again, I rode over to Urdo. Most of the foot soldiers were scattered across the battlefield, but fifty or so were drawn up in the sort of churning I now recognized as the Isarnagan notion of order. A woman came up from among them with a red cloak, which she handed to the leader. I had guessed who she was by this time, though I could not imagine how or why she was here.

"Well met, King Urdo," she called loudly and cheerfully, in Tanagan accented like Conal's, settling the cloak around her shoulders. "I am Atha of Oriel." Her voice was chillingly calm for a woman who had been fighting like a demon only a few minutes before. Yet there was an edge to it that made it quite clear she was not entirely in her right mind.

"Well met on the field of battle, Atha of Oriel," Urdo replied, in even tones. "What brings you to my country in arms?"

It was hard to tell under the war paint, but I thought Atha seemed surprised. "I am here in arms to avenge my herald, Conal the Victor," she said, as if this was only to be expected. "Sulien ap Gwien and Conal's kinsman, Lew ap Ross, were kind enough to send me his body and all the details of his betrayal and hero's death." Emer would have known all the details, I thought, and she must have made Lew say more than I had said in my carefully worded letter. I could just imagine Conal's face if he saw this reaction. I wondered if his father had come.

"I mustered my forces at once," Atha went on. She waved her spears, both bloodstained now. Those of her forces who were near enough to hear cheered. "Keeping my oath not to invade Demedia again, although it was in rebellion against you, I sailed south to Magor, only to learn from Golidan ap

Dorath that you had already killed the traitor Aurien ap Gwien. So we sailed onto Caer Tanaga to consult with you. When we reached your city three days ago it was to learn that it had been taken by Arling Gunnarsson and the traitor Ayl Drumwinsson. We could not stop this, but we have been preventing their traitorous allies from joining them from the north. Today we have been reinforced by boats coming upriver bearing your faithful ally, Ohtar Bearsson, and his men. Seeing all the armies hurrying up the highroad, we followed them in secret and came to your aid."

"My deepest thanks, King Atha," Urdo said, bowing as best he could from horseback.

She laughed. Her laugh somehow reminded me of the tale I had heard that her feasting hall was decorated with the heads of her enemies. "If I had known we would find you so hard pressed I would have brought more than these few warriors you see around me. Fortunately, some of those rebels have fought us before and remember the howl of our wartrumpets and the bite of our swords."

"I shall send my herald to them to make a truce until tomorrow," Urdo said. "I am glad to hear of Ohtar's arrival, and I have more forces coming to me here."

"We shall beat them out of the land, and avenge Conal and all our fallen friends!" Atha said in a great shout. All her warriors blew their trumpets and beat on their shields, and the armigers cheered.

Urdo sent for Raul, who rode toward the enemy under herald's branches. We dismounted and made a kind of camp on the hill and in the little valley. We saw to our wounded and gathered the dead. Urdo talked quietly to Atha while we were doing this. I hoped he was finding out exactly how many troops she had brought and how many boats. It always astonished me how quickly people traveled by water. She must have called at Magor after we left it, and still she had been here for days, having battles with the rebel lords.

I went back to Urdo when I saw Raul coming back. I was tired from battle and from the healing charms, which had seemed much harder to sing than usual, and to work less well, as if some part of them was falling short of the ears of the listening gods. It was not that the gods could not hear—I had reattached ap Padarn's foot, which had been held onto his leg only by the knife which was stuck through his boot, which could never have happened without the Lord of Healing's aid. There were far fewer dead and wounded than there had been in the battle against Marchel. Still, I was weary. I frowned and rubbed my head between my eyes where an ache was starting. My only wound was a little scratch on my arm from the edge of a spear. It itched. I drank some water from my flask and stood in my place beside Urdo.

Raul looked very grave. He bowed to Urdo and then to us all. Then he turned back to Urdo and addressed him. "We have a truce until tomorrow, when we shall meet to see whether the truce shall last longer or if we shall fight again," he said. "Cinon is eager to fight, but Flavien wants to negotiate. Cinvar looked a little shaken, like a man who knows what it is to be charged by armigers. Angas looks sick, as if he has aged twenty years in the two years since he was last at Caer Tanaga. He said nothing at all, but looked only at me and not at his allies. Cinon called you 'the tyrant Urdo' every second sentence."

"He has never forgiven me for telling him the truth about his father's death," Urdo said. "As for Angas, that is bad news but what I expected. Did they mention the city?"

"They have not been able to reach the city," Atha said.

"Then if we want to negotiate we will need to send separately to Arling and give him a safe conduct to and from the negotiations," Urdo said. Raul made a note with his patterned stylus.

"Why negotiate?" Atha asked, pushing back her hair with both hands. "Why not wait until your reinforcements arrive and then crush them?"

"They have my wife hostage in the city," Urdo said. "And while it is necessary to fight the rebels, I will keep the Peace and the Law as far as I can. We will talk to them. I have hopes that Angas, at least, will realize what he's doing. He did not fight against me today. Was Morthu there?"

"I did not see him," Raul said. "I saw all four kings, and many of them had priests and war-leaders and counselors with them, but there was no sign of Morthu ap Talorgen."

"Good," said Urdo, but he frowned as he said it. I would much rather have known where Morthu was myself.

"Negotiations should go more smoothly without him," Raul agreed.

"Let us hope they have learned a lesson from this battle, and are prepared to beg forgiveness and make peace," Cadraith said.

"I don't know what they might have learned from this battle," I said. "They broke, but really, nobody won. As for begging forgiveness, it's too late for Cinvar, anyway; they fought Urdo himself, there's no possible excuse."

Atha jerked up her chin in emphatic agreement. "We want vengeance," she said.

"Aurien is dead," Urdo said, very firmly. "She is the only person who has wronged you directly. We very much appreciate your help, and when peace is restored we will make you and your army fine gifts, discussing at that time what will please you. But I will not make my kingdom a desert for vengeance for your herald."

"Very well," said Atha, and tossed her head. The spikes of her limed hair did not move at all. I wondered if it was actually stiff enough to hurt someone.

"I will go to them again in the morning," Raul said. "And I will speak to them about sending someone through to Caer Tanaga."

"Double sentries tonight, and a wide sentry-ring," Urdo said. "There is a stream here, so we have water. Let us all rest as best we can; tomorrow is likely to be another busy day."

" 'We will keep to our old ways and the traditions of our ancestors, and you cannot make us change. Such is the law on this island, old man!' said Sulien Glynsdottar, putting down her cup, and
glaring fiercely about her."
—From *The Life of St. Cinwil*

We made camp on the hillside, with the stream inside
our inner sentry-ring and a strong outer sentry-ring
set all around. Govien managed to get our ala sorted out
smoothly. All the same he rolled his eyes when I came up to
him by his tent. "I wish Emlin were here," he said. "Emlin
would have known all the answers to Dalmer's questions
without needing to ask Nodol."

"No he wouldn't," I said, as reassuringly as I could. I also
missed Emlin's cheerful competence. "You're doing very
well, Govien. We're finished before Cadraith's ala." I started
to swing my arms to stretch the weariness of battle out of my
shoulders.

"But not before Urdo's," he pointed out, truthfully. "I don't
think I'm suited to be a tribuno," he said, putting down a wax
tablet. "I find it so hard to keep track of everything."

"Everyone does," I said.

"Not thinking of running out on ap Gwien, are you?"
asked Masarn, coming up behind us and stepping carefully
around my turning arms. "Can't do that, you know. It's an
emergency."

I laughed, and bent to touch my toes.

"I wasn't thinking of running out," Govien said quickly.
"I'm just not so good at doing Emlin's job. He's really the tribuno. I'd rather be just looking after my own pennon."

"Well, I'm not really a praefecto," Masarn said, twitching
his white cloak into place. "But, fortunately, I only have to do
the tribuno's work because Urdo's his own praefecto. And

whatever Gormant may think, he has been ever since you left us, Sulien."

"And I'd much rather never have left you," I said, straightening up and rolling my shoulders. I could feel muscles loosening all the way down my back. "I can't say I'm not really a king, though."

"Indeed you can't," Masarn said. "If you were only a praefecto, the way I am, you could get out of having dinner with Atha on the grounds that you were exhausted from the battle, or because your ala needed you. As it is—"

"Masarn, if I have to eat with her then you do too!" I said.

"I wouldn't miss it for anything," he assured me.

I looked at him suspiciously.

"That's where the best food will be," he said. "And if we get to talking about the next battle I won't have to suggest strategies. I can leave that to you and just agree with everything you say."

I laughed. "If I see you doing any such thing I will take your plate away."

Masarn made the face he made at his children when they were misbehaving, the one that made them stop and laugh at the same time.

"I can manage here," Govien said. He even managed to smile at Masarn, but looked worn and weary. What he needed, what the whole ala needed, was a good rest.

"We're none of us young anymore," Masarn said as we walked together through the camp.

"None of us who fought through the War," I replied. "There are plenty of young armigers still." As if to prove my point, a young groom ran past, laughing, holding a blanket, one of Hiveth's pennon chasing after.

"It's easier for the young," Masarn said, watching them giggling and tussling.

"But don't you miss it?" I asked.

"Miss what?" He looked at me. "I'm here, aren't I?" He hesitated for a moment. "Did you ever know a veteran who left an ala and settled near it who didn't come to practice sometimes? That's why I'm still fit to fight, and all the other veterans in the ranks. The thing is, you hear the trumpet for practice at dawn and you roll over and thank merciful God you're not out there in the rain. Then a sunny day comes and you hear it blowing. Then you think, why not, it would be a change and you can see your friends. Maybe that's missing it. Maybe. But the important thing is when you hear the trumpet blowing the alarm.

"*Then* you know where you belong. I could have stayed home. I could always have stayed home. Nobody ever made me join the ala, it was my own choice. But if the trumpet's blowing the alarm, well, how could I? How could anyone who knew how to ride and use weapons?"

"Why did you join in the beginning?" I asked, curious. It was a question we never asked. Once you had sworn to ride as Urdo's armiger then that was enough.

"Why do you think?" he asked.

"Well, I always thought everyone joined for the excitement, or to win a glorious name for themselves."

Masarn laughed. "And how old were you when you realized not everybody was just like you?"

I squirmed a little. "So you were fighting for the Peace all along?"

"No." Masarn looked serious for a moment. "Now, yes, but not when I joined; I didn't have any more idea what Peace was then than anyone else. I thought I was lucky to have a wife who had a trade, and that's as far as I thought about anything past my own nose. I was in the city guard at Caer Tanaga, before Urdo took the crown. He asked us if any of us would like to become armigers. Garwen thought I was mad, but I did it. She kept saying that fighting wasn't any trade for a man who likes his food the way I do, and she was right. But it was the only chance I was likely to have to be near the horses." His face relaxed as he thought of them. "Marchel taught all of us recruits to ride. When Urdo gave me White-foot it was as if the world had found harmony and the White God had set me in my right place already."

"I have always loved horses," I said.

"They're easier to love than people," Masarn said, and before I could think of anything to say to that, we had arrived at Urdo's big tent.

All our banners were flying outside it and it all looked very splendid. This big tent was made of very fine Black Isarnagan leather. Instead of being put up with whatever wood could be found around, like a normal tent, it had special support poles. It was carefully made of sewn leather, and almost entirely weatherproof. It even had a curtain that could be set up inside to make it into two rooms. It could hold twelve people, at a push. Glividen had designed it during the war. It needed a packhorse to itself, but it was worth the trouble. Most tents had barely room for two people to sit and talk, but with Urdo's big tent there was room for a council with maps spread out, even in the rain.

I followed Masarn inside. Urdo was sitting with Cadraith, an old man with unbound hair and the long shawl of an oracle-priest, and a middle-aged woman with a shawl over her head in the Demedian manner. Darien was standing to pour wine. Everyone rose as we came in, and bowed.

"Sulien, you know Atha ap Gren," Urdo said, presenting the woman. I blinked. I had not known her. She had dressed and washed her face, and with her hair covered she looked just like anyone else.

"I am honored to meet you," I said, and bowed. Darien handed me a cup of wine. I smiled at him.

"And this is Inis ap Fathag," Urdo said, introducing the old man.

I bowed, but the old man shook his head. "I shall go no more by the name of my honored father, although I have carried it all my life. I shall be known henceforward as Inis, Grandfather of Heroes." He turned to Atha. "Do you hear that, girl? Have that worthless poet my daughter married put that into the praise song he makes over my ashes this autumn."

Atha laughed, sounding unamused. "Will you set me impossible tasks even beyond the grave, Grandfather?"

"Ah, so you count yourself a hero?" he asked. Atha looked

furious, as well she might. She had as good a claim to be considered a hero as anyone I had ever met. "Amagien will be delighted to do it. He is pulling mourning around him like a cloak. Nothing poor Conal did for him alive was good enough, but he will use his death to build the son he imagines he should have liked to have." Inis turned back to me, and bowed in formal greeting. "I owe you a great debt, Sulien ap Gwien."

He was bent with age, but he had been a tall man. I had often thought, looking at Lew, that Conal must have got his looks from his mother's family. Inis was very old but he was still a handsome man, even with his hair disordered and the front of it shaved in the fashion of oracle-priests. I thought that I was seeing not only where Conal got his pretty face but also where he learned his way of talking.

I bowed again. "If one of your heroic grandchildren was Conal the Victor, then it is I who owe you a debt, for Conal saved my life."

"You saved him from many other, more foolish, deaths," Inis said. "And you sent the memory of his honorable death home, for which I honor you, as Conal's wretched father Amagien bade me honor you. He stayed in Oriel writing the poem to make his son's memory immortal."

"Is he a very bad poet?" I asked.

Cadraith looked horrified, but Inis laughed. "I almost wish he were, for if so it would be very easy to dismiss him altogether as someone who needs no consideration. But in fact he is a good poet, when he is honest, which is seldom enough. He was a very bad father, and so poor Conal grew up thinking he could never be good enough. Conal was a very good warrior; it was his great misfortune that his cousin Darag was a better one."

Of course, I realized, this old man was Darag's grandfather as well. That was why Atha, Darag's widow, addressed him so. I looked at Atha. She was frowning. "I never met Darag, but he must have shone very brightly to outshine Conal," I said.

"He did," Atha said flatly.

"And he is dead, and Conal is dead," Inis interrupted. "Dead, and here we are to avenge him, for what good everyone imagines it will do."

"If you keep on like this I shall send you back to Thansethan," Atha said between her teeth.

Urdo closed his eyes for a moment. "Have you been to Thansethan?" he asked Inis politely.

"I have just come back from a visit to the hospitable monks," Inis said. Darien set down the wine jug. You would have had to know him to see that he was doing it with extra care. All the same Inis shot him a shrewd glance. "You need not fear, young hawk, they will do nothing for or against anyone until all is decided. Well, they will take in the queen whenever she gets so far, which is sometimes before that, but that is scarcely action to shake our path. I spoke to them about the gods of Tir Isarnagiri and about the way the worlds will go. Father Gerthmol was terrified." He giggled, very high-pitched, almost like a woman. "I told them what a thread we are all hanging by. I think they are praying I am mad."

"You *are* mad, of course," Atha said, as if it were an accepted thing. They both laughed. The rest of us looked at them awkwardly. Masarn rubbed the sides of his head as if they hurt. "Be careful, Grandfather, you are getting near where you will lose the thread of words."

"I have seen eighty-nine summers, forty-two of them across all the worlds. I will be dead before midwinter," Inis said. "Of course I am mad."

"You said the queen will escape to Thansethan?" Urdo asked, leaning forward.

"Most of the time," Inis said. "After you are dead, of course. It's where she wants to be, after all. They'd be fools not to take her." He shook his head a little as if to clear it. "But every world is different," he said, rocking on his heels a little. "You have changed so much here that it is only the great patterns and events that are certain. It is possible she will choose to die instead."

"Is she well now?" Urdo asked.

Atha raised a hand. "The more you press him the less precise he gets," she warned. "He really is mad, you know, and the more he thinks about this sort of question the further he gets from being able to talk sensibly."

Inis cackled again. "She's right, she's absolutely right. What I see is not what is or what will be. Often enough you married Mardol's daughter, and she was not so proud. She bore you two sons, but the monks took her in at the end just the same."

Cadraith gasped. Urdo looked as distressed as I had ever seen him.

"Hush now, grandfather," Atha said. "You're getting confused."

He looked at her. "You always die old," he said. Atha looked as if he had slapped her.

Masarn cleared his throat. "I think the food is here," he said. Sure enough, Talog was hesitating in the tent entrance with a large steaming bowl. It was porridge, of course. We sat down to eat. Inis was mercifully quiet, rocking to and fro, though the rest of us exchanged a little chatter about the weather and the camp. When we had finished the porridge, Talog brought in two chickens, jointed and fried over the fire. I wondered where they had come from, and hoped they were bought at the roadside rather than stolen. I knew there could not have been enough for everyone. That didn't stop me from enjoying my share. After we had finished and wiped our hands Urdo drew out a map of the southeastern part of Tir Tanagiri from the heap on his box.

"So where exactly is Ohtar?" he asked Atha.

Atha looked intently at the map. "This blue line is the river, yes?"

"The blue line is the river, this black line is the road we are on, and this circle is Caer Tanaga, where the other roads join."

"Then he is—" Her finger circled and stabbed. "Here. Between the road and the river, and also on the river in boats, some his and some ours."

"I wonder what our enemies are doing," Cadraith said.

Then he looked at Inis in alarm, as if afraid his question would be answered in horrible and dubious detail. Inis ignored him, ignored all of us, gnawing away on a chicken leg that seemed already bare of meat.

"The same as we are, I expect," Urdo said, setting down his bowl. "Making camp, eating. What I wonder is what they want."

"The kings want not to pay taxes," Cadraith said. "Not to have to maintain the alae now the Jarnsmen aren't such a threat. Not to have to keep to the Law when it doesn't suit them. To rule the barbarian way their fathers ruled, and their ancestors back before the Vincans came." He looked at Atha, who just smiled.

"They would not have gone to war for that," I said. "They want that, yes, but they can see that the Peace is good for everyone. They remember what it was like before."

"Do they?" Darien asked. "I don't. Cinon is only seven years older than I am. Flavien was his father's youngest son and a young man at the time of Foreth. I'm not sure how old Cinvar is—"

"He's a year or two younger than I am," I said.

"Even so, that's not old enough to remember the wars at my father's death," Urdo said. "You're right. That generation is almost gone. Of all the kings who fought then, only Guthrum and my mother are left. But Flavien and Cinvar must remember the War."

"They remember we won it," Masarn said.

"That's right," said Cadraith. "They don't think of Peace as something that needs to be won fresh all the time, the way you said at Foreth. Even though it's written down in your law code. My father would have loved that. He believed that, and old Duke Galba. It was the Vincan way, even though your Peace is a new Peace. But what does it mean to Cinvar, except that you stopped a Jarnish invasion?"

"That thought is nowhere in Tir Isarnagiri," Atha said. "Each king makes the Peace, and it dies with them, and their law with it. It was an unusual thing that I kept Darag's peace and his laws after he died, although he was my husband. Next year, when our son takes the crown, if he keeps them it will be considered amazing."

Urdo sighed. "Still, I don't think I pushed the kings too hard. I doubt they would have risen up, however resentful, or allied with Arling, if not for Morthu."

"Black heart and poisoned tongue," Inis said, in a confirmatory way, without looking up.

"What does Morthu want?" Atha asked.

"Power and importance," I said. "He wants to make himself High King. He calls himself the grandson of Avren; he schemes and makes alliances with whoever he thinks will help him."

"If he wanted that and was prepared to put all that effort into it he could have had a good chance at becoming Urdo's heir," Cadraith said. "That way he'd have got to take over something whole, not something broken."

"I think he wants it broken," Darien said quietly. We all turned to look at him. "I know him; I knew him when he was young, at Thansethan. He hates all of us. He thinks we killed his mother and poisoned her memory. He doesn't want to take over the kingdom, though that's probably what he told Arling and his other allies. He just wants death and destruction and everything broken to pieces." He paused, and looked at Urdo. "I said years ago that I would ask your permission before fighting him. I am asking that permission now. I am a man grown, and a trained armiger."

"You are also the person we can least afford to lose," Urdo said slowly, with a strange expression.

"That is a heavy burden you lay on me," Darien said.

"I know," Urdo replied, smiling faintly. "I have been carrying it for long years without realizing how heavy it was, until now when I set it down."

Inis laughed, and looked briefly at the two of them. "Better than any old bowl," he said.

"It's not as if the whole war could be settled champion against champion," Atha said, looking at Darien speculatively and ignoring Inis entirely. "If everyone would agree to put the weight of the war on that, it might be worth risking, if we had someone very good. Darag won a war that way."

"And hated himself for the rest of his life after, all his lives," Inis said, rocking backward and forward, eyes tight shut.

I wondered if he were seeing into other worlds now, looking for one where his grandchildren were happy and alive. I looked away from him uneasily. Darien and Urdo were still looking at each other. I could not read their faces. "Can I fight him, if it comes to that?" I asked.

Urdo looked at me, and back to Darien. "Neither of you may challenge him. He is no fool to settle for a single combat. What happens in the field is different. Certainly if he were dead this war would be a very different matter."

"He should be mine to kill," Darien said, like someone who knows their argument has been incontrovertibly countered.

"He is a talker, not a famous fighter, that I have ever heard," Masarn said. "He was in my pennon and he learned as well as most, but not better. I'd say Sulien or Darien could take him, or I could, come to that."

"They say he knows sorcery," Cadraith said.

"Who says so?" Urdo asked.

"He says so himself," Atha said, surprising me. "He claims the reputation of his mother in his letters, trying to awe and overpower his would-be allies."

"Has anyone seen him doing sorcery?" Urdo asked.

Darien stirred, but did not speak.

"He read Gunnarsson's dreams," I said. "You did not want to believe him an enemy. He may claim to be a sorcerer to make himself seem more powerful. I would not give him reputation he does not deserve, but better that than be caught unawares and burn like tallow the way poor Geiran did at Caer Lind."

"Very well," Urdo said. "We will consider that he may be a

sorcerer. That is another good reason for not fighting a single combat, even if he would agree to it."

Cadraith shifted uneasily. "We don't know for sure that Darien's right," he said. "Morthu is more dangerous if he wants to destroy everything, but I've seen no signs of that, only of wanting to make himself High King. We've gone straight onto talking about combats as if we were sure that was the truth."

"I know it is," Darien said.

"If he is a sorcerer it makes it more likely he wants to destroy everything," Masarn said. "It would take a powerful lot of hate to do that."

"It's a terrible thing to want," Urdo said. "Even his mother just wanted to be safe, in her way, walking the path she saw in her madness. But I think Darien is right even so."

"It makes no difference," Atha said, glancing at Inis, who was staring at his hands in his lap and ignoring us again. "It sometimes helps to know what your enemies want, but it's rare enough to be able to give it to them, and we would be wanting to deny him all of it in any case. If Suliensson turns out to be right we may be able to separate Morthu from his allies in negotiation. We don't lose anything by trying."

"He's very good at talking," Masarn said. "He always has been."

Urdo yawned. "Tomorrow we will meet with their leaders. At worst we will buy enough time for ap Meneth and Luth and ap Erbin to join us, and maybe Alfwin as well if he can. At best we will come to an arrangement. Raul is visiting their priests even now to see if they can help—most priests of the White God will negotiate to save lives."

"Let's hear what they say they want," Cadraith said. "They might not be foolish enough to fight now they've seen us on the field."

"Cinvar has lost that army," I agreed. "He might want to slink off home himself now."

"We will have to fight Arling," Masarn said. "We will have to get him out of the city and fight him."

"It does seem unlikely that he will just agree to go away," Urdo said.

"And only six stood scatheless at the battle fought at Agned, and the bloody hand of battle brought dark death to both the islands," chanted Inis gleefully. Then he began to cry like a baby, and Atha made apologies and led him away.

— 13 —

Lady of Wisdom,
guide thou my thoughts,
aid thou my strategy,
let my words fall clear on the air
from my lips
to listening hearts.
Let me be lucid.
Let me be heard.
         —From "Charm for Rhetoric"

The ala doctor, ap Darel, woke me. He was arguing with Govien outside the tent about whether it was too early to wake me or not.

"If it's an emergency you can call her," Govien was insisting, loudly, right outside my tent.

"It's not an emergency, but I've never seen anything like it before, and I wish Sulien would come and see," ap Darel said firmly.

I yawned, stretched, sat up, and poked my head out. I obviously wasn't going to get any more sleep this morning.

"Oh, Sulien," Govien said in obvious relief. I had slept longer than usual. The sun was well up, and visible, too, in a blue sky.

"Anything urgent?" I asked. Both men shook their heads. "Then is there any chance of hot water?" I asked.

Govien frowned anxiously. "If you really need some, I expect so. The cooks have the fires lit."

"I'll use the stream," I said, pulling myself to my feet. "I see you, ap Darel. If it isn't urgent I'll speak to you when I'm clean."

I walked down to the stream. The cooks' assistants had marked off a place upstream for drawing drinking water. So many had come down to bathe that it seemed as if a whole ala was in the water together. Even Cynrig had shaken off his modesty for once and was splashing about with the others. I plunged in to join them. It was a warm morning, but the water was as icy as if it had come straight from the twin peaks of fire and ice on the island on top of the world. Rigg had been there, I thought. Emrys had. I knew then that however vast the world might be I would never leave the island where I was born. Then Masarn splashed me and I whirled around to splash back. I went back up the slope goose-pimpled and needing to rub myself down, but with a much clearer head.

Ap Darel was still waiting outside my tent. "I can show you here, quickly, I think," he said. He took my arm and frowned at the scratch I'd taken yesterday at the battle. "Yes. Look at your arm."

I looked. The scratch was red-rimmed and slightly swollen. I looked at him in sudden alarm. "Poison?" I asked. "Is there much of it?"

"No poison I recognize," he said. "And ineffective for one. But it must be something like poison. It seems as if everyone who was hurt yesterday has a wound that looks angry and is healing more slowly than it should."

My scratch hurt, now I was thinking about it. I frowned down at my arm. Normally I would expect something like that to have scabbed over already. My arms bore the light scars of a dozen similar scratches I had taken over the years, and there had been at least as many that had healed without leaving any mark. I remembered how tired I had been after the healings the night before. "I will come and see some of your cases after I have eaten," I said. "I've never seen anything like it either. It might be they poisoned the weapons. Though I wonder how Cinvar could have persuaded his people to agree to that. Or maybe they cursed them? Now I think of it I have read of a curse called the weapon-rot. It is named in the charm I sing over any cut that bleeds."

"It is in my charms too. And I have read of it in Talarnos," ap Darel said, looking horrified. "He says the Malms suffered from it long ago. He says their wounds turned green and full of pus, and then their blood became poisoned, the wounds turned black, and the patients invariably died. He treated it with spiders' webs and salt water, and said it was not found among civilized people but only among the barbarians from across the Vonar. He thought it not a curse but a disease."

"How could it be a disease? Diseases spread between people, they don't infect wounds!"

Ap Darel shook his head. "Talarnos was a frontier army doctor two hundred years ago. The useful half of his book is charms for when you haven't picked up the weapon. Maybe he didn't know much about disease."

"Well, now," I said, as briskly as I could. "Whether it is poison, curse, or disease, it is nothing like what Talarnos describes. It is at least a red swelling, not a green one." The thought of a green wound was too horrible to contemplate.

Ap Darel frowned. "Can you see if there is anything you can do?" he asked hesitantly.

"We are not in Derwen," I said. "And I do not think it is a disease. But I will look."

I closed my eyes and felt for the scratch on my arm. Then I reached out for the Lord of Healing. He was there, part of the structure of the world. Concentrating, I tried the charm for preventing weapon-rot. It was the same as when I had tried to send Darien back before he was born. My will could not connect to the god's power. I tried to see what was preventing me, but I could not. The gods were there. I knew better than to call on them for no reason, but I could feel their presence threaded through the world where they needed to be. There was some invisible barrier preventing that one charm from reaching the Lord of Healing. Another god? Somehow it didn't feel that way. A person? I tried to push against it but it slipped away from me. Eventually I opened my eyes to see ap Darel watching me curiously.

"The charm isn't working," I said shortly. "It is not a disease, whatever else it is. I will see the wounded, and then I will speak to the High King."

I dressed, ate, and visited the wounded. I learned nothing ap Darel had not already told me. When I went to see Urdo he was sitting in his tent with the side laced open. The sight of him sitting there so solidly in the sunlight reassured me that the world was going as it should.

I found that he knew of the problem already. "I knew it before I woke," he said. "The weapon-rot ran through my dreams. I think it is a curse, or something like one. It is something done by black sorcery, not by the power of any god. The worst news is that it covers the whole of Segantia."

"The whole of Segantia?" I repeated, feeling sick. "What can we do? How could anyone do that?"

"Who is king of Segantia?" Urdo asked.

I blinked. "You are." I hesitated. "Or your mother is?"

"Exactly." Urdo pushed his hair back wearily. "It has never been an issue. I am High King. Rowanna has been ruling Segantia for a long time. I have never taken up the land or taken it from her. There is a crack we left there, meant in kindness, but used for ill. Through that crack this curse came. I can do nothing to break the curse, and I do not know whether Rowanna can. It is not a matter of the whole land, or I could break it, but of Segantia alone. I have sent a messenger to her at Caer Segant, asking her to come."

I remembered Rowanna fasting for the White God. "Will she know how?"

"I don't know," Urdo said. "Her father was a king, and she has been ruling Segantia well for a long time. But this is not a disease. And she has often relied on Teilo to stand beside her on what is holy."

"Will Teilo come here as well?" I asked.

"Mother Teilo is close on ninety years old," Urdo said. "And I don't know if she is with my mother, or off in Aylsfa with Penarwen, or even up in her monastery in Demedia. She was in Caer Segant the last I heard though, so maybe she will come with Rowanna. Even if she is there and she comes, I don't know if she could do anything about this. I don't know if anyone could. Maybe only killing the sorcerer would release the land, if blood has bound it."

"Morthu," I said, quietly and with loathing.

"We should not assume that," Urdo said.

I looked at him incredulously. "Why do you always think the best of him? What doubt can you possibly be giving him the benefit of now? He is a sorcerer and he hates us."

Urdo put his hands together and looked down at them, pushing his long fingers together. "We do not know if Arling has brought any sorcerers from Jarnholme," he said, after a moment. "I could not see who had cast this spell, try how I might. And consider the power it would take, to stop a charm reaching to the gods. It would take more than the strength of anyone's soul."

"Morwen used the power of other people's souls, killing them for it," I said, lowering my voice, although there was nobody near enough to hear. "He could be doing that."

"I can't imagine how many it would take," Urdo said. "Not just one or two. And they would all be our people. But it may yet be a group of Jarnish sorcerers."

"Most of them scarcely know enough charms to light a fire," I said dubiously. "But I suppose it could be any sorcerer or group of them on the other side." I was still sure it was Morthu.

"If it is Morthu it might explain why Raul didn't see him last night or this morning," Urdo said. "Doing something like that would exhaust him almost completely, even if he was stealing souls to do it."

"It is the worst thing I have ever heard of anyone doing," I said, remembering my relief when Ulf had told me he had killed Osvran. "How can Flavien ally with him when Morthu's mother took his father's soul for sorcery!"

"New times make new alliances," Urdo quoted Dalitus. "They are none of them best placed for logic. Cinon accuses me of favoring the Jarnsmen overmuch, and not only makes alliance with Ayl, but invites in Arling Gunnarsson and his army."

"We haven't seen Ayl," I said. "I don't think he wants to be allied with them at all. If Arling landed there, that might have startled him into being on the wrong side."

"It's family," Urdo said. "He is married to Penarwen, so he

is standing with Angas, who is standing where Morthu pushed him."

"Family," I said slowly. "Just like it has always been in Tir Tanagiri; family, and connections. But we have made the Jarns part of that pattern as well."

Urdo shook his head. "That pattern is there, it isn't something it's possible to change. But with the alae, and with the oaths that reflect the patterns going up from the farmers to the kings and from the kings to me, I have tried to set another strong order that supports the Law. If it is given time I think it will hold."

We had talked about this in our letters, and I knew it was important to him. I wanted to say something about different kinds of loyalty, and was turning the words in my head when Raul came up. His skin was very dark around his eyes and his cheeks were hollow. I wondered if he had slept at all.

"They have agreed to meet at noon in the next valley east," he said, without any greetings at all beyond a bare acknowledgment.

"And what is wrong?" Urdo asked.

"Father Cinwil is one of the priests acting as a herald for them," Raul said, sitting down on the grass just outside the tent.

"I thought he was in Derwen?" I said, surprised.

"With your mother?" Raul asked, raising his eyebrows.

"He was escorting Amala and Gomoarionsson to Caer Tanaga, along with a handful of my wounded," Urdo said flatly.

I bit my lip. "Did you ask about them?"

"He assured me they are all safe," Raul said, looking up at me. "But he did not say where. Amala and Gomoarionsson are valuable pieces to lose."

"I wonder where Thurrig is," Urdo said, gazing southwest in the general direction of Caer Thanbard.

"And Custennin," Raul said. "And Guthrum, of course."

"Guthrum will do nothing, as usual," Urdo said. "He has family ties on both sides and he has not grown old by taking risks. And before you say it, he keeps his sons firmly under his hand and we cannot guess what will happen when he dies."

Raul smiled. "Then let us leave what is out of our control and consider what is close at hand."

"Do you think there is a chance we can split them?" Urdo asked.

Raul shook his head. "Not likely, not today, unless you can get through to Angas somehow. Arling and Ayl should be here tomorrow. So should Ohtar, all being well. Then, possibly. Cinon and Flavien may feel uncomfortable to see themselves sitting beside the invaders, and beside Ayl. But today will just be posturing, I think."

"I do not know if Angas will listen to me at all," Urdo said.

"He was so confused in his letter," I said.

Urdo raised his chin. "He has raised his banner but not yet fought against us," he said. "I think he will find it difficult. I will speak to him if I possibly can."

"Who will go with you today?" Raul asked.

"You must come, of course," Urdo said. "I will take Darien, so they can see him. I will not take Atha, so they can see that there are only Tanagans there today. Cadraith and Sulien should be there, to show Flavien and Cinon that they do not speak for all the kings of the island."

Raul looked at me. "You will bite your tongue before speaking?" he said.

I laughed, I couldn't help it. "I'm sorry. I know I'm one of the least tactful people in the island of Tir Tanagiri, but yes, I will do my best to be quiet unless Urdo tells me to speak."

"There is no need for that," Urdo said, looking vexed. "Sulien is not seventeen any longer, to say what comes into her head without thought. She has been ruling Derwen very well for five years."

"Forgive me," Raul said.

I looked at him. "Have you eaten?" I asked.

"Eaten?" he said, as if the word were an obscure Jarnish one he could not quite recall. "No, not today."

"I will fetch you some porridge," I said, and went off to the cooks, letting them sort out the details of who would accompany Urdo to the afternoon's talks. After delivering Raul's breakfast I dealt with all the problems Govien had saved for me, and then visited the wounded again, though I could do no good.

The talks that afternoon were as useless as Raul had said they would be.

Someone had set up a splendid awning in the little valley, to keep off the sun. It was blue, which was as neutral a color as possible under the circumstances. The banners of all the kings we had fought yesterday stood on the far side of the awning, the Brown Dog of Tathal, the Snake of Tinala, the Crescent Moon of Nene, and the Thorn of Demedia. Angas's Thorn looked to me as if it had been set up a little back from the others. On our side, although we might have flown all our banners and the ala banners as well, Urdo had chosen to set up only the green-and-red banner of the High Kingdom of Tir Tanagiri. The contrast was striking. Urdo, Darien, Cadraith, and I walked down behind Raul and sat in front of our banner. We were there first and so we watched as the others approached.

Father Cinwil brought them. He was wearing a plain brown robe, so he and Raul matched. Flavien walked first behind him, wearing a dark red cloak and a jeweled belt and looking impassive. Then came Cinvar, wearing very splendid armor and looking defiant. Cinon had got fatter since I had last seen him, but his face was just like his father's. His clothes were very splendid and he had the moon embroidered over his heart in silver. He and Cinvar both wore their pebbles prominently outside their clothes. Angas came last, wearing his praefecto's cloak over ordinary clothes. He looked distant and reserved. He looked at me when he bowed to me, and then looked away as if he could not bear the sight of my face. He did not look at Urdo at all.

They all sat down, opposite us, and proceeded to say nothing whatsoever in many words while the sun slowly moved down the sky behind us and our shadows lengthened. Cinvar spoke first, calling Urdo a tyrant and a usurper, ruling without the support of the land and people. He also called him a heretic, which sounded very strange to me. Urdo replied that neither land nor gods were unhappy with him, and only a very few people, whose grievances he would hear. He added that they were in rebellion against him, as rightful king, and in alliance with foreign invaders. He said they must surrender to his mercy and make their oaths again. He said that if they did this he would hear their grievances at the council of the kings. Then Darien, so smoothly that I would hardly have guessed it was rehearsed had I not known already, suggested that the council of the kings should be held twice a year at regular times, so that grievances and the governance of the land could be discussed. Angas spoke in favor of holding regular councils, but demanded that the Breghedan question be settled at one. He said that Urdo must give up his tyrannical practices and return to honor and moderation. I do not remember anything else of substance being said at all that day, though many words were spoken.

When we rose at sunset, agreeing to meet again the next day, Urdo and I tried to speak to Angas. He looked straight through me and turned away to walk off after Flavien, his head high. There were tears glittering in his eyes; I saw them.

"I think we made some progress," Raul said.

"Did you see how Cinon winced whenever we mentioned Arling?" Darien said.

I stared after Angas. I realized I was rubbing the scratch on my arm only when Urdo put his hand on my shoulder to stop me. "He feels trust has been betrayed," he said.

"I killed the one messenger he could trust to come to me," I said. "I can't blame him. But it is hard when friendship turns to hate. It's much worse with him than it is with Flavien, who I never liked."

"He was wearing his praefecto's cloak," Cadraith said, touching his own cloak. "He still knows what that means."

"He may yet see clearly," Urdo said. "Poor Angas. I feel I was unfair to send Morthu back to him."

"I wish he would just talk to us properly," I said.

Raul and Darien were still discussing how they would split the kings when we walked back to camp. The rest of us were very quiet. When Atha and Masarn asked at supper how it had gone, I could find no words to tell them.

— 14 —

Be trustworthy and you will be trusted, seek out associates that
are trustworthy and you will not be betrayed.
    —C. Dalitus, *The Relations of Rulers*

The next day Morthu was there, and it was only then I realized how wonderfully well the negotiations had gone
without him. Whenever he spoke he insinuated, changed the
meaning of what had been said before, twisted words, and set
people arguing. The worst of it was that so few people
seemed to notice. Old Inis's words, "Black heart and poisoned tongue," kept coming into my mind as I sat listening to
him putting in a word and sending the discussion awry. He
had come from Caer Tanaga with Arling, apparently. He sat
between Arling and Angas, dressed very finely, with his hair
and beard silky smooth, smiling, always smiling.

Arling looked like his uncle Sweyn, except that when I had
last seen Sweyn he was pinned to the ground by Galba's
lance. We had not been talking for long before I had decided
that such an accoutrement would have suited Arling well
enough. He wore a pebble prominently on his chest, and
from the way I saw Cinon eyeing it I wondered if this was
part of their alliance.

Urdo raised the issue of Caer Tanaga and the return of the
queen. Arling, avoiding the question of the city, said the
queen was safe, but he would first see the hostages Urdo was
keeping in the alae; and gave a list of names, first among
them Ulf Gunnarsson, Cynrig Athelbertsson, and Pedrog ap
Cinvar.

"These men are not hostages, but my sworn men. I will not
surrender them to your demand," Urdo said, very sternly.

"Then I will keep your queen as pledge of your good conduct toward them," Arling said. Morthu smiled, and I caught
myself shivering to see it. "As heir of Sweyn Rognvaldsson I

am King of Jarnholme and of all the Jarnsmen on this island, and I claim dominion over them all."

Ohtar, sitting beside me, made a little growling noise in his throat. "Bereich does not accept your dominion," he said.

"The men you name are scattered among my alae, but tomorrow I will bring those who are here to speak for themselves," Urdo said.

Then Angas spoke for a long time, prompted by Morthu, about Urdo's supposed high-handedness in dealing with the kings.

That day we achieved even less than the day before.

Again, none of the others would stop and speak to us personally when we finished for the day. We walked back up the hill toward the camp through the warm evening air. We picked up our weapons where we had left them that morning. The guard looked glad to be relieved of them. It had been a very hot, weary day and I was looking forward to bathing in the stream.

"You need to master your hate," Raul said to Darien. Darien had spent most of the day saying little, looking straight ahead, entirely expressionless.

"I *am*," Darien said, through gritted teeth.

Urdo laughed. "I think we would all have been at Morthu's throat several times today if not for the herald-peace."

"Oh, *yes!*" I said, and sighed at the thought of how satisfying his throat would feel under my hands.

"Yes. I do not like being referred to, even sideways, as someone who is loyal because he cannot think for himself," Cadraith said. "And as for Arling's claim over the Jarnish kings, where is Ayl?" We passed through our outer sentry-ring, giving the signals.

"Ayl is coming on as slowly as he can and not be seen as deliberately dragging his feet," Ohtar said. He, too, had been very quiet all day, apart from that one comment and growl. "I spoke to him. He would like to think about Aylsfa and his harvest. He wants nothing more than for Arling to vanish in a puff of air and never have troubled him."

"Then why did he not stay loyal?" Urdo asked.

"It is twelve years since Foreth," Ohtar said, looking at Urdo sideways under lowered eyebrows.

"Yes?" Urdo asked.

"Do you know how many of his huscarls Ayl lost at Foreth?" Ohtar asked. "Most of the men who fell were those he could rely on, the trustworthy great men of his kingdom. He lost a brother and a nephew there. Those who were left, including his brother Sidrok, were those who were less competent, or those he could trust less. Now the sons of the men who died are old enough to fight and to want vengeance. Ayl has done his best to invite in families from Jarnholme who will be loyal. Without them he would be in sad straits indeed. His marriage alliance has helped him a great deal, also. But now that is pulling him in the wrong direction. It is not easy for Ayl. If Arling had landed in Tevin he might have managed it, but with him right there, handing out rich gifts and promising glory? Ayl would have been torn apart by his own people if he had called for loyalty."

"But Aylsfa has prospered in the Peace," Raul said, frowning.

"That is true, and Ayl knows it. His farmers know it, too. But the huscarls? They would find it hard to see from close up, especially those who were thirteen years old at the time of Foreth and are fighting men of twenty-five now, who never have struck a blow in war," Ohtar said. He shook his head at the thought. His hair and beard, grizzled when I had last seen him, were silver now.

Darien raised his chin. "It is like the kings. They would not have risen, but given an excuse to rise, they have."

"What Arling didn't say in front of his Tanagan allies is that he has been offering gold and plunder to any Jarnish king who joins him," Ohtar said.

"You weren't tempted?" Urdo asked, in the calm tones in which he would ask to be passed a jug of water.

"I am too old to be such a fool," Ohtar said, and grinned unexpectedly. "Bereich is firmly under my hand, I have learned the benefits of Peace, I don't believe they can win, and besides, I keep my oaths."

"I never doubted the last," Urdo said. He and Ohtar smiled at each other. "It is good you were there today to give a good example of Jarnsmen living within our Peace. And it will not hurt us at all to have Ulf and Cynrig there tomorrow to do the same."

"Everything Arling said about that is nonsense," Darien said. "If Sweyn had heirs and left them anything, then they would be his son and daughter, who are alive and well in Caer Lind."

"Nephews inherit in Jarnholme," I said. "I know it sounds crazy, but they think better a grown nephew than a half-grown son."

"Oh, and no king would ever die in bed at the age of seventy with their son nearly forty and a father himself," said Cadraith, whose own father had done just that.

Ohtar laughed. "It's not the usual way for kings in Jarnholme, though some of us are hoping to set new traditions on this island. I am four and sixty, and my grandson and heir is two and twenty."

"How old was Alfwin's father, Cella?" Cadraith asked. "His son followed him."

"His youngest son, at that," I said. "But Cella was murdered, and so was his heir. That hardly counts."

We crossed back into the camp then, and almost at once Atha came toward us. "It's strange to be allied with her," Ohtar said, gesturing. "I would guess it would be something keeping the Lord of Angas ranged against you, seeing Atha ap Gren here. We had a hard time of it in Demedia ten years ago."

"I have thought of that," Urdo said. "But she came with help in a time of need. I know you fought against her then, but will you eat with her now?"

"I will," Ohtar said. "I have fought beside her since, and been glad she was there." I wondered what they had said to each other beside Caer Tanaga. They were unlikely allies to find fighting together for Urdo's Peace, who had both fought separately against it.

I went off to bathe and to visit the wounded, who were suffering strange fevers and swellings of their wounds. Some of them were seriously unwell. My scratch was healing, uncomfortably, but definitely healing. These more serious wounds did not appear to be improving. Ap Darel tried to be cheerful in front of the patients but was clearly very worried.

"I think we should send the worst cases out of Segantia," he said, when we were alone. "If the curse is on this land then the charm should work and they should heal when they are out of it."

"If we could send them anywhere," I said. "There are enemies around us. The whole army could move, but a handful of wounded people would be stopped."

"Then the whole army should move out of Segantia," said ap Darel hopefully. "We could be back in Tathal in a day, or in Magor, or even Munew."

"I will suggest it to the High King," I said. "But do not hope for too much. I think we will wait here while these truce talks continue."

"Will they achieve anything, do you think?" ap Darel asked.

"Time for ap Erbin and Luth and ap Meneth to join us here, at the very least," I said.

"More troops will do us little good if the ones we have die of plagues out of the history books," ap Darel said, and walked off, leaving me staring after.

Urdo, as I had expected, said that we could not move without breaking the terms of the truce.

The day after, Ulf and Cynrig came down to the talks with us. Cynrig had asked me what to wear, and I had suggested his ordinary decurio's clothes. Ulf also wore his usual armor, but with his hands bare. This made it very clear that he was wearing the huge worked-gold armring he had worn at Foreth, but which I had never seen on him since. Ohtar wore twice as much gold, and his bearskin cloak, but somehow he did not look anything like as barbaric.

The other side had brought two more people than the day before. One of them was clearly Ayl; I recognized his walk before he was near enough to see his face. The other was a man dressed in red. When he came nearer I saw by his pale skin and dark hair that he was half Jarnish. His cloak had a white walrus embroidered on it, and from that I guessed who he must be. I glanced at Ohtar, whose sign this was, and saw that his normally pale face was so red as to be almost purple. Ohtar's son Aldred had married Rheneth ap Borthas, Flavien's aunt, and after the birth of a son, Aldred had died of poison. This man, who had been brought up in Tinala, must be Ohtar's grandson.

Urdo put his hand on Ohtar's arm. We waited while they seated themselves. The man in red was introduced by Flavien as "Walbern ap Aldred," a form of name which seemed to incense Ohtar still more. In looking at Walbern I had missed seeing how Arling took Ulf's appearance; if it had surprised him he had got over it. He was looking sneeringly at Atha. He hardly glanced up when I introduced Ulf and Cynrig, though Morthu gibed that it was strange to see a Jarnsman prefer to be known as "Fairbeard" than by his father's name.

Most of the morning was spent dealing with Cinvar's supposed grievances, including allegations that we had mistreated his mother at Caer Gloran. It was not until late in the afternoon that Arling made his claims.

"As for Caer Tanaga, I claim it by right of conquest," he said. "I am Sweyn's heir and so High King of the Jarnish Eastlands of Tanagiri. I will rule the Jarnish kings and keep them in order under our own law."

Cinon and Flavien, and Cinvar too, the idiots, all raised their chins affirmatively at this, as if this was what they wanted. This must be how they had justified their alliance, of course. I could hardly believe it. I could feel anger rising up, almost enough to choke me.

"The Jarnsmen will be ruled by their own king in their own place," Cinon said. "And the only time we will need to speak to them will be when there are border disputes."

Arling smiled wolfishly, and I could imagine what sort of speaking and border disputes he was imagining. It was hard to believe anyone could be so stupid. They thought Arling would keep the Jarns out of their lands and didn't care about the law in any others. I tried counting slowly, backward, in Jarnish. I put my hands together in my lap and set my tongue firmly between my teeth so I would not forget and say what I was thinking.

"Bereich denies your overlordship," Ohtar said, rapidly and emphatically, as Arling was drawing breath to say more. "Bereich recognizes Urdo ap Avren as High King of Tir Tanagiri and says that we all live under the King's Peace and the King's Law, Jarn and Tanagan alike."

"If you will accept Arling as your overlord and your son's son here as your heir, Bereich will not be pressed hard," Flavien said smoothly, making a gesture toward Walbern, who smiled and crossed his arms across his chest.

Ohtar raised his head, and the bearskin cloak he always wore moved with his shoulders almost as if he were a real bear. "For thirty years," he said mildly, "you have denied me so much as sight of my son's son. Now you present me with a Tinalan stranger dressed in the shadow of my banner and expect me to give up my loyalty to my land and to the High King?" He drew a deep breath, and raised his voice a little. "The very hills of Bereich would rise up against me if I were such a fool. If you want my kingdom you will have to fight me for it, the same as ever you have needed to, and your father before you. My daughter's son stands ready to defend it after me." His eyes moved to Walbern, who was looking puzzled. "As for you, Walbern Aldredsson, it is too late for you to be my heir. But if you choose to come to Dun Peldir without your uncle's armies, it is not too late for you to find a welcome."

Walbern looked at Ohtar, openmouthed, and then at Flavien, hesitating. Before he could speak, Morthu stepped in.

"Would that be a proper Jarnish welcome, with a sword, or a Tanagan welcome, with poison?" he asked, and laughed, and Cinon and Cinvar laughed with him, and the rest of them laughed one by one, until all that side of the table were laughing, except Ayl and Angas. My hands were trembling with suppressed rage. Aurien was the only one who had tried to poison anyone, and Tanagan or not, she had been their ally. Violation of hospitality should never be something to laugh about. I was shocked to see Cinvar, who had eaten in my mother's hall, laughing at that.

"We were talking about just that difference in the laws," Arling said, with laughter still in the lines of his face. "My uncle Sweyn—"

"Sweyn never claimed what you say you inherited," Ulf interrupted fiercely. "Sweyn was king of Jarnholme by right of birth and by right of acclamation by the assembly of fighting men. He went through the ceremonies of kingship. He left Jarnholme and came here and tried to take this whole land by force, and by blood sacrifice, and he failed, failed utterly. Sweyn was buried with his fallen defenders, on the field of Foreth, which you fled. He did not even win so much as a man's width of the earth of Tir Tanagiri to himself. But he died honorably, as befits a man of the house of Gewis, trying to win himself a wider kingdom. He never claimed any such title or any such overlordship as you claim to have inherited from him. You blacken his name by saying so." I wanted to cheer.

"Blacken his name, brother?" Arling asked, leaning back. "Why should I listen to a traitor telling me so?"

"Oh, go back to Jarnholme and be content," Ulf said. "Aunt Hulda will die one day and let you rule for yourself; you need not cheat and lie your way to someone else's kingdom to do so. To what do you say am I traitor? To you as self-appointed king of all Jarnsmen everywhere? It is no treachery to be in the losing side of a battle. Sweyn was dead, which takes back all oaths I made to him. I made my peace with the High King, I swore to serve him, and I have."

Cynrig raised his chin. "I too. And I have prospered in Urdo's service, and will marry a Tanagan girl of rank at Midwinter." I kept my eyes straight ahead. I had been told about his betrothal already. I suppose decurio is a rank, and she was serving as key-keeper, but that was not what was normally meant. Bradwen's parents were farmers in Derwen. Arling locked eyes with Ulf and ignored Cynrig.

"Will you still claim dominion over all Jarnsmen?" Urdo asked. I happened to catch Ayl's eye, and he squirmed. Then he looked away and set his jaw.

"Yes," Arling said. "Even of these traitors." He sounded as if he meant it absolutely.

"Now that you see they are not hostages, we could speak of ransoming the queen," Darien said. It was the first time he had spoken for hours, and everyone turned to look at him. The blood rose in his cheeks, but he did not look away from Arling.

"What ransom would you give for her?" Arling asked.

"Yes, what are you prepared to give to get her back?" Morthu echoed.

It was a difficult question. With Caer Tanaga Arling had captured the greater part of our treasure. "Safe passage for you and your people back to Jarnholme, with what coin you have gained of this expedition, and peace between us thereafter," Darien said.

Arling laughed. "That I could have already, boy, if I wished it," he said. My hands twitched, sorry my sword was set down outside the bounds of the herald-peace. He turned to Urdo. "Acknowledge me king of the Jarnish Eastlands, and I will return both your queen and your city."

It was so quiet that I could tell that Ohtar was holding his breath.

"You set a high price on one woman, to think you could have what otherwise you would have to fight a war to gain," Urdo said. Ohtar exhaled, audibly.

"One woman?" Morthu said, and looked at me insolently.

"Yes, we have heard you have another, but the queen is prettier," Arling said. I gritted my teeth. Darien gripped the table in both hands, so hard that his knuckles whitened.

Urdo, amazingly, laughed. "Talk about things you understand," he said. "Arling Gunnarsson, I will offer you gold for the queen's release. How much would you have? In the old laws of Jarnholme the price is half that of a king, the same as for a huscarl. Will you take four panniers' worth of gold?"

"I will consider it," Arling said.

"It is time," Father Cinwil said. We all rose and bowed.

"A word, brother," Ulf said, in Jarnish, as we left the shade of the awning. "A word here, outside the peace-holy place." Arling hesitated, and turned and came toward Ulf. We all waited, standing in two uneasily wavering lines.

"Yes?" Arling asked. Now they were standing, everyone could see that Ulf was a hand taller than his brother.

"You will not go back to Jarnholme?"

"No. Will you give up this foreign king and come and serve me?"

"Never, so long as you are a fool," Ulf said, and the contempt was clear in his words. "Will you persist in this breaking of the Peace, this taking guidance from the sorcerer?"

Arling glanced at Morthu. "He is no sorcerer but a holy man," he said, touching his pebble. "And what should I care for your Peace?"

"You should be king enough to care," Ulf said, turning the armring he wore with his fingers. "This is our grandfather's armring. I am your brother still, your older brother, and though I cannot be king, I am still head of the family."

"For what that is worth to a childless man who limps," Arling agreed, cautiously.

"By the blood we share," Ulf said, facing Arling and raising his hands, palm up, so that his arms were spread wide. Behind me somewhere, Ohtar made a noise, and the late light of the sun caught and burned on the great gold armring of the House of the Kings of the Jarns, bright enough to make my eyes water.

Ulf's voice was strong, and very clear. "By my death, I curse you; by the shades of the fallen, I curse you; by the graves of our fathers, I curse you; the cold hand grasps you strong—never shall you lead to victory, never shall you rest hallowed, never shall your line survive. Thurr smite you; Frith wither you; Fritha spurn you; Uller hunt you; Freca blind you; Noth drown you; Tew slay you; Hel rot you; Fury rend you; Doom find you."

Ulf turned his palms down, slowly. All the time he had been speaking, color had been leaving Arling's face, until the pebble he wore was darker than he himself was.

Ulf lowered his arms to his sides and spat hard at the feet of his brother. Arling bent almost as a man struck hard in the stomach would bend, though the spittle did not touch him but only landed on his shadow. His pale eyes flashed. "You have no power, no power to curse me," he said, but his voice cracked. He looked to Morthu, who smiled and made a gesture with his hands.

"There is no harm in such cursing, it is nothing but words," Morthu said, also speaking Jarnish. What Emer had told me about curses came back to me, and I knew he was wrong. "If it will hurt anyone it will be himself. Let us think no more about it and go back to Caer Tanaga, and see whether the queen wishes to join these traitors and tyrants and adulterers."

Anger had been building in me all afternoon, and I was angry then. But that was not why I leapt. I could have taken one more meaningless insult, and I hardly knew for sure what the Jarnish word meant. But I was nearer than Darien, and out of the corner of my eye I could see him preparing to move. Before he could do anything to break the truce beyond mending, I leapt toward Morthu. I did not touch him. There was triumph and just a little fear in his eyes. I could tell that he had been hoping to provoke me, or one of us. I could see that Arling and Ayl were both moving to help him. As much as I wanted to, I did not break his neck. I moved my hand very slowly and put it on his arm, just at the edge of his cloak, where it was bare. We must have looked like people about to go in to dinner together. He stayed absolutely still, but there was no hidden laughter in his eyes now.

"You say there is no harm in cursing?" I said, as loudly as I could. I saw Arling stop, then take a step away. "Well then, I, Sulien ap Gwien, will curse you, by the gods of my people, and we will see what comes of it. I will curse you, Morthu ap Talorgen, such that if you go to Caer Tanaga it will be your death."

As I said it I reached out to the Lord of Light and to the Mother and to the Shield-Bearer, and I wove their names with mine and Morthu's into the curse. Then I felt the threads of the world shifting so that what I had said was true, and if Morthu went to Caer Tanaga he would die. I knew this as clearly as I knew that if I dropped a stone it would fall to the ground. I need not drop it, but if I did, it would fall. He need not go, but if he did, that would be the end of him. I don't know why I picked going to Caer Tanaga especially, except that he had just said he would go there, in his insult to the queen. As I spoke the last syllable there was a blinding flash of light. I dropped my hand, and stood blinking.

Morthu was lying on the grass. He must have dropped suddenly while everyone closed their eyes. "I am slain!" he wailed. "The demon ap Gwien has attacked me!"

"A demon!" Cinon shouted. "A demon, I always said she was."

I looked around. Morthu was on the ground. Everyone else in front of me was backing slowly away. "I didn't touch him," I said.

"Does this break the truce, Father Cinwil?" Morthu asked, in a faint but clearly audible voice. I could have stamped on his throat right then. I was ready to do so if the truce was broken.

"I shall have to consult," Father Cinwil said fussily, coming to Morthu and checking him for wounds. Naturally he found nothing.

"I didn't touch him," I whispered to Raul as he came past me to join the other priest. He looked at me as if I were a toad someone had put into his bed.

"Morthu ap Talorgen is unhurt," Urdo said loudly, in the voice he used when he didn't want argument. "The Lord of Derwen may have been rash to curse him, but he himself said curses have no power. Sulien ap Gwien is the queen's champion, and it was too much for her, as it was hard for all of us, to hear ap Talorgen so malign her."

"But the light!" Angas said, his voice accusatory. "All that you say is well enough maybe; I do not think much of Gunnarsson and Morthu's treatment of the queen myself. And anyone can lose their temper. But that light!"

"That was not my light," I said. Ayl was making a Thunderer sign with his fist, and moving away from me.

"I will never sit down again with that demon," Cinon said, clutching at his pebble.

"Ap Talorgen is unhurt," Father Cinwil said, at last, helping Morthu to his feet. "We will consult, and inform you."

We walked back up the hill, without Raul. "I'm sorry," I said to Urdo as we picked up our weapons.

"That's all right," he said. "If you had killed him, we'd have had to fight right away, and probably on bad ground."

"I wasn't apologizing for not killing him," I said.

Urdo grinned. "I don't think they will conclude that the truce is broken. And if you are a demon you won't have to sit under that awning in the heat listening to all of that."

"Can I be a demon, too?" Ohtar asked in a deep rumble. "I don't understand what they think they'll gain. Do you think Arling will take gold for the queen?"

"It's possible," Urdo said, not looking at any of us.

"Do we have that much gold?" Cadraith asked. "Back in Caer Asgor I have some, but not here."

"Caer Segant is nearer, and not lacking in gold," Urdo said. They went on up the hill. I was fumbling with the buckle of my sword belt.

"That was a real curse," Darien said to me, waiting.

"Yes," I said.

"Gunnarsson's was a real curse, too," he said.

Ulf had only gone a few steps up the hill, his ax in his hand. He stopped and looked up for the first time since he had cursed Arling. "It was," he said. He looked at Darien, and then at me. "I am so angry with Arling for being such a fool, for spoiling everything we have been building here. And I'm so sorry I killed your brothers, Praefecto. If I hadn't, none of this would have happened."

He was right, of course. If my brother Darien had lived, everything would have been different.

"It was not by your own will," I said awkwardly.

"I killed your brother Galba, too," he said. "I don't know if you ever knew that. At Foreth."

I hadn't known. But it was a battle; we had been on different sides. It was a good thing nobody had told Aurien. "Why are you telling me this?"

"He wants you to be the instrument of doom that kills his brother," Darien said, as if this should be obvious to a gatepost.

I looked at Ulf, who was swinging his ax nervously.

"Oh," I said. "Oh. All right then. If I get the chance, I have no least objection in the world."

Delightful is a tree in full leaf
a wonder are the roses of Summer,
when a beautiful woman passes near
somebody is watching.

How can I sleep when your soft breathing
fills the air of the hall?
Alone in the dark I long for you.
Everything reminds me.

Delightful are the golden leaves
a wonder are the berries of Autumn,
when a beautiful woman speaks
somebody is listening.

How can I see when you are my horizon?
When your shadow falls
between me and the wide world?
Everything reflects you.

Delightful are the bare branches
a wonder are snows of Winter,
when a beautiful woman is sad
somebody takes notice.

How can your insolent husband ignore you?
How can he slight your honour
when I would long to give you
everything your heart seeks?

Delightful are the buds on the trees
a wonder is the promise of warmth,

when a beautiful woman looks up
somebody is waiting.
    —*Spring*, Cian ap Gwinth Gwait

Emer and her troops had come into camp while we had been at the discussions. She and Atha were glaring at each other over Masarn's head as we approached Urdo's tent. Emer had her hand pressed to her face, which was usually a sign that she was unhappy.

"Good Merciful Lord, have they ever been on the same side before?" Darien murmured to me.

"Briefly, when they invaded us after Foreth," I replied. Darien rolled his eyes and we went forward with Urdo, Cadraith, and Ohtar to greet them. Ulf and Cynrig left us to go back to their friends. I envied them.

"I have settled the troops from Dun Morr near your ala, by the stream," Masarn said to me when we had all exchanged greetings.

"A good idea," I said. My ala were more used to them than the others, at least. And that arrangement would keep them far away from Atha, which was nothing but good news. Most of Atha's troops were still around Caer Tanaga, but enough were here to make it very awkward if Isarnagan rivalries took fire.

After a little while of exquisitely painful politeness, I excused myself to bathe and visit the wounded. Cadraith went off to his own ala. Emer came with me, to settle her troops, she said. I noticed she was still limping a little from the wound she took in the fight in the woods. "What is that woman doing here?" she asked, as soon as we were out of earshot.

"She has come to avenge Conal," I said.

Emer laughed and tossed her hair back in a way that made me think that she was very near tears. "Avenge Conal," she said. "Atha the Hag to avenge Conal?"

"He was her herald," I said reasonably. I stopped walking, and so did she. "Emer, I know you want to avenge Conal yourself. I value your troops being here very greatly. The help you and Lew have given me in this time of trouble is beyond reward. I understand that you are from Connat and have a long-standing quarrel with Oriel." I did not say that she had put aside this, and much greater causes for quarreling, in the case of Conal. "But do not quarrel with Atha now. Urdo needs her."

"I will not quarrel with her if she does not quarrel with me, but do not ask me to eat with her," she said. "And when we fight, do not put me next to her in the battle."

"Battle command will not be up to me, but I will tell Urdo what you have asked," I said. "As for eating, that should be easy enough, if there is a bloodfeud between you."

Emer put her hand to her scar. "Does this count?" she asked.

It didn't, of course, as long as it had happened in the usage of war. But she knew that as well as I did. "Emer—" I began hesitantly.

"Conal would never have wanted Atha to avenge him," she said quietly.

"Conal would not have wanted you getting yourself killed, either," I said bluntly. "He said so to me, when he was dying."

"It isn't his choice," she said, staring straight ahead. "You don't understand. When you love somebody that much and they are gone." She shrugged.

"But you have responsibilities still," I said. "Dun Morr, your daughter, Lew."

She looked at me as if I were reminding her that the floor would need sweeping and the eggs gathering. "Have you ever known someone and when you are with them it is as if the sun has come out?" she asked. "And when they are not there, you are in the shadow? So that a room that does not have them in it is the same as an empty room? And when you see them you know that here the patterns of the world make sense again, because you are together? My whole life—"

It had been a very difficult day. I was fighting down the urge to tell her she was talking like a spoilt child, and not like an adult and a queen who should understand duty. It was a great relief to me when she stopped talking, in the middle of the sentence, with her mouth still open. I turned around to see what had startled her so much.

Teilo and Inis were walking toward us, talking furiously. Inis was waving his arms about with great emphasis. Otherwise the camp seemed much as usual. Someone was cooking lamb not far away, and the smell made me hungry.

"Inis ap Fathag!" Emer said, hardly above a whisper.

"He's calling himself Inis, Grandfather of Heroes, now," I said. "He came with Atha."

Emer laughed. "Oh, that is so like him. He's as cracked as a pot; he has been for years, though if you don't ask him questions he sometimes talks sense. I knew him when I was young and was fostered in Oriel, before the war. But I am amazed to see him here. I thought he'd never leave his trees again. Conal told me he hasn't left the grove since Darag died."

They were almost close enough to speak to, and I could hear Teilo's raised voice: "I don't believe that God has turned against the High King, but how can I blame people for questioning?"

They came to a halt next to where we were standing. "Greetings, Mother Teilo, Inis," I said, bowing.

"Well met with the Merciful Lord's blessing, ap Gwien, ap Allel," Teilo replied, bowing to us in turn. She was looking well. She had been lined and ancient ever since I had known her; five years had not made much difference. She looked like a hazel tree, old and gnarled but still capable of standing up to the winter wind. The brown robe she wore only emphasized the comparison.

"Greetings, Mother Teilo," Emer said. "And a good day and a welcome to the island of Tir Tanagiri to you, Grandfather of Heroes."

"Greetings, Granddaughter," Inis said, smiling at Emer.

"What, will you claim every hero you meet as a grandchild now?" asked Teilo, smiling. "What about ap Gwien, here?"

To my surprise Inis bowed deeply to me. "Greetings, hero," he said. I could feel my cheeks heating. "But as for little Emer," he said, turning back to Teilo, "I am entitled. There are more worlds where she marries one of my grandsons than worlds where she doesn't. Even in this world—" Emer took a rapid breath. I closed my eyes, expecting him to blithely betray all Emer's secrets to Teilo. "—she was betrothed to Darag, before he so rashly married Atha," he concluded, smiling wickedly at Emer.

"Is the Dowager Rowanna here with you?" I asked Teilo, to cover my embarrassment.

"She is here in the camp," Teilo said. "We arrived from Caer Segant only a few hours ago. She is resting from her ride and will greet her son later. I have been to visit some of the wounded." She shook her head sadly. "Inis and I have been discussing this terrible curse."

"Urdo told me it lay on the whole land of Segantia," I said.

"What curse is this?" Emer asked.

"It is the weapon-rot," Teilo said. "Those who took wounds in the battle are not healing as they should because the charm to protect against the weapon-rot is not reaching the gods."

"All the gods?" Emer asked, clearly appalled.

"Ah, there you have put your finger on it," Teilo said approvingly. "It is not reaching the White God, Ever Merciful."

"It is not reaching the Lord of Healing either," I said.

"No?" Teilo looked at me sharply. "And by what name are you calling him?"

"Graun," I said, surprised that she would ask such a personal question.

"Graun," Inis echoed.

"And have you only sung the charm, or tried to reach for him as well?" she asked.

"Yes, both. My way felt blocked. It was very unusual." I did not want to tell them about trying to send Darien back, or when Morwen was trying to kill me, but those were the only other times I had ever met anything that blocked my way to the gods.

"I have been looking for some heathen Jarnsman in the

camp who knows enough of healing to do more than sing the charm by rote, and who will speak to me enough to name what god they are calling, but I have not found one yet. Either they clutch their pebbles tightly and ask me to pray for them, or they will hardly speak to me at all."

"Ohtar will know," I said. "I will take you to him and ask him to speak to you."

"But the charm is not working for the heathens, either," Teilo said. "So whatever name they are using, that god is not hearing their request."

"That is much too wide in scope to be a curse," Emer said. "Unless a God has cursed us."

"I don't feel the Gods are angry. And Urdo said it was a spell," I said. Over Emer's shoulder I could see some of Cadraith's ala exercising their horses and laughing as if the world were nothing but sunny evenings on grassy slopes.

"It is some sort of sorcery, clearly enough," Teilo said.

"No spell could close all the eyes of all the gods," Inis said.

"I agree, but why are people's wounds rotting in front of our eyes?" Teilo asked. "The same charm will reach any god, if you weave their name into it. It is rare enough to do it, for anyone. What use to ask Graun for help fishing when it is Nodens who understands how to fill your nets? But there are charms I was taught as a girl to sing to Breda, which I have been singing to the White God and having them answered."

"There are a lot of people in Tir Isarnagiri who know all about that, since you sent St. Chanerig to us," Inis said.

"Saint, indeed. I didn't send him, and well you know it," Teilo said, unperturbed. "The dear Lord never spoke a word to me about your island; my concern has always been with my own people."

"Are you saying that it makes no difference what god you worship?" Emer asked.

Teilo and Inis both turned on her so fiercely that she took a step backward. "It makes all the difference in the world!" Teilo said. "When I came to realize that there was one God greater than the others, who we could all worship together, whose mercy and forgiveness could set all things right, it changed everything."

"It is people that are the same," Inis said.

"The charm is the same, you mean?" Emer asked, almost timidly. Hardly like a question at all.

"Yes. The charm itself is the same, except for the name, though the answer may be a little different. How could a charm be stopped?"

"So is the spell stopping the charm?" I asked. "As if it were a spear I reached toward the gods and the spell blocks the spearpoint?"

"If you pray to Graun, and if I pray to the Merciful Lord, and Inis prays to Miach, and none of the charms are heard, then yes, it seems as if the spell is blocking the charm itself from working," Teilo said. She was very free with the names of the gods in her speech. The gods are not people who need to keep their names close, but it made me uncomfortable all the same. It didn't seem polite.

"The charm, or the shape you make in your mind," Inis said, looking sharply at her, more focused on the moment than I had yet seen him. "The spearpoint ap Gwien spoke of is the shape your mind makes to reach. If something is preventing people making that shape, that is just mind clouding."

"If it is clouding minds all over Segantia, why isn't it affecting Cinvar's wounded?" Emer asked.

I had not thought of that before. "Maybe Morthu has taught them a different charm," I said. "Arling said he was a holy man; he must have done something to get that reputation. If the shape of the usual charm is being blocked then a different charm might work."

"Can Rowanna find a different charm?" Emer asked.

"Rowanna?" Teilo frowned. "It will be very hard for her, but I will help her if necessary. I was hoping we might find somebody who knows a different charm. Do you know any other charms that might work? Do you think Ohtar might? How about you, ap Allel?"

"I have never made much study of healing," Emer said.

I tried to remember. Every charm I knew seemed so specific, and useless for anything else.

"The elder charm for health," Inis said, his voice remote.

I looked at him cautiously. "The charm that begins 'The elder tree grows near the water's edge'?" I asked, trying not to make it sound like a question. It was a charm Garah had taught me, not one of my mother's. "But it is no protection from weapon-rot, it is just a charm for strength against sickness. I sing it over people who are ailing, to help them recover."

"It keeps infection from striking when someone is laid low," Inis said.

"I thought you said this was not a disease," Emer said, frowning.

"It is not a disease," Teilo said. "Disease does not strike the wounded. And that we would know how to deal with. Let us try this elder charm and see if it helps the wounded."

We started to walk on down toward the tents ap Darel had set up for the wounded of my ala. When we got there it was clear that things were worse even than they had been that morning. The moans and restless cries of the wounded came to us even from outside, and the air was heavy with the smell of sickness.

My trumpeter, Berth, happened to be the first of the wounded we came to. He was lying on a bed of bracken, in a light and uneasy sleep. The gash on his leg was bound up, but his flesh was swollen angrily red, even outside the bandages. "It would take tremendous power to do a spell that affects everyone like that," Emer said, looking at it.

"He has never had any hesitation about killing for power," Inis said.

"Who?" I asked, forgetting not to ask direct questions.

"The black-hearted poison-tongued son of the witch-queen who has courted pus to do this thing," Inis replied, unwinding the bandage to reveal poor Berth's festering cut. Berth stirred and muttered in his sleep, but did not wake. I wished Inis would tell Urdo that it was Morthu who had done it.

I put everything out of my mind except the need for healing. I put my hand on Berth's shoulder and sang the elder charm, which addresses the Lord of Healing as Rhis, planter of the elder tree, most beneficial of all trees for the making of medicines, asking for strength and protection against infection, and a return to ease and health. I put Berth's name into the charm, and my own, and called on the Lord of Healing with all my heart. I felt tired when I finished, but I had felt my call being answered.

Berth opened his eyes and looked at me. "Lord Sulien," he said, and then he yawned. "I am terribly thirsty," he said. Emer quickly brought water for him, and as he drank it I looked at his leg. It looked much like the scratch on my arm, a cut that was being slow to heal. The skin was pink and a little shiny, but the puffiness and festering had gone out of it.

"I will tell Flerian you are feeling better," I said as we left Berth to move on down the tent.

"She will come to see me later; she is a good girl," he said. "I will tell her you healed me. Thank you, Praefecto."

I got on with singing the charm over the wounded. I realized after a little while that Inis had moved off to sing the charm himself, where he was most needed. Teilo listened to me singing the charm a few more times before she moved ahead to sing it for herself. Emer stayed with me, her lips moving. As I left the side of a woman who seemed to me to be dying she stopped me.

"That is the hardest charm I ever heard," she said. "I am not usually slow at learning such things, but the words and tune of that one seem to run straight out of my head. I am no use here; I will go and see to my troops."

I found it was the same with ap Darel, when he came to me. He tried his best to learn the charm but could not. I sang it over as many of the wounded as I could that night, and then rolled into my tent very late, absolutely exhausted. It was only when I was lying down quietly that I realized I had forgotten to eat.

The next day I was not wanted at the negotiations. Urdo

and Darien came down to my tent and ate breakfast with me. Urdo invited me to eat with them in the evening and hear about the progress of the talks. Then Teilo dragged me off to heal Cadraith's wounded. It seemed that some of them refused to let her near them, and the rest refused me. Theological arguments were almost as thick in the air of their tents as the flies. I tried to ignore them and concentrate on the charm, but Teilo kept being distracted and drawn into them. Doing the healing tired me much more than it usually would. It was almost evening when I went to visit my own wounded, and found Berth's slash reddening again and all the work to do over again. I could have wept. Nobody was as bad as they had been the day before, but the wounds all seemed on the point of turning bad again. I sent ap Darel with my excuses to Urdo, and sang the charm until my voice cracked.

I was far down in sleep when Urdo woke me that night. I came awake bone weary from a dream of training long ago. I thought for a moment it was Osvran come to drag me off to a night exercise. I blinked at Urdo while he explained that Raul was sick. "I know you're tired, but it seems the only people who can sing this charm are you and Teilo and Inis. Teilo is ninety years old and Inis is—"

"An unpredictable loon, and asleep among Atha's Isarnagans," I said, sitting up and running my fingers through my hair. "I am coming; there is no need to apologize. I didn't know Raul was wounded."

"He's not," Urdo said. "That's what worries me. He has a fever."

"A fever?" I was still slow with sleep.

"I cannot heal it," Urdo said, simply.

I pulled a shift over my head and stood up as I stuck my arms through. "Where is he?" I asked.

"In my tent," Urdo said. We walked through the sleeping camp, answering several challenges from sentries. I was glad to see them so alert. The moon was almost half full and from her position I could tell it was well after midnight. It was chilly, even though it was high summer. I should have brought my cloak. I stifled a yawn.

There was a lantern in Urdo's tent. Darien sat cross-legged in the circle of light, washing Raul's face. Raul looked terrible. His skin was almost gray, and looked tight and stretched. I put my hand on his forehead and pulled it away almost as if I had been burned.

"When did he get like this?" I asked. "He was fine yesterday."

"He fell asleep after dinner," Urdo said. "I thought he had tired himself out with the negotiations and let him lie where he was." He indicated the overflowing box of papers where they had been working. "Then he woke me, calling out in the night, and when I came over he was as you see him."

"He hasn't been right for days," Darien said, very quietly. "He hasn't been eating or sleeping, he's been driving himself too hard. This fever is new, but he hasn't been well. He's been rubbing his head all day as if it aches."

"I don't know if the elder charm will do any good," I warned. "And even if it does, it only seems to work for a time, as I sent ap Darel to tell you earlier."

I reached out to Raul again and began to sing the charm. As soon as I did he opened his eyes and started to struggle feebly. "No," he muttered. "No. Not her. Never. Tell Father Gerthmol." I stumbled in the words and hesitated as he fought against my touch.

"Father Gerthmol is in Thansethan," Darien said calmly, taking hold of Raul's shoulders. "And he is too old to ride out this far. My mother knows a charm that can heal you."

"No," Raul said, struggling against Darien's hands. "Not her. No heathen charms. The demon. The one-eyed demon!"

"Mother Teilo says the charms are the same," I said, but he didn't seem to hear me.

"No!" he said, shrinking back and whimpering.

I looked at Urdo, who sighed tiredly. "I wish you wouldn't be such a fool, Raul," he said. "You know Sulien isn't a demon."

Raul muttered something with a lot of "No" and "not her" in it, which finished, "Always trying to come between us."

"Teach me the charm," Urdo said to me. I sang the charm through, feeling it a very fragile thing against the weight of fever pressing on Raul. Strangely, my singing it without touching him seemed to quiet him; he stopped struggling and lay quiet.

Then Urdo put his hand on Raul's head and sang the charm through, naming both the White God and the Lord of Healing. It was obvious at once that it had helped; Raul's breathing was easier and his color was almost normal. He seemed to be sleeping gently.

"Did you hear it?" Urdo asked Darien.

"I think so," Darien said, smoothing Raul's forehead and drawing a blanket over him. "Why is it so hard to hold onto? I heard it through twice and it is as if the words want to slip out of my mind."

"I think that's this curse on Segantia making it difficult," I said. "I can sing that charm, but it makes me very weary. Emer and ap Darel and the others who have tried couldn't remember it at all."

"I am glad I can hold it," Urdo said. "I can help you with the healing when I am not at the negotiations."

"I will try," Darien said. "Do you want me to stay and help with Raul?"

"I think he will sleep," Urdo said, looking down at his old friend. "I think we should all do the same."

"I will go back to my tent, then," Darien said. "If you need me again, just call me."

"You won't need me either," I said, standing. "But how did the negotiations go?"

Urdo shook his head. "The only good thing is that they all want to air all their grievances, and it is buying us time. You are doing more good here."

I could not see Darien's face now that he was out of the circle of light. "Arling looked like a broken man today," he said. "We mostly heard Cinvar's grievances, none of which were worth the air he wasted on them."

We said good night and I walked back through the sleeping camp to my tent. Dew soaked both the grass and my feet. Even though I was tired it took me a long time to get warm enough to go back to sleep.

— 16 —

Where are my weapons, where are my warriors
where are my walls of strong stone set with iron?
  —From "Queen Alinn"

The next two days I spent singing charms while people squabbled about theology. How the charm worked or didn't work; why the charm was hard to learn; the difference between charms, hymns, and praise songs; who could have cursed us and whether we deserved it: all were suddenly subjects of widespread and immediate interest. People who scarcely thought about charms except when they'd cut their finger, lost their blanket, or wanted to light a fire, suddenly had urgent opinions on how they worked. The theory that the White God had turned away from Urdo seemed to be more popular now that Raul was ill. Teilo took his place at the negotiations, which was good, Darien told me, because she bullied Father Cinwil and they made some progress in getting small points settled. This did not compensate me for the loss of her charm-singing ability and theological authority in the sick tents. When the negotiations were over every day, she and Urdo and Darien came in and sang charms until we were all too weary to sing any more.

Others went down with the same sickness Raul had. The elder charm seemed to help, but they remained weak and feverish, and found it hard to digest food. Feeding the invalids was made more difficult by the lack of food. We were in no immediate danger of starvation, but we were down to salt fish and acorn cakes, which are hardly palatable at the best of times. On the second day more supply wagons came in from Caer Segant, which meant we could give them gruel. In the evening of the same day, Luth and ap Erbin arrived with their alae. Ap Erbin seemed more horrified that we were allied with Atha than by the plague. After talking to Urdo about it at great length over dinner, he and Alswith came to my tent to complain about it just as I was going to bed.

"I can't believe it!" he said. Marriage, or just the passing of time, had caused ap Erbin to gain weight. He looked now as if it would take a very substantial blow to topple him. Combined with his missing ear it gave him the look of a formidable warrior. "You weren't in Demedia, you don't understand, but how could Urdo bring himself to do it?"

My hair had come unfastened and was straggling over my face. I pushed it back wearily. "I think you don't understand the desperation of the situation down here."

"I do," he said. "I don't know why we're talking instead of fighting, now that the Peace has been broken, but I do see how bad it is. But even so; Atha ap Gren! The soldiers who stoned the White God would be a more popular choice of alliance with my ala."

"We didn't invite Atha in, as Urdo already told you," I said. "She just came. And we were glad enough to see her on the field. As for why we're talking, it was to make time for you to come up." I struggled to swallow a yawn.

"Yes?" Alswith asked. Unlike ap Erbin she seemed almost unchanged since I had last seen her. The flame-colored hair that gave her her usename was bound tightly against her head; she had been wearing her helmet for riding. She frowned. "So why are they talking? Who are they waiting for?"

"That's a chilling thought," I said.

"Where is my uncle?" ap Erbin said, leaping on the implication.

"Custennin of Munew remains at home in Caer Thanbard, so far as anyone knows, and Thurrig is with him," I said.

"I suppose they could be waiting for Marchel," Alswith said.

"I have no idea where she is, but I don't think she could bring enough force to make any difference, unless she has fresh troops from Narlahena," I said. "We broke her alae pretty thoroughly; she doesn't have more than a couple of pennons worth of armigers."

"Fresh troops from Narlahena might land at Caer Thanbard," ap Erbin said. "I should ask Urdo if he wants me to go down there and talk some sense into my uncle."

"If he would risk as much," Alswith said, biting her lip.

Ap Erbin put his arm around her. "Urdo knows my loyalties," he said.

"He must have thought he knew Angas's," Alswith said. "Sulien, I can see you're exhausted, but do you think we'll attack tomorrow?"

"You'll have to ask Urdo. I've been up here all day," I said. "But Alfwin should be here in three or four more days. Also the militia of Derwen are on their way; they should be here soon. Urdo said something about being able to agree to fight even if we couldn't agree to make peace."

"I could go to Caer Thanbard and back in four days," ap Erbin said.

"You'll have to talk to Urdo," I said, and yawned.

"Does he really think they'll agree to give back the queen?" Alswith asked dubiously.

"I think Urdo still hopes he might split their alliance if they can only see sense," I said. "What we must avoid is anything that would split ours."

"Oh, don't worry, I won't insult Atha to her face," ap Erbin said, picking up my meaning immediately. "If Urdo says we need her, then we do. But it's a bad pass if it's come to this, fighting our old friends with our old enemies at our side."

"I wonder if Angas feels the same," I said, and felt sure that he did. I still wished I could speak to Angas.

Urdo must have told ap Erbin he was needed at the talks, because that was where the two of them spent the next few days. The work with the wounded became a little less terrible as some of them recovered. As long as someone sang the elder charm over them daily they healed slowly and naturally. I still spent all my time at it, but it felt less like trying to dam a river with a pair of stirrups. On the second day after ap Erbin came in, Raul was well enough to leave the sick tent. On the third day Alfwin arrived, and so did the militia of Derwen. I was glad to see them. With all this force of infantry we were as strong now as the other side. Urdo thought so, too. The day after that he spent the day thrashing out an agreement for a pitched battle to be fought the next day. They were arguing over location, Raul told me when he came up briefly to fetch some maps.

Rowanna came down to the sick tent to remind me to be ready for her feast that night. In the alae the custom was to feast after battle, not before it, but she had argued that the militia of Segantia would expect to feast before. Urdo had agreed, on condition that she arranged everything and provided the food. She had been fussing about it ever since. I looked down at my clothes, stained with blood and worse things from the sick tents, and agreed that I would come, as befitted the dignity of my position.

In the afternoon, when Urdo was still at the truce talks, Garah arrived.

Masarn came to the sick tent to fetch me. He waited until I had finished singing the charm then put his hand on my shoulder. "Sulien, can you come with me please? It's an emergency."

I knew immediately that something was really wrong, because he said the words without even the lightest touch of irony. I washed my hands in the bowl ap Darel insisted on bringing me. It made no difference, of course, as the plague was not a disease, but it hurt nothing. Ap Darel said it raised the patients' hearts, and anything that did that was worth the bother. I followed Masarn out of the tent, leaving behind me a rising murmur of speculation. "What is it?" I asked.

"Ap Erbin's scouts thought they'd caught a spy sneaking in, and she insisted on being taken to him personally before she'd speak. As she didn't have any weapons, they did it. It's Garah, and she refuses to say anything until you are there," he said. "He's taken her to Urdo's tent. She wants Urdo too. I'll go down and see if he can come; I think it's that important from the way ap Erbin was looking."

"Garah?" I blinked. "Where has she come from? Why is she alone?"

"I have no more idea than you, but I'm sure she wouldn't have come if it wasn't important," he said. "You go up to Urdo's tent, and I'll go down to the truce talks and see if I can get Raul to recognize me. I can't just interrupt, but that might work."

I walked up through the usual bustle of the camp. Rowanna and Atha were sitting together by Rowanna's tent. I bowed to them as I passed. When I came to Urdo's tent I scratched at the flap, drew back the curtain, and went straight in.

Garah and ap Erbin were sitting just inside. I recognized her at once, though she was dressed as the lowest sort of servant, and absolutely filthy. Under the dirt on her face were marks of bruises. Her eyes were red-rimmed as if she had been weeping. She looked up when she saw me, but she could barely manage a smile. "I tried to get her to come, but she just wouldn't," she said.

"What?" I blinked. "Who? Have you come alone all the way from Bregheda?"

Now it was her turn to look at me stupidly. "Bregheda? I came from there almost a month ago, as soon as Urdo sent for me, just in time to be captured with Caer Tanaga. I escaped from the city last night."

"From the city?" I echoed. "Are you all right? Is that your disguise?" I sat down and let the curtain fall closed, leaving just one bar of sunlight across the floor of the tent.

"Disguise?" She looked down at herself. "Oh, no, this is Morthu's idea of how to treat people as they deserve. He's been having me scrub floors for the temerity of pretending to be queen of Bregheda, as he put it. I admit I did spend a little while thinking of what Glyn would do to him for that, and how the muster of Bregheda, such as it is, would avenge the insult, and how you would, Sulien. But he's quite right that my parents are farmers and I used to be a groom, and I have scrubbed plenty of floors before and it just isn't as awful as Morthu imagines. It doesn't do any good to stay angry about that sort of thing. And it did give me a chance to move about, rather than being stuck in the one room like the others. Elenn

tried to stop him, but by then I'd realized it made more sense
to do it and I told her so. That's the least of what he's been
doing anyway. It doesn't matter."

"It does matter," I said, ablaze with indignation. I wished
I'd killed Morthu when I'd had the chance.

"I'm sure Alswith has some clothes she can lend you," ap
Erbin said, a little tentatively.

"I don't care about clothes!" Garah said, so loudly that it
was startling, almost a shout. "How long will Urdo be?"

"It depends whether he can leave the talks now," I said. "If
he can't then he might be an hour or so yet. Please tell me,
what's been happening? Who wouldn't come?"

"Elenn. She refused to come with me. Morthu and Amala
have been telling her lies and she believes them and she
wouldn't come out."

"Amala?" I said, amazed.

"She was brought in a while ago, with some idiot Narlahenan prince. She was treated well, and Elenn has had to entertain them. You know what she's like, ever gracious, doing
her duty. She's doing that still, even though the city has been
captured. She and Amala have been condescending to each
other. Amala told her in my hearing that Urdo was treating
you as his wife, letting your mother embrace him as family
and leading you in to dinner."

My heart sank and I tried to speak, but my voice caught in
my throat, so Garah went on talking. "I told Elenn afterward
that it was a nonsensical lie, as if you'd ever do anything like
that. I told her everything I could think of about how honorable you are and how you don't mean her any harm and how
you would never do it, but she believed Amala, because it fitted with what Morthu had been saying, and you know how
Morthu convinces people. Elenn said Amala had never been
known to lie. I don't know why she was, either. I know she's
Marchel's mother, but I would never have thought of her as
being on Morthu's side."

"It isn't like her," ap Erbin said.

I took a deep breath and spoke as evenly as I could. "Actually, those things did happen, but without any such intent.

Can you imagine trying to stop my mother embracing Urdo?" Hot blood rose beneath my skin at the memory.

"Oh, Sulien, you idiot," Garah said. "You know Elenn's pride; even you must have seen how stupid that was. As for Urdo, I don't know what he can have been thinking."

"I think my mother was trying to say that he was Darien's father," I said feebly.

"As if that needed saying," ap Erbin said disapprovingly. "Weren't you thinking about the queen at all?"

"I knew Elenn wouldn't be pleased," I said. Garah snorted. "But I thought we could explain. I didn't realize it would be this bad."

"Who could?" Garah agreed. "To be fair, if Urdo had explained it properly she might well have accepted it. She likes Darien, after all, and it's not as if it's more than an acknowledgment of that, really, I suppose. It's how Amala put it, and what Morthu had been saying about Urdo putting her away. I knew you wouldn't do anything like that, but I didn't think about your mother. She would want acknowledgment, of course."

"Yes," I said, feeling wretched. "It was just impossible. You know what Veniva is like."

"It was just Morthu making it sound as bad as it could possibly be, and maybe making her believe that," Garah said, and sighed. "In any case, I told her that even if it were true fifty times over she would still be better off out of Caer Tanaga, and she could go back to her father's house if she wanted to."

"She's taking it as badly as *that*?" I asked, horrified.

"Worse," Garah said. "She hates Morthu, you know she does, but she still wouldn't leave, even when there was the chance, because she wouldn't risk the insult to her pride. She said something about an argument with her sister? She said Emer and Atha were allied with you and they were her personal enemies. She said she couldn't trust any of you. She said terrible things about Emer."

"What?" ap Erbin asked, sounding merely interested.

"Is this relevant?" I asked.

"Not really," Garah said. "The important thing is that Elenn is still in Caer Tanaga and she wouldn't escape with me."

"How did you get out?" ap Erbin asked.

"Through the old heating tunnels under the citadel," Garah said. "Glyn found an entrance in a storeroom years ago, and it was near the room where they were keeping those of us who weren't noble but were hostages. I would have come days ago, but I was trying to persuade Elenn. Then yesterday, no, the day before, Morthu came and—"

"Morthu was in Caer Tanaga the day before yesterday?" I interrupted.

"Yes, why?" Garah asked, her voice in the gloom sounding puzzled. "Did you think he was here?"

"So much for curses," I said, disappointed.

"Oh, as for curses, that's much worse than you think," Garah said, leaning forward into the bar of light so I could see her bruised face clearly. "Morthu is killing people, sacrificing them for his sorcery to put curses on us all. People in Caer Tanaga. He burned a hundred people in one night on the dark of the moon." The dark of the moon. I counted backward. That would have been the day we left Caer Gloran. "He took all the armigers who didn't die in the fighting and made up the numbers with wounded and guards and just people of the town, and he tied them up in the courtyard and burned them alive. He made us watch. Elenn stood stock-still with her hand on her old dog's head, more like a statue than a woman. I tried to protest when I saw what he was doing. He dragged poor Edlim out by his feet, with his head bumping, and it was too much for me. But he only beat me and said that if I said another word I would be out there with them." She shuddered.

"What did he do with them?" I asked.

"I don't know what he was doing. He sang in strange languages, and it was dark sorcery. Everything went very dark, even the fire, though it was still burning and still burning them. Then there was a strange light, and it looked as if something was coming out of all of the bodies and Morthu was gathering it up." She lowered her voice. "I think he was taking their souls. I prayed to the Mother to help them, with as many of their names as I could, but I didn't dare do it aloud, and I don't think it helped. I was sick, afterward; but then I couldn't move even to retch, I could only watch." Her voice shook. "Everybody was too afraid to talk about it afterward, but Garwen said she didn't see anything except the people burning. Since then, almost every night he's been there he has killed one or two people. He didn't make us watch again, but we knew what was happening. Then, the night before last he came to our room, and I thought he'd kill me then and I was terrified. He looked at me as if he liked me being afraid and smiled in that horrible way of his. But he didn't take me, he took Garwen and her youngest daughter."

"Garwen?" I asked stupidly. For a moment the name meant nothing to me.

And then Masarn opened the curtain and came in with Urdo, and Garah burst into tears.

"Garwen?" Masarn asked, glancing around the tent. And then I remembered his quiet, uncomplaining wife, who had lived in Caer Tanaga, and made candles and borne children and looked at me as if I were an exotic beast.

"Oh, Masarn, I'm so sorry," Garah said, through her tears. "Morthu killed her, and little Sulien, too. I sang the Hymn of Return for them. But your other three are safe. I brought them out myself; they are hidden on a farm I know outside the city."

Masarn stood completely still and all the expression drained out of his face. I stood up and put my arms around him, and he turned and held onto me as he wept, as if he were a child and I his mother. Urdo embraced him too. Ap Erbin stood up and pressed his mead flask into Masarn's hand. Masarn looked at it as if he didn't know what it was, then he gave a great sobbing howl and took it, and drank.

"Masarn?" I asked gently. Masarn didn't show any signs of having heard at all. It had hit him hard, and I didn't know what to say. I couldn't say what we always said in the alae; that she had been brave and died well, that the cause was good, and that she had learned well and would be swiftly reborn. None of it was true, and the unspoken words were like ashes on my tongue.

Urdo went to Garah, who was wiping her face. He squatted beside her. "Are you hurt?" he asked. "How did you escape? Where is Elenn?"

"She just wouldn't come," Garah sniffed, and repeated her story, this time without the incredulity at my stupidity.

"Morthu must have clouded her mind. But even so, what makes her think she's safe there, where Morthu is slaughtering people for power?" Urdo asked angrily.

"Morthu and Arling have both offered her their protection if she were free," Garah said. "Arling has a wife, of course, but Jarnsmen do sometimes have more than one. And she still hates Morthu, she has told me so. But I think Morthu has somehow persuaded her that we're going to lose. They took her to see the war machines, and she came back very shaken. I don't know everything they said to her. I wasn't there most of the time. I only know what I heard them say and what she told me. But I tried really hard to get her to stop being an idiot and come with me." She glanced over at Masarn, who was still weeping in my arms. "I tried too long, Urdo, and that's why Garwen and little Sulien died, and that's why I came now, before he took the rest of us."

"You did the right thing," Urdo said, his voice very stern. "Sometimes there are no choices that harm nobody."

They arose early and saw the Tigran armies spread out on the plain before them. No more support had come to help them hold the pass. They knew at once that although they saw the sun rise they would not live to see it set. It was immediately clear to everyone that the most it would be possible for them to achieve would be to win a little more time for Satea and the other cities of Lossia to prepare for the onslaught. So, without discussion or lamentation, they took sweet oil and combed each other's hair and bound it up as was the fashion for feast days, so that their bodies would be seemly in Death's Halls when they came there after the battle.

— Fedra, *The Lossian Wars, Book V*

Garah and I went down to the stream. Ap Erbin took Masarn off with him. There wasn't anywhere to bathe that wasn't in full sight of anyone who happened to wander by, of course. The news of Garah's condition raced through the camp. When she was clean the bruises showed much more clearly. We went back to my tent, where I trimmed the ends of her hair so that they were even.

"At least I used a knife, not a sword like you did at Caer Lind," she said, smiling at the memory.

"I'm not nagging at you for doing it, either," I said, stepping back a little to make sure it was straight. I had never seen her with short hair before. It made her whole head look different. It looked quite good now that it wasn't sticking up in all directions.

"I don't know if it's what Garwen would have wanted. She was a Tanagan, and she really loved the White God." Garah took a deep breath and swallowed hard to stop herself crying. "But it seemed like the right thing to do."

I embraced her. "Oh, Garah, I'm so glad you got out!"

"I am, too," she said. "I wish I didn't have to go to this

feast. I could just sit down and sleep, now that I'm clean and I've told you and Urdo what's happening."

"You do need to be there, and to look like the queen of Bregheda," I said. "It's important."

"Well, what can I wear? I said I didn't want to borrow anything of Alswith's, but nothing of yours will fit me."

"A drape fits anyone," I said, remembering Amala telling me so in Caer Gloran.

"But if I wear your drape, what will you wear?" Garah asked doubtfully. "Or do you have more than one?"

I had four, back at Derwen, but only one with me. "I shall wear my armor," I said. "I told Rowanna I'd wear what was suitable for my position, and what is more suitable than that?"

"Is it clean?" Garah asked as I unfolded the material. It was green, not the pale green of beech leaves that Elenn often wore but dark, like a pine forest. Dying linen dark colors was my mother's latest obsession. It required treating the cloth in some special way before soaking it in the dye. She had discovered it when trying to work with Ayl's pink. There had been several months last winter when we had weavers and dyers to dinner every day and it seemed as if she could talk of nothing else.

"Of course," I said. "I have only worn it once since I left home, at Idrien's awful meal at Caer Gloran."

"I meant the armor, but I'm glad about the drape. What was awful about Idrien?"

I told her about Idrien and Cinvar as I folded the drape into the right pleats and pinned it for her. She was horrified. "You mean to say he sent everyone who could fight up to the fort with Kerys and left Idrien just sitting there?"

"I think he was hoping we would kill her and give him an excuse for fighting us," I said. "He said something at the truce talks that made me wonder about that."

"I would never have guessed he was as bad as that," she said. "My opinion of human nature is lower than it was, and I thought not much could shock me after coordinating all the news of the island for Urdo for all those years."

I put my armor on. It was clean, and even polished, ready for the battle. Although it was a warm evening I settled my white praefecto's cloak on my shoulders. "Ready?" I asked, twitching it so that the golden oak leaves hung straight.

Garah looked down at herself critically. "I don't suppose you have anything to cover my head, the way they do in the north?" she asked. "I don't have the height to carry it off as Vincan elegance the way you do."

I laughed. "I like the way my legs can move in a drape, that's why I wear one. And yes, I do; hold still and I'll fasten it for you."

I wound the cloth around her head and fastened it with my amber brooch. She looked splendid, with a matronly dignity I never aspired to.

"I know it's no use asking you, but I wish I had some powder to cover the bruises on my face," she said.

"You only look as if you've been in battle," I said comfortingly. "Why are you so nervous about how you look today?"

"Rowanna terrifies me at the best of times," she admitted. "And I've been hearing Morthu calling me worthless for days on end, I suppose. I feel a fraud. I am a farmer's daughter, after all."

"You are a farmer's daughter; your parents were well when I left Derwen. And you are the queen of Bregheda, and you look it," I said. "I'm sure Elidir will have some powder you can borrow. She uses that sort of thing." Some of the armigers of Galba's ala did, too, but I felt Garah would be more comfortable with someone she knew.

We went through the camp to find Elidir. Before we reached her tent we came across Darien, wearing a dark blue drape, talking to Ulf. As we came up to them Ulf put something into Darien's hand and went away rapidly. I quickened my pace. Darien was standing staring after Ulf as if dazed. My first thought was that Ulf had made some claim of paternity. This was strengthened when I saw what Darien was holding, which was Ulf's armring.

"Oh, hello," he said, when he noticed us.

"Are you all right?" I asked.

"Oh yes," he said. Then he shook his head a little and looked at me as if he was just seeing me. "I just had a couple of surprises. Ulf gave me this." He lifted the armring so I could see it, then pushed it on and up his arm, where the gold was just visible under the fold of the drape. It was just how Ulf had been wearing it at the truce talks. "I know why, of course, but it still surprised me."

"Why?" Garah asked. I was choking down astonishment and anger. Darien wasn't supposed to know. As far as I knew, he believed Urdo was his father.

"Well, because he's sure he's going to die tomorrow, and this is the armring of his family, and by giving it to me he's giving his claim to be the king of the Jarns to Urdo." He hesitated and turned the ring a little with his other hand. "Or rather, giving it to me because giving it directly to Urdo would be too obvious, I suppose. But I wasn't expecting it at all." He blinked again. "When did you get here, ap Gavan?"

"This afternoon," Garah said.

"Can I see the armring?" I asked. Darien put his arm out and I looked at the worked gold. As long as Ulf had done it in a way that didn't make Darien suspect, then it was all right. Seen as Ulf's claim to be king of the Jarns it even made a sort of sense. "Is it very heavy?" I asked.

"No heavier than this," he said, touching his throat self-consciously. He was wearing a heavy gold torc, twisted in the old style from before the Vincans came. "It seems to be my day for being given strange heirlooms. The dowager Rowanna found this in Caer Segant. She said it was Avren's and Urdo should have it. Urdo said I should have it. He insisted. And that I don't understand. He wasn't like himself."

"Did he tell you about the queen?" Garah asked.

"What about her?" Darien asked.

"She refused to escape from Caer Tanaga with Garah," I said. "Urdo's very distressed about it."

"What do you mean refused?" Darien asked.

"She's been listening to Morthu," Garah said. "He told her that Urdo had been treating Sulien like a wife, and she believed it."

"Damn Morthu and his poisoned tongue!" Darien said, immediately furious. "I need to talk to Urdo about this."

"Not now," I said. People were already moving through the camp. "After the feast."

"Yes. Will you come with me?" he asked.

"Of course," I said. "But as for strange heirlooms, will you have one from me?" I hadn't known I was going to say it until the words were out of my mouth. But it felt right. I had given him so little, all these years. "If you can spare one of the brooches on your drape to stop Garah's hair falling down, this amber brooch is an heirloom of our house, given to me by my father from his treasure."

Garah put her fingers up to the pin immediately, but Darien did not move. "Thank you," he said. "I have often seen you wearing it. But if you don't mind, I won't take it now. I have this awful foreboding of being weighed down by gold and with nobody to give me good advice. Give it to me another day, if you will."

With that he walked away from us. Garah shivered a little. "He has grown up," she said.

We went on through the camp. By the time we found Elidir, Garah only just had time to pat her face with some powder before we had to make our way up the hill to the feast.

The sun was sinking toward the clouds massing in the west, and the camps were full of cheering people. There were too many of us for everyone to eat together. The five alae, the two Isarganan armies, the militias of Derwen and of Segantia, and Alfwin's army all ate in their own camps. Their food was what it would have been any day, with the addition of some fruit and ale from Caer Segant. All the same, they seemed to have caught the festival spirit. Even the sick and wounded had come out of their tents to participate. Maybe it was the sight of our massed banners on the hill, making a brave array. Maybe it was the music, for everywhere I went I seemed to be tripping over a Segantian musician. Or it might just have been the relief that we were going to fight at last and leave this camp. However it was, they cheered me and

Garah as we made our way toward the hill, and they called our names.

Garah stopped unexpectedly. "They've got a Breghedan banner," she said, and tears welled in her eyes.

They had indeed, just one, but plain to see among all the other colors. "Don't cry, you'll wash off all the powder," I said.

Garah gave a choked laugh. "Yes, but a Breghedan banner! Wait till I tell Glyn."

As we came nearer I saw that it was a gold charge banner hastily tacked onto someone's red cloak. I don't know how Rowanna managed to make it so quickly even so, and the effect from a distance couldn't have been better.

We sat in a circle to eat, sitting where Rowanna put us. One of her servants filled our cups with Narlahenan wine. Most of us drank from leather or wooden cups, but for Urdo Rowanna had set out a gold cup and a gold plate. I had never seen such a thing, and had heard of them only in old tales. I wondered what else she had hidden away in chests in Caer Segant.

Everyone was dressed in their best. Masarn was sitting between ap Erbin and Alswith, clearly, but not indecorously, drunk. Alswith's hair was caught up in a net of silver mesh on top of her head, which looked spectacular. Alfwin sat on Alswith's other side, wearing even more gold than Darien. Atha sat next to him, with a patterned shawl over her head. One of her captains sat beside her, a quiet sensible man called Leary ap Ringabur. Raul was next, wearing his brown robes as always. Then came Ohtar, in all his barbaric finery. Garah was beside him. Then Darien, in his blue and gold, between her and me. Urdo was on my other side. I wondered how Elenn would take this when she heard. Urdo was dressed in white linen with a purple silk cloak. Rowanna sat on his right, veiled and formal, a captain beside her, in armor. Cadraith was next, in red velvet fastened with gold Vincan pins. Then came Teilo, in her robes. On her other side sat Inis, in his crazy colored shawl. Emer sat up very straight on his right, clearly having been persuaded to eat with Atha after all,

though I didn't see her eating anything. She was wearing a
white dress that was a little large for her, and which I suspected of being borrowed from Alswith. Her two arm rings
were her own though; I had seen them often before. Between
her and ap Erbin sat Luth, in his famous blue breastplate and
his praefecto's cloak.

It was a strange meal, half tactical discussion of the coming battle and half diplomatic exercise. Urdo did not indicate
by any word or sign that his heart was less than entirely in
what he was doing. The earlier distress might never have
been. I felt strangely detached, as if I were watching everything rather than participating. It seemed we were to fight
down the road a little way, near a branch of the river called
Agned, where the road crosses the river on a bridge. Urdo explained it all very clearly, and made sure everyone understood what the ground was like and what their part in the
battle was going to be. A lot of it depended on how the enemy arranged themselves. I kept realizing I hadn't said anything for a long time and ought to speak, but I didn't have
anything to say. Inis, too, spoke very little, and that little
mostly to Emer. When we got up to leave he came up and put
his hand on my arm. "Bear up, hero," he said. I stared after
him as he went off down the hill with Atha. They even got a
cheer from the armigers who were waiting to see us come
down.

Garah went off to bed. Darien and I went with Urdo to his
tent.

"I'm glad that's out of the way," Urdo said, stretching and
yawning. "It was important to my mother, and I have done it,
but I would rather have had a conference about tactics, as
usual."

"So would I," I agreed, sitting down. "Do you think the Isarnagans will understand what you want them to do?"

"Atha seemed to. But it's hard to plan much in advance. So
much of it depends on how they use Angas's ala," Urdo said,
lighting a little lamp and pouring more wine. "And whether
we can make a difference right at the beginning."

"I wish I could have spoken to Angas," I said, remembering his face on the first day of the talks. "I'm sure he's not there entirely willingly."

"Morthu has bewitched him with his voice," Darien said.

"People cannot be persuaded by things against their will," Urdo said, and there was pain in his voice.

"They can by sorcery," Darien said. "I could get angry to think how you will believe anything rather than face that, but I know it is more sorcery affecting you. Think. I wanted to talk to you about the queen, and it is the same for Angas. It isn't that Morthu persuades people, though he does, it is sorcery. He weaves a spell of words. He takes the way people are, and takes their weaknesses, and makes power for himself out of them. If they have no weaknesses he turns their strengths against them, as a knife can be turned. He does this with words, with some power of his voice, but it is sorcery, I am sure of it. I have been hearing him do it since I was a child at Thansethan. It works on everyone around me and nobody will ever see it. He infects people with despair, and he twists their hearts. He has done this to Angas, and to the queen. He has done it to you, to both of you. He hasn't persuaded you to join him, but you are thinking better of him than he deserves, or than his actions merit. You know he can do it, but you don't think of it clearly."

"He twists people's strengths?" Urdo asked. "How?"

"Your mercifulness and your desire to be fair, to give the benefit of the doubt, and to keep to the Law," Darien said, the lamplight reflecting on his gold as he leaned forward.

"I had never thought of those as faults in a king," Urdo said, his voice very strange.

"They are not. That is what is so terrible about Morthu," Darien said, jumping to his feet and pacing the tent as if he could no longer bear to be still. "They are strengths, I said they were. But think how you exiled Marchel after Varae, but how you have spared Morthu time after time."

"There was never clear evidence before the Law, which there was for Marchel," I said, to save Urdo saying it. He was weeping, and futile though it was I wished I could spare him some of the pain.

"He knew that and used it," Darien said. "And he made you feel sorry for him and that he could change. I have seen him doing this time after time. He did it at Thansethan. He made Father Gerthmol's kindliness into weakness, and his love of order into rigidity. I didn't understand at first, but then I saw enough of it. The worst of it is that people can't see it. You would rather think the queen a fool and a traitor than believe in his sorcery. Elenn could never betray us, there is no treachery in her. She is everything a great queen should be: beautiful, clever, diplomatic, skilled at logistics. Consider how honorably she has always treated me. But Morthu has leaned on the queen's strength and pride, and her doubts that she is worthy to be loved, or to be your queen, when she has given you no children." Darien looked so angry I wouldn't have been surprised if his eyes had flashed fire, the way they do in stories.

"She knows that doesn't matter, that isn't what's important," Urdo said.

"You might have told her so, but she still feels she's failed you that way," Darien said. "It's a weakness and a way in for him. He is so good at finding the little cracks in the wall we have built, and using them to force a knife blade, and after it an army."

"He won't succeed," Urdo said. "There's one thing I've learned in this war, and these truce talks, which is how well we have all learned Peace, how well it is rooted in all of us. We will fight this battle, and this war, and we will win in the end because Morthu is one man and his cause is only his own. He may have stuck his knife blade into our small cracks, but he only persuades by his own sorcery. The gods are on our side." He looked at me and grinned, though his face was still wet with tears. "Remember the night before Foreth? When I die, you have to take her back my sword."

"You're no more likely to die tomorrow than in any battle," I said gruffly.

"And no less," he agreed. "The risk is always there. I've always taken it, even when Mardol and the others called me foolhardy to fight in the line myself. It's necessary, I told them. Life is in the moment when you're living it, one moment at a time. If the Peace was to be anything, it could not all rest on one man. But all the time I have known that if I die then my Peace would break with me. Before Foreth, I felt sure we would win, but I did not know what victory you could make without me, if I fell, and still I fought. But now, it is different. There are enough of you I trust that no matter if I am here or not I feel sure the Peace will go on without me, which is how it should be. I have never tried to make bargains with Fate, but I have always felt that she is not opposed to the Peace. Seeing it spreading, my work is done, if need be."

"It would be better with you," I managed to choke out.

"And I would rather live to see it," he agreed calmly.

"I wish you'd let me fight Morthu," Darien said. "One man or not, he's a sorcerer and ruthless and powerful."

"We'll have to see how the battle goes tomorrow," Urdo said. "Full tactical conference in the morning before we move into position to fight at noon."

As I stood up to leave, I thought that something about the tent seemed different. I looked around, and caught sight of the box Urdo used to carry papers. It was closed, and the top was completely empty.

— 18 —

Before Gorai,
defender against tyranny,
I saw war horses
covered with blood.
After the howl of battle-cries
the green grass grows long.

Before Gorai,
defender against the heathen,
I saw a mighty shield wall
steel swords clashing.
After the howl of battle-cries
plenty of time to think.

Before Gorai,
defender against dissension,
I saw the thick of the fight
many killing, many being killed.
After the howl of battle cries
time to sleep easy.

— "Gorai ap Custennin" by Aneirin ap Erbin

At the end of our discussion after a skirmish or an exercise, Osvran would always finish off by saying, "Right. And we're not going to make the same mistakes again, are we?" And we'd all chorus, "No, Praefecto!" I can see us now, Galba looking thoughtful, ap Erbin slim and with both his ears, and Enid grinning because there was always something she couldn't resist. There is so much of that training I have not set down, so many happy times. All the same, it is Agned I must write about. Agned, and mistakes that shouldn't have been made and were, beyond hope of getting it right next time, because there isn't always another chance.

Agned, not happy days; Agned, whether it's easy or not, however many excuses I find to sharpen my pen and moisten the ink and stare out of the window dreaming and wondering when the flax will be ripe. The battle of Agned happened fifty-five years ago. It hasn't been possible to change it in all that time. Anyone might think I would have got used to that by now.

The River Agned rises in the hills of Segantia; it runs down into the Tamer, and thus to the sea past Caer Tanaga. The river is navigable. There were occasional Jarnish raids up it in times when the raiders were very bold. I suppose it might have been fordable if you were prepared to go to a little trouble. But there was no need. The highroad from the west crosses it at a solid stone bridge called the Agned Bridge. There is a farmhouse there that was ruined in the wars and patched up again clumsily. I used to stop there to water the horses when I was riding from Derwen to Caer Tanaga, and I would sometimes exchange a few words with the farmers, and buy bread from them if they had been baking. If it hadn't been for that I doubt I would even have known the river's name. But now I will never forget it, though the name means the battle and not the river.

It's not an easy battle to remember in order. It began at dawn with a tactical meeting in Urdo's tent. A fine haze of rain was falling. The camp was breaking up around us as we spoke, the tribunos and decurios getting everyone in order. Almost everyone but the sick and wounded was going forward with us, even the doctors. Those of the wounded who could walk would have to look after the others. Mother Teilo was the only person staying who could sing the elder charm.

Cadraith had gone up to the battle site the day before with Raul and Father Cinwil to view the ground. He told us about it; the road, the river, the gently rolling slopes, forested on the heights. He drew a detailed plan of it, and we agreed where we would draw up our troops.

"After we charge there's going to be a gap at the end of our line here, across the road," ap Erbin said, putting his finger on the spot. "An ala could come up there and turn the line."

"Maybe we could put the wagons there," Ohtar said. "The ones that have been coming up from Caer Segant with supplies. That would make a defensible point, if there were some troops there, too."

"A good place for some of the militia," Cadraith said.

"You said the rest of the Tanagan infantry go with us in the middle?" Ohtar said, moving his finger over the drawing. "Are you sure they all understand how Jarnsmen fight? They will stay with us? They will follow orders?"

"I talked to my troops about it last night," Rowanna's captain said. "Half of them are Jarnsmen themselves, and I have made sure the rest understand."

"Then we will put the militia of Derwen around the wagons," Urdo said. Raul made a note.

"They know the ala signals," I said. Raul noted that, too.

"I've fought with Tanagan levies before," Alfwin said. "They do startle easily, but there's not much chance of them breaking and running if we're in the center."

"I am glad you are here. I could wish Guthrum had come," Ohtar muttered, smiling at Rowanna's captain, who smiled back a little shakily. He was a Tanagan, not a Jarn. "Arling is here in strength, and by now Ayl will have brought up all his troops."

"I wish we could have made Ayl see sense," said Darien wistfully. Then he shook his head. "Sorry. Where were we? Who else is in the center?"

"My people," Emer said. "We will be next to Alfwin."

"I think the folk of Dun Morr who are mounted could look to the defense of the road and the carts, with the Derwen levies," Urdo said. Emer looked as if she was about to object. "It's essential to have some strong defense there, and you're used to each other," he went on. She subsided. "And that way it'll be all infantry in the center."

"And we Isarnagans will be on the left, with the slope down to the boggy ground in front of us," Atha said. She looked most alarming, being normally dressed, but with her hair limed and her face and arms already painted. She had not brought her captain this morning.

"I'm sure you can hold the left," Urdo said, and smiled encouragingly. "The alae will begin on the right, mobile, and ready to go where they're needed. Just give them room if they need it. If they don't shift them with the first charge, we'll rally, and I'll try to hold the second one back until there's a really good moment to shift the other side."

I stared down at the drawing. I had slept badly. I had learned late how to wield an ala as one weapon, even though an ala trains together and uses the same weapons and knows the signals and commands as second nature. These troops didn't even all speak the same language, but Urdo could see them all as one weapon to strike the blow he wanted struck.

"What about the farm?" I asked.

"The farmers have left it," Raul said.

I knew it had come to that, and I could imagine it only too well; the little family fleeing, clutching their children and livestock. I hoped they had somewhere to go. "Not that," I said, putting the thought of the breaking of Urdo's Peace as far out of my mind as I could. "I meant to say that it's here, down the slope from where we said we would put the wagons. Won't it be in our way when we charge?"

"Only if we go straight down," Urdo said. "We can go around, down the center."

"And from where will you direct the battle?" Atha asked.

"We will make a command post here," Urdo said, pointing to a spot uphill from the main Jarnish line. "I will be there with scouts and signalers. I would rather be mobile with my ala, but in a battle like this, I need to be able to see it all."

"That is wise," Darien said.

"Take some strong defenders in case they get through," Alfwin said, very firmly.

"I will have bodyguards there, of course," Urdo said. "But right up here is well out of anyone's path."

"I will send you some more bodyguards," Ohtar growled, and I saw the other infantry commanders raising their chins in agreement.

It seemed to take all day moving everyone up to Agned

and getting in position. It was raining harder, and the grass was wet and slippery. The other side was doing the same, shifting about, getting ready for noon. They also took up a position about three quarters of the way up the slope opposite us. I wondered why it always had to be charging uphill. There was no sign of Angas. The troops I could see clearly all seemed to be Cinon and Flavien's militia. There were very few banners flying on the other side, in marked contrast to every other time I had seen them. I wondered about it idly. I could see Ayl's red-ribboned standard way over to the other side, on the bridge, but that was the only clear signal of identity, though there were clearly Jarnish troops behind the militia in several places. Directly in front of us I could see some Narlahenan horses, and some war machines. I squinted at them through the rain. One of them looked like the way Antonilla described a javelin-hurler. Others were clearly stone-throwers. They looked as if they belonged on a city wall, not on a battlefield.

"Are we going to have to charge at those?" Govien asked, seeing me looking.

"If we do, we'll be going too fast for them to hit us before we hit them," I said, as reassuringly as I could.

Raul went down in the rain to confer with Father Cinwil, and came back. I noticed that Father Cinwil was riding one of the old greathorses we kept at Magor for teaching recruits to ride, a black mare blotched with white unkindly known as "Old Cloak," because she fitted anyone but not very well. I wondered who had said he could take her. I almost rode over to ask Nodol if he knew, before I realized what a ridiculous thing it was to be worrying about.

I made sure my ala ate the food they had brought with them, and dealt with the last-minute rash of problems. I sang the elder charm over three armigers who thought they might be coming down with fever. Then, at last, we got the signal to mount, and got into position, in front of the wagons.

Just before noon, Raul and Father Cinwil rode down, exchanged a few words, and rode back up toward their own sides. As Raul reached us, he turned his horse to face the enemy. He waited for Father Cinwil to do the same on his side, Old Cloak taking her time as always. Then, when they were facing each other, they each threw down the herald's branch they carried, and that was the signal that the truce was over and the battle had begun.

Almost at once the signal came for us to charge. In that one moment there seemed to be freedom and the chance to make a difference. I could almost forget that I needed to direct the whole ala and see it all as an extension of my spear. They were waiting for us, ready and defiant, and we were charging uphill, and against a hail of thrown spears and stones. All the same, we made an impact on them. However good infantry are, they can't withstand a five-ala charge without noticing it. The front row went down under the impact, but the men behind had long spears and did not break. As soon as the charge had stalled I signaled for the rally banner to be flown, and heard from the trumpets that the other alae were doing the same. Soon we were back up the ridge again. To my surprise I had been right; most of us had gone too fast for the war machines. We had only lost two riders in Galba's Ala, with half a dozen more wounded.

Meanwhile Ohtar and Alfwin and the rest of the central infantry block had advanced under the cover of our charge, and were attacking to the left and center. They seemed to be doing well at first, but then to my horror I saw fire erupting into their lines. There were more war machines down there. Each warrior who was touched by the evil clinging fire burned up, as Geiran and Morwen had burned at Caer Lind, burning everyone they touched. I had not known machines could work sorcery. I had to look away. I took a drink from my water bottle and caught ap Madog's eye. "Is there a word for more horrible than horrible?" he asked. I shook my head, sickened.

I looked toward the command point, hoping to be ordered to charge, even though the turmoil below still looked terrible. It was so hard to wait for the right moment. I looked back to it and saw that some of our Segantians had broken and were running uphill. Ayl's troops on the bridge had attacked them unexpectedly from the side, which had been too much for them. Alfwin's men were fighting steadily and evenly, but clearly retreating, and so were Ohtar's. Some of Flavien's men, or so I assumed, for they were fighting under his snake banner, rushed forward in pursuit of the scattering Segantians. Then, at last, I saw Angas, leading his ala down through the massed infantry. They were going very slowly; there was no chance for them to build up the momentum for a charge. They were moving through Jarnish infantry, which I thought at first must be Ayl's or Arling's, but then they raised their banner at last and I saw the silver swan of Cennet. Guthrum had come, but not to us. After almost forty years of keeping quiet unless attacked, Guthrum had finally moved. Clearly his family ties to Angas had won out above those to Urdo. Maybe, like Ayl's, his own men had been so eager to fight that he could not keep them home. I ground my teeth and wondered what Rowanna would say to her sister when next they met.

Our troops were still retreating, at different speeds. The Bereichers had hardly moved at all, but the Segantians and the Isarnagans of Dun Morr were well back. Flavien's militia were pursuing them wildly, but the Jarnish infantry were either engaging with Ohtar and Alfwin or advancing slowly and steadily. Right in the center a group of them had come right past the retreating and disorganized militia. I looked desperately toward Urdo and the command post. It couldn't be long before Angas was through, even with all those troops in his way, and once they had an ala out there things would be desperate. If it had been my choice I would have been charging already. The ala were ready to move on a twitch.

After what seemed an age the command came. The trumpets blew the five notes of "I'm coming to get you" and we charged right into them. The relief of doing it was tremendous, even with the wind blowing the rain right into our faces. This time the timing was exactly right. We hit them at the right speed and they broke. Even Angas's ala retreated before us. I led my ala straight toward them, and they skulked away behind the infantry.

I don't know how many of them we killed in that charge. It was almost like Foreth again. I thought for a moment that we were going to knock them right back. We pushed them down into the valley bottom. Then Atha and her Isarnagans came running down the hill to help. They were better suited to fighting on the broken ground than we were. Masarn and Cadraith stayed down to support them while Luth and ap Erbin and I rallied and prepared to go back to make sure the Jarnsmen we had seen before had not got any further up our hill.

Then came a great blast of trumpets from some ships that had been slipping unnoticed up the river, brought by the same wind that had brought the rain. They were flying the dampened banner of Munew, and they disembarked in good order, not far from us, below the bridge. Thurrig was there, and Custennin, and his young son Gorai, and a fair part of the levy of Munew, and Thurrig's fighting sailors. I sat and gaped at them for a moment, as the battle slackened around me. I signaled that we should wait for a little while. Nobody moved toward them. I did not have the least idea whose side they were on. From the look of things, neither did anyone else. Then I saw ap Erbin call up his signalers and deliberately raise their ala banner high. Gorai saw it and pointed excitedly, saying something to his father. He couldn't have been more than fifteen or sixteen; he looked far too young to be on a battlefield. I couldn't imagine what Custennin was thinking. The battle was still going on, but with the ala around me I could safely pay attention to the disembarking troops.

Thus I saw Marchel ride confidently toward her father. She was at the head of a pennon of Narlahenan horse. Although I was behind her and away across the battlefield I saw by the casual arrogance of the way she held her head that she knew these troops were on her side. I drew breath to give the signals that would gather the ala to ride back and be ready to charge again. But Thurrig said something to a sailor by him. I saw the woman look at Custennin as if for confirmation. Young Gorai waved his arms enthusiastically. Then the red-and-green banner of the High Kingdom rose over the ship, and at the same moment Thurrig drew his ax with one smooth movement and stood waiting.

I didn't see what happened when they met, because a pair of maniac Jarnish monks threw a bucket of water over me at that moment, while shouting praise to the White God. I don't know what they expected to happen. They and their friends had pushed and fought their way through to me, but the two with the water didn't even have any weapons. Cadarn killed one of them and I killed the other. The rest were dead already. I wasn't much wetter than I had been already, from the rain, but I was much angrier. When I looked toward the ships again everything was a confused melee.

I decided that it had wasted enough of my time. Luth and ap Erbin and I exchanged signals and headed back up the hill.

There was a disruption then as a great flaming ball fell in the midst of ap Erbin's ala. Ap Erbin and his horse were caught right in the heart of it. I don't know if the horse went mad or if ap Erbin did it on purpose. Unlike everyone else there, he and I had seen the fire before. I have always liked to think he had time to decide what to do. They ran clear of the ala without touching anyone else, making for Guthrum's line, near the flame machine. The enemy faltered and fell back before him, as well they might. His bones and the horse's bones shone through the fire, and his sword flashed blue as he brought it down one last time before his bones scattered as he fell.

Then Alswith raised a great cry of "Death!" She stood up in her stirrups and threw off her helmet, letting her long red hair loose. It did not fly out behind her as it had at Foreth; the rain flattened it to her head. Still, we all recognized it as the mourning sign it was.

Ap Erbin's ala, who really should have known better, followed her as she turned and raced back to the main part of the battle, where the Jarnish shield wall was reforming. They were calling "Geraint," which was ap Erbin's name, though he didn't like it and I never used it, and "Flamehair" and "Death." They fell on the flame machine and hacked it and the crew to pieces, and then set about hacking all around them with no discipline or order. This kind of thing is what Duncan always used to say would happen if husband and wife, or even lovers, fight in the line together and one of them is killed. In all my years of fighting this is the only time I have ever seen it. I'll agree it's reprehensible, but it's human, and I have felt the same when I have seen a friend killed. It might be possible, if cruel, to separate husbands and wives in the alae, but it isn't possible to fight only with people about whom one feels dispassionate. At the time I understood Alswith entirely, and the rest of the ala better than I should. I had tears on my face and I missed ap Erbin already. Shouting "Death!" and laying about me blindly would have been such a relief.

Luth and I looked at each other for a moment, then I wiped my hand across my eyes and gave the signal to continue up toward the Jarnsmen who were harassing Ohtar and Alfwin, which was where we were needed.

Some of Ayl's troops from the bridge had met up with some of the advancing Jarnish troops, and I saw that Arling was there. They were pressing our people hard. We took them on both sides, while our Jarnsmen stood firm against the enemy. There, even as my first pennon hit and their line wavered, I saw Walbern ap Aldred, fighting in the Jarnish line but with Tanagan weapons.

I looked for Ohtar to see his reaction. He was among his men, not far back. He was taking off his armrings and giving them to his companions, who seemed to be protesting. Then he handed over his sword, sheath, belt, and all, and murmuring something to the man he gave it to. I heard afterward it was "Make sure this gets to Anlaf if it needs to, and don't disgrace me." Then, unarmed, he looked at the sky, and raised his hand to the bear's head on his cloak. His line stepped back a little, leaving him half a step ahead of them. Ayl's troops rushed into the gap, but almost as soon as they moved forward they were moving back again, tripping over each other in their hurry to back off. Quietly and calmly, without any fuss at all, Ohtar had turned into a bear, his great cloak billowing over his skin and his face pressing forward to become a bear's mask. It didn't seem the least bit startling at the time, merely inevitable. He was still Ohtar, he was just all bear now, and that was only how it ought to be. He stood fully four foot high at the shoulder; he was a great bear of the woods of Norland or Jarnholme such as had never been seen in Tir Tanagiri. He was taller than I am when he stood up on his hindpaws and roared. Ayl's men began to retreat in earnest then, even though Luth's ala were ready behind them.

Then Walbern stepped forward from his lines and copied his grandfather's gesture. The two bears both rose on their hind legs, roaring and growling. Within seconds they were biting and buffeting at each other. The men of Aylsfa steadied and drew up their line again. Some of them even grinned and made rude gestures at the men of Bereich. I wondered whether to intervene, or how to intervene. There was no possibility of confusing the two bears. Ohtar was taller and darker. He seemed to be getting the best of the fight, too, though they both had blood on their fur. I happened to catch sight of Luth's astonished face over Ohtar's shoulder as I was looking and couldn't stop myself laughing out loud.

Ohtar somehow seemed to grow ever taller and more bearlike as the fight went on. It ended very suddenly, with Walbern dropping to all fours and running off through his own lines, setting off another panic there as he bowled over some of his former companions. Ohtar followed him, loping steadily after, striking out at men of Aylsfa who tried to hinder him. Before long they were all in flight. Luth, wide-eyed and gaping, gave way for the bears, and they loped off toward the northeast, Walbern still ahead and Ohtar following.

Luth's ala seemed to be dealing well enough with the men of Aylsfa who had broken. The Bereichers gave a cheer and took a few ragged steps forward, but before they could do anything rash, Alfwin began shouting commands and they steadied their line.

There were those who said later that they found the bodies of grandfather and grandson among the slain. But nobody ever claimed to have found Ohtar's cloak, or brought any token of Walbern's back to his mother's kin.

— 19 —

She hewed him down, the hell-cursed woman,
with Wulfstan and Wolmar, his shoulder companions,
his faithful followers who long in life
stood at his side waiting his word
fallen before him led the way forward
back from the battlefield down into death.
      —"The Battle of Agned"

After Ohtar had gone and they had closed up again, we had a hard fight to shift the enemy. After a while, when it seemed that we were winning for the time, I caught sight of Arling making a stand, his house lords around him. I gave the signal for each pennon to fight as seemed good to them and led mine in toward him.

That was when I killed Ayl, getting to Arling. I didn't mean to, and I've been sorry ever since. Ayl was a friend, and I had broken bread with him, and he was a good man, for a Jarnish king. Furthermore, we had to deal with his awful brother Sidrok for years after until his son was grown up. I didn't think of any of that then, only that he was between me and Arling. He stepped forward thinking that I would hesitate, and the look on his face as I pulled my sword out of his chest was comically surprised. I went on, laughing, and took down two more of Arling's house lords before we crossed swords at last.

He called himself the Lord of Jarnholme and Tir Tanagiri and High King of all Jarns everywhere, but the best I can say of Arling Gunnarsson is that he was brave enough to stand still and fight back when it came to it. He did not flinch, though I was mounted and he was not, and though he knew he was doomed to die. I did not see the gods Ulf had named come to claim him, but I do not doubt they were gathered around him. I saw them in his eyes when he fell at last. Smitten, withered, spurned, hunted, blinded by his own folly, rent and slain, he died at last, drowning on his own blood. I left him to rot on the field.

Alfwin rallied his troops and Ohtar's, and they went forward now downhill with new heart, while the men of Jarnholme and Aylsfa faltered. I looked toward the command post for orders, but I could no longer make it out through the rain and mist. I sent a messenger for orders, and gathered the ala around me. I rode off uphill toward the wagon wall so that we could change horses.

Before I came up to it I began riding through fallen armigers and horses. The spear-hurlers and stone-hurlers had found their range here, and many of Urdo's Own Ala had fallen to them. Everywhere were fallen friends. I saw the doctors tending to Beris, who had a spear through her arm. A little way on up the hill I saw Masarn on the ground, wounded but still alive, with some of his armigers around him. Elwith signaled that I was needed, so I rode over and dismounted. I handed an armiger Brighteyes' reins and knelt in the mud by Masarn.

His legs had been crushed by a great stone flung by a war machine. There was clearly no hope of survival. The part of my mind that was calm was surprised he wasn't dead already.

"Ap Gwien!" he was murmuring. "Tell ap Gwien," he said, looking straight up at me.

"I'm here, Masarn," I said. "What is it? Tell me what?"

"Tell ap Gwien I did it. I take full responsibility," he said. "She will understand. I hope."

"I understand, Masarn," I said, though I didn't have the faintest idea what he was talking about. I don't know if he heard me, or if he even knew I was there.

"Oh, Sulien!" he said, sounding exasperated and pleased at the same time. Then the life went out of him as he was speaking. Although his eyes were open he was no longer behind them.

Another fall of machine-hurled spears came down among us just then. I only just got my shield up in time, and Brighteyes was nicked on the hindquarters. "We need to get away from here; they have the range," I said. "Take the wounded to safety, and the rest of you ride with me for now."

I mounted again, biting my lip, and only then wondered who was leading Masarn's ala. Masarn was the tribuno, really; Urdo was the praefecto and he was at the command post. Then, too late, I understood what he had wanted to tell me. Darien was the signifer. He must be leading them.

We still needed to change horses. I led the ala on uphill. When we came to the wagon wall we found Angas's ala pressing it hard, and Darien leading what was left of Masarn's ala, about three pennons' worth. I saw Ulf and Rigol in decurios' positions. I signaled for trumpets to be blown and we charged in support. The horses were very tired and we didn't have much speed, but Angas's ala turned and fought us. They were fresher than we were, they were as good as we were, and almost every pair of eyes that met mine over a spear had laughed with me in better times. I saw ap Cathvan come howling toward me on the left; ap Madog took him down. Each moment was a bitter struggle. I tried to direct the ala as best I could, but the fight soon degenerated into a furious skirmish. When they eventually withdrew and rallied we had lost many armigers and horses. So had they, of course. I had not seen Angas himself during the fight, but I caught sight of him as they rallied. He had lost his helmet in the fighting and had a cut on his temple. His jaw was set and his eyes shadowed.

I desperately wanted to charge again, but changing horses was now a necessity. Brighteyes was sweating and laboring to breathe. Angas was trapped where he was, between us, the wagon wall, and the command post. I could see it now, but there were no signals for me, all of them concerned the battle below. I had no idea what was happening down there. I did not want to send for Luth or Cadraith in case they were needed more where they were. The levies by the wagons were looking mauled, but had held. I saw Emer, still mounted, and unscathed so far. I signaled for the grooms to bring up our spare horses. Once we had them we could take Angas. Even though we had lost so many, with what was left of Urdo's Own Ala reinforcing us I had a full-strength ala. As the horses were led out I called Darien, Ulf, and Rigol over to explain where they were to fit.

We had changed horses in battle and in practice hundreds of times. It was something we could do almost without thinking. I kept four pennons mounted, the three newcomers and my own, between those changing horses and Angas, so that he could not charge unexpectedly and take us by surprise while we were unhorsed. He did not charge but sat there, staring at me and Darien as we spoke. Then, as our fresh horses were led up, and as three remounted pennons started to come through to be in front of us, he raised his banners and charged, not toward us but directly away, reversing their direction, toward the command post.

I should have known what he had been planning. It was like a nightmare. Practiced order became churning chaos. Brighteyes just didn't have a charge left in him. I threw myself onto Glimmer's back and spurred him after Angas. Darien and Rigol and I were in front and the rest of the ala followed close behind. We went as fast as we could, and were soon on their heels.

Urdo was as well defended as he could have been. Ohtar, Alfwin, and Atha had all sent troops to extend his regular bodyguard, all of them house lords, all of them strong and valiant veterans. I looked at that line of shield wall as I came near them and thought how strange it was that they were our side being charged by an enemy ala, not enemy that I was charging. They were mostly heavily bearded pale-skinned Jarnish faces, with a sprinkling of people from the levies of Derwen and Segantia, and here and there a blue-painted Isarnagan. They stood as firm as they could against Angas's onslaught, spears ready against the horses.

Just before I reached the line I saw Angas break through them and then fall, his horse killed under him. Glimmer stumbled over Angas's fallen horse. I leapt clear as he fell and almost fell myself from the shock as my legs hit the ground. I ran on through the mud.

I was in the gap right behind Angas, who was cut off from

his ala. I was only a few steps behind, but Urdo was in front of him and everything was happening horribly slowly. Angas had his long ax in his hands, the one Thurrig had been teaching him to use when I had first come to the ala. Urdo had his sword, the one the goddess had given him on the top of Foreth. My lungs were burning as I ran. Angas swung his ax forward toward Urdo's head and Urdo turned to punch block the ax head with his shieldrim. He almost made it; he was strong and fast, and he might have spitted Angas before he could get in another blow. But he turned too far on the wet grass. The ax came down on his shoulder and on down past his collar bone, before I was there to stop it.

In battle there is no time to mourn and in this life there is no undoing.

Urdo slid to the ground, dead, or so near to death that there was no chance of recovery. Angas froze as the stroke went home, as if he couldn't quite believe what he had done. As Urdo's body touched the ground, he dissolved into it as if he were rain. Where he had fallen there was no sign that anyone had ever been there. In that instant I reached Angas, who was still staring. Darien reached him in that same moment, and he would have died then if his ala hadn't come up around us. I got in one good slash at his leg before someone flung himself off his horse between us. We were very hard pressed there for a little while. Darien and Ulf and Rigol and I made a stand back to back over the place where Urdo had fallen. The ground was slippery with mud and blood. We had most of an ala coming against us, most of Urdo's defenders were down already. Rigol fell, and Ulf took a blow in his side which slowed him considerably. Then Govien brought my ala up and relieved the pressure. After a while what was left of Angas's ala fled as Cadraith's ala came up and chased them off.

Only then, when there was no enemy immediately in front of me, could I look to Urdo. He was there, lying on the ground, looking up at me, smiling a little, certainly wounded but seeming alive. Then I blinked, and looking again I saw only a pile of damp leaves, shaped vaguely like someone lying down. Cadraith had dismounted and was kneeling beside

Urdo, weeping. I was too amazed to move for a moment. I could see Urdo and the leaves together or separately, as if they were both there and both as real as the rain on my face. Urdo signaled for Darien, who went to him and knelt. Then he looked around. He did not move his head. Only his eyes moved. "Raul?" he asked, as if forming the word was a great effort.

Raul had been in the command post, and I feared the worst. But he came limping up. Angas's ala had concentrated on the place where I had been, and more of the defenders were alive than I had guessed. Raul's hood was back and his sparse hair was soaked on his head. He bent down to Urdo, who said something to him quietly.

"Garah?" Urdo said, and again his eyes moved, and Garah came up from behind him. I knew he could see her before he possibly could have seen her if he had been looking out of his eyes. I could hardly breathe.

"Alfwin?" he said. "No, too far. Cynrig will witness for the Jarns." Cynrig dismounted and came forward. Unlike most of the ala, he didn't have a scratch on him.

Urdo smiled, and before Cadraith and myself, before Raul and Garah and Cynrig, before the remaining members of the militia and the waiting circle of the ala, he took Darien's hand. The rain slackened as he did so and became a light haze, the way it had been in the early morning.

"Let this be heard," he said, raising his hands palms up and then down, just above the ground. "Here between earth and sky, bound by my own will, to promises, to expectations, I, Urdo ap Avren ap Emrys, High King, offer you my heir, Darien Suliensson. Hear me, my princes, my people, and all gods of earth and sky and home and hearth and kindreds of people, and hear this, White God Ever Merciful, who holds all oaths." He paused, and seemed to draw breath, but the breath he drew was the wind that sighed around us. The rain had stopped entirely. "I offer Darien Suliensson to you as High King of Tir Tanagiri, and as War-leader of this island, and I tell you he has the right of birth; the blood of Vinca runs in his veins, and the blood of the ancient Tanagan kings, and the blood of the kings of the Jarns. What is more, he will keep the Peace and the Law I have established for my land and my people, he is my heir and my considered choice. Will you have him?"

We all roared our acclamation. "Darien!" we shouted. The clouds parted to the west and a few rays of late-afternoon sun came through.

Darien stood, and pulled off his helmet. There were tears on his face, but he looked like a grave young god. "I do not know how I shall serve as king, but I shall do the best I can," he said. We roared again, though my throat was tight and my eyes were burning.

I looked back to Urdo and again saw nothing but a pile of leaves and twigs. Nobody else seemed to see anything unusual. Then I could see Urdo there again and he gave me a hand signal to come up.

"We must find out what is happening with the battle and fight on," Darien said, and began giving a series of sensible orders.

I walked over to Urdo and knelt beside him. I wanted to say something, but I didn't know what; it seemed as if I had said everything already or that what I wanted to say could never be said. I didn't even know if he was there or if what was happening was the land gods doing what they could for Tir Tanagiri. He had sworn by his name, but I could see that what he was now was part of the bones of the land. Still, he was Urdo, my king, looking at me with patience and confidence. I know he saw me and understood me, as he always had. I still couldn't speak, nor weep either. I put my hand on his and under the leaves I felt the hilt of his sword. I knew what he wanted then. I took it and laid my bloodied and battered sword at his side. Raul looked at me curiously but said nothing. I don't know what I would have done if he had tried to stop me.

The groom had brought me Glimmer, who had not been hurt in his fall. I mounted and took my place in the ala. We went back to the battle. Angas's ala had taken refuge in the farm. Guthrum and some of Ayl's men were still holding the bridge. Flavien and Cinvar and Cinon were fighting against Alfwin and our infantry in the center. Custennin and Marchel were dead. Gorai and Thurrig were holding out at the ships. The flame thrower was entirely destroyed, but the rest of the machines were still a danger.

I was told we fought on until darkness forced us to a halt. I was told we charged three more times, and Govien organized Galba's ala as well as any tribuno could, until he was too badly wounded to ride. I was told that I screamed like a demon and slew hundreds of enemies (and some old friends who had changed sides) without hesitating or getting a scratch myself or even getting the sword bloody. It may be so. It may even have given me some comfort at the time. It's gone now though, except for what people have told me since. I don't remember a thing about the rest of the day after getting up on Glimmer's back, gritting my teeth, and settling Urdo's sword in my hand.

20

The weakness of monarchy lies in the character of the king. It lies in the hands of the gods to send us the king we deserve.
—Aristokles of Lossia, *"The Just City"*

"My son Anlaf will become king of Bereich, if the land consents," Alfwin was saying. I couldn't quite remember why I was lying on the grass, but I wasn't uncomfortable. "He is there already. As for the land around Thanarvlid, Alswith can hold it until her son is old enough."

"Alswith can hold it in her own right, and her son after her," Darien said. I opened my eyes. It was night. In front of me, Darien, Alfwin, Raul, Emer, and a group of people were clustering around a lantern.

"It is not our custom," Alfwin said. He had a bandage around his leg and he looked even paler than usual.

"I know that," Darien said patiently. "But it is not your custom that a woman should ride to war and avenge her father and her husband, and Alswith has done that. The land was given to her and to ap Erbin together, it is not the land of his ancestors where she is a stranger. She is of the royal kin of Tevin. She has the skills. In Tir Tanagiri she can be a king, and she shall be."

"We are in this land now," Alfwin said, agreeing, and although he was speaking Tanagan he used the Jarnish word for land.

I sat up, carefully. I did not seem to be wounded anywhere. "Have we won or lost?" I asked.

They all turned immediately toward me. "That is what we are trying to determine," Raul said.

"We don't know where all of them are," Darien said. "Urdo is—" He hesitated, and I knew that he knew what I knew. "Very near to death. Ap Erbin is dead, and Ohtar, and Custennin. We have lost many of our troops. More than half.

But they have lost more, two thirds perhaps. As well as the kings you killed, Marchel is dead. We think Flavien is alive, at least his forces retreated in some order. We don't know where Cinon is; he may be dead and unnoticed. Guthrum was still holding out on the bridge when we called a night-truce. Angas and what is left of his ala are still in the farm."

"What about Morthu?" I asked.

"Nobody has seen him all day," Emer said.

I grimaced. "And how about Cinvar?"

There was an uneasy silence for a moment, and they exchanged glances. After a moment Darien spoke. "You killed Cinvar," he said gently. "You killed three kings with your own hand today. It will be remembered forever."

Remembered forever, even if I didn't remember doing it. I didn't even particularly care about Cinvar, who was an idiot. "It wasn't enough, if Morthu's still alive," I said.

Darien raised his chin.

A messenger came running up. "Father Cinwil wants to speak to someone," he said, his words falling over themselves in his hurry.

"Where has he come from?" Darien asked, without hesitation.

"From the bridge," the messenger said.

"Then speak to him, Raul," Darien said. "Tell him we will take Guthrum's surrender if he will return to the Peace. When we have done that we will have the more difficult task of dealing with Angas."

There was some coming and going then as Raul and Father Cinwil negotiated. Atha came and spoke to us. She asked how Urdo was, and Darien told her he was near death. "I must go and sing the elder charm over my people," she said as she left us.

"Does the curse still hold?" I asked. The looks on their faces were enough to tell me it did. I pulled myself to my feet. "I should go to the sick tents."

The first person I saw there was Ulf. Ap Darel was sewing up the gash in his side and berating him for fighting on all day with it. I tried the charm against weapon-rot and felt the same block that had been there all this time. The elder charm worked, and soon I was back in the routine of the sick tents, moving from comrade to comrade, singing the charm, exchanging a few encouraging words, and moving on. Padarn was there, and Beris and Govien and many other old friends. It seemed everyone wanted to ask me about Darien, whether the sun had really come out when Urdo proclaimed him his heir and whether he was really High King now. They wanted to know if they should call him Darien ap Urdo or Darien Suliensson. I told them they would have to ask him.

I came across Thurrig in the third row of the walking wounded. I was more pleased to see him than I could have said. "What brings you here, you old pirate?" I asked.

"Just scratches," he said dismissively. "Barely that. I wouldn't be here if not for the terrible stories people are telling about a curse that makes any scratch go bad and kill you."

"Not if I can help it," I said, and sang the elder charm over his cuts, which were more than scratches but none of them serious. "I saw you getting out of the boats with Custennin," I said.

"Undecided to the last minute, as always," Thurrig said, and gave a great rumbling laugh. "Linwen and Dewin would have kept him in Caer Thanbard until things were sure. Young Gorai wanted to fight for Urdo and Peace and Honor and his uncle ap Erbin, the hero. He needs his romantic notions knocking out of him, but he'll be a better king than ever his father was even so. Custennin knew he wanted to do something, but he wasn't sure what. He thought he might want to join the rebels and fight for the White God. Well, he's safely praising him now. We wrangled all the way upriver. It's hard in civil war when you have friends on both sides. I didn't make up my own mind until I saw Marchel coming towards me, looking to profit by her oath-breaking. Well, she's learned better now. I don't know what made her think I'd taught her all my tricks."

"Oh, Thurrig," I said, knowing how much he cared, however lightly he spoke. "I saw your grandsons at Derwen half a month ago. They are fine men, sensible men, and one of them might have a child of his own by now, from the way his wife looked then. I saw Amala, too; she looked well."

"Amala is in Caer Tanaga," Thurrig said. "She's been writing to me, telling me to come and join her and bring the ships so that we can go off to Narlahena. She thinks that because she's been forgiven there that I will be, forgetting how long memories can be."

"I've always wondered what you did to be exiled there," I said.

"It's been almost fifty years, and I haven't told anyone; do you think I'll tell you now?" Thurrig asked. He grinned. "I didn't even do what they think I did. Or, at least, I did half of it. I went against orders and won a sea battle against the Skath. The other half, killing king Thudimir, I didn't do, but I know who did, and I've always let everyone think I did."

"Who did?" I asked.

He gestured to me to lean over, so I put my mouth to his ear. "Amala!" he whispered. I looked at him skeptically. I could not imagine her killing anyone. Thurrig chuckled. "Talk to me if you're thinking about a way of getting into Caer Tanaga, because if Amala is expecting me to come, that might be one." We exchanged serious looks and he moved his eyes to indicate the people around us. "I'm very sorry to hear about Urdo," he said. "I served his father and his grandfather and I'll be glad to serve his son."

Then Darien came through the press of doctors and wounded to stand beside me. "You have served my house and my country well, all these years, and never better than today," he said, taking Thurrig's unwounded hand. "Has my mother sung the charm over you?" he asked.

"I have," I said. "We were just talking."

"There is nobody else waiting," he said. "I want to talk to you for a moment, if you wouldn't mind."

"Where?" I asked. We had set up camp on the hillside. The camp was, of course, full of people.

"Let us go out among the trees," Darien suggested.

"I'll speak to you soon, Thurrig," I promised. Then I followed Darien out. The moon was only a day or so away from full, but clouds scudded across her face, making the light change from moment to moment even before we came to the trees.

"What is it?" I asked.

Darien stopped. "I just feel so strange," he said. "Being the heir is different from being the king, and it's really hard to understand what's happened to Urdo."

"He's dead," I said, feeling the weight of it. "You're the High King, and everyone wants you to be."

"There is so much I still had to learn," he said. "But I have to decide what to do. Angas wants peace. Angas always wanted peace. Morthu inflamed him against Urdo. He was quite happy to agree that Morthu should stand trial for sorcery. But he wants me to forgive him for killing Urdo, and he wants me to marry his daughter. In effect he wants to say he was justified in fighting, and his grievances have been settled. Can I forgive him?"

I hesitated. I knew I ought to say that he should forgive him and make peace. Angas could keep it, if Morthu were dead. I had always liked Angas. I couldn't think straight on about Urdo's death yet, but even though the killing tide that had risen in me was stemmed for now, and I might let him live, I could never forgive Angas myself, never again embrace him as a friend. "I can't," I said, at last. "I understand what Morthu did. I know why Angas was fighting against us. I pity him. But I can never forgive him."

"I don't know," Darien said, very quietly. "I have to marry somebody, and soon, and it would be a very good way of settling the north, although the girl is twice my cousin."

"Twice your cousin?" I asked.

"Missing a generation both times," Darien said, and the moonlight let me see him smile. "Eirann was Rowanna's niece, and Angas is Avren's grandson."

He sounded like Veniva, who I knew would approve wholeheartedly of such a match. Also, as he was not Urdo's son, there was no relationship at all. I couldn't say that. "I think it's sufficiently far," I said.

"Raul thinks so, too," Darien confirmed. "Marriage is such a big thing, as well. Why didn't you marry Urdo?" he asked, abruptly.

I blinked. It had never crossed either of our minds, but I could hardly say that without telling him that Urdo wasn't his father. All the same, I didn't want to lie to him. I thought back to the night in the stables in Caer Tanaga when I'd heard Urdo talking to Mardol. "Urdo wanted to make a diplomatic marriage," I said. "And I wasn't really anybody."

"You were the daughter of the Lord of Derwen!" Darien said.

"Well, yes," I said, feeling myself on safer footing. "But that didn't mean then what it would now. Derwen was a tiny, insignificant place back then. A lot of the growth it's had since is a consequence of Urdo's Peace. Back then almost nobody had heard of it. Urdo himself had to stop and think for a minute the first time I told him where I came from." I smiled at the memory. "Now, Derwen is a kingdom worth mentioning. We have a large ala, and a militia; we have trade." I bit my tongue to avoid going on to explain all the things we made and shipped. I didn't want to sound too much like Veniva, even if I was proud of how Derwen had grown. "But back then, we were nothing, really, out of the way down there. I wouldn't have had an alliance to bring to Urdo. And he was very young, and he had a lot of lovers."

"All the same, having a child means something," Darien said.

"Yes, but I didn't have any idea what," I said truthfully. "I was very young, remember, younger than you are now." Hard as it was to believe. But he was twenty, and I had been eighteen when he was born. "And Urdo was young, too, he thought he had plenty of time. And even more than Urdo's need for a diplomatic marriage, he needed a queen. When he found Elenn he had that. He loved Elenn, I know he did. She has been a really good queen for Tir Tanagiri, while I would have made a really dreadful one. Also I didn't want to be one. I wanted to be what I am. Oh, not Lord of Derwen, I do that as well as I can because it's my duty. But I wanted to be an armiger, to ride for Urdo. If I had ambition, I wanted to be a praefecto, and I wanted to be the best."

"You are," Darien said seriously.

I stopped and looked at him, but the moon had gone behind a larger cloud. "I am what?"

"You are the High King's Praefecto, and you are the best."

"One of the best," I agreed cautiously. It was true that there weren't many people who could touch me at practice.

"You killed three kings today," Darien said. "I would say you got what you wanted. You didn't have to be queen. You got to be the best."

"Sometimes when you get what you wanted it turns out not to be what you want anymore," I said, heavy-hearted. I wanted Urdo to be alive again, and I wanted to be riding free with a spear and a sword and companions around me.

"I know," Darien said. "I wanted to feel as if I was unquestionably Urdo's heir, not the second-best choice, not a bastard. We talked about proclaiming it in a few years when all the kings knew me, when I was a praefecto. He made me feel there wasn't any question he would have chosen me even if there had been a choice, but I wanted everyone to feel like that. I wanted you to feel like that," he said, in a lower voice.

"But I do!" I said. "I'm so proud, Darien!"

"But now I have that, it isn't anything because what I want now is to talk to Urdo. But he is—" He choked.

"He is dead, and you are High King," I said.

"He is dead, but there is no body, and he is lying there with his bones sunk into the land but still speaking sometimes. I am not High King yet, I have taken nobody's oath," he said. He looked so young, biting his lip in the moonlight.

So I knelt to him there in the moonlight and made him my oath for Derwen. I did not make my armiger's oath again. Although it, too, is ended by death, I still feel bound by it in my duty to Urdo.

When Darien had spoken, I stood again, and then, as a cloud moved away from the moon, I saw Darien's face, transfixed. "Mother, the trees!" he whispered, as if he hardly dared speak.

I turned to see what he was looking at. The trees were moving; one of each kind was growing taller. They formed a circle around us and bowed to Darien. There was a music rising and growing around us that was the song of the green and growing things of the island. I could feel the land then, as I could at home in Derwen, but this was the whole island speaking to Darien, the mountains of Bregheda and of Demedia, the fens of Tevin, each river and forest and rock and farmstead making itself known to him as part of the pattern, part of the music of the island, whether he had known it before or not.

The moon shone steadily now, for we were out of the time of clouds. I found myself mounted on Apple, as always when the land saw me, and as always, although I knew he was dead, it felt so right that it did not have time to feel strange. I moved back a little from Darien as they came through the trees, the protectors of Tir Tanagiri, as I had seen them all once before when I went home to Derwen and took up my lordship. Urdo had been beside me then as I was beside Darien now. Turth was there, and Hithwen the white roebuck, Hithun the stag, Hoivar the great owl, Palug the cat, and many others, coming out of the shadows and the moonlight to make themselves known to the new king. I sat there calmly on Apple's back, looking down at Darien as they came one by one and greeted him. His face shone with wonder in the moonlight and he put out his hand to each of them in turn, before they went back to the trees to wait. Last came Ohtar Bearsson, protector of the Jarnsmen of Tir Tanagiri. Darien embraced him, though Ohtar was taller now than any man or bear that had ever walked the waking woods.

Then Urdo was there, leaning against an oak tree on the opposite side of the clearing from me. I looked again; maybe he was the tree. It was as if the whole wood, the whole hillside, the whole country, was Urdo's body now, as the lake had been the Mother's body the night we had visited her. He was not dead, no more than Ohtar was, for he would not return to live other lives. He was Urdo forever, not as a man but as part of the land. It was small enough comfort in my grief for the man who was my friend. He looked at me, but we did not speak. There were no words, there could be no words in this time, only the great chords of the music of the land as his new awareness pulsed into Darien's veins and moved the air around us. If every musician in the country had played at once it would not have made a harmony like the swelling of the themes of that music.

After a while there was a moment when we were waiting, and then the high gods were there, above the trees, as if they had always been there, as of course they had. Gangrader was there among them, with Heider and Tew and others of the Jarnish gods I did not recognize. Darien bowed to them all, courteously, one by one, and they stood there above the trees, waiting again.

Darien stood alone in the center of the grove, for Apple and I were away toward the edge of the trees. He lowered his head for a moment. Then he touched one hand to his pebble. He reached out his hands, palm down, then palm up. There was a hushed expectancy, although the music neither stopped nor slowed, and then there was the light, limning everything with clarity that was neither sunlight nor moonlight, making everything seem larger, more distinct and more clearly itself. Everything glowed with benevolent light, and the music which had been all the parts of the island became one song, praising the light, the God made Man whose sacrifice had enabled all beings to become more truly themselves. Everything was love and warmth and safety, everything was in its place and growing there. The song was an affirmation rising from the heart and filling the soul.

For a moment I felt it, as Darien raised his arms. The light was made up of all that I loved; the land, the Peace, even my gods were singing. But inside me something was still cold, and my heart said no. It may have been my stubborn nature that would not turn from the old ways. Or it may have been my grief that would not let me wholly give myself to rejoicing. I turned Apple's head away from the light, and stared out into the darkness behind me. The song was subdued at once, little more than a memory behind me. It seemed I was staring into a desolation, a plain of ashes, and out in that plain I could see a city of darkness, gray against black, a city whose towers were spikes and whose heart was malice. Morthu was out there, and his kind, those who would rather do harm than good. It wasn't only Morthu and I knew it, but Morthu was the heart of the spite I could see and name. There were dark gods there, too, some formless and some with shapes and names that I feared. I almost turned back to the light. I had no desire to hate and spoil like Morthu. But Apple whickered, and there came an answering sound of crows, and I knew that Gangrader was behind me.

My heart said no again. I absolutely refused to yield Morthu the darkness. This was a false choice and no choice and I would not be forced to make it. I raised Urdo's sword. Light moved on the blade before me. I drew a deep breath and remembered starlight on the sea. Without the darkness there would be no light. Every light casts shadows, too, and without the shadows there would be no light because everything would be light. I remembered sun through the clouds, and I remembered every dark night I had stood a night watch on a cold camp and the beauty there was in darkness. I remembered the colors of morning when I had come to them through night.

With every memory I pushed my darkness out onto that plain. My darkness had trees and wind and the splash of the sea. I heard a bear's low growl behind me. My darkness was a welcome friend, different from the light. I remembered a light seen in a farm window on a night ride long ago, somebody dying or being born. I remembered the dark on top of Foreth. I could smell the water weed of the Mother's lake high in the hills of Bregheda. I held the sword high and looked at it, knowing that a sword can kill, but that some people must be prepared to kill to keep the Peace. My darkness was not an attack on the light but something else real and good. Lightning split the sky before me and thunder crashed around me, and the lake was in front of me, dark under the sky, between the blue flashes. I threw the sword out into the water as I had promised Urdo. I saw her hand come up to

catch it. Then I felt a hand on my shoulder, and it was not
Gangrader's but the Lord of the Cunning Hand. He pressed a
spear forward into my empty hand, and the spear shone with
blue light. As I looked at the spear I knew it was a great treasure of the land, as great as Urdo's sword, and greater in my
hand because it had been meant for me.

As I took it I heard the music again, another upswelling
behind me, and this time it sounded more resonant, like a
light shining in darkness or a harp played in a hall when the
wind blows cold outside.

The dark citadel was almost surrounded by my wholesome
darkness. It now seemed to stand on a crag far off in the distance. Then I saw Morthu standing on the walls and aiming a
war machine at me. Darien moved up beside me, armored in
blue and gold, shining. Ohtar was on my other side, a huge
bear snarling defiance. Behind me were Urdo and Gangrader,
Turth and Bregheda, the Lord of Light, the Lord of the Cunning Hand, Sky Father, Heider, the Lady of Wisdom and all
the gods in their ranks, and the White God himself, a slight,
bearded Sinean wearing a loincloth.

Morthu's war machine sent a great ball of dark fire toward
us. I raised my spear to block it, but saw too late that it was
aimed not at me but at Darien. As fast as thought, Apple and
I moved between Darien and the ball and it burst around us.

21

> She rides through battle, dealing death,
> choosing which warriors to invite,
> steel cold eyes, cold steel sword,
> selecting those who feast tonight,
> she may laugh or howl as she stalks,
> picking the ones she will smite.
> —From "Walkurja"

The world around me went out like a blown candle and I was crushed by despair that fell on me like a heavy weight. I was running full tilt through the wood, in the dark, entirely alone and entirely desperate. I had already been running for a long time and I was tired. There was no possibility of rest or refuge. It was hard for my thoughts to get any purchase on the surface of my mind. Whenever one did it immediately began to spiral into a terrible, despairing loop. It seems that I went around each loop more than once, some of them many times, so that they were both terrible and terribly familiar. I ran, without really seeing the woods around me, accepting what I saw without thinking about it. There were trees and the shadows of trees stretching out all around me however far I ran. I saw eyes, more than once, regarding me from the undergrowth; a boar, a cat, a great silver hound. I veered away from them less in fear than in self-loathing. I ran heedless for a time without measure, until at last I caught my foot on a tussock and sprawled headlong, bruised and sobbing. I almost poked myself in the eye with the spear. It had stopped glowing. My fingers were cramped from clutching it. I was almost ready to cast it away uncaring, but I knew there was a reason I had to keep it. I looked at it for a while before I remembered that it was given to me in trust.

What had I thought I was doing standing there among the gods, taking gifts from them, thinking myself almost one of them? Alone in the dark, cold wood I knew myself all too human. My mistakes had led to Urdo's death, and now he was dead and there was nothing in the world worth living for. I could help keep the Peace and rule Derwen, but they would be hollow, joyless things. The weight of my grief and loneliness made me double over. Duty was a thin shield indeed against it. Still, the spear had been given to me and I would guard it. Though their purposes were beyond me, I knew I had been there and I refused to fail in my trust. I had been there, even if it was hard to hold it clearly.

What had I thought I was doing, sitting on Apple's back? Apple was dead, long ago in Caer Lind. Alone among the strange trees I knew myself far from home. These were not my familiar woods and this was not my land that remembered him. I was a stranger here, alone, uninvited, and unwelcome. I pulled myself to my feet to seek a way out and ran again, blindly, lurching, blundering into trees. After a while I stopped and threw my head back and howled.

What had I thought I was doing, trying to change the shape of the world when not even my family trusted me? Alone beneath the rustling branches I knew I had no real family. I hardly knew Darien, and now he was about to forgive Angas for killing Urdo. My father was dead. The brother I loved and the brother I despised were both dead, my sister had died after trying to poison me, my mother was old and had never really found me worthy of her. I howled and scrabbled at the fallen leaves and loam of the forest floor, stirring up a smell of damp rot that almost made me gag.

What had I thought I was doing, surviving the battle? Alone in the moonlight among the falling leaves I understood Emer, going forward to die. Almost I envied her for her illusions. I had long understood that a valiant death in battle is still only death and pain and blood and an end to life. Urdo was dead. I had outlived my lord and my purpose in life. I had failed in my duty to defend him. I had not been there in time. I wailed and wept and rocked to and fro. Again the spear got in my way, reminding me of its existence.

What had I thought I was doing, throwing away Urdo's

sword? Alone in the chilly glade I knew I had nothing left to remind me. I had been clutching the spear all this time, now I hugged it to me and sobbed over it. For a moment it was comforting, then it was hateful to me. It was a reminder of how I had failed in my responsibility. I longed to throw it away. I considered killing myself with it. I hated it. I hated myself. I hated the whole world. In that moment I even hated Urdo for failing me by dying. He was supposed to tell me what to do, and now I would never be sure again. I tore at my hair, tearing it out in great clumps. Somehow the pain steadied me. Pain, a part of my mind thought, is my ally. I saw a raven sitting on a bare branch in front of me, dark against the darkness.

What had I thought I was doing, being here at all? Alone beneath branches reaching like needy hands I knew I should have stayed at home and taken care of my responsibilities and my own people, who were my duty even if they hated me. I knew I would never find myself again, never find my way home to the people who had trusted me and who I had abandoned. I was worthless. I caught at the spear to hurl it away, and caught my thumb on the blade, a beginner's mistake. I had not done that since I was twelve years old. What a stubborn fool I was, without even the skill to handle a spear properly. I sang the healing charm over my thumb, by reflex. I wasn't at all surprised when it didn't work, and the wound continued to sting and drip blood. It was what I deserved, after all, to be abandoned even by the gods.

As I put my cut thumb in my mouth I looked up through the pain and saw that it was not entirely true that they had all abandoned me. Gangrader was here, leaning against a tree in front of me and looking down quizzically. I realized that he had come to claim me at last. I was here to die of exposure in the wood, to complete the sacrifice Ulf had made of me.

What had I thought I was doing, living my life? Alone with Gangrader in the cold, wintry glade, I knew that my whole life since Ulf had dedicated me had been like a brand drawn back from the fire to be thrust into it on the next cold night. I had fought and ruled and laughed and thought myself alive, but really I had been dead all this time and not known it. I looked at him and hated him. He was standing in a patch of moonlight, leaning against a great ash tree. There was a grizzling of snow on the ground. He had his dark cloak clutched around him and a raven perched on his shoulder. One eye socket was shadowed and empty. He stared at me and did not speak. I stared back, despairing.

He continued to stand there looking at me until anger moved in me. Anger is another ally, came a thought somewhere at the back of my mind. I pulled anger around me like a warm blanket until fury filled me. "What did you think you were doing, claiming me against my will, Lord of the Slain?" I asked. My voice sounded dull and flat and hopeless in my ears. I did not ask how it would be worse to be claimed by Gangrader than to run mad in the wood. "Here you are in the wood, come to get me, yet I have never worshiped you or called on you, and so the sacrifice Ulf Gunnarsson made was worthless, being unwilling."

Gangrader laughed harshly, making me furious. "The unwilling are no less welcome," he said, in Jarnish.

I stared up at him, filled with indignation. "Of all the ridiculous, barbaric ideas I've heard from the Jarns over the years, that is the worst. How can it be? The whole purpose of a sacrifice is that it be made wholehearted. That's revolting."

"Long it would take to ask consent of those you left behind you for the battlecrows," he said, in Tanagan now.

"That's different. They would have killed me as quickly," I said, rocking back on my heels and staring up at him. "That is not sacrifice."

"What difference if my servant throw a spear to hurtle past the waiting swords and eyes, and dedicate the harvest reaped to me?"

"All the difference in the world!" I shouted, getting to my feet. "The gods have power but people have will. You may not claim me against mine."

"Has Ulf no will?" he asked. Before I could answer that Ulf's will did not bind me, he went on, "And would you count no worth the service you have done me all these years?

They name you with my Choosers of the Slain." The shadowed side of his face seemed to be smiling.

"I have never served you, and you have no right to claim me now," I said.

"Do you call me when you desire aid?"

"I never have," I said. I shifted the spear loosely in my hand. I had no idea whether this weapon could hurt a god. I was not used to fighting them. Nobody was. I wasn't used to standing screaming at them for that matter. I began to wonder what I was doing and why I was doing it.

"Yet here I am when you have need of aid," he said. "And what is there that you will offer me?"

"What aid?" I asked cautiously. I remembered Ulf telling me never to believe Gangrader's twisted promises. I had told him proudly that Gangrader had promised me nothing.

He laughed, and the raven rose a few beats above his shoulder before settling again and fixing me with its dark eye. There was another on the leafless ash above his head, I realized, which had been staring at me all the time. I looked uneasily away from its bold gaze. "Are you come back so far beyond despair that you have reached the shore where caution lies? With time you would have found the way yourself. Shall we leave thorny points of who serves whom and now discuss how we go on from here?"

"You have not come to claim me?" I asked, still uncertain and confused. I was not quite all the way back from the despair Morthu had thrust me into.

"Who shall say what is mine?" he asked, in a very different voice, in Jarnish, smiling his crooked smile.

I wept then, with no warning, remembering not Gangrader saying that to Morwen but Urdo repeating those words in Caer Tanaga so long ago. On Foreth Ulf asked me if I had had no good of my dedication. Gangrader had come twice now to save me. Still he was no patron god of my choosing.

With those tears, which were from my heart and caused by no sorcery, I washed Morthu's despair from my eyes. As I wiped the back of my hand across them to dash them away, I could see clearly again. I shivered, and for the first time saw what I was looking at; the bare branches, the sprinkling of snow. "It's winter," I said stupidly. I remembered the three days' night on Foreth, and Darien spending a day following Turth when it had been five days for me in my waiting anxiety. "Has half a year passed as I ran mad? Is Urdo buried already? What has happened about Morthu? Does the curse still hold?"

"Time is rent from the worlds," Gangrader said, still in Jarnish, making me wonder why he had been speaking Tanagan before, and why he had changed. "Nor are you friendless outside time."

I didn't understand in the least. "Am I still in the time of the gods?"

"You stand in time here now as we feel time," he said, back to Tanagan again. "Leaves and snow fall as worlds turn into time. This wood is not the world until we choose, not until someone looks and fixes time. Then there is going on but never back, for us as you, the pattern set in time. That blackheart would have thrust you out to wail and gained the time himself, without you there. He little thought that all of us would wait. No one has looked, and time is waiting yet; it hangs upon the moment when you came, that instant when the king bowed to the trees."

"So this time isn't real?" I asked, trying to puzzle my way through what he had said. I looked at the raven on the bare branch. They seemed as real as anything I had ever seen.

"It will be real in time," he said.

"So, is there a way back?" I asked.

"Many ways," he replied, smiling again.

"And is there a way back before that moment?" I asked, knowing it was hopeless, but needing to ask anyway. "Back to the morning of the battle?"

"There is no power can bend or break that law," he said.

I drew breath, then stopped. This was where he supposed I should ask for help, so that he could bargain with me. He looked as if he were expecting it. What he said about unwilling sacrifices could have been meant to trick me. If I spoke, if I said anything at all now, it would be to ask for his help, and to make myself what he said I was. I took a firmer grip on the spear and said nothing, just looked at him evenly. Pain had been my ally, anger had been my ally. In the same way I had understood my allies even through the muddle of despair, I recognized that, although he would trick me if he could, Gangrader was my ally, too. I was myself again, and the heavy emptiness of despair had no more hold on me.

I kept waiting. I kept my breathing as even as I could, though I couldn't control the speed of my heart. I was past being afraid, past hope and despair into true recklessness. I did not know what Gangrader wanted or whether it was the same as what I wanted. Being his Walkurja was better than despairing in Morthu's power. I understood that now, but it was not my will, and my will had been forced too much this night already for me to give in now.

I stood there and looked at Gangrader's unmoving face. I did not even know if there truly was a way back. If not then I might have lost seven months, or seven years, or worst of all seven times seven years, like people in stories who went under the hill and feasted for a night only to come back to find their friends dead and their children grown old. If so, then I would have to endure it. I faced the possibility then, and though I hated it I thought I could bear it if I had to.

As I stood there, leaning a little on the spear I had been given, I mourned. Urdo was dead, and Masarn, and ap Erbin, and so many friends. I mourned in silence for all who had fallen at Agned, running their names through my mind. I mourned even for Ayl, who I had killed, though not for Marchel or Arling. I mourned for Masarn's wife Garwen and his daughter who had shared my name. I mourned for all the people Morthu had slain in Caer Tanaga to get the power to curse Segantia, and I mourned for all those who had died of the curse, naming all those I knew. Then I mourned for Duncan and Conal and all who had been killed in this war since Aurien poisoned me. I mourned for Aurien as she had been. I went back further and mourned again for Galba and those who fell at Foreth, and back through the war and mourned my father, Gwien, and beyond to Caer Lind, to Enid and

Geiran and Bran and Osvran and Apple. Still I stood there and still I mourned for those who had fallen in skirmishes or in training, and at last I mourned for Rudwen and my brother Darien.

When I had held them all in memory I began to go forward through all my battles, each victory and defeat. When I reached Agned it was as painful as touching a fresh wound, but still I held it again in my mind. When I had done I was still staring at Gangrader, and he at me, as if we would never move.

I thought over my stewardship of Derwen, of my love for the land and my care of the people. I thought how Urdo had said I had done well, better than he would have thought. I remembered how Darien had said I was the best armiger. I thought how I had hated myself under Morthu's despair and pushed that away as I had pushed away his darkness in the night. I remembered Veniva looking at me approvingly on the steps of the hall. I remembered little Gwien jumping up and down while he was waiting for me to rub down Beauty, because he was so glad to see me at Magor. Osvran used to say that we should never be arrogant, but we were right to be proud of what we were. I had repeated this to my own armigers for years, but never until now had I understood it for myself.

"Will you ask for help?" Gangrader said, in Jarnish. I was almost startled to hear the silence broken after so long.

I frowned at his smile, and then I laughed. Only now did I consider what he had said before. None of the gods had looked, so that I could go back into time when I had left it. I did not understand what it meant not to look into time, when the gods are part of the structure of the world, but it must mean that this was something they wanted. The laugh echoed strangely and some snow slid off a high branch. I drew a deep breath. "Oh yes, I will ask for help," I said. I raised my arms, palms down and then palms up, as if to make an oath. There was no hymn for this, no words to help me find the way. "Albian," I said, "Shining One. If ever I have served you, send me light to show me the way back to the sunlit world where I belong. Merthin, Lord Messenger. Aid me now, show me the right path out of this wood to my own time. Mother Coventina, who brought water on the hilltop at Foreth, help me find a way back to your world I left."

Gangrader wasn't there any longer. Where he had stood was a faint beginning of a path curving away around the ash. I looked up and saw the raven on the branch was still staring at me. I stuck my tongue out at it. The moon went behind a cloud, leaving the sky very dark.

I took a step on the path. Nothing happened. The trees were not very thick here. I went forward cautiously. My feet almost seemed to know the way, as they might at home in Derwen. I ran over what I had asked—might they have taken me back to Derwen instead of back to the night I left? I walked on, and found myself scuffing through strewn drifts of fallen leaves which crackled beneath my feet. The air smelled autumnal. The sky was beginning to lighten ahead of me. The path seemed to be tending downhill. I saw antlers through the trees, and dappled flanks moved past me in a rush as a herd of deer ran by, almost close enough to touch. Last came the great stag with the pair of brown eyes like pools and I knew I had seen Hithun again. I walked on, carefully, and now in the early dawn light I was walking on ferns and celandines and passing the last of the dead bluebells. I saw wild roses and brambles in full bloom, showing very white before color came back to the world.

I came at last to the place at the edge of the trees where I had stood with Darien. The sun was rising before me. My fingernails were broken and bloody, and my hands and arms were engrained with dirt and criss-crossed with scratches from brambles. The cut the spear had given me around the base of my thumb was a white healed scar, like something I had got years ago. The spear itself was also encrusted with dirt, but whole and safe. I could see the camp below me, as I had left it to walk with Darien. I gave heartfelt thanks to the gods.

Two people were walking up from the camp toward me. I didn't feel as if there was any hurry to go toward them, so I stayed where I was. It occurred to me all at once that I was ferociously thirsty. I lifted my water bottle to my lips and drained it dry. By the time I lowered it they were close enough for me to see that they were Ulf and Garah. The expressions on their very different faces were identical.

22

I have been where were slain the warriors
of Tir Tanagiri, I have seen them fallen,
myself alive, they in their grave.
     —"The List of Battles"

I sat down on a fallen elm, thickly grown with moss, ivy, and great brown tree mushrooms. Garah and Ulf only took a few minutes to come up. They sat down on either side of me in the watery sunlight.

Garah began to give fervent thanks to the Mother for my safety as soon as she was sure I was really there, mostly unharmed, and in my right mind.

Ulf, characteristically, just grunted. "People have been catching glimpses of you for days," he said. "But you were gone a moment later."

"Days?" I asked, my heart sinking.

"This is the morning of the third day since the battle," Garah said gently.

It could just as easily have been a hundred years. I should have been grateful, and I knew it, but all the same I was furious.

"The first morning half your ala were up here beating through the woods," Ulf said.

"What has happened?" I asked, pushing my straggling hair back out of my eyes.

"Wouldn't you rather go down and bathe?" Garah asked. "And aren't you hungry?"

Bathing would have been wonderful, and my stomach rumbled at the thought of food, but I wasn't ready for the amount of well-meant fuss there would be when I got back to the ala. Besides, I wanted to know what I'd missed. "Tell me now," I said.

"Morthu and Cinon are in Caer Tanaga," Garah said.

"Elenn's still there and I don't know what anyone has told her. We're a bit stuck as to what to do about them. We can't easily get them out of there, but they can't do much as long as they're in there. We're not really in a position to besiege them."

"We could," Ulf contradicted her. "It would mean having people on both sides of the Tamer and blockading the river, but we could do it."

"Everyone from Bereich is eager to get home," Garah said. "And the same goes for Atha and her ships. They'll stick it out, but they have had enough already."

"What about the other side?" I asked.

"Flavien is camped not far away and has sued for peace," Garah said. "Raul and Mother Teilo and Father Cinwil have been beating out the terms with him, and the same with Hengist Guthrumsson for Cennet, and Sidrok Trumwinsson for Aylsfa. Those of Arling's folk who are left around here have agreed to go back to Jarnholme as soon as they might. Some of them are in Caer Tanaga with Morthu though."

"What have Flavien and Hengist and Sidrok agreed to?" I asked.

"Well, they have all agreed about the council, and about Glyn being king of Bregheda," Garah said, and rolled her eyes. "What business it is of theirs to disapprove I don't know. It has been agreed that in future if there is no clear heir, then the council will decide." This was exactly the sort of thing Urdo had wanted the council for, of course. "They spent yesterday arguing about ransom for those killed, and today they were ready to move on to accepting Tereg ap Cinvar as king of Tathal."

"Tereg? I thought his name was Pedrog?" I asked.

"Tereg is the younger brother," Ulf said. "They were both in ap Erbin's ala. Pedrog was a decurio. I knew him quite well. He was killed when they charged against the war machines. Tereg is a sequifer. You must have sung over his wounds, because he was quite near me in the sick tent on the night after the battle."

"We are going to have a number of very young kings," I

said, inadequately. I ran through them in my mind, and realized who hadn't been mentioned. "What about Angas?" I asked. Garah hesitated and gave me a curious glance. I gave the best smile I could. "What has he agreed to?"

Garah hesitated again. "It's all right," Ulf said. "Ap Gwien does not pursue vengeance on past the limits of sense."

"I know that!" Garah snapped. "Here you are, alive to prove it, when vengeance would have had you dead in the dust five years ago after you killed Morien." She rolled her eyes.

"Ap Theophilus stood witness that Morien challenged Gunnarsson. It was a judicial combat, and did not break Urdo's Law," I said.

"But if you were vengeful past sense you would not have forgiven the bloodfeud," Ulf said.

"Oh, I forgot to tell you, I killed Arling in the battle," I said, suddenly reminded.

Garah laughed. "Everyone knows that," she said. "The tale of how you killed three kings has not diminished in the telling."

"Thank you," Ulf said, simply. Garah looked at him, puzzled.

"We were talking about Angas?" I reminded them.

"Angas has made peace," Ulf said.

"Darien told me on the night of the battle that Angas had offered him a marriage alliance," I said.

"And that wasn't what sent you mad?" Garah asked cautiously.

I laughed, completely taken off balance. "It was Morthu who sent me mad," I said, when I had recovered myself. "Didn't Darien tell you?"

"Not in any detail at all," Garah said.

"Was Morthu here?" Ulf asked. "I thought he was in Caer Tanaga from the evening of the battle."

"He was in Caer Tanaga," I said. "He reached here and sent me mad, by sorcery. Then the gods showed me the way back."

Garah frowned. "You saw them?" she asked tentatively.

"I really am in my right mind again," I said, and patted her arm. "I saw them all with Darien, but at the end they only helped me as they might help anyone who is lost in a wood. I had conversation only with the Lord of the Slain." Ulf gave a little growl. "I struck no bargains with him," I hastened to assure him.

Ulf muttered something into his beard in Jarnish that might have been "Good!" or might have been something else entirely. I decided not to press him about it. The memory of Gangrader's eyes fixed on mine was still fresh.

"What did he want?" Garah asked gently, looking as if she suspected my wits were still wandering.

It was an impossible question. I wondered if I even knew what the answer was. "I think," I began tentatively, and then I was sure. "He wanted, all of them wanted, wanted very strongly, for me to come back here and now. There is something I need to do. I don't know what it is, but I know it's important."

They both gaped at me, and again their expressions were identical. I did not laugh. "So why are you two together and looking for me?" I asked.

They looked at each other guiltily. "Actually, we weren't looking for you," Ulf said. "We were just walking up here to have a private conversation."

"Don't let me stop you," I said, slightly hurt.

"I was hoping we might see you up here," Garah said. "I have no idea what it was Ulf wanted to talk to me about."

Ulf looked at me cautiously. "It doesn't matter," he said.

"Go on, what is it?" I asked, curious.

"Getting into Caer Tanaga," he said at last, lowering his voice, though there was nobody anywhere near us. "You got out, ap Gavan. There must be a way back in. Not a way suitable for a whole ala, of course, and not honorable for the High King to be doing it, but if you got out then there is a way one person could go in, and kill Morthu. I could do it. And that would stop this plague killing everyone, and stop him hurting anyone else."

"Elenn, and the people still in the city, you mean?" Garah asked.

"He is doing terrible things there. Right outside the usage of war. Darien said that to Angas, and Angas agreed."

I remembered ap Madog asking me about the safety of the people of Magor, and how I had said they were unlikely to wander onto a battlefield. I could hardly believe I had ever been that naive. I shuddered.

"Them, yes, but everyone else as well," Ulf said. "Morthu was asking for a ship to get away to Narlahena, the last I heard. Think what he could do there. And he could plot from over there, like Marchel. He could come back, in ten years or fifteen, when he was ready, and there would be all this to go through again. And even if he doesn't do that, he can curse us all with plagues like this one, and the Grandfather of Heroes says it can only be ended when he is killed. Segantia would be a desert. Berth ap Panon is dead of the wound-rot, and he is not the only one. While Morthu lives we are none of us safe."

"Did Inis definitely say it was—" I began, and then I remembered that I didn't need to convince Urdo about that anymore. Sitting up here I had almost forgotten he wasn't down there in the camp. "Where have they buried Urdo?" I asked, abruptly.

"He is near death, but not quite dead yet," Garah said. "He is in his tent. He hardly speaks or knows anyone is there, but sometimes he can hear what Darien says, and replies."

I could not imagine why this had gone on so long. Since he was dead, surely it would be better for everyone to know he was dead and for Darien to be ruling clearly in his own name? "I see," I said.

Garah put her hand on mine sympathetically, then took it back. "I really think you need to bathe," she said. "You're all over scratches and grime, even worse than at Caer Lind."

"I'll go down soon," I said. "But you were about to tell Ulf how to get into Caer Tanaga to kill Morthu."

"You're not going to stop me?" Ulf asked.

"Stop you?" I took a firm grip on my spear. "Far from it. I'm going to come with you."

"But will Darien allow it?" Garah asked.

"Probably not, if he is negotiating," I said. "Also, he wants to kill Morthu himself, though he knows the risk is too high. But we could do it without troubling him with it until Morthu was dead."

"I am nobody," Ulf said. "I am one Jarnish armiger. Darien could disown me if I were caught. You are the High King's mother. You can't risk giving Morthu a hostage like that."

"High King's mother nothing—" I began angrily, but Garah interrupted me.

"You are Lord of Derwen," she said. "You would leave another very young king if you are killed."

"That's true," I said slowly. "My lady mother would cope, I suppose, but it will be five years before little Gwien is old enough to be king for himself. All the same, I fought in the battle and could have died, and did not count that a hindrance."

"The battle yes, but nobody else could have done what you did; you had to fight," Garah said. "This sneaking into Caer Tanaga is something anyone could do, if it is necessary that anyone do it."

"I can go alone," Ulf said. "It will be safest. There is least chance of being seen. I would have gone already without telling anyone, except for needing to know the way."

"How will you get him to fight you?" Garah asked. "He will not agree. He will use magic and twist your mind against you if you are close to him."

Ulf shifted uneasily. "I wasn't planning to talk first," he said. Garah and I just looked at him. "Yes, I'm prepared to murder him if that's the only way to kill him!" he said after a moment, too loudly. Some startled pigeons flew up from the trees behind us.

"I need to talk to Darien," I said, turning the spear in my hands.

"You just said he wouldn't let me go," Ulf said.

"He must not negotiate a settlement where Morthu lives on

to work malice," I said. "But sneaking in and murdering Morthu breaks the Peace and Urdo's Law. I cursed him, and I felt the curse take hold. It will take him." I felt sure of it.

"But we can't just sit and do nothing and wait until it does," Ulf protested. "The gods send aid to those who put themselves in the way of it."

"And while I don't agree with murder either," Garah said, "I did wonder ever since I heard about your curse whether he might be keeping himself alive against the curse by sorcery, and by murdering people to get the power for it."

My gorge rose and I swallowed hard against it. Had Masarn's wife died because of my curse? I remembered her long ago, on a cold winter morning at Caer Tanaga, eating chestnuts and smiling, surrounded by children. "We have to stop him," I said, getting to my feet. "A siege is too long, even if it's possible."

"Murder is an ugly word," Ulf said, looking up at me. "But it is not breaking the Peace for one man to break the Law and afterward come to justice. Remember how after Arvlid died, Urdo persuaded us not to move against Morthu? If I had done what I wanted to then, Morthu would have been under the earth eight years now, there would have been no war, and many good people would still be alive. It was what you wanted to do as well." He looked steadily at me. It was true. I had regretted it ever since. I raised my chin. "If the gods have brought you back for a reason, maybe you should come with me. Maybe you could kill him with honor. But with or without, the world needs to be rid of him, as it is rid of Arling."

"Not like that," I said. "I want him dead as much as you do. But we must not begin Darien's reign with murder. That is not what the gods want." I looked at the spear, which just seemed like any spear, and at the thin white scar on my thumb, which looked as if it healed ten years ago at least. "The Smith put this into my hand for some purpose, and it was not to kill Morthu. It might be to rescue Elenn and the people of Caer Tanaga. But I need to speak to Darien. There might be a way to do it without going through the heating system."

"It might not even be safe," Garah said. "He will know I escaped, and Elenn might have told him how. You know how it is, when you're talking to him what he says sounds like the most reasonable thing in the world and you almost agree. If he told her I was a traitor she might have shown him the entrance, and he might have blocked it, or have someone waiting there to get anyone coming in that way. Also, some parts are quite narrow—I'm not sure either of you would fit."

"I'd take that risk," Ulf said stubbornly.

I shook my head. "I'm going to find Darien," I said, and turned to walk down toward the camp.

Garah hurried after me. "Aren't you going to wash first?" she asked. "He'll be busy with the peace talks, but he'll probably come as soon as he hears you're here. You probably have time to wash in the river."

"That seems like a good idea," I said. I glanced back at Ulf, who was sitting with his hands on his knees, looking thoroughly dejected. I felt an urge to throw something at him. "Come down to camp," I called, startling the pigeons again. He got up and trudged down after us.

"I'm going to bathe, then I'm going to talk to Darien," I said. "When we have a plan for a group to go in, I'll make sure you're part of it."

"Thank you," he said grudgingly.

"And if anyone is to go through the old heating system, it should be me," Garah said.

"But you just said how dangerous it would be!" I said.

"It would be more dangerous for anyone else who wasn't sure of the way, and especially if they were bigger," Garah said, and shrugged.

We went on down into the camp. People immediately began fussing around me, as I had known they would. I told them I had been driven mad by Morthu's sorcery, and didn't say anything about what happened with time, or the gods. I might as well not have troubled myself. To this day they say that wood is haunted, and who is to say it is not?

At last I came down to the River Agned. They said it had flowed red with blood after the battle on the bridge, but it was back to the usual clear brown of river water by now. Ulf had gone off somewhere, probably to sulk about not being allowed to murder Morthu on his own account. Elidir was pressing soap on me and Govien was trying to explain exactly how he'd arranged the ala while I was away and Garah was fussing about my armor when they suddenly all went quiet. I looked up to see why, halfway through unbuckling the strap under my arm.

Angas was there. He had not long come out of the water, and had a towel in his hand. He had a nasty cut on his thigh, which he had taken from my sword; he was bruised around the shoulders, and his hair was streaming wet.

His eyes looked bruised, too, as if he had not slept for days.

"Sulien," he said. "My old friend—" He trailed off, and tears welled in his eyes.

I just looked at him. I realized I was reaching for my sword only when my hand closed on my empty scabbard. "Traitor," I said.

He stepped back a little as if I had struck him unexpectedly. "Must we be enemies?" he asked. I caught sight of Garah's horrified face out of the corner of my eye.

"No," I said. "No, King of Demedia, we have no bloodfeud. The High King has made peace with you. If you can keep the law then assuredly I can. You need have no fear that Derwen will seek revenge." The tears ran down into his beard, but I stayed absolutely cold.

"Urdo made us embrace as friends when we had quarreled about his birth," he said. I remembered it well, the first night I rode with the ala, the spears against the sunset. "Sulien—"

"Derwen will keep the peace with Demedia," I repeated.

He bowed his head. "I hoped you would understand," he said.

"Oh, I understand," I said. "I even pity you. I know about Morthu. But you could have spoken to me like this at the truce talks, you could have stopped giving in to Morthu; you killed Urdo by your own will and with your own hand and I cannot forgive that. As for my own private self, well Angas, old friend, if you don't get out of my sight right now I am going to do my best to kill you barehanded."

It would have given me a great deal of pleasure. But he left, not looking back, and I took off the rest of my armor and went down to the river.

23

Greatest of all living men is Aulius
who has restored the state
the great soldier, the great patron of art,
the great administrator,
Aulius, most renowned son of mother Vinca.

Fresh from his victory over the Sifacians
(and their adherents, our treacherous fellow-citizens,)
he returns to Vinca to march in triumph
to be proclaimed the father of his country,
bringer of peace, saviour of the state.

From the Northern snows to the Southern desert
from one end of Empire to the other,
everyone takes notice of his goodwill,
his mercy, his benevolence.
Everyone offers flowers, or writes praise songs.
> —"The Civil Wars Are Over Forever,"
> Flaccus, *Aulian Ode 2*

As soon as I was dry and dressed in clean clothes, I dealt with Govien's most urgent queries. I wished that Emlin was here, or Masarn for that matter, or ap Erbin. I decided that from now on I would train all my decurios so that they could do a tribuno's work at need. The problem wasn't that Govien couldn't do it; he could, he just didn't trust himself with it. I agreed with his dispositions and reassured him. Then I went to find Darien.

He was sitting outside Urdo's tent arguing with a round-faced man wearing a torn and soot-stained drape. As I came up he made a gesture of dismissal, and the man grabbed his hand. I stepped forward. I had brought the spear with me, without considering it, and now I found it ready in my hand.

Before I could reach him two of the guards had dragged the man away from Darien. They heaved him up and slung him down in a patch of mud, then watched with their hands on their weapons as he backed away.

"Who was that?" I asked, curious.

"Ap Alexias of Caer Custenn," Darien said, his eyes on the man. He beckoned to the guard. "Send someone to follow him and make sure we know where he goes. He should not leave the camp. If he attempts any mischief, bring him to me."

"Yes, my lord," the guard said, and strode off.

There were other people waiting to speak to Darien, but he dismissed them. "Come back later," he said. "I would speak to my mother alone for a while. If Raul comes, send him to me."

"Ap Alexias was one of the men who worked the war machines," Darien went on quickly, when we were alone but for guards and messengers, who waited where they could catch hand signals but not overhear quiet conversation. "He knows nothing about their construction, only their operation. He is the only survivor of their Lossian crews. He expects me to provide a ship to take him back to Caer Custenn."

I snorted. "Really?"

"I told him he was free to take passage on any Narlahenan trading ship, as far as Narlahena, where he would doubtless be able to find a ship going east into the Middle Sea. He said his money and possessions were lost when his camp was looted. He seemed to expect I would make restitution."

"Can he know so little about war?" I asked.

Darien shook his head. "Sheer effrontery, I think. But he is a long way from home. If he had known how to build war machines I might have found a place for him."

"He has surrendered?"

"They have all surrendered, except Morthu and Cinon. Now they have lost, now at last they will talk peace terms sensibly. It is enough to make me tear my hair. We could have been at this stage half a month since if any of them would listen. Though Morthu not being here makes that much easier."

"It's Morthu I wanted to talk to you about," I said, and hesitated.

"Certainly he is the worst outstanding problem," Darien said. He looked seriously at me, and then suddenly his face changed and he looked ten years younger, no longer the confident young king, only an uncertain boy. "I have not welcomed you back. Where have you been, Mother?"

"It took me a little while to find my way back here," I said.

"That thing Morthu threw at me—" he began.

"I was caught up in it," I said, without explaining what it was. "The gods helped me find my way back."

"Great thanks to them," Darien said. "And thank you," he added.

"I should have blocked it with the spear, if I'd been quick enough," I said awkwardly. "But Morthu, who sent that thing, is still there, still in Caer Tanaga and still making trouble. I have heard that you have been negotiating and he may escape?"

"He has offered to go to Narlahena and not come back," Darien said. "He has refused to fight a single combat. He has the Queen, and the people of Caer Tanaga as hostages."

"He must not escape," I said. "He must be brought to trial. I am glad he refused the single combat, because that would not do either. It wouldn't be much better than sneaking in and murdering him, now that we have won and we must rebuild the Peace. He must be tried for his sorcery and his treason in public. His poison can't be allowed to spread, and if he lives or if he dies quietly then it might not die with him. It's not just his curse that is still killing people; it's the lies he's told and will still tell. You know how insidious they are. You know how much he can harm the Peace. He has to stand trial, and soon."

Darien's eyes gleamed. "But how could we make him stand trial?" he asked.

"Make him," I said. "Take Caer Tanaga, and capture him, and force him to come to trial, quickly, while everyone is still here."

"But how can we take Caer Tanaga?"

"The same way Arling did. Quickly, and from the water, when it is lightly held. This is Thurrig's idea, he suggested it to me the night after the battle. Amala is there, and Gomoarionsson, and what's left of Arling's house lords. Amala has been writing to Thurrig, asking him to come and take her back to Narlahena. If Thurrig's fleet came, or some of Thurrig's fleet that is here, with Thurrig visible, then they might think they were friends and let them get close and dock. And then we would have people inside the defenses and could take the city."

Darien raised a hand and one of the waiting messengers came up. "Find Admiral Thurrig and ask him to come here," he told her. She ran off, her loose hair flying about her face. Everyone's hair seemed to be loose or cropped, according to their custom. There were few enough in camp with nobody to mourn, after Agned. "If that worked, it would get us inside the defenses, but not inside the citadel," Darien said. He started scratching lines in the dust, ships and numbers of fighters they could carry. "And they will know that Thurrig fought on our side in the battle."

"They will, yes," I said. "But it might still work. He could fly his own banner, which would confuse them. It doesn't need to fool anyone for very long. As for the citadel, I have just been reminded that Garah got out. Someone could get back in that way and open the gates, though it would be very dangerous because Morthu may know how she came out. She has insisted on volunteering to go back that way."

"How long have you been back?" Darien asked.

I stopped, confused, and glanced at the sun. "Two hours, maybe a little more," I said. "Why?"

He grinned at me. "Because already you have a plan, and not only a plan but volunteers. When were you planning for this expedition to leave?"

"As soon as possible," I said. "If you agree, tonight. The Agned flows into the Tamer below Caer Tanaga, so we could sail down and then up, and they would not know where we had come from. At the same time the alae could be riding down to go inside and help when they could."

"It will take longer than that to move the alae up, and they would really be needed," Darien said. "How many ships were you planning on taking?"

"I think three. More than that would be suspicious, and with three we ought to have just about enough people."

"I'm not sure how many defenders they have there," Darien said, frowning. "Cinon's there, too, and I don't know how many they left when they came here for the battle."

"A sudden attack taking them by surprise," I said. "And the people of the town would be on our side as soon as they saw who we were."

"Do you have volunteers ready for the ships, too?"

"I have promised Ulf Gunnarsson he can go," I said. "I don't have any others." I hadn't thought about it in detail, but it came to me as I was speaking. "Perhaps half armigers who have been trained to fight in close quarters, and half Jarnish infantry who had some experience fighting in the Isarnagan war. Atha's people probably know the most about fighting in towns, but I wouldn't really trust them to know how to stop."

"I was teasing, about volunteers," Darien said. "I'm amazed you even have one. Is Ulf still looking for death? I was surprised he survived the battle. He can certainly go if he wishes it, he deserves it. He took a blow meant for me just after poor Rigol fell, and we might have all gone down to be Urdo's honor guard if not for Ulf."

"That was a bad moment there," I said.

"I didn't get a scratch from it," Darien said. "I think you and I and Father Cinwil are the only people on either side who didn't get at least a minor wound in the battle."

I shook my head at the thought of it. "As for Ulf," I said, after a moment. "I don't think he's looking for death so much as wanting to kill Morthu. Mostly I think he just wants to be doing something, anything. I feel some of that myself, but that's not the real reason why I want to go on this expedition. I feel as if there's something I need to do, something the gods made sure I would be here to do, and this is it."

"If Masarn were still alive I'd make you stay back," Darien said. "You're needed, and this is dangerous. But there is nobody else capable of commanding a force like that, unless Thurrig takes charge of it all himself, and he's an old man now. Sending any of the other kings would be as bad as sending you. The new decurios are too new to send. And of course poor Luth needs a month to get hold of a new idea."

"Who will bring up the alae?" I asked.

"I'll do that myself," Darien said off-handedly.

"What about the peace talks?" I asked.

"It's almost all agreed, and Raul can cope," he said. "In any case, we will want the kings at Caer Tanaga for a trial, if we can capture Morthu alive."

"What about Cinon?" I asked. "Dead or alive?"

Darien paused. "Dead might be better," he said softly. "He is a fool from a line of fools, he has a daughter who is about two years old and no other heir, and it might be better to put all of Nene under Alswith's rule, along with her own land. Her son could marry Cinon's daughter when they are both old enough, if they can bear each other, to make it formal. He hates anyone with Jarnish blood beyond reason, and many of them are his own people now. Urdo has heard so many appeals from the Jarnish farmers of Nene this last five years. I would rather do without him if I can."

Before I could say anything more I caught sight of Thurrig, coming up the slope toward us.

"I am glad to see you better," he said to me, before he bowed and greeted Darien.

"My mother is well, and has a plan," Darien said, and explained it briefly.

Thurrig smiled at the thought of taking the city quickly, and grunted at Darien's figures, but roared with outrage at the thought of getting there that night. "Impossible," he said. "The wind, the tide, the currents at the confluence with the Tamer! Have either of you ever been in a boat? They're not like horses that you can just point the right way and get there, or change direction on a knife edge. With a fair wind a ship is the fastest way to get anywhere, but without one it's slower than walking. And if the wind is with us for going down the Agned, it will be against us when we go up the Tamer, or the other way around, which is more likely at this time of year. I could get to Caer Thanbard faster than Caer Tanaga, from here. Dusk! We would be lucky to get there at sunset tomorrow."

"Sunset tomorrow it is, then," Darien said. "When will you start?"

Thurrig stopped, in mid-rant, and spluttered wordlessly for a moment, so much he almost choked. I laughed. "Oh, laugh, will you," he said, when he had his breath again, laughing himself. "I have been too much with Custennin, I had forgotten what a king's decisions sound like."

"You do understand the danger?" Darien said. "They may know at once you are loyal to us."

Thurrig gave him an appraising glance. "I knew that when I suggested it, Suliensson. It seems like a good chance. As for when we should start, I will answer decision with decision and say we should start as soon as we can get everyone ready to leave. I have taken on water already."

The spear seemed to move a little in my hand, as if eager for the fight to come. "Shall I gather up volunteers?" I asked.

"In a moment," Darien said. "I want to speak to you about another matter."

"I'll leave you to that and see you at the ships," Thurrig said, and bowed to us both.

I smiled, watching him go.

"He has served four generations of us now, and remains his own man," Darien said. He was smiling too.

"He is a good man and an honest one," I said. Then I turned to him. "What did you want to discuss?"

"If I am moving the alae, I shall break this camp and have everyone follow us to Caer Tanaga," Darien said, sounding very sure. "If we take the city, good. If not, then it will mean a tedious siege, and better conducted from as near as possible. There is the question of Urdo."

"He's dead," I said.

"Dead, but with no body to bury or burn." Darien looked as if he was looking at something far off. "People think they see him, still, as we saw him in the leaves. He speaks to me sometimes. He is one of the powers now. Nobody seems to question how he can stay near death so long. But we need to bury him or do something so that everyone knows he is gone. Do you think I should do that here and now, or at Caer Tanaga? And what happens if people see him in the land after they know he's dead?"

I opened my mouth to say that the longer it dragged on the worse it was, when suddenly Urdo was sitting there with us. I could tell that it was just the shadow of the tent and the rise of the hill, but at the same time I could see his face in the shifting light and the way his knees bent as he sat. What I felt was contradictory, as it had been when he gave me the sword. There was so much to say that I couldn't speak, and instead I felt my mouth close with all of it unsaid. He was looking at me as if he knew it all anyway, all the things I could never find a voice to say. He did not speak to me, but turned to Darien, who was watching him silently.

"Caer Tanaga," he said. "Let the women lay me out." It was the Jarnish custom for women to prepare a dead body. "Then set me in a boat and let me go."

"They will say you are not dead," Darien said unsteadily.

"Some will always say that," Urdo said, smiling a little. Then he was gone, the sunlight and shadow no more than that.

"That would appear to settle it, then," I said. My voice sounded a little hollow even to myself.

"People shouldn't say that," Darien said, talking to the space where Urdo had been. "It will make them wonder about the White God."

The White God, of course, who the Book of Memories says came back and walked among his friends after his death, appearing and disappearing when they needed help, until he moved on to become an entirely new kind of god.

"Whatever happened long ago in Sinea, the White God is a real presence," I said, remembering the light that united everything and made all the music into one music. "I think the priests sometimes sound very sure of things that nobody can be sure of. People who understand the gods sound like Inis, not like Father Gerthmol."

"Urdo sang with us in the light," Darien said, as if this reassured him about something. "And Father Gerthmol may sound too sure, but nobody can understand Inis."

"I think that's the state you have to get into to really understand the gods," I said. "And if by then nobody can understand you, that's how it is. When they have dealings with us they do it at a level we can understand without needing to try to understand them. Their purposes are strange to us."

"You said they showed you the way back," Darien said. "Sometimes I feel they want something from me and I don't know what it is."

I thought of Gangrader standing leaning against the ash and staring at me in the moonlight. I remembered how he had arranged for Darien to be born. I had stood in the icy stream and scrubbed off the mark Ulf had written on my stomach in blood, yet here he sat, twenty years later, regarding me evenly. I felt an urge to protect him from all of that; absurd, because he was High King and needed to stand between the gods and the people.

"They showed me a path through the wood," I said. "They gave me this spear. We were standing with them against Morthu. They may know more of things than we can, but we were all standing there together."

He looked at me solemnly. "I will never forget your darkness. I will keep to Urdo's Law, that no one god and no one faith shall be set above another."

"I will never forget your light," I said, and smiled.

24

"Our strength is not in stones, but hearts,
but stone-strength shows how heart-strength holds."
—"The Outwall," Naien Macsen of Castra Rangor

The first time I ever saw Caer Tanaga, I was riding down from Thansethan with Garah. My breasts had been painfully gorged with milk and she had made me drain them in a ditch at the side of the road where we had been hiding for fear of Morwen's pursuit. We came out of the ditch and rode on down the highroad looking as dirty and disreputable as any two girls on greathorses ever did. Then we came over a rise in the land and saw Caer Tanaga below us, the glazed walls and towers of the citadel shining in the morning light. I thought from the first that it was the most beautiful place I had ever seen. Caer Gloran had impressed me with sheer size. Caer Tanaga won my heart with its red and white towers standing on the hill by the river like banners flying.

Since then I had lived in it and come back to it a hundred times at least, in war and in peace, from the north, from the west, from the east. I had grown used to it, but it had never failed to lift my heart when I first caught sight of it. Whether it was the end of a weary day of training, or to defend it against Ayl in the war, or on a visit from Derwen, coming here had always felt special to me. In all those years this was the first time I had ever come to it by water. It looked very different from below, angled against the hill as we came toward it in the sunset.

I had been bracing myself to see the enemy banners flying from the tower. So many times I had looked up to see what alae were here, or if Urdo was back from somewhere. I looked up deliberately, and frowned. I looked at Thurrig, who looked as mystified as I did.

"Arling's a Jarn, of course; he doesn't have a banner, only

a standard. Banners are a thing for civilized people," he said slowly. "Maybe they didn't bother changing it."

"Then why would they take the kingdom banner down, and why are they flying the Moon of Nene, too?" I asked. "Arling's standard is up there, anyway. I can make it out."

It became visible whenever a gust blew Urdo's gold running-horse banner clear for a moment.

"Maybe they want to surrender," Thurrig said, but he was shaking his head as he said it. "No. They'd have flown the kingdom flag for that, more likely than Urdo's horse, I'd have thought."

"It isn't Urdo's horse," Garah said. She had both hands on the rail and was staring fixedly upward as the ship moved. "The running horse is the sign of the House of Emrys. I expect Morthu's flying it as his own banner."

"But he shouldn't be," I protested.

"His mother used to have it embroidered on her clothes, don't you remember?" Garah said.

"Morwen was entitled," I said. "Well, sort of." I stopped and thought about it for a moment. "She was Avren's daughter. Even after she was married she would have been personally entitled to use her own family things. It's unusual, but she was of higher birth rank than Talorgen. But that doesn't mean she had the right to pass it on to her children."

"Was he flying it when you were there before?" Thurrig asked.

"I didn't see it," Garah said. "But I didn't go outside the citadel at all. Nobody said anything about it. But what else could Morthu fly? Angas isn't there, and doesn't approve of what he's doing, so the Thorn of Demedia would be wrong. He doesn't have lands or a banner of his own."

"If he isn't a king or a great captain then he shouldn't be flying one at all," Thurrig growled, glancing up complacently at the red ship on blue that had been his own banner for fifty years.

While we were talking the ship had been creeping closer and closer, so that the city was all around us and we were almost at the wharf already. We were too close now for the war

machines on the walls to reach down to us. The troops were
all under the canvas awnings, ready but not visible.

I turned to Garah. She was smiling at me in a resigned sort
of way. "Yes, I really am sure I want to go through the tunnels," she said, before I could speak. "Yes, I know the dangers. Morthu may have found out how I escaped and be
expecting me. Yes, I have a sharp dagger. No, you can't
come, you're too tall, and you're needed out here."

I sighed. "Am I really that predictable?"

Garah and Thurrig both laughed. "You might have been
about to say that you wish you had just one horse with you,"
Thurrig put in. It had been a long trip.

The landing was almost easy. We had not been able to tell
what degree of opposition we might meet. The important
thing was to have all three ships at the wharf, if we could, so
that we could have all our forces ready. We had discussed
such things as leaping across from one deck to another if necessary. As it happened there was no need. There were a score
or so of Arling's soldiers on the quayside. One of them hailed
us in Jarnish as soon as we were near enough.

"Who comes to Caer Tanaga?"

"The Admiral Thurrig, at his wife's invitation, come to
help some of you get back to where you belong."

"Can't be soon enough for me," the Jarnsman said.

Thurrig laughed, his hand twitching on his ax. They kept
up a constant banter, all of it double-edged, as we came in.
One of our sailors threw a rope and a man on the wharf
caught it. He was one of the usual dockworkers of Caer
Tanaga; I had seen him often enough when I had come down
to cross the river into Aylsfa. He knew me, too, of course.
When his eyes met mine they went wide. I put my finger to
my lips, but it was too late. He let out a great whoop and leapt
on the Jarnish soldier who had been talking to us. The other
workers saw what he was doing and hesitated. I stood up on
the side of the ship, almost overbalancing, and gave a battle
cry. Before we were even off the ship there was nobody in
sight to oppose us.

We disembarked as rapidly as we could. Garah rushed off

straight away to try and open the citadel gates. As we were forming up, crowds of townsfolk came pressing around us, telling us how delighted they were to see us. When they heard that the alae were coming, some of them rushed off to open the town gate. An old fat priest who had a church near the wharf embraced me as kin and actually wept for joy at the sight of me. More and more people poured out of their houses, roused by the cheers. Caer Tanaga had suffered under the invader, and now that we had come to lead them, the people were more than ready to fight. They didn't really need us, they just needed to believe they could win. They came armed with whatever was to hand: wooden clubs, old rusty infantry swords, spades, pitchforks, kitchen knives. I don't think there was an occupying soldier alive in the lower town in half an hour. As we went up through the streets toward the citadel the little company Thurrig and I had brought swelled to become a great mob.

As we went on I heard hoofbeats on the cobbled road behind me. It sounded like a messenger, so I called a halt. The disciplined troops halted, and the mob surged and seethed around us. They let the horseman through. It was one of the grooms from the stables. He was riding Urdo's mare Prancer, who Urdo had left here when he rode away to war.

"What news?" I asked the groom.

"Where is the king, ap Gwien?" he asked.

"Urdo is wounded in the battle, and very near to death," I said, though the words stuck in my throat. "Darien, his heir, is High King of Tir Tanagiri."

The mob gasped, and the gasp spread out in ripples as people behind told each other what I had said.

"They told me the king had come back," the groom said, looking as if I had struck him in the face. "They came down to open the gates and they said that he had come on a boat. I thought he would need his horse."

Prancer put her dark head down to nuzzle my shoulder. She was in wonderful condition, though she was twenty years old and had borne seven foals. She had carried Urdo in the charge at Foreth and seemed ready to do it again at a moment's notice. I stroked her nose. She was caparisoned in all her finest armor.

"He isn't coming back and he won't need his horse," Thurrig said. "But ap Gwien will ride, and the rest of us will all walk. We need to free this city in Urdo's name."

This seemed very harsh to me, but the crowd gave a great roar. It was on a different pitch from the cheering they had done before; now there was anger in it. The groom slid down and gave me Prancer's reins. I swung up onto her back and set my spear straight. Then I was doing my best to keep her from trampling anyone underfoot as we all surged forward again.

I hesitate to call what happened a battle, or even a skirmish. There was a gate before the great gate, which we called the sally gate. It led from the street into a practice yard and was most inconvenient if you actually wanted to be anywhere else, so we seldom used it. It was always kept closed. I had considered going in that way and dismissed it almost at once. It was just too difficult to get open, and too easy to defend inside. Cinon was directing the defense of Caer Tanaga, and he thought otherwise. He must have massed as many troops in the practice yard as he could, both his own militia and some of Arling's Jarnsmen. As we came up to it, the sally gate opened and the troops rushed out, well armed and armored, fresh and ready to fight. There might have been a thousand of them, but they could not use their numbers in the street. The people of Caer Tanaga fell on them as a pack of starving wolves falls on a lame deer.

I saw two women with kitchen knives take down a Jarnish warrior a head and a half taller than either of them. After that one of them had a spear and the other his long knife and shield. That was the pattern of the whole fight. It was brief and very bloody. Prancer snorted with excitement, just as Apple used to do. She was too well trained to try to charge where there wasn't room, but she took out one man with her hooves. I killed a man of Nene and saw King Cinon being hacked into pieces in front of me. One of the people hacking was a cobbler I recognized. "There isn't time for that! He's dead already!" I bellowed. To my relief they dropped the corpse and looked about them for more live enemies.

As I did the same, I noticed that they were trying to drag the sally gate closed again. I shouted orders and my disciplined core of troops rushed to oppose them and keep the gate open.

When the fighting appeared to be over for the time being, Thurrig strode over to me. He was splashed with blood, but none of it was his own. He did seem a little out of breath. "Shall we go in this way?" he asked. "I know it is inferior to the great gate, but it is at least open."

"I doubt we could stop them," I said, leaning down and speaking quietly and gesturing to indicate the mob. "You lead the troops in with them. As I'm the only one mounted, I'll ride up and see if ap Gavan has managed to open the great gate. She should be there by now."

"When you know, come and tell the rest of us, eh?" Thurrig said. He blew a huff of breath up out of his mouth as if to cool his face. Prancer stepped back, delicately.

"Remember we want to take Morthu alive if we possibly can," I said.

"I don't know if I can restrain them," he said. "But I'll bear it in mind."

"Back soon," I said, and turned Prancer's head uphill.

I heard Thurrig shouting orders and the crowd roaring behind me as I left. I rode around the curve of the hill. It looked very empty without the usual rash of stalls outside the houses. It seemed eerily deserted, after the press of people lower down. It reminded me of the first time I saw Caer Lind. I could see almost straightaway that the great gate was shut, and slowed Prancer's pace. There was someone standing on top of the gate. I had stood there myself on many a patrol. It was part of the circuit of the walls. There was a stairway there running down into the citadel. What was strange was that it looked like Elenn. I rode closer, cautiously.

Elenn was standing in the middle of the gate, right over the arch, leaning on the parapet, which was waist-high there. She was perhaps twice my height above my head. The gate below was tightly shut. I remembered her standing down in the gateway years before, with the gold welcome cup in her hands. Now her hair was loose and tangled and her eyes were red-rimmed. She was wearing an undyed linen shift with no overdress. She looked down at me with a hatred I did not know how to answer.

"Elenn," I said.

"What do you think you are doing using my name?" she asked. At once I recognized in her the madness of self-hatred and despair that Morthu had set upon me in the wood. I could draw her out of it as Gangrader had done for me by turning the hate outward, away from herself. Knowing this didn't help me know what to say.

"I have done nothing to harm you," I said.

"And did you not have my husband take a husband's place to you before all the world at Derwen?" she asked. "And did you not share his bed at Caer Gloran? And did you not bear him a son?"

"My mother embraced Urdo as kin at Derwen, that's all," I said. "My son Darien was born three years before you married Urdo. And will you not believe his word that since you were married he has lain with no mortal woman else?"

Her brow creased a little at this, as if she were thinking it through and finding a thin thread through the maze of lies.

Then Morthu stepped from the shelter of the stairs. He was dragging Garah in front of him, holding her like a shield. He had one hand around her waist to force her to move and the other around her throat, and a knife in that hand. He could kill her before I could kill him, no matter what I did. "You are no mortal woman, but a demon. Everyone knows it," he said.

I was so angry I could have ripped his throat out with my teeth if he had been close enough. "Unhand the queen of Bregheda," I said. I was surprised to hear my voice sounding perfectly calm. "And then, Morthu ap Talorgen, we can talk about whose soul is given to evil, though I think you would prefer to discuss how to stop the people of Caer Tanaga tearing you limb from limb."

"Do you say so?" he asked, stepping nearer to the edge, still holding Garah in front of him. She looked irritated and almost resigned.

"They have already done it to Cinon ap Cinon of Nene," I said. "They are inside the citadel already."

At this Elenn started, but Morthu smiled mockingly down at me. "And if you have brought an army, why are you not with them?" he asked. "Why have you come here alone with only your groom—" Here he jerked Garah's head. "—and your horse and your lapdog?"

"I am no dog of ap Gwien's, but hunt on my own accord," said Ulf from behind me. I did not turn to look at him, though I had had no idea he had followed me. Elenn frowned and rubbed her forehead as if it hurt, then she leaned forward and looked at Ulf earnestly.

"Does my husband live?" she asked.

"He is near death," Ulf replied, stepping forward as he spoke so he was between me and the gate.

"Let the dog bark," Morthu said carelessly. But Elenn looked as if she believed what Ulf said. "What have you come to offer me, Sulien? If you have troops they will never think to come here until I will it."

"I will not offer you anything at all until you release the queen of Bregheda," I said.

"But then you will kill me with the treacherous spear you clutch so tightly," Morthu said. He tightened his grip on Garah's throat so that she winced, and closed her eyes for a moment. Elenn also winced when she saw it.

I had hardly noticed that the spear was in my hand. I looked at it, and then up at him and I laughed. Elenn started again when I laughed, and looked at me in astonishment and then back at Morthu. "This spear is too good for your blood," I said. As far as I could tell, he looked surprised. "I come to offer you a fair trial before the Law," I said.

"Before the High King?" he asked.

"Yes, of course," I replied.

"And when I am acquitted will I be free to sail to Narlahena, or where I would?"

"If you were innocent, you would be," I said.

It was then that Elenn moved. I think Morthu must have read it in my face, because he could not have seen her himself. She drew a thin dagger from her sleeve and stepped deliberately toward him. She was aiming for the side of his neck, but as she struck he took a step back.

"Oh no, my love," he said, softly and caressingly. Their eyes met. For a moment Elenn's arm remained poised with the dagger. It fell very slowly, like bark peeling back off a tree. The terrible thing was that I could do nothing. I could hardly breathe until it was at her side. Then I tried to speak, and could not, my voice caught in my throat. Morthu did not relax his gaze. "What are you doing?" he said, very gently. "Who has bewitched you so that you attack me, your own true love?"

Just as slowly as her dagger hand had fallen, her left hand rose and touched Morthu's face. Elenn moved forward a step, her face held as if for a kiss. The stillness as she moved was excruciating. I was caught up in the spell, unable to interrupt, unable to move away. I didn't want to kill Morthu, I wanted him to stand trial, but I would have killed him then if I could. I brought up the spear. The only reason I did not throw it was because there was no clear shot that would not have chanced killing either Garah or Elenn.

When Elenn's lips had almost met Morthu's, Ulf let out a great wordless howl. He was so pale that his lips looked like blood on his skin, and his nose was paler even than that. His nostrils were flaring like a horse that has run to the edge of strength. His shout broke the spell for a moment, and Elenn brought forward the dagger; and her hand trembled as Morthu began to will it down again.

Then Ulf rushed forward, his mouth open as if he wanted to howl again, but no sound came out. He crashed into the gates with all his strength, and shook the wood a little in the stone gateway. Prancer took two steps back and shook herself. Ulf stepped back and slammed himself into the gates again. Morthu was still staring at Elenn and her hand was wavering, the dagger poised as if she could not decide whether to plunge it into Morthu or into her own heart. He stepped nearer to her. Garah twisted in his arms, trying to free herself as he moved. In the same instant, Ulf flung himself on the doors a third time. This time he spoke, calling on Gangrader in a deep and terrible voice. Garah struggled and twisted half away from Morthu's knife.

In that moment I was poised, spear ready. I was free to move now, free to do whatever seemed best. It seemed as if I had plenty of time to think and consider whether I should risk the shot. If I did, I could probably kill Morthu. That, I knew, would have consequences far beyond those I could see. I could have done it then in that clear moment. I drew my arm back and aimed carefully, then threw, with all my heart and strength. The spear the Smith made and gave to me struck true where I had sent it, right in the keystone of the gateway arch beneath their feet.

The spear struck with a great booming sound. Prancer reared and then backed. She probably wouldn't have done it if I'd been Urdo, but though she knew me she didn't trust me enough to sit quietly for a noise like that. It only took me a moment to bring her back under control, but that was too long. The stones of the gate were falling, ponderously, collapsing like a child's set of blocks that has been built crooked. They hung for a moment and then came down with a series of great crashes, sending up dust that hung in clouds before it settled. For a few minutes I couldn't see any of the people I had been looking at before the wall fell, only a heap of stones and the dust, rising and falling again. Then I saw Elenn, sitting on a block at the side of the pile of crumpled stone that had been a gate. The white of her dress was stained with stone dust, but she seemed unhurt. She had her dagger in her hands and she was turning it over and over.

I nudged Prancer closer. "Are you all right?" I asked, as if this were some ordinary accident and we were friends.

"Ulf Gunnarsson broke my fall," she said, and gestured.

Then I saw Ulf, crumpled on the ground near her. His leg, the one I had lamed, was caught beneath one of the great stones and crushed. His arms were outspread. He must have caught her and thrust her aside but been crushed in doing it. I dismounted and bent over him. His eyes were open.

"Ah, come to claim me at last," he said, so quietly I could hardly hear him. It clearly hurt him to talk. "Kill me quickly, Sulien."

"Don't be a fool," I said. "You'll lose the leg for sure, but you'll probably live."

"My back is broken, and something inside," he said.

"Even that doesn't mean you're dying," I said.

"Gangrader brought down the gate," Ulf said, and smiled. There was blood coming out of the corner of his mouth. Then, in Jarnish, and even more quietly, almost confidentially, he said, "I should have been a carpenter, if I had been born to any other house. It was what I wanted, and where my skill lay, we all knew it. Even as it was, I would have gone to learn woodworking and let Arling have it all, if he had been worthy. The year my mother died, I was seventeen. I was a fool. I bound myself to the Raven Lord, hardly thinking. I sailed with Ragnald to learn the art of war. I wronged you then, and broke my own luck doing it. But he has kept his promise, all his twisted promises, and now he came when I called.

I couldn't bear to tell him it was the spear that had brought down the gate. "I'm sure he will come and speak for you, and help you make a good return," I said. "Do you want me to get Elenn? She's here. You saved her."

"Did you ever believe that?" he asked. "Surely if you had you would never have fought Conal. I am glad she is safe, and I am very sorry about ap Gavan."

"Garah?" I asked, blankly. I looked around. On my left I saw her hand under the keystone block of the arch, which still had my spear trembling in it.

"I couldn't catch them both," Ulf said.

I should have been there to catch Garah, though even then

I knew I might more likely have got myself crushed under the stones trying it. "You did very well," I said.

Ulf shut his eyes for a moment. "Where is Morthu?" he asked.

"I'm right here," came Morthu's voice from the pile of rocks, as smooth and assured as ever. Elenn jumped at the sound of it, almost cutting herself. There was no sign of him.

"He's caught in the stone-fall," I said. "Don't worry about him. His plans have come to nothing. He will have a fair trial, and a fair death."

"The gate is broken, but I trust you will keep up the guard at the outwall," Ulf said. A big bubble of blood burst on his lips, and just like that he wasn't there anymore, only his empty body. I mourned for him almost as if he had been a friend.

"We were discussing a boat for Narlahena for the queen and myself," Morthu said, comfortably, as if nothing had happened. I looked at Elenn, who was now sitting as still as a statue, looking toward the fallen stones. She had tears running down her face but she neither moved nor made any sound.

"We were discussing a fair trial for sorcery," I said. I waved my hand in front of Elenn's face to get her attention, and gestured to Prancer. She looked at me blankly. Then she seemed to see the horse. She looked back at me, her eyes hard and untrusting. I offered her Prancer's reins. She took them dubiously.

"You see, it is so unfair," Morthu said. "When you do it and bring down whole walls, you call it an honest charm. When I do any little thing you call it sorcery."

With that, he pushed aside the rock as if it had been soft cheese and stood in the sunlight. At the sight of him Elenn was stirred into action. She pulled herself up so that she was standing on the stone where she had been sitting and used it as a mounting block to get astride Prancer. She looked tiny on his back, the way Garah's children used to look when I put them on a greathorse for a ride.

"It is sorcery because you have undone your soul to have the power to do it," I said, looking at Morthu to distract him from Elenn.

"And what was I to do, after you had killed my mother and she could teach me no more?" he asked. "Oh, I forget, I am supposed to say that she was a black sorcerer, too, and malign her memory the way the whole world does. Even her other children do it. What is sorcery after all but self-reliance, refusing to be bound by the careful limits the gods set because they fear people growing to be stronger than they are. They are no better than we are. The only difference is that they know how to use power. They would make us take baby steps where we could run, because we have will and they do not. We are greater than the gods, if we dare to use the power we can have."

Through all this I deliberately did not look at Elenn, so she could get away, yet I heard no clatter of hooves. "And is bending minds and killing innocents to get power being like a god?" I asked.

"They were enemies and people of no account," he said.

"What do you want, Morthu?" I asked. "Is Darien right that you want to destroy us all and all we have built? And why? Just for hatefulness?"

He laughed. "Because you were all so proud of what you were doing," he said. "You all cared about the war and the Peace so much, and never about people. I care about people. I know what they want."

"You may know what they want, but you do not care about anything except yourself," Elenn said. She was sitting very still on Prancer's back. "You are still the nine-year-old boy who lost his wicked mother. The love and attention of the whole world would never be enough to feed the hole that is inside you." She actually sounded sorry for him.

"You were just playing games for attention?" I said incredulously. "All of this?"

"Do you call it a game?" Morthu asked, his voice rougher than I had ever heard it. "A game, when I have killed Urdo?"

"Angas killed Urdo," I said. "Where were you on the battlefield of Agned when the river ran red with the blood of the brave fallen on both sides? Skulking here?"

"You speak only at my pleasure," Morthu said. "If I wish it your tongue would cleave to the roof of your mouth and never free itself."

"I think you understand less of the way the world works than you think you do," I said, as if I were entirely undaunted by such a threat from a man who had just parted stone like clay.

"Oh, do I?" he sneered. "The gods cannot help you now. By bringing you back from where you ran, they have bound themselves by their own rules. I could have your legs freeze and the muscles die. Before the gods could act again they would be withered, so that you would be a cripple forever, riding only in a special saddle and never fighting again. Yes, I think I shall do that. It would be better than killing you to see you live without everything you live for."

On my left the spear was sitting in the keystone arch. On my right was Elenn, on Prancer. She still hadn't moved. Morthu was certainly good at reading people's fears. I had feared paralysis ever since I had drunk the henbane. I slapped Prancer's flank hard. "Gallop for the stable!" I shouted, to the mare, not her rider. She was a wise horse, and did as I told her. At the same moment, as Morthu was distracted by Elenn getting away, I grabbed for the spear. I pulled it from the stone and brought the blunt end around to smack into Morthu's belly. He went down the way anyone would. I reversed the spear and put the point on his neck.

"I want you to live to be tried," I said. "But I am not so very set on it that I will not kill you if I must."

There was a blessed clatter of hooves, and Luth was there with a pennon around me. He grinned cheerfully. "We couldn't find you," he said. "We looked everywhere, but we didn't think to look here until we saw the queen riding out. We have the city and the citadel."

"Good," I said. "I have the sorcerer Morthu ap Talorgen. I

do not know how we can imprison him until we try him, unless I stand here with my spear on his neck the whole time. Get Darien. And get the Grandfather of Heroes. He may know a way."

25

An iron protection,
a mountain eyrie,
how can we recognise truth?

This is not a riddle,
so we will never understand it.
      —*The Oracular Riddles of Lafada ap Fial*

Darien didn't come himself. He sent Raul and Inis. They came up bearing lanterns, and only then did I realize how dark it had become. Raul suggested imprisoning Morthu in one of the rooms on the top of a tower, and guarding the stairs. Inis suggested stopping the guards' ears with beeswax.

"Also, there is a charm against sorcery," he said. "It will not work on him, but I could sing it in the room where he is kept, and over the guards."

"I am ready to face a fair trial," Morthu said, sounding dignified and persecuted. "I have no idea why everyone has taken against me so. I will submit to a fair trial where accusations against me will be made in the open and not by insinuation. A fair trial, judged by the kings."

"The High King will judge you," Raul said.

"That will not be a fair trial," Morthu said. "The demon's brat will listen to his mother and not to me, and it is all her word against mine."

"You have great trust in the restraint of the faithful hero Sulien," Inis observed.

I laughed. I would never have thought of it, but it was true, not many people would accuse someone of being a perjured demon while under their spear, not if they really believed it.

"Will the kings at least be there to witness that it is done fairly?" Morthu asked.

"They will," Raul said. "Everyone who wants to witness

may; it will be done before the people. There will no doubt be many who wish to witness."

"I will submit to a fair trial and need not be treated like an honorless outcast," Morthu said.

"Nevertheless, you will wait in the tower room overnight," Raul said. Several of Luth's armigers took Morthu off, and he went with them reluctantly.

"I will go and watch with them and sing charms for what good they are," Inis said. "You go to see your family."

"I do want to speak to Darien," I said.

"Your mother is here," Raul said. "A ship has come from the west, bringing both bishop Dewin and the wife of Gwien."

"Together?" I asked apprehensively. Inis laughed.

"On the same ship, at least," Raul said.

"I must hasten after the blackheart before he poisons his guards," Inis said, and left without another word, his shadow huge and wavering in the lanternlight.

"Do you think he meant with poison or with words?" I asked.

Raul shook his head. "I don't know why he talks like that."

"There are many truths that can only be told like that," Inis said, popping his head back around the door.

Raul jumped. Inis took his head back. We both waited for a moment before speaking again.

"I'm not comfortable about this trial idea," Raul said. "Morthu's right that a lot of it is your word against his."

"Garah and Ulf are dead, yes, but Elenn was there all the time."

Raul shook his head doubtfully. "She may not speak," he said. "And the stones cannot speak, though I can read something in them." He lifted his lantern and peered at them, lighting up the place where Morthu had pushed them apart, and then the hole where the spear had struck.

I had felt awkward with Raul ever since he had shrunk away from me in his fever. "I am not a demon," I said baldly.

He looked embarrassed. "I do not say you are," he said.

"But enough people say so that your word alone might not sway them."

"You did say I was," I said. I was too tired to be diplomatic. "We have always stood on the same side, Raul, on Urdo's side. You know I am not a demon, why do you also feel that I am?"

Raul looked at me in the wavering light. "I thought about that as I was getting well after my fever," he said, at last. "Partly, like the queen, it was jealousy. I knew this was wrong and I struggled against it. Urdo had room in his heart for all of us. But the other part I did not face until then. How can I admit that you are a good person, if you refuse to accept God?"

"It means having a place in your world where people can be good and still not worship your god," I said.

"In Thansethan they do not teach of any such possibility," Raul said. "Urdo tried and tried to explain it to me. It was easier for me to believe you a demon than to believe it." He shook his head. His face was wracked with doubt. "If I admit in my heart you are not a demon then it shakes the way I have lived my whole life. For if worshiping God is not the highest good, the only good, the only source of honor, then what is life for? Still, these doubts are between me and God, between me and my god." He smiled shakily. "This is far from the point. I know you are not a demon. But your word will not hold that weight with the pious even so."

"The queen will have to speak, too," I said.

"If she will," Raul said.

"I will speak to Darien about it," I said. "And besides, there are many people of the city who will have seen him doing sorcery, and killing people for power."

Just then a party came to collect Ulf and Garah's bodies for burial and to begin moving the stones. Glividen came up and began tutting about the gate. I didn't want to talk to him, so I left Raul with him and went down toward the sally gate. When I reached it I didn't feel ready to go in and face Veniva and Darien. I went on down the street toward the stables. I would see if Prancer was safe back where she should be, and also see my own horses and help them settle.

It had always been a good idea before. Even after Apple was killed I found visiting the stables calming. Now every stall and bale of hay spoke to me of Garah as she had been when we had first come to Caer Tanaga. I had not yet had time to take in her death. Now I remembered how we had joked as we rode from Thansethan. "Here lies Garah ap Gavan. She was brave and she loved horses and she listened to Sulien ap Gwien one time too many." How could I possibly explain it all to Glyn and the children? I was blinded by tears as I walked among the gentle huffing and munching of contented horses. I remembered how Garah had tended Starlight in this stable, and how I had sat here late and overheard Mardol and Urdo talking. I felt old. It wasn't my fault that she was dead. She had volunteered to go and open the gate. It may have turned out to be useless, but we had no way of knowing that in advance. I did not weep for guilt or self-pity, but because I would never hear her teasing me again.

I don't know how long I wept on Brighteyes' patient neck. The grooms and occasional armigers politely ignored me as they went about their business. After a while I began to groom Brighteyes, getting the dust of the road out. It was soothing. When I was done I moved on to Glimmer. As I reached behind me for the bigger brush someone put it into my hand. I did not turn or stop. "Thank you, my lord," I said, and went on currying in companionable silence.

After I had finished with Glimmer I went back up to the citadel. The streets were full of cheerful people. I returned all their greetings. When I came to the sally gate the guards let me in at once. "Do you know where my mother is staying?" I asked the nearest, one of Alfwin's men who had been in the ships with me.

"I don't know," he said. "But the High King was asking for you. He's in the upper room." He gestured with his hand and I thanked him.

The courtyard bore the signs of the fighting earlier. The bodies had been moved, but it was slimed and bloodstained in places. As I came to the door that led to the stairs I almost fell over something small and sticky. When I peered at it I saw that it was half of someone's hand, the palm and fingers. For no good reason Conal's ironic voice came into my head, saying, "There will be rather less sword fighting, or rather more one-handed people." Friend or foe, I wondered. There was no way to tell. I kicked it into a corner where it wouldn't be in anyone's way. Time enough to clean in the morning.

Darien was in Urdo's study, sitting on one of the spindly chairs. The table was full of papers already, but they were set in neatly squared stacks. Veniva was sitting in the other chair, reading a piece of unrolled parchment, holding it out at arm's length to see it clearly as she always did. They both looked up when I came in.

"There you are at last," Veniva said. Then she came forward to embrace me, and so did Darien.

"What brings you here?" I asked.

"The news that the battle was won and that Darien would be crowned and want oaths," she said. "I have brought Galbian and little Gwien. They are asleep in our room now, but they are longing to see you, Gwien especially."

"I will be delighted to see them," I said. "As I am to see you. This is only the second time I have ever seen you away from home."

"It is only the second time I have come further from Derwen than Magor since I was married," Veniva admitted. "I left Emlin in charge at Derwen. I came on the ship, which called at Caer Thanbard and Caer Segant before coming up-river. Bishop Dewin and Linwen ap Cledwin are here, too, come to advise young Gorai."

"Is Gorai here?" I asked. It had been difficult to restrain him from joining in the river expedition.

"He will be here tomorrow, with all the infantry," Darien said. "We will try Morthu at noon. Alfwin and Flavien and Hengist and Sidrok will all be here by then."

"What witnesses have we?" I asked. "Raul was saying there might be a problem with my word. Garah is dead."

Darien's face fell. "I heard," he said. "I shall miss her. She was always here, until last year. When I first came to Caer Tanaga she was very kind to me when I was lonely. She taught me a lot about horses. She was a good friend. But she knew the risk when she volunteered to open the gates. That is why she wrote down a sworn statement and had it witnessed by Luth and Cadraith."

"I have just been reading it," Veniva said. "It could not be better put. Did you really teach her to read, Sulien?"

"Yes," I said. "But that was such a long time ago I'd almost forgotten. She's been reading and writing for years." Making lists, I thought, remembering her crossing things off them decisively in this room.

"There are also the servants," Darien said. "We have plenty of evidence."

"And Elenn?" I asked.

There was an awkward little silence. "She wanted to speak to Urdo," Veniva said. "She did not seem herself."

"Morthu had her under an enchantment," I said. "She is only halfway back from it. Where is she?"

"She went to see Urdo," Darien said, frowning a little. "Halfway back? I have never heard of such a thing. I thought the spell might not be broken until Morthu died. Do you think she will feel better tomorrow? Far enough back to speak against Morthu?"

"I don't know," I said. "I wouldn't count on it."

"We have plenty of evidence even without her," Darien said. "My concern is why he agreed to be tried. Do you think he has some trick prepared?"

"It wouldn't surprise me," I said. I walked over to the window seat and sat down. I was more tired than I had thought. "He kept asking if you would be there and if all the kings would be there. He may mean to bewitch you all."

"Teilo will be there, and Raul," Darien said. "And Inis, too. He must be tried before the Law and seen to be guilty, and then executed for his crimes."

"I know," I said. "Inis said there is a charm against sorcery, but he did not seem very sure of it. Will Angas be here, too?"

"He is here already; his ala came up with us," Darien said.

"It has been very complicated fitting everyone in. Dalmer and Celemon have been rushed off their feet. And as for the citadel it has been a nightmare, without Garah or the queen to set it in order. I need a tribuno to see to it for me."

"You need a key-keeper," Veniva said crisply. "Which is more like a quartermaster for your fortress than a tribuno. And you are getting one, getting a wife indeed, who will also be here tomorrow if the wind stays good for boats coming up the Tamer."

"Tomorrow?" Darien said blankly. "Even if Angas had sent to Demedia the moment we agreed, the message could scarcely be at Dun Idyn yet, let alone the girl returned."

"If she had been in Dun Idyn, you would be right," Veniva said. "But she was in Cennet with the grandmother she is named for, and you will have the two Ninians here tomorrow, by the news I had at Caer Segant. So you can be crowned and married, and begetting great-grandchildren for me and heirs for the kingdom."

"She has been key-keeper of Dun Idyn for Angas, but she will have to learn the ways of Caer Tanaga," Darien said, sensibly ignoring the last comment.

"She is only just eighteen," Veniva said. "Don't count on her being good at it straightaway. All the same, I think of the available princesses she was a good choice, even considering she is your cousin."

"Yes," Darien said. "I was thinking mostly about settling the north."

Veniva began to go into a long genealogical digression. I yawned, and she interrupted herself immediately. "You should be in bed, Sulien."

"I think I will go to the baths," I said, deciding as I spoke. "I am stiff and tired and dirty from being on the boat. Afterward I will sleep. Where am I sleeping, do you know? In barracks?"

"You should be here in the citadel," Veniva said.

"I think Govien has already taken your things to the barracks," Darien said. I embraced them both and left them.

The baths were deserted. There were a few candles lit but

no attendants. The water was pleasingly hot, and there was a whole rack of dry towels. I looked into the weapon room. It was empty and there was nobody there. I took the spear into the baths and left it on top of my clothes and armor, plainly in my sight, and only an arm's length from the pool. I did not want to take risks with it, even for the marvel of hot water.

I scrubbed myself all over with soap, rinsed, then got down into the water to soak my aches away. I did not swim, just lay back in the running water with half an eye on my spear. I felt my aches melting away. When I heard someone coming I tensed immediately. I was standing up in the water with my hand on my spear when Emer came in. She snorted.

"You Vincans. You really don't seem to notice that you don't have a stitch on, as long as you have your weapon ready."

I laughed, and lay back again. "The weapon is the important bit. Come on in."

She took off her clothes and slipped into the water. "This is truly one of the great blessings of civilization," she said as she relaxed into the warmth.

"You weren't wounded at Agned," I noted. She had the old scar on her face, the scars on her foot from the wound she had taken when Conal had been killed, and nothing else apart from two or three pale seams on her arms and legs, also clearly very old, and the dark lines of childbearing on her stomach.

"I'm the only one of my people who wasn't," she said. "I could feel bad about it, five hundred people coming to war so I could die, and here I am, alive and untouched while half of them are dead and the other half wounded."

"Do you really think anyone needs to go out of their way to make Isarnagans fight?" I asked.

She laughed. "You have a point," she admitted. "They wouldn't have come if they didn't want to."

"And you fought in a good cause, whatever your personal reasons were for fighting," I said.

She ducked down under the water for a moment and then

came up again. "The trouble is that it doesn't make any difference to how I feel," she said.

"Do you really think that you're the only person who has lost someone?" I asked.

"It isn't the same," she said. "I met Conal when we were both eight years old. There had never been anyone else."

If you didn't count her husband and daughter, of course. "I've been mourning Garah this evening," I said. "She came away with me when she was fifteen years old and I was seventeen. She lived her own life and died her own death, and they were both good ones. Without me she might have stayed in Derwen and been quiet, and that might have been good as well, who can tell? She has been making my life better for twenty years, twenty years of friendship. And the same with Masarn, and ap Erbin, and—" I paused a little. "And Urdo. You miss him, yes, of course you do, you will never forget him, but you can go on and live your life."

"You are speaking of my husband," Elenn said. I jumped. She was standing against the back wall of the room, next to the candle sconce by the door to the changing rooms. I had not heard her coming. She was wearing the same stained shift and her face looked ravaged.

"I was speaking of my friend," I said. I wished the words back as soon as I had impulsively uttered them. I knew Elenn didn't understand friendship between men and women. As smoothly as I could, I brought my feet under me so that I could reach my spear immediately if I needed it. It seemed ridiculous to think I would have to defend myself against Elenn. I was more afraid she might grab the spear and hurt herself with it by mistake than that she might hurt me.

"My husband," she said again, sounding both bereft and angry.

"Come into the water, Elenn," Emer said.

"With two women who hate me and mean me harm? I think not." She sounded imperious.

"Morthu has cast a bewitchment on you," I said. "He has been lying to you. We don't hate you. I certainly don't."

"I don't either, sister," Emer said.

"Everyone has been lying to me," she said. "Why did Ulf tell me Urdo was near death, when he is dead already?"

"Death has two sides to be near," I said. Emer choked back a horrified laugh. "And Ulf didn't know. Near death is what we have been saying, because although he is dead he has been talking."

"He talked to me," Elenn said, shifting uneasily and most uncharacteristically. "He said he had not talked to you."

"Not talked, no, not since he died," I said, choosing my words carefully. "He has spoken to other people when I was there."

"I asked him if Darien was his son," Elenn said. "Morthu told me he was not, that he was the product of your incest with your brother."

"He told Angas that as well," I said. "I really don't know how people can think of these things. It's so far-fetched that I didn't think anyone could believe that one."

"Do you know what Urdo answered me, about Darien?" she asked.

"No, I don't know," I said, honestly. Darien was Urdo's son in every important sense except that of blood. I spared a thought for poor Ulf, lying cold, waiting for burial. The part he had had in Darien seemed to me the least important, over in minutes, bound to flesh only by Gangrader's will.

"He said 'he is now,'" she said. "Even Urdo twists his words so that I don't know what they mean. 'He is now.' 'No mortal woman else.' What can I make of that? Morthu took my will, yes, but how can I trust anyone when I cannot tell truth from lies?"

I was thinking how to answer when Emer spoke. "Do you remember when we were children?" she asked, her voice soothing in its cadences. "Do you remember how Maga would command and organize the three of us, and Allel would always be ready with his arms open if we were hurt? Maga would scoff and call him weak and foolish, and he would say 'Yes, my dear, you see right through me, I am weak and foolish and you have caught me with a pocket full of plums I have brought for the children.' Maga would make promises and twist them, but you know you could always trust Allel to do what he said, though what he said would never be as marvelous. And when you were nine years old and I was eight and the fosterlings were come from Oriel, Darag pushed you out of a tree and you had a great cut on your knee. There was a scab on it, and Maga saw it one day when it was nearly healed, and she said you should pull it off because it was hanging loose. And you asked if it would hurt, and Maga said no, it wouldn't. But Allel interrupted and said that yes, it would hurt a little now, but it would be a good little pain to make your knee better."

"I could trust my father," Elenn said, as if discovering something fine and precious. "He is far away in Connat." Her face had relaxed a little from the terrible twisted mask it had been when she had first come in. "But I can go home if I want. I can do anything now. I am queen no longer."

"I have sometimes left out parts of the truth when speaking to you," Emer said. "But I have never lied to you. I told you the truth about Conal when you asked. You know I don't hate you."

I crouched still in the warm moving water and tried to be inconspicuous. This was best left to Emer. I wished I had gone straight to bed and never been here at all.

"I don't know," Elenn said. "You hated Maga, and she didn't know. You were glad she was dead. You embraced her killer."

"It wasn't like that," Emer said. "I loved Conal for being Conal. You know I always loved him. I just didn't care that he had killed Maga."

"How could you betray the family honor like that?" Elenn asked. "How could you love a man who killed your mother?"

"If we are speaking truth here, then I should say that if not for propriety I would have cheered and given him the hero's portion for killing my mother," Emer said defiantly. "Yes, I hated her. She used us, you and me, and she was even more cruel to poor Mingor, forcing him to be what she wanted and never what he wanted."

"You and Min did not know how to deal with her," Elenn said. "I loved her. She never did me any harm. She taught me a lot about how to deal with men and how to run a court which has been very useful. She fought you because you fought against her."

"Yes, and even though you were her favorite, you shut everything away inside where she couldn't get at it, do you think I don't know that?" Emer said. "I saw that. I didn't want a shell like yours. By the Raven, Elenn, she wed you to five men who promised to kill Darag, one after the other. How can you say she didn't do you any harm? The shell itself is harm, however useful it may have been. It's a defense, yes, wonderful, but how can anyone get close to you? It's cracking now, but the last time before tonight when I saw a human expression on your face was when ap Dair came back and said that Urdo wanted to marry you and you knew you would be getting away from her."

"I was eighteen years old," Elenn said. "Any girl of that age is glad to be married, and I was to be a High Queen. And there were not five. I was betrothed to Ferdia, but Darag killed him before I could marry him."

"He was too honorable to live," Emer said.

"Yes," Elenn said. Her face was back to normal, as far as I could tell in the candlelight. I relaxed a little. "I could have trusted Ferdia, if he had lived," she said. She put her hand up to her chest, but it fell away empty. I looked at Emer, and she gestured to me to speak.

"Where is your pebble, Elenn?" I asked quietly.

"Morthu made me—" she said, and stopped. "I'll get another one. I'll go to Thansethan and get another one. I can trust Father Gerthmol. I can trust them at Thansethan." She stopped again, and looked down at me. "I love Darien, you know," she said. "I don't blame him for anything you did."

"I'm glad you love him," I said calmly. "He loves you, too. He was very distressed when Garah told us what had happened to you. He knew straightaway that Morthu had bewitched you."

"I always thought he was Urdo's son," she said.

"You know, when it comes to believing Morthu's lies, I think he's contradicted himself there," Emer said. "If Darien isn't Urdo's son, then Sulien isn't Urdo's leman. The two things can't both be true."

Elenn thought about this for a moment, and then smiled. I suddenly saw what Emer meant about her shell cracking. Every other smile I had seen on her face was suddenly revealed as controlled and deliberate, compared to this one which seemed as if it could crack her face. I wished Urdo could have seen it. She took three steps forward and, still in her shift, jumped into the water, between me and Emer, sending splashes right across the room. She looked the least beautiful I had ever seen her, and the most human. "The truth comes clear at last," she said, and embraced Emer. Then, after a little hesitation, she embraced me. I embraced her back. Oh well, I thought, feeling old, it is the truth now.

26

As for sorcery, any that are convicted of it shall suffer death.
And any who teach sorcery or offer to teach sorcery to another, or
any oracle-craft, shall suffer death, that the knowledge of it may
pass away entirely.

    — Vincan Law

When we gathered in the central courtyard for the coronation and trial the next morning, Elenn was dressed in green and gold, and her face was as beautiful and unreadable as ever. Her midnight black hair was brushed and shining in the sunshine but left to fall loose on her shoulders. Seeing this, I took off my helmet and shook out my own hair. Alswith, waiting beside me, with the other kings, looked at me curiously.

"What are you doing?" she asked.

"I am letting my hair loose for mourning," I said.

"Don't you usually cut it?" she asked, frowning a little.

"That is the Vincan way," I said. "We cut our hair short and cast it on the pyre, and the time it takes to regrow marks the time of mourning. After Foreth, Galba's whole ala cut their hair. I have always cut mine before, but there hasn't been time. Seeing Elenn like that, it seemed like the right thing to do it the Tanagan way now."

"Do you think I should let mine loose?" she asked. Behind her head, which was wrapped in a grey scarf, I saw Veniva coming out into the courtyard, bringing the boys. Glividen intercepted her and started to ask her something. Gwien started jumping from foot to foot on the cobbles, then stopped and stood sword blade-straight at a word from his grandmother.

"You did at Agned," I said. "What is the Jarnish custom?"

"Baring your head is usually a sign of surrender," she said.

"Women are supposed to surrender only to their husbands, that's why all the veils and cloth. For mourning we wear dark colors."

"Nobody thought you were surrendering at Agned," I said.

"I meant it for defiance, as well as mourning," she admitted. "I was surrendering to fate, to death that had come from nowhere to take ap Erbin like that. If he had been killed in the ordinary chance of battle I wouldn't have been so angry and led the ala back like that."

"You destroyed the war machines," I said. "I don't think anyone saw it as surrender. For that matter, I've seen plenty of Jarnish farmers with bare heads." Off on the other side I saw Thurrig and Amala engaged in a furious debate, with much arm waving. Amala seemed to be getting the best of it, but Thurrig was smiling.

"They have surrendered to their masters," she said, and shrugged. "It doesn't make sense when you think about it, especially here where they needn't have a master except the king. Most of the farmers in Nene are like that." Elenn walked over to stand on the turf almost directly opposite me, next to Mother Teilo and Raul and a little knot of other priests of the White God. I looked for Emer, and saw her in the crowd, with Inis.

"They'll be so delighted to have you instead of Cinon that they won't mind about you being a woman," I said reassuringly. I hoped Flavien couldn't hear. He was right at the other end of the space marked out for the kings, talking to Rowanna. The courtyard was a mixture of organized and disorganized bustle.

Alswith bit her lip. "The Jarnish ones, I hope so," she said. "It is the Tanagan ones who felt like Cinon and who are still alive that will be the problem. It's going to be so hard. I miss ap Erbin every minute. He used to say he was getting old and fat and no fun anymore, and I would tease him, and now he's dead. I can't even take time to mourn him properly because I have all this responsibility and work to do, and I won't even be going home, but to Caer Rangor."

"It's hard work being a king," I agreed.

"I feel like I shouldn't be standing here, but lined up over there with the alae," she said, gesturing.

"Me, too," I admitted. Govien had Galba's ala under control. My ala, Urdo's Own Ala, looked very understrength. They had lost yet another decurio yesterday. Darien would have to give a lot of attention to getting them back to the force that they had been. Elwith stood in the praefecto's place, looking a little apprehensive, the way everyone is when they start. She kept straightening her oak-leaf cloak as if she couldn't believe it really belonged to her.

"And there are the children, too," she said. "And all these people in Nene who don't know me. Alfwin said I should rule for Harald, but Darien said I could rule in my own name, and Harald after me."

"I think you should let your hair loose," I said. "You are standing here for Nene, and Nene is a mixed kingdom. You are Jarnish in blood but your son is of both people, and you mean to be king of both people."

She raised her hands and unwound the cloth and shook her hair free.

Gorai came out of the doors, walking with his aunt Linwen and Bishop Dewin. He bowed to them, clearly making farewells. They walked across to stand by Raul. Gorai came on past Glividen, who seemed at last ready to let Veniva go. As he went past Luth's ala, his uncle Aneirin ap Erbin hailed him, and they spoke for a few moments, before Aneirin clapped him on the back and let him come on.

"It's clear to see where that young man is going to get his advice," Alswith said approvingly.

"Do you like Aneirin?" I asked.

"He's far and away the best of the whole family, apart from my ap Erbin, of course," she said. "There's more to him than his songs, though they are very good songs."

Gorai came up to us then, and we bowed and made him welcome. I was very glad of his presence a moment later when Veniva brought my nephews up. He was only a year older than Galbian, and they found much to talk about together. I did not then guess that that was to be the beginning of a friendship and alliance in Council that would last until their deaths, and even beyond, since Galbian's daughter Veniva married Gorai's son Cledwin. Then I was only glad that they occupied each other. I noticed Glividen standing talking to Inis, waving his arms about.

"What did Glividen want?" I asked Veniva.

"More nonsense about the heating system of the citadel running underneath here. I told him Garah had come up through it yesterday so it must have been clear then. He gave me a long explanation of how it worked. He says the ducts run under where we are standing."

"You were stopped a long time, for that," I said. Inis had called to Teilo, and she came up to them. Glividen was still gesturing, and Teilo seemed to be trying to calm both of them down. I wished her luck.

"I was telling him about Ninian," Veniva admitted.

"Where is she?" I asked.

Veniva looked around, then back. She would never even consider doing anything as vulgar as pointing. "There, near Atha, with Angas and her grandmother Ninian. She is wearing a scarf on her head, so you can't see, but her hair is red." I looked. As far as I could tell she looked like a sensible girl. She was tall and slim; she would not have had the weight to be an armiger. I hoped Darien liked her.

The trumpets blew then, warning us that Darien was about to come out.

Veniva went to stand with Emer and Inis. Angas came hurrying over and took his place.

"Some people said Darien should have waited until all the kings could be here," Gorai said.

"Who isn't here?" Galbian asked.

"Glyn of Bregheda, and Anlaf Alfwinsson, Ohtar's heir of Bereich," Gorai said. "And some are here, but their heirs are not."

"The kings of the north who could not come so far so fast will swear to the High King when next they are in Caer Tanaga," I said. We had spent a long time discussing this. If

either of them had been less sure allies it might have been
worth delaying. As it was, we had most of the kings here already, and as Darien insisted, a formal oathtaking in Caer
Tanaga such as Urdo had taken at the beginning of his reign
was a good way to affirm the Peace. Everything was arranged
the same way. It made everything feel connected at root
when I thought that I was standing where my father had
stood with my brother Darien to make his oath to Urdo.

Only Rowanna had been here for the last coronation, and
stood then where she stood now, upright and alone. Tereg
was standing where Uthbad would have stood. The elder
Cinon had stood where Alswith was standing now. He
might have been here then as his father's heir, I didn't
know. Duke Galba would have stood where Galbian was,
and on my other side there would have been nobody. I
turned my head. Alfwin bowed a little. Sidrok was smirk-
ing, but stepped away when I looked hard at him. He was
not half the man his brother was. He would not have killed
Ayl himself, but he was clearly delighted he was dead. He
had Ayl's son Trumwin with him, who was ten years old. He
began to smile at me before he remembered that I had killed
his father, then he looked away with dignity. Hengist
Guthrumsson stood next. I could not remember if his father
had taken oath to Urdo at his coronation or later. Ohtar
would have taken the end place, or his grandson Anlaf
Alfwinsson, if he had been here. I wondered what had become of Walbern.

There was another blast of trumpets followed by a hush as
Darien came out. He was wearing the dark blue drape he had
worn for the feast before the battle. He had the gold torc
around his neck, and Ulf's armring on his arm. The drape
was pinned with my brooch from the hoard of Derwen—this
time I had insisted. He came forward in silence with the
crown in his hands. He walked straight up the clear strip of
turf between the crowds until he stood on the stone under the
oak, the Stone of the Kingdom in the central courtyard of
Caer Tanaga, the heart of the High Kingdom.

He crowned himself then in the words and form that Urdo had used, and Avren, and Emrys, but naming the White God as witness and overseer of his oath and his marriage to the land. I looked over at Veniva, who was smiling with tears in her eyes. She and Raul had spent half the night working out the exact words of the oath.

When it was done the kings and kings' heirs all went up and made our coronation oaths. It was a renewal for me, but a fresh oath for the others. After the oaths, Darien embraced the kings as they rose. He barely touched Angas, but his hug for me was real and warm. Then Darien walked down to the alae, and each ala made their oath together, each armiger naming whatever gods they would and Darien welcoming them in the name of the White God. When that was done he turned to the people, who were packed in down the long colonade, as many of them as could squeeze in. They gave a great cheer, and the rest of us joined in.

Then Darien spoke for a little while about the Council, about the Law, and the Peace. We cheered whenever he paused. At last he came around to Morthu. "He will be brought before me and tried," Darien said. Those of us who had brought weapons for the coronation took them off for the trial, and there was a general shuffling as people took their weapons to the weapon room and came back. Darien gave his sword to ap Caw to take to safety; the old groom walked as proudly as if he was carrying a baby.

Another hush fell. Darien walked back to the stone. Inis came out of the crowd and began sprinkling water everywhere and chanting his charm against sorcery. Bishop Dewin pursed his lips disapprovingly, but nobody left. He stopped here and there and poked at the holes which were the vents for the heating system. I wondered if they had such things in Oriel and if he was confused by them.

After a little while, two guards brought Morthu out, walking between them. He paced up very deliberately over the grass until he was directly opposite where the kings stood. He was wearing the armor of an armiger. I wondered who had given it to him. Maybe it was the only thing that would fit him. The guards walked back away from him, leaving him alone in the center.

"Who accuses me, on what charge?" he asked, sounding like a prince who had been wronged.

"I, Darien ap Urdo of the House of Emrys, High King of Tir Tanagiri, accuse you, Morthu ap Talorgen, of black sorcery and seditious treachery."

"What right have you to that name?" Morthu asked. "Your mother was not married to your father, and who is to say who your father is? Will she come and swear to it before the gods?"

I thought for a moment that he had cast the spell on me to make my tongue cleave to the roof of my mouth, for I could not speak. There was an indrawn breath among the kings around me, and many of them glanced at me.

Then Darien laughed. "Here we see an example of the sedition I spoke of, from your own mouth," he said. "It is no news that my mother has never been married to my father, but likewise it is no news that they were lovers at Caer Gloran before my birth, that my father has acknowledged me his son all my life, and that he proclaimed me his heir before gods, princes, and people on the field of Agned as he lay dying. Nor has my mother's name ever been linked with another man, in all her life. Yet, if you like it better, I will call myself Darien Suliensson, for that is the name my father used when he proclaimed me his heir, and in that name I took the crown and mean to reign."

Chins were being raised around me. "Absurd," Gorai murmured to Galbian. Alswith patted my arm.

"Will Sulien ap Gwien so swear?" Morthu asked.

"We are not here to embarrass my mother, but to inquire into your treachery," Darien said. "Before we begin, will you swear before the gods to speak the truth?"

"Of what am I accused?" Morthu asked again.

"Sorcery," Darien said. "That is, burning your own soul to power your spells. Sedition, that is plotting to stir up the kings of Tir Tanagiri to fight against their rightful king. And treachery, that is plotting with the enemies of your country, and specifically inviting Marchel ap Thurrig and Arling Gunnarsson to invade."

"By all the gods I care for," Morthu said, "I swear that I am innocent of those charges, and I will speak nothing but the truth."

Angas stirred uneasily, and I wondered if he was also thinking that there were very few gods Morthu cared for.

"It is customary to ask the White God to witness and hold your oath," Darien said.

"But it is not the law," Morthu said. He was right, of course. I gritted my teeth.

We then went through the procedure of evidence being given against Morthu. Veniva read out Garah's statement. Several servants and people of Caer Tanaga made statements. Then Flavien made a statement about Morthu's sedition, enticing him into rebellion. Sidrok made another, almost identical, as was Hengist Guthrumsson's. Then Atha came out, looking subdued and just like anyone else, and spoke about the letters he had sent her. Then it was my turn. As briefly as I could I explained about Aurien, and Daldaf, and that he had confessed the plot and the stolen letters. Then I gave an account of the events of the day before, which should have been sufficient evidence of sorcery all on their own. Lastly Elenn came forward, with Teilo at her side, and gave evidence quietly, confirming what I had said, confirming Garah's statement about the sacrifice, and saying that she had been bewitched and forced to act against her own will.

When she had stepped back, Morthu raised his head. "May I speak now?" he asked. "Can I defend myself, or am I to be condemned unheard by this conspiracy of my enemies?"

"You can speak," Darien said patiently.

"In the first place, the kings who say I wrote to them seditiously are twisting the events. There were letters between us, yes, and we did discuss rebellion. But as they stand pardoned, that is not in itself a crime. I did not begin writing to them, as they said. They were the ones who wrote

to me, and to my brother, stirring up the war because of
their rightful grievances, and not on my account. Secondly,
Sulien ap Gwien and her servant, Garah ap Gavan, are lying, out of the hate and mistrust she has always had for me
ever since she killed my mother. As for the last speaker, I
must explain my innocence. The Queen Elenn is a very
beautiful woman. When she fell in love with me and made
advances to me I tried to resist for some time, as she was
married to King Urdo. When he discovered this, I was banished to Demedia, although I was innocent. When I came
back, she said that since Urdo was as good as dead I could
have no more scruples, and threw herself at me. She is trying to escape blame and gain sympathy with this story of
sorcerous bewitchment. She should rather be pitied than
condemned."

Elenn stood completely still, her face as remote as if he
were speaking of someone else.

"And how do you explain the sacrifice of a hundred
armigers and townspeople?" Darien asked.

"Another lie. They tell you to go and see the circle of
ashes. It is true that we made a pyre to burn the dead, but
that is all the truth of it. My enemies are conspiring against
me, some out of hatred for me but most to shift the blame
from themselves to me. If you are not prejudiced because
one of them is your mother, you will judge the truth of it for
yourself. You may say that their conspiracy against me is
fantastic and unlikely, but on the same grounds consider
what it is that they say I have done and how plausible that
is."

"And why would Atha lie about you?"

"Who knows why Isarnagans do anything?" He shrugged,
and some of the crowd chuckled.

"And Rigga of Rigatona?" Darien asked.

"Who?" Morthu asked, but I could tell he had not been
prepared for this.

"Rigg, of Rigatona. She writes from Caer Custenn of your
conspiracy with Arling." Darien waved the letter I had sent to

Urdo when all this began. It seemed like years ago, but it was hardly a month and a half.

"Probably a forgery your mother made," Morthu said, and stared at Darien as if daring him to condemn him.

This was the first public act of Darien's reign. He had not only to do justice, but be seen to do it. If there had been a vote among the kings then, I am not sure whether Morthu might not have swayed enough of them to set him free.

"And sorcery?" Darien asked.

"Where is your evidence of sorcery?" Morthu replied.

"We have given our evidence," Darien said, coming forward toward Morthu. "Garah's written evidence and Sulien's spoken evidence you deny as lies. Shall I have Raul and Glividen tell us how the stones of the gate were fallen? Shall I have everyone who has ever dealt with you tell of one thing and another that are individually very small but together are incontrovertible proof?"

I was looking at Morthu, so I saw his eyes narrowing as Darien approached, and I saw his face tighten as if he was waiting for him to be near enough. He didn't have a weapon, but neither did I. I didn't really think he was going to jump Darien, it wasn't that sort of expression.

As I was trying to think what sort of expression it was, Inis leapt forward. "The blackheart has come to Caer Tanaga!" he shouted. "Hear me, oh Earth!"

Then everything happened at once. Darien took another step forward and there was a muffled *crump* sound, and gouts of fire exploded up through the ground in a wide band across from where I was standing to where Elenn was standing, opposite me. Almost before I had seen it, there was a loud bang and the fire was gone. A wave of warm fog expanded quickly outward at knee level, and rolled away along the ground. I wasn't sure at the time if any of it had been real, but I found afterward that the hairs on my legs were singed off, so it must have been.

Morthu was staring at Inis with incredulous hate on his face. "That wasn't sorcery!" he said.

"Not a bit of it," Inis agreed cheerfully. "That was the fuel for the flame-machines which you had stored in the heating-system tunnel, and you set it off with a perfectly ordinary spark charm. Do not condemn this man for sorcery, Kings and Princes; he would have killed you with innocent burning oil."

Gorai actually laughed.

"We would have been just as dead," Darien said, sounding a little shaken. "And murder is also a capital crime," he added. "Thank you, Inis, whatever you did."

"I just took away the air around the fire, and the life from the heart of it," Inis said, as if this made sense in the first place and as if it were possible in the second. He sounded a little bashful.

"Well, Morthu," Darien said.

Morthu tried to take a step toward Darien, and stumbled to his knees. "My feet," he screamed.

Teilo stepped forward from the crowd. "The curse has him," she said. "He could not do sorcery, and the charm he did has opened the way for the curse to find him. And every life he has taken to keep it away is making it stronger now."

Morthu kept screaming. I leaned forward to see. It looked as if the grass had caught Morthu by the feet and ankles and was holding him tight. Now it was twining up his legs to his knees. "Cut me loose!" he screamed, tearing at the grass with his fingers.

Inis cackled. "You just tried to kill them all, and you think they'll cut you loose?"

I looked to see if anyone would. Flavien was patting his clothes, looking appalled. Everyone else seemed stunned. Gwien was gazing, eyes wide. "His foot's come right off," he said. It had. The bare bones were lying separately on the innocent grass like the bones of someone long dead, each toe bone separate from the other bones like an illustration in one of ap Darel's books. Morthu's scrabbling fingers had been caught, too, and he was pulled forward on his hands and knees, with the grass reaching up his arms.

"Help me!" Morthu shouted. "I'll teach you all my spells. I'll make you High King if you help me. I'll show you how to be like a god! Whatever you want, power, lovers, comfort. Just get me away from this grass. You're standing on it too, you know. How do you know it won't turn on you when it has done with me? Cut me free and lift me up!"

"And will you be carried in a chair all your life, or walk in shoes with springs on their heels?" Inis asked, still full of maniacal cheer.

"This is not deadly grass you have stumbled on," Teilo said. "This is the vengeance of the Earth you have scorned all your days."

Alswith was looking sick. Even Darien looked pale. The worst of it was that there wasn't any blood. I was at the same time both intensely glad of it and absolutely horrified by seeing it. Only Inis seemed to be enjoying it, laughing and dancing about. He went back into the crowd and took hold of Elenn's arm and dragged her forward. "Elenn!" Morthu screamed. "Help me! Cut me free!"

She spat on his face. "So perish all who malign my honor," she said coldly.

Even I shuddered. She shook off Inis's hand and walked over to Teilo, who held Elenn against her shoulder like a child, hiding her eyes. Teilo was not afraid to look herself. On the faces around me I saw hatred and nausea and disgust and, on some, a furtive pleasure. Raul looked incredulous. Dewin looked confused. Father Cinwil looked as if he might be sick at any moment. Only Teilo watched entirely dispassionately, as if she needed to be able to give an account of it to someone later.

When Morthu stopped begging for help and his screams became gurgles, Teilo gave Elenn to Raul and came forward again.

"It is time for mercy," she said to Darien. "Kill him now."

Darien raised his chin, and reached for where his sword should have been, then remembered he didn't have it. All of us were patting our clothes now, and discovering the same thing. By the time a guard came up at Darien's signal, it was too late; there was nothing left of Morthu but his neatly piled bones.

I was very glad he was dead, and so perish all poison-tongued traitors and sorcerers. But all the same, I have never cursed anyone since.

27

Let the dead be carried gently;
let them wonder, who are living,
what choice shall be tomorrow.
　　　　　—Roland Poem, Number 5

When it was almost sunset, a servant came and asked me to go to Elenn for the laying out. I had almost forgotten about it. Darien had told me in the morning that there would be a boat ready, but it had gone out of my mind. I was the last to arrive in the little room where they were preparing the bier. Elenn welcomed me, looking very composed. My mother was there, and Alswith, arranging cornflowers and roses around the piece of wood that was, when looked at in a certain way, Urdo lying still with closed eyes. It was a gnarled and weathered oak log with the bark still on. I don't know where they found it.

Emer stood a little apart, as if unwilling to touch it. Rowanna was fussing around and wiping her eyes. Her sister Ninian was not there, and clearly not invited, although she had been at the coronation. Ninian ap Gwyn was there, casting very uncertain looks at Elenn and at the piece of wood. I got to see her hair, which was as red as Alswith's. It looked strange with her darker skin. I have heard people call Ninian a beauty, which seems to me too kind of them. All the same, her looks were certainly striking when she was young.

Alswith was still wearing the grey overdress she had worn at the coronation. The others were all wearing very splendid clothes and whatever gold they had. For a moment I felt out of place in my armor. Then I reminded myself that Urdo had given it to me after Caer Lind and that it was fit to wear anywhere.

The log on the bier both was and wasn't Urdo. Sometimes it could look like him to me, and other times it was only the wood. He was a hero of the land now. He could look however he chose and make any part of the land resemble him. When we were done to Elenn's satisfaction the other six of us picked up the bier and carried it out. Emer and I had the front, Ninian and Alswith the center, and Veniva and Rowanna took the end. Elenn walked in front, carrying a bunch of flowers tied up with hair of all colors which people had sent.

In the citadel Darien and the kings waited to see us carry it by and then followed us down through the streets of the town. Many armigers joined in behind, and many people of the town. It was like a procession. People opened their doors to see us pass. Some of them were crying. Some called out farewells to Urdo as if they thought he could still hear.

"Where are they taking Urdo?" I heard a little boy ask his mother.

"They're taking him away to a magic island where he can be healed," his mother said, mopping at her eyes.

The bier wasn't heavy, nothing like as heavy as it would have been if we had really been carrying Urdo's body. We came at last to the wharf. Elenn directed us to lay the bier in the center of the boat on a prepared box. Then she stepped in and went and stood at the prow. Alswith went to the steering oar. Emer and Veniva and Ninian and Rowanna stepped away, back into the crowd. I hesitated. Nobody had told me what to do next. I looked at the bier, and it was Urdo, unquestionably Urdo. He looked as if he were asleep. I remembered a night journey long ago, going to Derwen after Morien's death, when Urdo had fallen asleep crossing the Havren. He had looked just like that. I stepped into the boat and stood in the stern, near his feet. If I could guard him in death, as in life, I would do it.

There were people lining the wharf. The sun was setting, and I thought that they would sing the Hymn of Return. They did not, they just stood there, some weeping, some waving, and all watching.

Alswith steered out into the center of the stream and let the current take us. We slipped downstream fast. We had not discussed where we were going, or what we were going to do when we got there. We did not talk now, not even when we were away from the city and the crowds. We just let the boat drift on, as if for as long as it was doing that we did not need to think of the length of time stretching ahead down the dark stream that would be afterwards.

Life went on, of course. We kept the Peace. That is the important thing.

Darien was a good king, and Ninian a good queen. They had children, and their son is High King of Tir Tanagiri today, uniting in his veins the blood of Emrys and of Hengist and of Gewis and of my own family, who have been Lords of Derwen back to the trees. Darien died twenty years ago, the way my father did, finding a cure for a plague. He never learned that Urdo was not his blood-father, or if he knew he never told me. He had a stone put up for Ulf at Caer Tanaga, which says just what is proper.

The Council was a matter of great tedium for me, but also a way of keeping the kings from open war, so it must be accounted a blessing. Angas and I sat and glared at each other across the table, even when we were agreeing, for thirty years. He did a lot to promote the stability of the kingdom, and he is probably the best king Demedia ever had. He was my good friend, and I never forgave him.

There have been no more wars. Most Jarnsmen who come to Tir Tanagiri now come to settle in Tevin, Nene, Aylsfa, and Bereich, where they know they will be welcome. Instead of spears and knives they bring their wives and families, their plows, and their good woodworking tools.

The priests of the White God are everywhere. It is unusual not to wear the pebble. But worship is still free as it always has been, and it is still allowed to swear an oath by any god you choose. More kingdoms have followed Munew, but the whole land has not been given into his hand like Tir Isarnagiri.

Once Morthu was dead, the charm against the weapon-rot worked again. Those who had been sick got well, and the world was restored to the way it should be. There has never been any trouble with it since, or with any other charm I know.

Elenn went to Thansethan, becoming a sister, and later the leader of the community. So at last she came to sit on the Council in her own right and in her own name, and I saw her again. I never spoke to her of it, but I think from the way she spoke of other things that she found trust and healing with the monks.

I ruled Derwen and bred horses, and sat on the Council until I grew too old and yielded my place to my great-nephew. Gwien died in an accident in practice when he was barely fifty. I have lost my health and my strength slowly. I kept them longer than most; I rode until I was over eighty. It seems to me now that I never valued as I should the days when I could wake in the morning and train all day, then fall easily asleep and do it all again the next morning.

I miss Urdo every day. Sometimes I see him still in a fall of leaves or a fold of the land. Sometimes even now he will put a brush into my hand when I am in the stables, or push the ink across the table to me as I sit here writing in the shaft of sunlight. We never talk, I don't know why; there is too much to say and it doesn't feel right. I miss my friends of those years, but, as I said, life does go on. I have other friends. Ap Lew is king of Dun Morr. She rides over to see me often. She understands the way my mind works. I trained her in the ala when she was a girl, and she went on to be the greatest armiger of her generation. She had to go to Varnia to fight her wars, for there were none left at home. Now that we have both grown too old to fight we sit and push pine cones and scraps of parchment about a table and tell each other how it was.

What it is to be young is to wake up in the morning with the belief that today can be better than yesterday. I never had that until I caught hope from Urdo and the ala. Now that I am ninety-three I spend a lot of time looking backward at my life. We kept the Peace. We preserved civilization, whatever

Veniva said. We have cities and libraries and waterwheels and scythes and plows and bathhouses. What more could Vinca offer? For my farmers to come and go in peace is a great thing. The world has changed and changed again, and the world I remember is like an age of legends. I tell myself this is a good thing. We won the Peace. Holding it is less exciting, but just as necessary. Keeping the taxes fair and building a highroad from Magor to Derwen and from here up to Nant Gefalion is not the stuff of stories. I am old, and I look backward very often. But when I look forward I do have hope for tomorrow.

So sometimes I say that I am still young, and nobody understands me. They don't want my thoughts on how they should teach their children to read. They want me to tell them stories of the days of King Urdo. But sometimes, when I hear them telling the stories to each other, it is the rumors that are remembered.

So I have set this down, even the things that I have never told anyone. Urdo would have said that only the Peace mattered. But I care also that his name is remembered and the truth is not entirely forgotten. It was a fine truth, and it is a good Peace, and a better world that we made.

I stood there in the back of the boat as it drifted down the stream. Elenn was staring straight ahead. Alswith had one hand on the steering oar, looking for a place to bring us ashore. She was always good with boats. I looked at Urdo's face, sleeping, dead, there, elsewhere. Alswith steered towards a landing place in the trees. I said then the only thing I found to say to him after he was dead, knowing that he heard it.

"Now sleep, my lord, and I will guard thy rest."

That is the last word my Great Aunt Sulien wrote, who was the daughter of Gwien Open-Hand. She was last seen on the tenth day after midwinter in the sixty-fifth year of Urdo's victory. I have had three fair copies made of her writing, and one I shall seal up and place in the wall as she wished.

Of her passing, and the tale that a tall black horse came to

her gate caparisoned in the colors of iron and gold, that she
mounted it with the grace and vigor of her youth, and that its
third step touched no ground nor none saw them after going
away, I can say only that none pious could believe it.

Coming soon in hardcover
from Jo Walton and Tor Books . . .

THE

PRIZE

IN THE

GAME

A new novel in the world of
The King's Peace

On the waking edge of sleep, Conal drifted a little, half-dreaming across the worlds. He held as tight as he could to place and time. Even deep down in sleep he had known he was in Edar. There was a smell to the place, the particular mixture of burning peat and heather bedding and hams hanging from the roof that told him he was home. He always slept better here than in his father's house at Ard-machan. Edar he knew as well as he knew anywhere. But this was not childhood. He could feel Emer curled up beside him, familiar and homely as his own heartbeat. Emer, in Edar, this place, this time and no others. Drifting, he held to time and denied the gift. Asleep, he turned away and strove to close eyes closed already.

He heard the door to the hall open, and came nearer wak-ing. It could still have been any time, anybody coming in. He was warm and Emer was safe beside him. But two pairs of footsteps came hurrying towards the alcove where his bed was made up. Conal's eyes opened, the struggle over, he was entirely and effortlessly there. When old Anla and Garth came to the foot of the bed he was awake, alert and sitting up. Anla was the steward, responsible for Edar in Amagien's ab-sence, but he was getting old and frail. For a year or two now more and more of the responsibility fell on his daughter's husband Garth. If they were both here now it must be some-thing urgent.

"Raiders," Anla said, his voice quavering. "Folk of the Isles. Six ships, coming in down on the shore."

"I was going to wake the folk and go out to fight them, stop them stealing the cattle," Garth said, sounding angry. "But your ap Gamal insisted we stay inside. She shut the gates. She demanded we get you."

"Thank the Mother of Battles that she did," Conal said, pushing back his hair. "If a straggle of you had gone running down the hill Atha's folk would have picked you off at their leisure."

"Then are we to cower inside without facing them?" Garth asked. "The cattle are all together in the near pastures, they were all brought in for the blessing last night. They will take them like reaping corn."

Conary had told him that no matter what good plans you thought you had, you almost always became alarmed when a crisis hit, which was why it was necessary to have everyone know the plans well in advance so they could stick to them instead of each going their own way. Conal didn't have a plan made in advance, it was all coming to him now and cohering as he thought of it. He didn't feel alarmed, though, he felt un-usually calm. Emer too seemed calm. She rolled over and be-gan binding back her hair. But he could see already how would have been helpful for everyone else to have known the plan before.

"Oh no, we must fight," Conal said, getting the order of things clear in his mind. "Anla, wake Nerva and tell her to get the paint ready. Garth, wake everyone who can fight and get them painted as quickly as you can."

Old Anla jerked up his chin and went off to find his daugh-ter, who was in one of the other alcoves of the hall. Emer stood up, stretched carefully, and reached for her armour coat. Garth hesitated, looking at Conal. "I hadn't thought we'd time for paint," he said, sullenly. "Nor need to bother with it. We could keep them from the herd if we were quick, if they thought there would be easier pickings elsewhere they might leave our cows alone and make for another farm. It isn't as if we can hope to stand and fight them all."

"We can hold them off for long enough for King Conary and the champions of Ardmachan to get here," Conal said. "We can do it better if they think we're a lord's household and not just a bunch of farmers."

Garth frowned. "It won't work," he said. "They won't come. They won't know they're needed. What do you know about it? You're the lord's son, not the lord, and even your fa-ther is only the lord because the king gifted him this land. He wasn't born to Edar. You're only a boy. Why should I take your orders?"

Conal didn't know what to do. He could kill Garth for saying that, but that would not make him obey him nor keep Atha from the herd. Garth was a foot taller than he was, and twice as broad across the shoulders, so knocking him down was out of the question. It was essential that the people of the dun obey, or he could do nothing.

"Conal ap Amagien is one of the king's champions of Oriel," Emer said, her voice as cold as steel. "He was armed by Conary himself this season. What you have said would be accounted treason in Connat, and my mother would have your head for it."

Conal blinked at her. He had never heard her sound the outraged princess of Connat before, though Elenn did it often enough. Garth looked at her in amazement. "In these parts we speak the truth to our lords," he said.

"And here I am speaking the truth back to you," Emer said. "Conal is young, true, but a king's champion."

"What is a champion but someone who has a chariot to fight from and need not be down in the crush with the rest of us?" Garth demanded, thrusting his chin forward.

"Someone who knows how to lead," Conal said, the words coming from his dream or from nowhere.

Emer looked cross enough to spit. "Conal is your lord's son, he is here, he has a plan to save you, and while you stand here arguing with him time is wasting that might mean all our lives, or the loss of all your herds."

To Conal's amazement, Garth hesitated only half a moment longer, gave a clumsy half bow and went off towards the door.

"I don't know how he dares speak to you like that," Emer said, twisting her hair into place behind her head with both hands. "I suppose it is from having seen you grow up and not really realising that you are a man now."

"No doubt," Conal said, still a little dazed.

"What is most needful for me to do first?" she asked. She was standing ready, looking at him expectantly.

"I love you," Conal said, surprising himself even as he spoke.

Emer gave a little surprised laugh. "I love you too, but—"

"I know," Conal interrupted. He stood up and buckled on his own armour coat. "Get the chariots harnessed. Find out where Meithin is and make sure she's ready. I need to see exactly where they are and how many of them there are. Six ships could mean two hundred warriors, but not if they are raiding and planning to take cattle back with them."

She bowed in acknowledgement and headed off without a backward glance. Nerva came in as she went out, carrying a great cauldron of paint and followed by most of the people of fighting age of the dun, naked and clamouring. None of them were blue so far.

Conal finished fastening his coat and went towards them.

Nerva made an awkward gesture with her head when she saw him. "We wanted to know what to paint," she said, swinging the big cauldron onto the hook over the fire. Nerva's daughter Hivlian, who was surely too young to fight, blew on the embers and started to add some wood.

Conal stopped. He had not the least idea. "What to paint?" he repeated, stupidly, wishing Emer was still there. He was a champion of the king's house of Ardmachan, but paint was a not something he knew anything about.

"Defence or attack, or which gods to call on . . ." Nerva said, stirring the paint. Then everyone started talking at once, each with their own suggestions and demands. Cevan slopped white paint onto the floor from the little pot he carried as he gestured too emphatically. Conal could not hear it all, and time was wasting in which he could be seeing how to stop Atha.

"Protection, of course," he said. "And beyond that, victory. Paint yourselves to win, and do it as fast as you can, time is short."

That sufficed to create enough silence for him to leave, though he could hear their voices being raised again before he was quite clear of the hall.

The dun outside was in uproar. Meithin was standing at

the gate holding a spear. Garth was beside her holding another and wearing an old armour coat. Another part of his plan came to Conal, and he smiled. Emer was harnessing the horses. Women and children were running everywhere, dogs were barking furiously, pigs and hens were loose and complaining. Conal ignored them all as best he could and went to the point of the wooden wall where, by long practice, he knew he could swing himself up to see down towards the sea.

Six boats, Anla had said. How many people could Atha have persuaded to miss the Feast of Bel for this raiding?

He was looking almost straight into the sun, he had to squint. He saw at once that they had brought no chariots. But there were more of them than he had hoped. He did not let himself be daunted, but counted them as Inis had taught them. He made it eight twelves two threes and two, a hundred and four, armed and on foot, but there might have been more. They were among the herd already, which made counting difficult. Still, that could work to his advantage. Few of them were painted; they were not expecting much opposition here. They would be about even for numbers, so he would need what advantage he could take. They would not all be champions, some would be farmers come for the raid and many of them would have come to sail the ships. But none of his people were champions except himself and Meithin and Emer. He squinted harder, looking among the cows, wondering.

He walked calmly over to Garth and Meithin. "Can you stand in a moving chariot?" he asked Garth.

Garth frowned as if he thought it some sort of test. "I never have," he said after a moment.

"Practice a little, once they are harnessed," Conal said. "I am not asking you to fight from one. That is a matter of years of practice. I just want you to stand in one until we are down there. Then you can get down and fight on foot. But you are the only one who has an armour coat and might convince them."

"Your lady was right to say I am no champion," Garth said, scowling.

"You are steward of this dun," Conal said, holding his ground.

"My father is steward," Garth replied.

"And shall we set old Anla bouncing down the hill to frighten Atha ap Gren and her chosen champions?" Conal lowered his voice. "I am not trying to punish you for insolence. I am trying to save the herds. We all want the same thing, Garth, and I know how to get it."

"I will stand in your chariot," Garth said.

"Very well," Conal said, and turned to Meithin. "Ap Gamal, when we are ready, take ap Madog here up behind you, go down the hill before the footmen, just a little behind me. At the foot of hill let ap Madog jump out, then wheel as fast as you can and make for Ardmachan. Tell them what is happening and bring them here to our aid as fast as you can."

"As fast as I can is going to take an hour there and back, which will mean closer to two hours than one, even if Conary listens at once," Meithin protested. "It's better for me to stay here and fight. We can't really use both chariots properly, but a chariot with a charioteer and without a champion is better than nothing. And I am a champion."

"They will come in time if you are quick," he said. Meithin looked as if she would have liked to argue more. If they had been anywhere other than Conal's father's dun, he was quite sure she would have tried to take over. In some ways he would very much have liked to take her advice, but everything screamed to him that doing so would be fatal to his already shaky authority. "Practice with ap Madog now," he said, and walked away.

Naked people stained blue and painted on top in black and white were starting to emerge from the hall.

A small child started to scream. Anla picked him up and started to soothe him. Conal could not wait, "Where is Old Blackie?" he asked. "Have they taken him already, or wasn't he with the herd?"

Anla blinked, and continued to rub the child's back as his cries subsided into gurgles. "He is here," Anla said. "He is in the calving house. He came up last night for the blessing, and he couldn't be left with the cows after, or they would all get in calf, and it isn't time."

Conal could feel himself smiling. "We really can do this," he said, and looked around.

Emer had harnessed up both chariots. Garth was practicing standing still as Meithin drove hers around in a small circle. Emer stood by theirs, holding the horses' heads. More painted people were coming out of the hall.

Anla had been talking, but he hadn't heard a word of it. "Where are the spears?" he interrupted. This wasn't Ard-machan. There wasn't a separate hall for weapons. But it wasn't the barbarian countries either, where people would take weapons in where they ate. How strange it was that he'd never needed a weapon at Edar.

"In the smokehouse," Anla said. "Shall I fetch them? Or shall I send Garth to fetch them? He has his own already."

"You fetch them, and take some people who do not fight to help you," Conal said. "Are there any weapons there besides spears? I know my father keeps most of his weapons beside him at Ardmachan, but did he leave anything here?"

"There is one sword of Amagien's, and there is another that belonged to Howel when he was lord here, and which his daughter did not want when she went to Rathadun. There are many slings besides which we use for hunting, and a few shots for them, and plenty of stones."

"Does anyone here know how to use a sword?" Conal asked, knowing the answer would be no.

"Lord, it is a champion's weapon," Anla said.

"Bring the swords to me," Conal said. "And share the spears out to those who are ready to fight. Give the slings to those who can best use them."

Anla hurried away and Conal walked over to where Emer was waiting.

"He has two swords, but I have no idea what size they are," he said to her.

"Give one to Meithin. I have a knife if I need one for the traces," Emer said, showing the little belt knife no charioteer would go without even on a peaceful summer night.

"Meithin is going to ride for Ardmachan as fast as she can," Conal explained.

"Then I will take one," Emer said, unruffled.

Anla came back with armloads of spears and started to give them to those who were painted already. It seemed to be taking hours for them all to get ready, though the shadows had hardly moved since Conal had come out.

"You should get them ready, or they will fight each other," Emer said, very quietly. "Shall I drive you to the gate?"

Conal could see that she was right. The young farmers were overexcited already and did not want to wait.

They looked up as he came over. He ran through what he would say to them in his head, but what came out of his mouth was his first thought. "Where are your shields?" he asked.

They were naked and painted blue. Across their chests, men and women alike though it looked more horrific on the women, was a great black battle crow. Down their arms and down their faces were white spirals. They had been boasting and teasing each other. Now they looked at each other in confusion at Conal's question, like children, and began to slink away to their houses to fetch their shields. By the time they came back their fellows had joined them, and at last Nerva came out of the hall, painted, and carrying the black paint.

Anla came back with the swords, which Conal took. "There were some throwing spears as well," he said. "Only five."

"My great thanks to you for keeping the dun so well," Conal said.

"It is Garth you should thank," Anla said, grudgingly. "I have kept it for many years, but he thinks it is his time."

"His time will come," Conal said. "Now, as soon as we are out, get Blackie from his house. Watch from the gate. When I signal by throwing both hands up in the air and calling his name, let him go."

Anla hesitated. "You know how Blackie can be," he said. "There's no promise he'd know his friends in a battle."

"Do it all the same," Conal said, as firmly as he could.

Anla draw breath as if he would speak again, but Conal stared at him. He didn't want a conversation about what Amagien would say if Blackie were hurt. At last Anla raised his chin in agreement and went off to help with distributing spears. Conal arranged the throwing spears in the slots in the chariot, so they would be ready to his hand. He set a long weighted fighting spear beside them, in case he needed it, then looked at the swords. They were both much bigger than the swords they had been practising with.

"Which do you want?" he asked Emer.

She looked at them. "They're both very old," she said.

"Anla said one of them was my father's and the other was left by the lord who was here before him."

"Which was your father's?" Emer asked, suspiciously.

"I really don't know," Conal said.

"Then I'll take the one that's a little shorter," Emer said. "I wish I had my own that King Conary had given me for my use."

"So do I, said Conal, buckling on his sword.

Nerva had been painting Garth's face. As soon as she was done, Garth climbed into Meithin's chariot and Nerva came over to Conal. "We are painted," she said. "Will you wear the victory sign yourself?"

He bent his head and closed his eyes and felt the pig-bristle brush sweeping across his face. Nerva murmured the charm as she painted, calling on the Mother of Battles for Victory, and he felt it taking effect, filling him with confidence, making him more ready to fight and kill. The calm that had filled him since he woke receded a little and although the paint was supposed to take away fear he felt a little fear for the first time.

"And you, lady?" Nerva asked Emer.

Emer looked at Conal, then shook her head.

Conal waited until Nerva had set down the paint and picked up her spear. Then he raised his hands palms up and then palms down.

"Branadain Mother of Battles, and Edar of the Spring, be with us now when we call on you. Right is on our side. These folk have come from the Isles meaning to take us by surprise, steal our herds and harm our people," Conal said. Then he looked at the waiting farmers. "Our plan is to hold them off for long enough for King Conary to come here with his champions and help us. Ap Gamal will be going to fetch him, so they will be back here almost before we know it, and well before the folk of the Isles can expect them. If I give a great howl like a wolf, break off and come back up to the dun, we will hold them off inside. We are fighting for time, and they have no help coming. And most of all, remember, the cows are ours!"

Anla swung the gate open, and Emer drove out, Meithin close behind with Garth clinging on to the side of her chariot. The painted farmers, giving a great roar, came boiling out behind. Conal saw heads turning down among the raiders. He gave his own battlecry as Emer headed the chariot straight down the hill towards them, and suddenly his feelings, which had been far away from him all morning came back and were close. He felt his love for Emer not as a distant knowledge but as a burning presence. His fear that he might disappoint his father, or die with nothing done, his joy at being alive and going downhill fast enough to rattle his teeth, and the love and comradeship he felt for Emer, so close beside him, all welled up in him at once and he thrust them all into the battle cry which rose up on the air above the howls and cries of the others.

Then they came up to them, and after that there was only the fighting.